Ally put her arm around Cody's waist. "Lean on me."

A bum leg was worth getting this close to Ally. He slipped his arm around her shoulders. Her fruity shampoo tickled his senses along with vanilla and that fresh hay scent that had clung to her for as long as he could remember. The smell of Ally. He'd missed it.

"We're gonna turn around nice and slow and take you back inside. Once you're on solid ground, I'll go warm up the soup and bring it over."

"That's too much trouble." He really should tell her he could walk just fine. Just needed his cane and to take it slow. But what he ought to do and what he wanted to do were two entirely different things.

"No, it's not." She helped him climb his steps. "I won't have you hurting yourself for no reason."

She cared and smelled good. But he couldn't get used to leaning on Ally. Couldn't get too close. Not until he figured out his future. If he had one.

Shannon Taylor Vannatter is a stay-at-home mom/pastor's wife/award-winning author. She lives in a rural central Arkansas community with a population of around one hundred, if you count a few cows. Contact her at shannonvannatter.com.

Tina Radcliffe has been dreaming and scribbling for years. Originally from western New York, she left home for a tour of duty with the Army Security Agency stationed in Augsburg, Germany, and ended up in Tulsa, Oklahoma. Her past careers include certified oncology RN and library cataloger. She recently moved from Denver, Colorado, to Phoenix, Arizona, where she writes heartwarming and fun inspirational romance.

Sweetheart Reunion

Shannon Taylor Vannatter

&

Tina Radcliffe

Previously published as
Reuniting with the Cowboy and
Rocky Mountain Cowboy

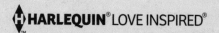

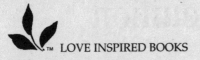

LOVE INSPIRED BOOKS

Recycling programs for this product may not exist in your area.

ISBN-13: 978-1-335-00782-7

Sweetheart Reunion

Copyright © 2019 by Harlequin Books S.A.

The publisher acknowledges the copyright holders of the individual works as follows:

Reuniting with the Cowboy
Copyright © 2016 by Shannon Taylor Vannatter

Rocky Mountain Cowboy
Copyright © 2016 by Tina M. Radcliffe

www.Harlequin.com

Printed in U.S.A.

CONTENTS

REUNITING
WITH THE COWBOY

Shannon Taylor Vannatter

To Dr. Mark Baker, DVM,
for keeping my pets healthy and for sharing
his stories during our many appointments.
Especially the mad mama cow episode, which
inspired a fictionalized version for this book.

Acknowledgments

I appreciate former Aubrey City Hall secretary
Nancy Trammel-Downes; Aubrey Main Street
Committee member Deborah Goin;
Aubrey librarian Kathy Ramsey; Allison Leslie; and
Steve and Krys Murray, owners of Moms on Main,
for all their help and support.

Commit to the Lord whatever you do,
and he will establish your plans.
—*Proverbs* 16:3

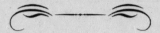

Chapter One

Fifteen dogs and twenty-one cats. The number of strays changed daily—but one thing didn't—they all depended on Ally Curtis. This *had* to go well. She checked her appearance one more time, spritzed on vanilla body spray.

A clatter echoed through the house.

"Mom, you okay in there?"

"Just digging for a Pyrex lid."

Ally hurried to the kitchen. Her two Pomeranians trailed behind, their nails clicking across the hardwood floor.

"Found it." Mom snapped the blue lid onto a glass casserole dish on the counter. Layers of cream cheese and chocolate were visible through the sides. "I knew you'd be too tired to make anything after vaccinating all that cattle and we need to win over our new neighbor."

"You really didn't have to do this, but I'm glad you did." A cramp shot through Ally's shoulder and she massaged the aching spot. "Thanks, Mom."

Every muscle she owned ached as if she'd spent the first day of September steer wrestling. And she pretty much had.

Vaccination day at a large ranch paid a lot of bills at her vet clinic in tiny Aubrey, Texas. But she always came home exhausted and reeking like a stockyard. The shower had removed the stench but not the twinges.

At least she had another vet in her practice and the new tech she'd hired would relieve some of their load tomorrow. But it was only Thursday night. Two more workdays until her only day off.

"You smell much better," Mom teased.

"Definitely. Now all I have to do is lay on the charm."

"My persuasive daughter bearing a four-layer delight. Who could resist?" Mom's eyes widened. "What if our new neighbor is allergic to chocolate?"

"Or pecans." Ally's heart stammered. "Should I make something else?"

"Forget I said that." Mom winced. "If there are allergy issues, just apologize and I'll bake a pie or something else."

"If there's any more baking to be done, I'll do it." Ally picked up the dessert. "You've done enough."

"It probably won't be necessary. I've never met anyone who didn't love four-layer delight."

"Neither have I." It was Daddy's favorite. And Cody had practically begged for it.

Thoughts of her father always led to Cody. It had been twelve years since her policeman dad had died in the line of duty. Twelve years since her good friend Cody's comfort had turned into an earth-shattering kiss. A kiss that had dug an awkward gulf between them.

Since then, she'd seen him exactly twice. When their mutual friend married his brother a few years ago and when he was in rehab for an injured shoulder and knee after his recent bull wreck. Her heart had clamored both times. But his apparently hadn't.

She sighed. By now he was probably fully recovered and back on the circuit. Even if he gave up bull riding someday, he was a nomad. A confirmed bachelor, he'd never settle in Aubrey. And she was way too independent for anything other than friendship. *So stop thinking about him.*

"You look pretty without the braid for a change." Mom smoothed her hand over Ally's hair.

"Thanks."

"Want me to go with you?"

"Tempting." Ally took in a sharp breath and squared her sore shoulders. "But what if the new neighbor's not a people person? We don't want to overwhelm. All we need is some animal-hating grouch to complain and try to shut down my rescue program."

"We're probably overthinking the what-ifs." Mom patted her arm.

"I hope so." Her shoulders slumped. "I just can't believe somebody bought the place. I almost had the owner talked into selling me a parcel. Can you imagine how many more strays I could have housed with the extra land?"

"I'm sorry I sold our land off over the years." Mom sighed. "It should have been yours."

"Stop, Mom. You were a widow. You did what you had to do. We'll just have to make the best of it. If I can get on the new owner's good side, maybe I can eventually convince them to sell me an acre or two."

Two canine puffballs—one orange, one gray— danced for attention at her feet. "Poor babies. I promise we'll have a good long cuddle when I get back. But right now I have to go butter up our new neighbor."

"Rotten babies." Mom picked up a Pom in each arm. "You'd think they never get any attention. Despite these little distractions, I'll be praying."

A lot of good that would do. But she couldn't let Mom know she felt that way.

Ally stepped out and strolled casually toward the farmhouse next door.

She'd just wanted to be a vet, not run an animal shelter. Yet after a client had brought her an injured stray, word had gotten out. And before she knew it, Ally's Adopt-a-Pet was born.

But she was running out of room. Thank goodness the inspector had already come for the year. If the state showed up tonight, she'd get written up for being over her limit. All she could do now was sweet-talk her new neighbor. And hope whoever it was liked animals.

Trying not to let her nerves show, she unlatched the gate between the properties and stepped through.

The horse trailer by the barn had to mean something. Ally's heart rattled. Surely their new neighbor wouldn't mind a few dogs since he, she or they clearly liked horses. Surely.

A cacophony of barks and yips echoed from the barn behind her clinic. Her volunteers—three girls from the local youth group—strolled the property walking several of the dogs. She waved a greeting and climbed her neighbor's porch steps.

Who was she kidding? There were way more than a few dogs, with a generous sprinkling of cats, plus the pets she boarded for her traveling clients. And if she tried to shush the menagerie, it usually only made the racket worse.

Maybe she should wait until the teens left and the dogs settled down a bit.

The door swung open.

Cody Warren—in the flesh. Tall, muscular, with hair the smoky brown shade of a Weimaraner and soothing aloe eyes.

Ally gasped. Twelve years since his kiss had changed her world. Twelve years since he'd left to follow his dream.

Twelve years of trying to forget.

The glass dish slipped from her hand.

Cody grabbed the dish, his hands closing over hers. His breath caught.

Ally. On his porch.

Same old Ally. Long waves the color of a dark bay horse's coat, usually twined in a thick braid but loose today and spilling over her slender shoulders. Cautious coffee-colored eyes as skittish as a newborn colt.

He'd succumbed to her charms once. It had rearranged his insides and altered everything. Who would have thought one kiss would put the wariness in her eyes, build an uncomfortable wall between them and cause Ally to spend all that time since avoiding him? All because of his disobedient lips.

"Cody?" Her voice went up an octave. "You're my new neighbor?"

"Looks like." And now he'd gone and moved in next door to her. Maybe not the best way to keep his distance. "Let me take this." He scooped the dish out of her hands.

"I thought you'd be back on the circuit by now." Her gaze dropped to his shirt collar.

"I…um… I decided not to go back to the rodeo." More like his doctor decided for him. And that little bubble in his brain had something to say about it, too. "Aubrey is home and I needed a place of my own."

"You bought the place next to me?"

"This was the only land available with enough acreage to start a ranch." Technically leasing, with an option to buy. If he decided to have surgery. And lived.

She hugged herself. "What happened to Aubrey not being big enough for you?"

"Things change." A brain aneurysm changed lots of things. "Does your mom still live with you?"

"She does." She bit her lip. "Okay, yeah, I still live at home. But it's the perfect place for my vet practice-slash-shelter and Mom's my office manager at the clinic."

"Come on in." He stepped aside, striving for casual, despite the drumming of his heart. "And tell me this is a pecan chocolate four-layer delight."

"It is. Mom made it, but I didn't come to stay." She glanced toward her place.

"You got a passel of kids waiting for you?"

"Um, no." Sarcasm laced her words. "Surely you know I'm not married."

"I meant the teenage girls out there walking dogs, but it looks like they're leaving."

"Oh." Pink tinged her cheeks. "They volunteer to make sure all of the animals get attention and exercise."

"Since they're leaving, I figure you can stay and help me eat this." He took her by the elbow and led her into the empty kitchen. Warmth swept through him.

Shouldn't have touched her. Not even her elbow. "Come on. Humor me. Catch me up on Aubrey happenings."

"I don't know any." She slid her hands in her pockets. "I pretty much stay to myself except for cattle calls and hospital visits with my dog program. I hope the Realtor told you about my small-animal shelter before you moved in."

"Like a good Realtor, she did." He set the dish in the middle of the kitchen island and rubbed his hands together. "Actually, she didn't have much choice. All the critters were serenading us when we arrived."

"Do they bother you?" She grimaced. "The noise, I mean."

"Not at all. You know I've always been an animal lover. In fact, once I get settled in, I plan to come over and adopt a dog or two, maybe a cat or three for the barn."

"Really?" Excitement filled her eyes for the first time since he'd opened the door for her.

"Sure." Maybe the way to reclaim their easy friendship was through her animals. Ally had always had a soft spot for all four-legged creatures. He could lend a hand with the critters in her shelter. Maybe help her find homes for them. But more than anything, he could use a friend about now. He opened a drawer and remembered he hadn't even brought his utensils in yet.

"Why don't you have any furniture or appliances?" She strolled around the large kitchen.

"My home's been in the living quarters of my horse trailer for several years." Maybe he shouldn't have kept his move secret from his family. A furnished house might improve his rep. "I never needed furniture until now."

Over the years, his humor had pegged him as the

class clown. His yearning for freedom and travel made everyone assume he had Peter Pan syndrome. His years on the circuit had only solidified his image as someone who refused to grow up, to take responsibility and settle down.

Now he was out to show everyone there was so much more to him. Maybe if he morphed into a mature adult before their eyes, they'd buy his cover. That he wanted to retire and be a rancher. Not that he was forced into retirement and might not live to tell about it.

"I'll be right back." He shut the drawer. "My silverware is still in the horse trailer."

"I have a better idea. Have you eaten supper?"

"Not yet." Why was she being so nice after making a career of avoiding him over the years? "But I can have dessert for supper." He gave her a sly grin. "I'm an adult."

"Jury's still out on that." She rolled her eyes.

Yep, he had a lot of convincing to do.

"Come on over and I'll warm up some taco soup." She scurried toward the door.

"You're making my mouth water. Lead the way." It would be hard to keep up with her with his bad leg. But he didn't want to let on, so he followed her out. He'd made it down the steps and a few feet farther when he stepped in a hole and his knee wrenched before he caught himself.

"Whoa." Ally grabbed his arm. "Are you okay?"

Heat crept up his neck. "My doctor warned me to be careful on uneven surfaces. I've got a little hitch in my get-along these days."

"Why didn't you tell me to slow down?"

"I sort of forgot when you mentioned taco soup." Actually, he'd wanted to hide his weakness.

"How are you going to run a ranch when you can barely walk?"

"Easy. With a great foreman and trusty ranch hands. I'll be the brains behind the operation." He shot her a wink.

"Okay, change of plans." She put her arm around his waist. "Lean on me."

A bum leg was worth getting this close to Ally. He slipped his arm around her shoulders. Her fruity shampoo tickled his senses along with vanilla and that fresh hay scent that had clung to her for as long as he could remember. The smell of Ally. He'd missed it.

"We're gonna turn around nice and slow and take you back inside. Once you're on solid ground, I'll go warm up the soup and bring it over."

"That's too much trouble." He really should tell her he could walk just fine. Just needed to use his cane and take it slow. But what he ought to do and wanted to do were two entirely different things.

"No, it's not." She helped him climb his steps. "I won't have you hurting yourself for no reason."

She cared and smelled good. But he couldn't get used to leaning on Ally. Couldn't get too close. Not until he figured out his future. If he had one.

A waft of steam rose from the bowl of warmed soup on Cody's granite counter. Cody's counter. How had Ally gotten herself into this? She'd had a momentary lapse of judgment—that was how. But if the way to a man's heart was through his stomach, maybe the way to getting him to sell land was, too.

If only Mom could have brought the soup over. But by the time Ally got back to warm it, Mom had already showered and was in her pajamas.

As long as he'd been in the hospital and then rehab, Ally hadn't worried about him. But obviously, she hadn't realized how banged up he was. With him living next door and unable to walk across his own yard, he was like a magnet. Seeing him again, and seeing him in pain, had brought old feelings flooding back.

Staying away from Cody was the smart thing to do. But he could barely walk, much less cook. Especially with no appliances. He needed her help.

"So where have you been since you left the rehab center?" She leaned her hip against the breakfast bar.

"I stayed with Grandpa in Medina until this morning." He stood across the island from her, making quick work of the soup.

"Medina is almost a six-hour trip. You should be resting." She scanned the open floor plan, just to keep from looking at those mesmerizing eyes. Large roomy kitchen with a peninsula and a big eat-in area. The former owner had installed new cabinets and tiled floors a few years back, but Cody didn't have a stick of furniture. No pictures or personal items, nothing on the paneled walls. Not to mention necessities like a refrigerator. "Do you at least have a bed?"

"Grandpa sent one with me from his spare room until I get my own."

"So instead of resting in your borrowed bed—" she rolled her eyes "—you try and walk to my house on uneven ground after your doctor warned you to be careful? What were you thinking?"

"Taco soup." He grinned, deepening the cleft in his chin. "And four-layer delight."

Her heart did a flip. He seemed a bit more serious and mature than the Cody she'd always known. Until it came to food.

He wolfed down another spoonful of soup. "Mmm."

Gravel crunched in the drive and vehicle doors opened, then closed.

"Expecting company?"

"No one knows I'm here."

Ally peered between the miniblind slats. "A blue pickup."

"Oh no, they've found me." Cody hung his head.

"Who?" Ally frowned.

"My folks." His tone was filled with dread.

Why? He'd always had a great relationship with his family. Unless something had happened between them. "They didn't bring you home?"

"One of Grandpa's ranch hands was headed to Fort Worth to buy a bull. I hitched a ride with him."

"Why?"

"I don't want to be fussed over."

Audra Warren, Cody's mom, entered first without knocking. "Cody, what were you thinking?" She splayed her hands. "Grandpa said you came home to surprise us."

His dad, Wayne, followed. "We were worried when you didn't answer your cell."

"I forgot to charge it."

Despite Ally's attempt to blend into the corner, Audra noticed her. "Ally? How nice to see you."

"You, too." She waved her fingers.

"Why all the secrecy?" Audra's attention swung

back to Cody. "We had to call the local Realtor to even find out where you were." Her eyes were teary, a testimony to a mother's love and worry over her recently injured son.

"I just didn't want a bunch of fuss." Cody hugged his mother, evidently feeling guilty now for upsetting her. "I'm pushing thirty—I don't need a lot of fanfare. And I figured y'all would insist I stay with you. I just wanted to come home. To a place of my own."

"We love you, Cody." Audra sniffled. "We merely want to help you get settled. But if you'd stay with us, we could at least gather the furniture we all have in storage and get this place livable for you."

"You should have called." Wayne's jaw tensed. "Your mother was worried sick."

"Sorry, Mom. I didn't mean to upset you."

"You don't even have a bed." Audra's voice cracked. "You can't stay here."

"That's the one thing I do have. I'm fine."

"I guess I should just be glad you're well enough to be home." Audra pushed away from him and gave Ally a quick hug. "Just like old times with you looking after Cody. Thanks for seeing to him."

"No problem." *Act natural.* She and Cody had been friends since grade school. That was all he was to her, a friend. "I brought a dessert to welcome my new neighbor, but once I saw it was Cody and he didn't even have a microwave, I brought soup over."

"Isn't this some setup?" Wayne winked at Ally. "You and Cody right next door to each other. Y'all could get into all kinds of mischief."

Like the mischief they'd gotten into twelve years ago.

No way. Ally's lips would steer clear of Cody Warren this go-round.

In fact, all of her would. "Since y'all are here, I'm gonna go."

Cody grabbed her hand. "I wish you'd stay. We've still got catching up to do."

Electricity moved up her arm. Ally pulled away. "I've got chores to do and a surgery in the morning. It's good seeing y'all." She aimed for the door and put it in high gear.

Distance. She'd have to keep lots of distance between her and Cody. Her heart couldn't take any more teasing.

Cody scanned his cozy house, grateful to have a loving family. Even though they sometimes smothered him.

Only twenty-four hours since his parents had caught up with him and his new house was already furnished. There would have been even more fuss if he'd told his family he was leaving Grandpa's. And if he'd accepted a ride *home* from his parents, he'd have likely ended up at their house. Yet because of them, he actually had a table to sit at to savor his last serving of four-layer delight.

In a day's time, his dad and his brother, Mitch, had brought over Mitch's old dining room set, appliances and dual recliner couch, along with Cody's old bedroom suite from when he lived at home. He'd moved out twelve years ago and Mitch had given up his bachelor pad two years ago, but they had kept everything. His family officially ranked as hoarders.

The rich coffee aroma still permeated his house, as they'd offered him countless cups throughout the day.

If only he could have the real stuff instead of the fake. The empty maker mocked him from the counter.

He'd die for a cup. Literally. He filled the carafe with water, poured it in the back, scooped decaf grounds into the filter and turned it on. It would have to do.

The doctor's list of aneurysm triggers included intense nose blowing, vigorous exercise and strain. Since he had no allergies, he should be okay unless he got a cold.

It was a genuine wonder the aneurysm hadn't ruptured during his physical therapy, which came to a screeching halt after his doctor found the bubble during a follow up scan after his last concussion. Hopefully, his leisurely walks on his new treadmill would help with his limp.

Anger and surprise would be easy to avoid since he was laid-back and not easily startled. But real coffee? He came from a family that joked about having caffeine in their veins instead of blood. Having his dark roast again just might be worth the surgery that could kill him or reduce him to vegetable status.

He scraped all the excess chocolate and crumbs out of the glass dish and polished off the last bite of the lip-smacking dessert. The tang of cream cheese lingered on his tongue.

Despite all the activity and furnishings, Ally had stayed away. Her mom had brought him a casserole, but he hadn't seen hide nor hair of Ally since yesterday.

Maybe moving next door to her hadn't been the best plan. It was the only land he'd found to lease, but it wasn't a good way to relieve the tension between them and get their friendship back on track.

He stood and waited until the stiffness eased in his knee before shuffling to the sink, then made short work of washing the pan and poured a cup of decaf.

Since they'd grown up in the same church, hung out in youth group and been in the same class, he, Ally and his now-sister-in-law, Caitlyn, had been best friends all the way back to kindergarten.

But Ally had avoided him at Mitch and Caitlyn's wedding. And after his bull wreck, when Ally had visited the rehab center with her dog program and had realized her patient was him, she hadn't been able to get out of there fast enough.

She was obviously uncomfortable because of that kiss that had spun his world into a blur faster than any bull ever had.

But hadn't affected her.

Maybe they needed to talk about the kiss. Agree to forget it. He dried the glass dish and tucked it under his arm. If he walked slow and careful and took the stupid stick, he could handle the uneven yard. He gulped the useless coffee, grabbed the cane and stepped out his back door.

Must have been after hours for her clinic. Only one other truck and a car were parked next to Ally's—probably one of her youth group volunteers. He continued past the house to the block structure with a neon open sign in the window.

A cowbell clanged when he opened the door.

"I'll be right with you," Ally called from the back. "Is it an emergency?"

"It's just me."

Silence.

A deep woof came from behind the counter. Cody eased closer. A male German shepherd lay sprawled on the floor, his ears perked up.

"Hey, buddy, don't worry—the vet's nice." He lowered his voice. "And she's a looker, too."

He set the dish on the counter, settled in a chair in

the waiting area, picked up a livestock magazine and thumbed through it.

"You know I'm on your side, Ms. Curtis." A man's voice came from the back. "I love animals as much as you do. But you're not in compliance with the cats. You're supposed to provide eighteen square feet per cat."

"The mama cat and two kittens just came in yesterday." Her words came fast, desperate. "Their owners moved and abandoned them. I just couldn't turn them away. I planned to buy some more acreage so I could expand, but someone else beat me to the property."

He'd tied up the land she needed. Cody closed his eyes.

"I'm sorry, but I'll have to write you up."

A pause.

"I understand." She sounded so broken.

And now she was in trouble.

Cody had to find a way to fix it.

Chapter Two

"**M**aybe you should consider revoking your no-kill policy." Mr. Humphries wouldn't even look at her as he flipped to the appropriate form on his clipboard.

"I can't do that." Ally's heart squeezed. Kill a perfectly healthy animal just because no one wanted it?

"You know I'm against it, too. Maybe you could take some of the cats to another shelter."

A lump lodged in her throat. "So they can put them down?"

"I'm sorry, Ms. Curtis." The inspector strolled toward the front of her clinic.

Come on—think of some way to change his mind. Ally hurried after him.

"Excuse me." Cody met them in the lobby, removed his cowboy hat. "I came to pick out those cats we talked about."

Mr. Humphries's eyes narrowed with suspicion.

Ally's insides lit up. "How many would you like?" She held up three fingers behind Mr. Humphries's back.

"Four."

"Four?" Mr. Humphries echoed.

Four? Her heart warmed.

"Just moved in next door. Cody Warren." He offered his hand and the older man shook it. "My barn is infested with mice. I'm thinking four cats should take care of the problem."

He sounded so convincing she wanted to hug him.

Mr. Humphries examined Cody a moment longer, then turned to Ally. "You run a clean operation here." He slid his pen into his pocket, tucked the clipboard under his arm. "I don't want to have to shut you down. See that you stay in compliance. I doubt that your neighbor can rescue you next time."

"Thank you, Mr. Humphries."

"And I trust—" he gave her a stern look "—that if I come back in an hour, you'll be down three cats."

"Four and they'll be in my barn." Cody clasped his hat to his chest. "You're welcome to come visit them."

With a slight nod, the inspector exited the clinic.

Ally waited, held her breath. A car door shut and an engine started. "Thank you, thank you, thank you." She jumped up and down.

"Just call me Ally's hero." He shot her a wink that made her heart take a dive.

Her fists clenched. Now he wanted to be her hero?

"You should have told me you were over the limit. I'd have taken the cats before your inspector came."

"It's really weird." She nibbled the inside of her cheek. "I've already been inspected for this year. Someone had to complain for Mr. Humphries to show up again."

"Who would do that? We don't have any other neighbors."

"I don't know, unless it was a client." She twirled the

end of her braid round and round her finger the way her dad used to do. "I've had a few new ones lately. Maybe someone didn't like what they saw." Not everyone liked her strays or her shelter. Some people could be so heartless.

"If that's the case, they should find another vet instead of hassling you." He gestured to the shepherd. "What's he in for? Armed doggery?"

She suppressed a grin. "Hoss is just staying with me while his family is on vacation. I didn't have time to put him in a run yet." The dog's tail wagged as she snapped a leash on his collar. "Why did you really stop by?"

"I brought your dish back. All washed and everything."

"You didn't have to do that." She raised an eyebrow. "You walked across my rutted yard for that?"

"I took it slow with my trusty stick." He patted his cane, cleared his throat. "I also wanted to discuss…uh… to ask you for contacts on some hands. Since you do cattle vaccinations, I figured you'd know the right people."

Nervous? Cody Warren nervous? About asking her for ranch hand contacts? She strode over to the bulletin board.

"A large ranch in the area just downsized. Lots of layoffs." She removed a business card and pulled two stubs bearing names and numbers, then passed them to him. "The card is the ranch owner for references. The numbers are hands." She rubbed the ache in the back of her neck.

"All your tension still lands in your neck and shoulders, huh?" Cody stuffed the contacts in his shirt pocket and limped around behind her. His warm hands grasped her shoulders, kneading her sore muscles.

She stiffened, almost pulled away. But when she began to relax, all thought of getting away left her. She had to focus on something other than the shivers he was stirring up. "I won't hold you to four cats. If you'll just take three, I'll be under limit."

"I want four. I was thinking I'd take the ones who've been here longest. But it would be a shame to separate the mama and her kittens, so I'll take those three plus one of the veterans."

Such a sweetheart. Not many men thought that way. If he ever grew up and settled down, he'd make someone a great husband. "That would be Bruno. His past shouldn't be a problem."

"You know his story?" His thumbs soothed away her aches.

What was she talking about? Oh yes, Bruno. "He killed his former neighbor's pet rabbit and chickens. We don't have any of either near here and he won't be wandering far from home anymore since I neutered him."

"Hear that, Hoss." The German shepherd's ears pricked. "You better stay on her good side."

"I need to get him in his run." She stiffened again, pulled away and dug four collapsed cardboard carriers from under the counter. "And we better go get the cats before Mr. Humphries decides to come back."

And before she melted into a pool of butter at Cody's feet.

Mama cat supervised her orange tom and gray female as they clambered and pounced on hay bales, while Bruno checked out the loft.

"You don't think they'll run away?" Cody still

couldn't muster up the courage to discuss their past, so he kept coming up with inane subject matter.

"You fed them." She scratched the mama calico along her cheek. "So they should stay close here."

Cody settled on a hay bale. Would his leg ever stop aching?

A breeze wafted through the barn, stirring strands that had strayed from her braid around her face. Absolutely beautiful. Why hadn't some man snapped her up? Was it because of all the homeless pets she kept? Cody loved animals as much as she did, but not everyone felt the same way.

If she'd found some critter-loving man and were living happily ever after, would it make whatever was left of his life easier or harder? "How come you never married?"

"Excuse me?" She propped her hands on her hips.

"Just curious." He shrugged. "Back when we were in high school, you dreamed right along with Caitlyn about getting married."

"I did, didn't I?" Her voice went soft and she settled on a hay bale facing him, elbows propped on her knees. "My parents married right out of high school and Mom never worked outside the home. She didn't have a clue about how to get a job, balance the checkbook or pay the bills."

She picked up the gray kitten and cuddled it. "Dad had done everything for her. For a while after he died, I thought I'd have to give up college and stay home to take care of her. It made me realize I never want to need anyone that much."

"Everybody needs somebody."

"Look who's talking." She caught his gaze. "Mr.

I'm-Never-Getting-Married-so-I-Can-Travel-and-Do-What-I-Want."

"I guess it got old." But it really hadn't. Not until he'd seen her again. Only one thing was certain. Being close to her drove it home. If he didn't have a bubble in his head, he'd go after way more than friendship with Ally.

He had to stop thinking about things he couldn't pursue. "I could build you a few extra pens above the ones you already have to solve your cat problem."

"I'd always planned to do that, just haven't had time." She bit her lip. "That would be great, but if you really want to help me, there is something else you can do."

"Just ask."

"Would you sell me a few acres? I had my eye on five, but one would get me out of a bind."

He'd have loved to. But the problem with that was that he was only leasing. Yet he needed his family to believe he was willingly retiring to become a rancher. Otherwise, they'd get curious and if they learned about his health situation, they'd hover and he'd have no peace while he decided what to do.

He couldn't burden her with his secret.

"Well?"

"Ally?" A man's voice called out, cutting off any response he might have given her.

"Over in the neighbor's barn," she yelled.

Footfalls crunched across the gravel and a shadow fell over the doorway.

A gray-haired man wearing scrubs stepped inside. "Everything go okay with the mastiff?"

"She'll be fine." She nodded. "The car just grazed her. Lacerations and contusions, but no internal injuries or broken bones. Most of her damage came from the highway."

"Ouch." The man winced. "Poor girl. I finished the vaccinations. Derek filled out all the records and he's putting the ranch file in the office. Just thought I'd check in before I go."

Ally gestured to the man. "This is Dr. Lance Bridges, the other vet here at my clinic. Cody is our new neighbor. He took Bruno and the three strays I got in yesterday, just in the knick of time. I'll tell you all about it tomorrow."

"Nice meeting you." Cody clasped hands with Lance. "Likewise."

"You go on home. I'm sure Erin has your supper ready."

"See you tomorrow." As Dr. Bridges turned away, a younger man approached. Blond, midtwenties.

"Some first day, huh, Derek?"

"I loved every minute of it." The younger man smiled, scratched the kitten Ally held under its chin. His hand dangerously close to hers.

Huh? Was he flirting with Ally?

Was this guy an assistant? Or working on being her boyfriend?

Ally pushed stray strands of hair away from her face. "You tell that sweet wife of yours I'll try not to keep you this late on a daily basis."

Whew. Thankfully the guy was married.

But what should it matter? Ally's love life was none of Cody's concern. It couldn't be.

"Don't worry. Brandy understands my work." The guy turned to the door.

"Where are my manners?" Ally stood, brushed the

hay off the seat of her jeans. "This is Cody Warren. We were friends all through school, and now he lives next door. Derek Tatum is my new veterinary technician."

"It's nice to meet you. I'll see you tomorrow, Ally."

"Make that Tuesday. Have a nice, long Labor Day weekend. With so many ranches in Aubrey, we have more cattle vacs scheduled as usual. But maybe there won't be any emergencies."

"But you're working tomorrow and Monday. If it's all the same to you, I'd just as soon do the same."

"If you're sure."

"I am." With a wave, Derek left them alone.

Ally set the kitten down and it curled around her ankle. "So what about the land?"

He'd hoped she'd forget about the issue. "I can't sell you any of it."

"Why not?" Her shoulders slumped. "Just an acre? A half an acre?"

His only option was to be as honest as he could. "I'm only leasing it." What were the odds of her talking to his parents about his land anyway?

"But yesterday you said you bought it."

"No, you said I bought it. I decided to test the ranching thing out before doing anything permanent." Great. He'd just reinforced her notion that he had commitment issues.

"Oh." The corners of her mouth tipped down and she stood. "I'm really tired and I can't wait to get cleaned up. Do you want me to walk you across the yard?"

It was tempting to lean on her. But not advisable.

"I'll be fine. I'll go nice and slow." He opened the door for her.

She exited and he followed. By the time he'd made

five steps, she'd already reached her back door. Not sparing him another glance, she slipped inside and closed it.

So much for talking about the kiss. It seemed as if without saying a word, they both agreed to forget it. At least things weren't quite as strained between them. Though maybe that would've been preferable.

Ally was his friend. And that was all she could be. So why did he have to keep reminding himself of that?

Ally stepped into the mudroom, where excited yips greeted her. "Hey, Foxy. Hey, Wolf." The two puffballs danced for her attention. "Did y'all miss me today?"

Peering through the blinds, she watched Cody slowly hobble to his house. He'd saved her from a written reprimand. But he wouldn't sell her any land, because he was only leasing. Which meant he probably wasn't staying.

He frustrated the daylights out of her. So she wouldn't coddle him. He was an adult. If he was goofy enough to insist on living alone and walking on his bad leg without any help, that was his problem. She didn't have the time or energy to babysit him while he played rancher next door. On the land he'd leased right out from under her.

She pulled off her manure-caked boots and picked a Pom up in each arm, snuggling them close. They stilled, except for their noses.

"Busted. Mama traitored—petting countless other dogs and cats again." The sniffing stopped and kisses took over. With both cheeks sufficiently licked, she set them down.

"Mom?"

"In the living room. Did the emergency surgery go okay?"

"Yep, she'll be fine. Derek was a great help to Lance with the vaccinations." She strolled into the living room. Home. She loved this house. The worn plank flooring and walls, beams across the ceilings, and ancient windows. Comfortable, unpretentious and cozy.

"Did Dr. Bridges leave already?" Mom was in her jammies, curled up on the couch with a book.

"A few minutes ago." Ally couldn't wait to soak in the bathtub for an hour. Except for Mom's weekly book club meetings, they both were usually in for the evening by six o'clock. Such exciting lives they led. Probably should get out more.

Maybe she'd have more oomph at the end of the day with Derek around. Most applicants would have waited until Tuesday to start work, but she was thankful for his eagerness.

Today's ranch vaccinations had been so much easier with help, and when she'd gotten the emergency call, Derek had been able to stay with Lance and finish. Best of all, she didn't ache quite as much with an extra set of hands at work.

Wolf and Foxy pranced circles around her, offering unconditional love—even though she'd been with other critters all day.

"Y'all don't care who I play with, do ya?" Her high-pitched tone sent the tiny bundles of energy into excited jitters and she settled on the floor, leaning against the couch. The Poms fought for lap space, then stilled as she stroked their soft coats. "You'll never guess who showed up after you left, though."

"I saw you with Cody after I got out of the shower."

"He arrived just as the state inspector was about to write me up for having too many cats. Cody took Bruno and the three I got in yesterday and saved the day." And rubbed her shoulders. She could still feel his touch.

"I wonder why the inspector came again. Good thing Cody was there to be your hero."

"Until I asked him to sell me an acre and he admitted he's only leasing the land." She picked up Foxy and rubbed noses with her. "What's up with that, Foxy?"

The only problem with furry friends—they never answered back.

Wolf let out a yip.

Not in people language, anyway.

"Maybe once his lease is up, you can buy the acreage. It'll work out." Mom gave her an encouraging smile. "Just have faith."

Mom's words stung. Faith was exactly what she didn't have.

Why couldn't her new neighbor have been someone else? A single woman living alone, or a family with a mom who needed adult companionship. Someone who could have at least sold her an acre or two. And who didn't stir such confusing feelings in her. Even some animal-hating grouch. Anyone other than landlocking Cody.

Though he probably wouldn't even stay put. Which, as her mom had pointed out, could be good for her. He wouldn't even be here if not for his injuries and she was sure he'd head back to the circuit just as soon as he could hobble there.

If Cody moved on, she'd get another chance to convince the owner to sell her a parcel of the land. But that meant Cody would run out on her like before. When she'd needed him most. She had to stay away from him in order to survive this go-round.

For as long as she could remember, Cody had gone from one obsession to the next, never sticking with anything for long. Baseball, basketball, fishing, hunting, soccer, football, racquetball and finally rodeo. He'd pursued rodeo far longer than anything else.

Wolf was hanging off her lap and Ally shifted her legs into a crisscross position to give the dogs more room. Closing her eyes, she twirled the end of her braid around her finger.

Sometimes she could still imagine it was her dad doing it. Even after twelve years, she longed for his presence, his sound counsel. He'd have known what to do about her shelter. But he wasn't here.

"Ally?"

She looked up. Mom had clearly asked her something. "What?"

"Are you ready for supper?"

"You can go ahead. I need a bath."

Her only hope was to buy the land once Cody got bored with playing rancher and his lease was done. And that would be best for her wayward heart, too.

A hot bath and a bowl of soup later, she crawled in bed thinking about her predicament.

And Cody. She wouldn't be his new short-term diversion.

Stop thinking about him.

She closed her eyes and snuggled under the covers— exhaustion fogging her brain.

Dogs barking. Ally opened her eyes. Lots of yapping. And they were close. How long had she slept— minutes or hours? It was still dark outside. She was used to the sound. In fact, she usually woke up only when they weren't barking. But this frenzied chorus seemed to come from right under her window.

She rolled over, squinted at the green digital numbers on her clock. Four twenty-three. Why were the dogs stirred up in the wee hours of the morning? And why did they sound so near? She threw the covers back, jumped up and hurried to the window.

Three dogs surrounded the live oak in her yard. Barks, yips and growls filled the early-morning air. As her eyes adjusted to the moonlight, she spotted a cat clinging to a gnarled, twisted limb high in the tree. In the distance, the lights were on in the barn.

What were they doing loose? Her heart lodged in her throat. She flipped her lamp on, tugged a warm-up suit over her pajamas and darted down the hall.

"Mom." Ally knocked on her bedroom door. "The animals are loose." Flashlight in hand, she bolted through the house and jerked the front door open. A light blinded her as she barreled into something solid.

Someone solid.

She screamed.

Chapter Three

"It's me." Cody's strong arms steadied her. The soft flannel of his shirt warmed her against the chill of the night air as his familiar spicy scent surrounded her.

Ally pulled away from him. "Are you all right? I didn't hurt your knee, did I?"

"No." He lowered the beam of his flashlight and she got a glimpse of his denim clad legs. "Why are the animals out?"

"I have no idea."

"I'll help you corral them."

"You can't." She stepped around him. "It's dark and you'll step in a hole or something and hurt your knee. If you want to help, though, go to the barn. I'll catch the dogs and bring them to you. Just put them in pens and I'll sort out who goes where later. Once I get all the dogs, then I'll be able to lure the cats back."

"I'm on it." He limped toward the barn.

She ran to the clinic. The door stood wide open. Odd. She grabbed several collars with leashes and a handful of treats, then scurried back out to the gathering under the tree.

"Here, Spot." The splotched mutt ignored her as he jumped, his front paws running up the tree with each lunge as he growled at the terrified cat. "I've got treats." She dug a biscuit out of her pocket and held it just out of the dog's reach. Spot's nose twitched and he lost interest in the cat long enough for her to clasp a collar around his neck. "Gotcha."

She stood on his leash while she went through the same routine with the Border collie mix and the terrier mix. With all three dogs leashed, she tugged them with all her might toward the barn.

A flashlight beam shone from the house. "What can I do?" Mom hollered.

"Catch dogs. Then we'll worry about the cats."

"I called Lance—I mean Dr. Bridges—to help."

A truck turned into her drive. Lance? No, he couldn't have gotten here from Denton so quickly. Who could it be? *Please not an emergency.* Pressure mounted in her chest.

The engine died and doors slammed. "Hey, it's Raquel. Cody called us to help."

Ally could have cheered. "Y'all are awesome." The Walkers were her closest neighbors other than Cody. Ally usually handled the health needs of their four-legged menagerie.

"How many are accounted for?" Slade, Raquel's husband, hurried to take the three unruly dogs from Ally.

"I'm not even sure." Ally scanned the area with her flashlight. "These are the only ones I've caught. I didn't want Cody hobbling around in the dark, so he's in the barn waiting to put them away as I catch them."

"Hunter, you help Mom catch dogs." Slade roughed up the young boy's already tousled hair with his free hand. Although the dogs fought against the leashes, he didn't budge. "I'll haul this rowdy handful to Cody and then Ally can see who's missing. I'll be right back to help."

"I'm so grateful y'all came." Ally surveyed the three-some clad in wrinkled jeans and jackets.

"This is gonna be fun." Seven-year-old Hunter darted around the back of the house.

"Watch for snakes," Raquel called.

"Probably too cool for them and I don't usually have any in the yard." Ally jogged to the barn, opened the door for Slade and took a quick inventory.

Some of the missing were boarders. She had to find them and keep this incident quiet. Strays roaming free could jeopardize her shelter. But if word got out that people's pets had gotten loose, her clients would lose trust in her.

As she stepped outside, another truck pulled in the drive. The door opened and shut. "How many are loose?" Lance's flashlight bobbed his approach.

"Thirteen dogs, nineteen cats—some strays and some boarders. Not all of them at least. I'm sorry to drag you out this time of night all the way from Denton."

"It's only fifteen minutes and we're in this together."

Over the next couple of hours, Hunter caught two dogs, while Slade rounded up three. Raquel manhandled a smaller breed and Lance nabbed another, while Ally wrangled an elusive wienie dog boarder who seemed intent on playing hide-and-seek.

"I heard some barking in the woods behind the barn." Slade headed back out. "Raquel, Hunter, y'all stay here—might be dangerous."

"Be careful." Raquel shuddered.

"I'll go with you." Lance followed.

Hunter and Raquel helped soothe the dogs, and as the sun began to rise, Slade and Lance returned with the last two Lab mixes.

"What about the cats?" Hunter helped her get the last two in their pens.

"They won't come out unless it's quiet and calm." Ally hugged Raquel. "Thanks so much for coming. I'd still be at it if y'all hadn't."

"We were glad to help. Hunter had a blast." Raquel tousled his hair. "You can tell all your friends about your dog-wrangling skills."

"Um…about that." Ally bit her lip. "Would y'all mind keeping this incident quiet? I don't want the people who board their pets here to lose confidence in my services."

"Good point." Slade gripped Hunter's shoulder. "Hear that? We're keeping this a secret." Hunter nodded and Slade turned to his wife. "We better go so Ally can tend to her cats."

The threesome waved goodbye as Ally thanked them again.

"Go home, Lance. Get some rest. I can handle things here today."

"Not happening. Saturday's always our busiest. If your mom will ply me with coffee, I'll be good to go."

"Great idea." Mom covered her yawn and the two strolled toward the house.

Leaving only Cody. "You should get some sleep. All I have to do is call the cats."

"I'll stick around." He scanned the pens lining each side of the long barn. "I doubt any of the dogs are in the pens they're supposed to be in. Once you retrieve the cats, I'll help you sort it out. Besides, I need to talk to you."

"Okay." *About what?* "Can it wait?"

"Go call your cats. It'll keep."

"I'll be back as quick as I can." She dug a stack of collapsed cardboard carriers from the storage closet, tucked them under her arm. "And thanks for all your help."

"My pleasure."

Ally stepped out. Cody seemed so serious. Had he talked to the owner? Would he sell her the land after all?

"Here, kitty, kitty, kitty." Ally's call was a gentle singsong as Cody watched from the barn window.

It took several minutes, but the cats started coming. From trees, from the roof, from the loft and from the woods. Soon she had them in cardboard kennels, and she pulled her truck near to load them.

Cody couldn't stand watching her do all the work. It had nearly killed him to let Slade and Lance play dogcatcher while he stayed in the barn. It was daylight now—easier to watch for holes. He limped out to help.

"What are you doing out here?"

"At least let me load them for you, save you a little work." He made his way to the truck bed.

"Fine." She picked up a kennel. "Stack them in twos and make sure they're stable. I don't want them tumbling around and scarring their delicate sensibilities for life."

"Cats have sensibilities?" He grinned.

"They most certainly do. Very delicate ones."

"I guess if anybody knows about it, it would be you."

Cody loaded a kennel she handed him. "You looked like the Pied Piper out there gathering them all up."

"Just call me the crazy cat lady."

"You must be exhausted."

"You, too." She adjusted a stack of kennels. "I can't believe the Walkers came over to help so early. How do you even know them?"

"Raquel's first husband was a Texas Ranger and Mitch's partner. A few years after he died, Mitch tried to fix us up, but neither of us was interested and she eventually met Slade."

He slid another kennel in place. "Slade used to be a chaplain on the rodeo circuit, so I'd seen him around. They're good folk. Since Raquel's the school nurse and it's Saturday, and Slade's a preacher and it isn't Sunday, I knew they could come without messing up the rest of their day."

"I couldn't even think of any of that. I was in panic mode."

"Speaking of panic, I don't mean to scare you—" A cat yowled at him as he hoisted its kennel on top of another "—but you don't have any enemies, do you?"

"Not that I know of." She stopped, caught his gaze. "Why?"

"That's what I wanted to talk to you about." Cody's heart thudded. He really didn't want to frighten her, but she seemed so oblivious. "Somebody had to have let them out."

"But why would they?" She hugged herself. "I must have left a couple of the pens open."

"Have you ever done that before?"

"No. But I've been distracted."

True. The almost reprimand from the inspector. The

land Cody couldn't sell her. "Even if you left a couple of pens open, that doesn't explain how thirteen dogs and nineteen cats got out. You don't really think one of each got out, then nosed all the other locks until they opened like it happens in the movies?"

"Of course not." She huffed out a sigh, shoved another pet carrier at him. "But I don't know why anyone would let them out."

"Maybe somebody wants to shut you down." He settled the last cat in place, striving for casual, trying not to let her see how worried he was. "Think about it— you said your state inspector must have gotten a complaint to show up when he did, and now your critters are loose in the middle of the night."

"But no one lives anywhere near here." She spread her hands wide, gesturing to miles of endless woods and pastures surrounding their properties. "Just you and me. Who would want to shut me down?"

"What about Lance?"

"No. I've known him a couple of years. He's a nice man, a member of our church."

"Maybe he wants to buy you out?"

"He had his own clinic in Denton and sold it to work toward retirement."

"What do you really know about Derek?"

"He's a great guy. I can't tell you how much it helped to have another set of hands on duty yesterday."

"You're sure he's okay?"

"Positive." She shook her head. "He has no reason to want to shut me down."

"Maybe he wants his own practice."

"No. He's a tech. The only way he can do anything is under the supervision of a licensed vet."

But Cody wasn't so sure. Maybe he needed his Texas Ranger brother to do a background check on Derek. And Lance. Ally's safety was too important to risk.

She was way too important to him. Way more important than he should allow her to be.

It felt good to attend the church Cody had grown up in. How many years had it been since he'd been here? When he'd visited home for the holidays while on the circuit, he'd often gone with his sister in Dallas, with his brother when he'd lived in Garland or with Grandpa in Medina. Over the years, he'd only attended his home church a handful of times.

As morning class dismissed, he caught up with Mitch. "Can we talk a minute?"

"Sure."

Metal chairs scraped the tiled floor and multiple conversations started up.

Cody waited until the classroom emptied. "Can you run a background check on Derek Tatum for me?"

"Why?"

"I think somebody's trying to shut Ally's shelter down."

"What gives you that idea?"

"This has to stay quiet." She'd tan his hide if she knew what he was up to. "Ally's worried it'll hurt her shelter's reputation."

"My lips are sealed."

"Someone turned several of her animals loose the other night," Cody whispered, even though they were alone.

"You're sure it wasn't a faulty latch?"

"Thirty or so faulty latches? How about Lance Bridges—know anything about him?"

"Isn't he the other vet at her clinic?"

"Can you run a check on him, too?"

"I need probable cause, little brother." Mitch folded his arms across his chest—his stubborn stance. "I can't just run a check on random citizens because you want me to."

"How much probable cause did you have when you ran a check on each of your wife's employees?"

"What makes you think I did that?"

"I know you."

Mitch's Adam's apple bobbed. "Touché."

Cody sighed. "I'm worried about Ally's safety."

"I'll see what I can find."

"Thanks."

The brothers exited the classroom, strolled into the sanctuary and claimed their seats on each side of Mitch's wife Caitlyn. Old-fashioned pews lined the church with traditional hymnals in the book racks, and prisms of multicolored light radiated through the stained-glass windows.

Even after his years away, it was still home. New preacher, new Sunday-school teacher, new pianist, even a new song leader, but the same timeless hymns. He still knew most of the congregation, and a lot of the new faces he'd seen on the circuit over the years. But the most important member—to him—was nowhere in sight.

"Where's Ally?" Cody elbowed Caitlyn, trying for casual.

"She doesn't come anymore." Caitlyn grabbed a hymnal from the book rack. "Not since her dad died."

"Really?" Why would Ally turn away from God after her dad died? That was when she'd needed Him most.

"You two are neighbors now. Haven't you seen her?"

"Well, yeah. But we didn't talk about church."

The pianist played louder as a deacon approached the pulpit to begin announcements. "Welcome. We hope you enjoy our services today. All of the announcements are in your bulletin, but we have one pressing need. Our volunteer couple who'd signed up to supply animals and oversee the petting zoo at our annual church carnival had a family emergency out of town." He checked his notes.

"Looks like they had most of the plans for the petting zoo in place, but with the carnival this weekend, we'll need volunteers ASAP. We have several gentle horses, but we still need a few more small animals and two volunteers to oversee both. If interested, see our director after services." The deacon turned the service over to the song director.

Ally could provide dogs and cats, and she'd probably know where to find more animals. Maybe he could talk her into volunteering to supply the petting zoo and help him oversee it. It would help the church, she might find homes for some of her strays, and it could get her back in church.

But how should he go about convincing her to agree?

At least the week started off quiet. Routine appointments. No emergencies. No state inspectors. No loose animals.

A tiny golden Chihuahua mix shivered in the corner of her crate. From nerves, not temperature. Ally fished her out.

"Poor baby Buttercup." Ally snuggled the tiny shaking body against her chest. "My poor little runt. Your brother and sister found families, but don't give up. You'll get your forever home. I promise."

"There you are." Cody's voice echoed through the long barn.

Ally's heart sped as yips, barks and howls started up. She stepped out of the pen into the alley between the kennels.

"What are you doing here?"

"I could ask you the same thing." Cody limped toward her, leaning on his cane. "It's Labor Day. Don't you believe in taking a day off?"

"Staying open was convenient for my clients who were off work today."

"Well, since you like staying busy—" he stopped beside her, too close "—I have a proposal for you."

Her breathing sputtered. Not that kind of proposal. And she wouldn't fall for it if it was.

"Who's this little guy?" Cody scratched the quivering puppy between her ears.

"She. Her name is Buttercup. She and two littermates were found in the baseball park this past spring. Her brother and sister were adopted, but she's the runt. No one has picked her yet."

"My sister, Tara, loves Chihuahuas and hers died a few months ago." He lifted the puppy out of her arms and tenderly held the quivering body against his heart. "Maybe she'll take this little darling."

"She's not all Chihuahua and that's probably why she got dumped."

"Tara's not a breed snob. Who could dump a sweetie like this?" Cody baby-talked the puppy as she buried her nose in his neck.

"I don't have a clue." Ally's frustration came out in her tone. "At least there was a ball game that night. One of the moms found them and brought them to me."

"So which of these dogs and cats are homeless?" The chorus of barks had settled as the dogs got used to him in their midst.

"I keep the first twenty kennels on the left for boarding. Their people are gone on vacation or out of town for work reasons."

"Their people?" Cody grinned.

"I don't call them owners. We think of animals as our pets, so I figure the pets think of us as their people."

"Why is she shaking? It's not cold in here."

"Chihuahuas have an abundance of energy. She needs a walk. I was just about to take her for one." The Border collie–spaniel mix stuck his white-and-black muzzle through his fence and whimpered. "I know, baby. You want some attention, too." She rubbed his snout.

"Can I take him for a walk?"

"Probably not a good idea with your leg. But you can sit with him if you want."

"I'd love that. In fact, point out the ones who need some attention and I'll take care of it while you're gone."

He certainly wasn't making her heart grow any less fond of him by being so sweet and concerned over her strays. "You sure?"

"It's not like I have anything else to do."

"Okay, hit this side." She gestured to the pens on the right. "Love on as many as you can or want to."

"Will do." He headed for the first pen, then snapped his fingers and turned back toward her. "I almost forgot my proposal. I went to our old church yesterday and signed you up to supply the pets and oversee the petting zoo for the carnival this weekend."

Her neck heated. Was that steam blowing out her ears? "Without asking me?"

"It was a spur-of-the-moment thing and they needed volunteers fast or the whole thing was threatening to fall apart." He shrugged. "They'd already advertised the petting zoo, so they have to supply it. And just think, it might be a chance to get some of your strays adopted out."

"But I don't go to church there anymore." She propped her hands on her hips.

"I know. Caitlyn told me."

"So did you ever stop to think maybe I'm tied up with my church this weekend? Or with work? Or with life?" Not that she had one, really, but he didn't need to know that.

"Your church? You still go?"

"Of course I go." She was a glorified pew warmer, just going through the motions, but she wouldn't mention that. "There are other churches, you know."

"I just assumed. Caitlyn said you hadn't been since…"

Her dad died. Her eyes stung. "I haven't. Mom and I switched to one in Denton."

"Did something happen at our church?"

"No." She sat down on a hay bale. "It was just overwhelming. Everybody was so sympathetic and sad for us. The sympathy almost smothered us. We wanted to go somewhere where nobody knew us. Where nobody knew Dad." Her voice wobbled. "Where they didn't feel sorry for us." Where Ally could pretend she was still leaning on God.

The hay bale gave with his weight as he sat beside her. "They were sad for you because they care."

"I know." She swiped at her eyes. "It was just too much."

He put an arm around her shoulders.

Ally's pulse thrummed at his nearness. In fact, he

could probably hear it. More than anything, she wanted to snuggle close, accept his comfort.

For a breath of a second, she let her head rest against his shoulder. But if she stayed, she might lose her heart. And he'd realize how she felt. But she couldn't feel that way about him or any other man. Self-sufficient Ally didn't need anyone. Wouldn't allow herself to. She pulled away from him and stood.

"I'll make a few calls, see if I can rustle up animals for the petting zoo."

"And think about overseeing it? It starts after school lets out Friday and ends at seven. Then ten till three on Saturday."

"Sorry, those are my work hours." She scooped the puppy away from Cody, touching him as little as possible. "I need to walk Buttercup. You start dog-sitting while I go." She grabbed a leash off the wall and strode toward the exit.

"Hey, Ally."

"Hmm." She stopped but didn't turn around.

"Are you mad at me?"

Yes. I'm mad at you for leasing my land. For that stupid kiss and leaving me behind all those years ago. But she couldn't tell him that. And that wasn't what he meant anyway.

Her shoulders slumped. "No. But in the future, don't sign me up for anything without asking me first."

"I meant about the kiss."

Chapter Four

Great. Cody held his breath. Maybe she'd think that break in his voice came from the awkward subject.

"What kiss?" Ally kept her back to him.

She didn't remember? Had it meant so little to her? Could the same kiss that turned Cody's world upside down be forgettable for her? Oh, how he wished he hadn't brought it up. Especially since his emotions had betrayed him. But he had and he couldn't let it drop.

"After your dad— I got carried away with comforting you. I was a kid and you were so close to me. You smelled good and I just wanted to make you feel better." You smelled good? Just shut up, Warren. Before you say something else stupid and make it even worse.

"It didn't mean anything." Her response was little more than a whisper.

"I know." To her, anyway. His heart crashed on the concrete between his boots. "I just want you to know— you're safe from me. So if you ever need a shoulder, I'm not a kid anymore. I can do just comfort."

"Good to know." She latched the leash on Buttercup's collar and vaulted out of the barn.

Cody stood and looked skyward. "You're safe from me?" he muttered and ran a hand through his hair. It sounded dumb, and with everything in him, he wanted to take it back.

But at least maybe things would be easier between them now. He'd help her with her animals and, if she agreed, the carnival so her strays might be adopted. And deep down, so he could spend time with her.

On top of everything else, he'd lied to her. He hadn't signed her up for the petting zoo. But telling her he had was the only way he could think of to convince her to participate. *But, Lord, it's for Your good. It'll help the church. And maybe some of Ally's strays will find a home. So yes, I lied and I'm doing it for the wrong reasons, but You can take my selfish intentions and work them for good.*

The Border collie whimpered.

"Hey, guy. What's your name?" Cody read the plate by the gate. "Oreo." He unlatched the pen and stepped inside. In the corner, he sat on a chair and the dog reared up on his knees. "A fitting name."

Ally was the kind of woman who named each stray. The kind of woman he could spend the rest of his life with. But how much life did he have left?

He had to be satisfied with being her friend. Only her friend.

Oreo settled his chin on Cody's knee. "You wanna come home with me, don't you, boy?" The dog's ears perked up. "I think I'll tell Ally to hold you for me until I get a bit more steady on my feet."

His phone rang and he dug it out of his pocket. Mitch. "Hello?"

"Those persons of interest we discussed. No record. Upstanding citizens."

"You're sure?"

"We're talking Boy Scouts. Literally. Any more trouble?"

"No." Cody scratched between the dog's ears. "Maybe I'm barking up the wrong tree—pun intended."

"I hope so. You let me know if there are any more incidents."

"I will. Thanks." Cody ended the call.

Maybe the other night had been an accident. Kids playing a prank or taking a dare. Doubtful, but maybe. Or maybe it was just a onetime thing. Just in case, he had to stick close to Ally. To make sure she stayed safe.

But how could he keep his heart in check while he protected her?

Her mom and the volunteers from the youth group traipsed the property with various dogs while Ally walked the Border collie spaniel.

The kiss discussion was a whole day ago, but her heartbeat hadn't gotten back to normal yet.

She smelled good. Cody thought she smelled good. Back in high school, anyway.

Now she smelled like…horse sweat, manure and worse.

But twelve years ago, had Cody been attracted to her?

No, she'd just been sad and he'd wanted to make her feel better. She knew it then and she knew it now. Why couldn't her heart catch on?

If he'd felt anything for her, he wouldn't have left for the rodeo, wouldn't have stayed gone so long.

And besides, she did not need a man in her life. Not Cody. Or anyone else. She had to stop thinking about him and concentrate on finding homes for her strays.

Gravel crunched in her drive.

Past her regular hours, clients with emergencies tended to make frantic calls first, and her usual volunteers had already arrived and were walking dogs.

"Let's go see who it is, Oreo." She turned the dog back toward the clinic.

As she rounded the building Cody headed toward the barn.

With a woman.

Her heart stammered. His girlfriend? Fiancée?

She couldn't do this. Meet the woman in Cody's life. Not with her hair more out of her braid than in. Not with manure on her boots. She turned away and tried to hurry Oreo out of their sight.

"Ally, there you are," Cody called.

Ally's shoulders fell. Out of all the horse ranches in Aubrey, why had the one next to her stayed vacant until Cody Warren decided to play ranch?

"Ally, over here."

Straightening her shoulders, she pasted a smile on her face and turned around.

"Hey." Feet forward, one step at a time.

Way too fast, the gap between them closed. The woman looked familiar.

"This is my dog." Cody bent to scratch Oreo. "Or he will be when I get a bit more recovered."

For you or for your girlfriend?

"We bonded last night, didn't we, boy? I'd take him now if it wasn't for my knee, but Ally's holding him for me." Cody looked up at her. "You remember my sister, Tara?"

His sister. Ally looked past the blond hair, recognized the familiar green eyes and smile. "Of course." A fit of relieved laughter clogged in her throat. Did she sound as giddy as she felt?

"It's great to see you." Tara hugged her.

"You, too. I didn't recognize you at first."

"Well, what can I say?" Tara patted her locks. "I'm a hairdresser. When I get bored, I change my color. So, where is she?" Tara rubbed her hands together much the same way Cody did when anticipating food.

"She who?"

"Remember?" Cody winked at her. "I told you to hold Buttercup until I could check with Tara?"

The wink rattled her already-shaky heart. "Oh. Of course. You'd like to see her."

"Actually, I want to take her home."

"Without meeting her first? She's not full-blood."

"I know and I was reluctant at first, but not because of her breeding." Tara's eyes misted and she pressed a hand to her chest. "I've still got footprints on my heart from Ginger and I initially said no. But Cody told me how sweet Buttercup is and showed me a picture. I couldn't resist, so here I am."

"That's wonderful." Ally transferred Oreo's leash from one hand to the other as the dog grew restless. "I know you'll provide a good home for her. But there are a few things to consider before you see her. Didn't you get married?"

"Yes. We live in Dallas."

"Does your husband like dogs?"

"Oh, yes. Jared is a major animal lover." Tara's

smile turned dreamy. "I wouldn't have married him if he wasn't."

"What about children?"

"Not yet, but definitely planned in the future."

"Chihuahuas aren't the best breed with small children." Oreo persisted in wrapping his leash around Ally's legs. "They can be protective of their people and aggressive, so they've been known to nip toddlers for simply climbing into Mommy's lap."

"I didn't realize." Tara's eyes widened.

"But she's not all Chihuahua. So it may not be an issue and if it is, if properly trained or kept separate until the child is older, there shouldn't be a problem."

"Oh, good."

"Now, what about where you live?" Ally stepped out of the corkscrew Oreo had created. "Apartment? House? Do you have a yard?"

"We're in a subdivision, a house with a fenced-in yard." Tara knelt to scratch behind Oreo's ears. "We kept Ginger in the mudroom with a doggy door while we were gone. Whoever got home first romped with her in the backyard and sometimes we'd take her for a walk in the evening. When we were home, she had the run of the house."

Ally offered her hand. "You pass. Buttercup is yours if you want her."

"I do. Let's go get her." Tara stood and rubbed her hands together again.

"Let me walk him back." Cody took Oreo's leash, his hand grazing Ally's. Electricity shot all the way to her toes.

While it took food to excite Cody, and Buttercup got Tara animated, it seemed Cody was Ally's source of excitement. His nearness propelled her right over the edge of her sanity.

Which was why she'd held off on agreeing to volunteer for the carnival. Spending a day and a half with him certainly wouldn't help her keep her right mind. But time at the church with her other two dozen or so four-legged friends who still needed forever homes would be good advertisement.

More than anything, she wanted to help the abandoned pets in her care. But could she survive working side by side with Cody?

It had taken Tara forever to finalize her purchases—a crate, a leash, a chew toy, along with tick-and-flea preventative—before she'd taken Buttercup and been on her way.

Cody loved his sister, but he was dying to spend time with Ally alone.

"So, you're holding Oreo for me, right?"

"I told you I would." Ally pointed to the boarding side of the kennels. "See, I moved him over to the boarder side last night. He belongs to someone."

"Do I need to pay you for boarding him?"

"No. He's fine until you can take him home."

"I wish I could right now." Cody sat on a hay bale and scratched the dog's head. "Let me at least provide his food."

"I'm just glad he has a home. Whenever you're well enough, he's yours."

"You hear that, buddy?" The pup's ears perked up at the enthusiasm in Cody's voice. He already loved the dog.

"And now that you're in the longhorn business, Oreo is great with cattle."

"So you know his history?"

"His former owner brought him here because Oreo insisted on herding her horses."

"His former owner? Not his person?"

"She obviously was never Oreo's person." Ally harrumphed. "I guess I should be glad she brought him here instead of dumping him. Thanks for finding Buttercup a home."

"I thought you weren't going to let Tara have her for a minute there."

"I was just being cautious." Ally raked hay out of a kennel and replaced it with a fresh batch. "I know Tara would never dump a dog, but a lot of the reason there are so many strays is because people aren't prepared to have a pet. Some breeds have more issues than others, so I make sure my potential adoptive families understand what they're getting into."

"I'm glad she passed. She'd already fallen in love with Buttercup."

"Actually, Tara got the brief version since she's owned a Chihuahua before. If she hadn't, I'd have gone into the chewing-on-the-couch issues." The barking around them reached a crescendo as the last of the volunteers exited. "If the potential adoptive family has thought through all aspects of having a pet, there's more of a chance that both the pet and their person will be happy."

"So why didn't you grill me about Oreo before you agreed to let me be his person?"

"Because I know you. I remember how much you

loved Duke. How patient you were with him. Even as a kid. And I know you'll love Oreo and take care of him."

Memories of his first dog warmed Cody's insides. That Ally remembered did funny things in his chest.

"You'll take care of him no matter where you end up."

No matter where he ended up? Apparently he hadn't convinced her he was settling in Aubrey yet. Even though his longhorns arrived yesterday and she was vaccinating them tomorrow. Maybe he should've had a little faith and bought the ranch instead of leasing it.

The phone rang and she hurried past the kennels to the desk. "*Ally's Vet Clinic and Adopt-a-Pet.* May I help you?"

Cody scratched Oreo's ears and cooed at him. How did animals reduce full-grown men to baby talk? Probably the same way babies did. Michaela, his niece courtesy of Mitch and Caitlyn, had him making silly faces and doing whatever it took just to get a grin out of her these days.

And made him think about having his own kids someday. If he lived long enough for it.

Ally let out a little whoop, whirled around and came running toward him.

"What?" He stood.

"You're so awesome!" She hugged him.

His arms slid around her waist, sending his pulse into orbit. "I've been trying to convince everyone of that for years."

"That was a friend of Tara's. She said you told her all about my shelter. She's coming tomorrow to get three cats and a dog, maybe even two dogs, for her kids."

"That's wonderful." But not nearly as wonderful as holding her.

She pressed her cheek against his chest, probably hearing his erratic heartbeat. Way too soon, she pushed away from him and their gazes locked. Her face neared his as she rose on tiptoe.

Was she going to kiss him? He closed his eyes in anticipation but her lips brushed his cheek. And then she was gone.

By the time he found enough courage to open his eyes, she was grabbing a leash off the wall.

"My volunteer walkers should get here anytime. You can stay and play with the critters if you want. Oh, and that carnival thing you mentioned. I'll oversee it. I've got ponies, rabbits, goats and, of course, cats and dogs lined up. Is that enough?"

"Sounds great. We still on for tomorrow?"

"Tomorrow? Wednesday? On for what?" She cocked her head to the side.

"You're supposed to vaccinate my cattle."

"Oh. Yes. I'll see you then." She hurried out of the barn.

He pressed his palm against his cheek, trying to capture the sweetness of her lips on his skin as all his dreams puddled on the hay-strewn barn floor.

At least she'd agreed to the carnival. A whole day and a half spent with Ally.

Sorry, God. I know that's not what the carnival is supposed to be about. Help me focus on the kids and not Ally. It's gonna take lots of work.

Sturdy camouflage muck boots with pink trim and brown coveralls dwarfed Ally. But somehow she looked beautiful in the late-afternoon sunlight.

"You sure we'll finish by Bible study time tonight?" Cody forced his attention to the corral, which teemed with longhorns, but his gaze bounced right back.

"Piece of cake. This is the last of them." The smudge of mud that lined her cheekbone didn't take away from her beauty. But it did give him an excuse to touch her.

He pulled his work glove off and wiped at the smear with his thumb.

She jerked away. "What?"

"Just some dirt."

She wiped at it with her gloved hand, depositing more grime.

"You're only making it worse." He chuckled. "And I think it's more than dirt."

"Eeeeeewwww." Her nose crinkled. "Get it."

Cupping her chin with one hand, he wiped with the other. And kept wiping long after the suspicious smear was gone.

Despite their surroundings—a barn lot populated by fifty longhorns, a dozen ranch hands and two of her employees, all covered in sweat and worse—he still smelled her fruity shampoo, a hint of vanilla and fresh hay. He could drown in her milk-chocolate eyes as she looked up at him with trust.

And there was something else in her gaze. Like she felt something, too.

She pulled away, pushed stray strands away from her face with her upper arm and opened the chute. The longhorn they'd just finished with shot forward and one of his ranch hands led the next cow into position with a feed bucket.

They continued that process, and an hour later, Derek gave the final injection, then turned the calf loose.

They'd vaccinated all his cattle. Except for stubborn Bessie. The only cow with so much personality he'd already named her. She still stood in the holding pen, refusing to enter the corral to the chute.

"I'll get her." Ally climbed the rail pen.

Halfway up and before she could swing a leg over, Cody caught her foot. "I don't think that's a good idea. Let me send one of my hands in."

"I've done this at least a thousand times." She rolled her eyes and yanked her boot out of his grasp, swung her leg over the rail. "I can handle her."

"You just ran her calf through that chute. Mama cows don't like it when you take their calves."

"Duh." She climbed down inside the pen.

"Be careful." Bessie eyed her warily, the cow's long horns making Cody wary.

"Come on, Bessie." Ally rattled the feed bucket. "Let's get this one little shot done and then you can get on with your day, be back with your baby."

Bessie lowered her head.

"Ally! Get out of there!" Cody clambered up the fence. Heat shot through his knee as his boot slipped.

Bessie pawed the ground.

Ally stood still.

The longhorn charged.

Chapter Five

"Get out, Ally!" Cody's heart stopped.

Derek launched over the rail just to the cow's left and Bessie wheeled toward him as Ally bolted for the opening under the pen. Just before Bessie gored him, Derek climbed the fence, then vaulted over as Bessie rammed her horns into the metal barrier. The steel pin stabilizing the temporary fencing held as Cody jumped down and pulled Ally under to safety.

Bessie spun toward them and charged. Had his ranch hands driven the rest of the steel pins deep enough to hold? *Please, God, keep Ally safe.* He covered her body with his. Would this scare trigger his aneurysm to burst?

Horns rammed against metal and Cody expected hooves on his back. Nothing. He turned to see Bessie staggering in the middle of the pen, shaking her head, slobber trailing from her mouth. He rolled off Ally, stood and helped her up, then dragged her farther away.

Lance pulled off his gloves. "Can one of the hands mount up and drive her?"

"Or a dog." Cody kept his eyes on Ally, making sure she didn't do something stupid again. But from the way she was shaking, she'd probably learned a lesson. "I've got a Border collie."

"Try the dog first. Ally, you go on home, Derek and I will handle her," Lance insisted.

"Be careful." Obviously rattled, she nodded and started for her house.

Cody limped after her, matching his hop-along gait to hers. Once they rounded the barn, out of eyesight, he grabbed her and pulled her into his arms.

She didn't resist, laying her cheek against his shoulder.

"Don't ever do anything like that again."

"I've done it—"

"Thousands of times. But this time almost got you killed." He held her away from him a bit, gave her a gentle shake. "And I couldn't do a thing. I tried to climb in after you. But this stupid bum knee—I slipped and all I could do was watch those horns barreling toward you. All I want is to keep you *safe* and I couldn't."

"I'm fine."

"Just don't do it again." Another scare like that could kill him. "You've got Lance and Derek to handle the difficult ones. Let them. In fact, why don't you stick with dogs and cats and let them deal with the livestock."

"It's part of my job."

"Your critters need you *safe*." He needed her *safe*. "And in one piece. If Oreo does the trick, you're free to take him on every cattle call you get. If not, I'll lend you a ranch hand and a horse. Okay? No more getting in pens with mama cows. Got it?"

"Got it." She searched his face.

Had he given himself away?

He couldn't. Couldn't let her know how he felt when he couldn't promise her a future.

"Now get inside and shower." His hands dropped away from her shoulders. "You smell like a barn lot." Mixed with the tantalizing smell of Ally. It was so tempting to hold her in his arms again. And never let go. He took a step back, gave her a light shove.

"Do me a favor and don't tell Mom about this." She spun away from him, bolted for her house.

He needed to take lots of steps back. The smartest thing to do would be to move. But the thought of staying away from her completely tore at his insides.

Ally hummed as she strolled toward the barn. It was early morning, barely seventy degrees as the sun warmed her back. Another hour before her clinic opened. Enough time to feed her crew. She turned as movement caught the corner of her eye.

A large dark gray cat with grass-green eyes hunkered near her truck. Oh, no. Were her animals loose again? She scanned the property. Nothing. And come to think of it, she didn't have any cats like this in her shelter right now. Or among her boarders. Probably male, from the size of him.

"Here, kitty, kitty, kitty." She knelt, held her palm up. "I won't hurt you. Here, kitty."

The cat stared her down a moment. Then its stance relaxed.

"Here, kitty, kitty."

The cat trotted in her direction, stopped a few feet away, then slowly inched forward.

"I won't hurt you, sweetie. Do you have a home? Surely no one dumped a pretty kitty like you."

It sniffed her fingers, then rubbed its jaw against her nails and started purring.

"You sure don't act homeless and you look well cared for. In fact, you look familiar. Charcoal?"

The cat looked up at her as if he recognized his name.

"It's you, isn't it?" She picked him up, checked under his tail. Neutered tom. "You are Charcoal. What are you doing all the way out here, boy? Your mama must be worried sick. Let's get you inside and call her."

She headed for the clinic instead of the barn.

"Are they loose again?" Cody stepped off his porch. "I saw you coaxing him."

"No. That's what I thought when I saw him. But I'm pretty sure he belongs to Stetson and Kendra Wright. They're clients and I've taken care of Charcoal since he was a kitten. I'm pretty sure this is him. He must be lost."

"I know them from the rodeo, but they live a good five miles away, clear on the other end of Aubrey."

"I know. It's odd."

"Maybe it's not him." He caught up with her, scratched the cat's chin. Charcoal's purr grew deeper. "All revved up, aren't you, buddy?"

"I was just taking him inside the clinic so I can call Kendra."

"I was fixing to head to the barn to visit the critters."

"Would you mind feeding them? That was my plan, but I need to see to this guy."

"I'm on it." Cody gave the cat one final scratch, his eyes met hers, and he turned away.

If she didn't know better, the way he looked at her... Nonsense. But he'd been really upset yesterday when Bessie had nearly taken her out. He cared and didn't want her to get hurt, because they were friends. Besides, it was his cow terrorizing her, so he'd have felt doubly bad if she'd gotten hurt. That was all.

It had to be all.

She unlocked the clinic door, stepped inside and set the cat down. "You wander where you want while I call your people." She pulled the W drawer, found the file, scanned for the number and dug her cell out of her pocket.

It rang twice and Kendra answered.

"Hey, Kendra, it's Ally. I've got a cat wandering around my place that looks suspiciously like Charcoal."

"How in the world would he get all the way over there? Let me check the barn, see if he's here."

Children's voices chattering in the background. Must be Kendra's young daughter and son. "Mommy's gotta go to the barn. Let's make a train."

Ally's heart took a dip. She didn't want to ever need a man, but that also meant she'd never be a mom. The thought didn't used to bother her. But lately...

"Charcoal," Kendra called. "Here, kitty, kitty, kitty. Charcoal."

The little voices helped call.

"He doesn't seem to be here." Kendra chuckled. "We've roused a barnful of cats, but no Charcoal. And he's usually here ready to eat first thing in the morning."

"I'll put him in a boarding kennel and you can stop by when you get a chance."

"Thanks, Ally. I really appreciate it. I know he prowls at night, but I never imagined him going as far as your place."

It was odd. Ally ended the call, pulled a temporary cardboard kennel from the stack and folded it into shape. "I hate to do this to you, Char. But I'm taking you to the barn and when you hear all those dogs barking, you'll be glad you're in a box." She picked him up and started to set him in the kennel.

He let out a yowl and braced three feet against the cardboard.

"It's just for a minute, I promise." She pried his feet loose and closed the lid before he could pop back out, then stuck her finger through one of the large airholes until she felt fur. "It's okay, big guy."

He squalled as she carried him out and toward the barn.

"You're heavy, mister. And you should be quiet. You're letting every dog in the place know you're here."

The yowling continued as she stepped inside the barn and hurried to open a boarding kennel, then opened the box. Charcoal planted himself at the back.

"First you want out, then you want to stay in. Come on, boy." She scooped him up.

By this time, the dogs were in full chorus, and the poor cat was so nervous he willingly dove for the boarding kennel. She fastened the latch in place, then rubbed his cheek through the wire but he didn't purr.

"You'll be okay. I promise. I won't let any of these yappers near you, boy."

"He's the one who started the racket." Cody.

She jumped, spun around.

"Sorry." He sat on a folding chair in Oreo's pen. "I thought you knew I was here."

"No. I called Kendra. She'll pick him up sometime today. Could you feed him while you're at it?"

"Sure. I gave Oreo a little extra after he worked so hard yesterday."

"I can't believe I never thought of using him for vaccinations."

"He's a pro. And I meant what I said—you borrow him for every cattle call. From now on."

From now on. But what about if Cody left? If he went back to the rodeo. Or followed whatever his next diversion turned out to be.

"What if this ranching thing doesn't turn your crank and you leave? What then?"

"If anything happens to me, I want you to have Oreo."

If anything happened to him? Like he might die? Her mouth went dry.

"I mean…if I end up…leaving, I want you to have Oreo for your work."

But he hadn't said *leaving*. He'd said *if anything happened*. Was Cody sick? No. Cody was way too tough. And except for the limp, he was the picture of health. He couldn't be sick. He'd just misspoken.

Cody was healthy as a horse. He had to be. Because in spite of everything, she needed him to be.

She searched his gaze a few seconds longer. If he was sick, he wouldn't be itching to get back on the circuit. No. Cody was fine.

But he wasn't the type to think of giving up a dog he loved. Was he so worried about her working with cattle that he'd leave Oreo behind?

The bright September day had cooled to comfortable temperatures. Ally scanned the area to make sure all the animals were in the shade.

Sheltered by two huge live oaks, the petting zoo spread across the church lawn with various animals in the temporary pens Cody had built. Carnival game booths covered half of the parking lot, with horseback rides occupying the rest.

"This is the best petting zoo we've ever had." Caitlyn stroked a silver rabbit inside a pen. "I tried to get Ally to do this over the years on numerous occasions. She turned me down every time, but let Cody ask and here she is."

Under the guise of securing the goat's tether, Ally turned away to hide her heated cheeks. Was Caitlyn suspicious? She'd been studying Ally all afternoon. Had she figured out Ally had feelings for Cody?

"Cody didn't ask." Ally shot him a glare. "He signed me up, leaving me little choice. Either do it or find someone else. It was easier to just do it."

"You signed her up?" Caitlyn frowned. "I thought you only suggested—"

"It worked out okay." Cody sent Caitlyn a panicked, wide-eyed "stop talking" look. "Dr. Bridges was able to fill in, your new vet tech is working this weekend, and when's the last time you took off?"

So he hadn't really signed her up. He'd only told her he had. She jabbed a finger at him. "Just don't try to make it an annual thing, buddy."

"I hated tricking you." He grimaced. "But it was for a good cause—to help the church and your furry friends. I hope you're not mad at me."

"I'm not." Ally managed to infuse lightheartedness into her voice. "But I'll be livid if you try something like that again." Though he'd probably be a memory by then.

"Maybe I'll have won you over with my charm by next year and you'll volunteer on your own."

"Uh, yeah, knock yourself out with that." Ally rolled her eyes, hoping to pull off the effortless friendly banter she and Cody once had. "Your charm bounces right off me." If only it were true. If only she could be immune to him.

"Kids should be getting home from school anytime." Caitlyn checked her watch. "Soon we'll be overrun. Are we ready?"

A car pulled into the lot, then another and another.

"Show's on." Ally stroked the horse's silky snout just as Cody patted her fingers instead of the horse.

Electricity shot up her arm and she snatched her hand away. Why had she agreed to this?

Because he'd gotten some of her pets adopted out and she felt she owed him?

No.

Because she wanted to find forever homes for more of her animals?

Partly.

But mostly because, try as she might, she couldn't resist Cody, and spending time with him was the highlight of her days. Even though he thought of her as only a friend. Even though she was happy on her own.

She was pathetic.

More arrivals, and in no time the parking lot teemed with vehicles and kids dragging their parents toward the games and zoo, along with a smattering of preteens trying to look bored.

"Wow, check him out." One of the girls giggled and elbowed her friend.

Ally's face heated. She knew who they were talking about without even looking.

Slade Walker and Mitch were helping with the horses and were both nice-looking men. But Cody drew females like a magnet.

Including her.

A day and a half spent with Cody. A beautiful kind of torture.

* * *

Half of day two at the petting zoo was behind them. Cody would go back to dropping in on Ally at her clinic, but this undivided time together would soon be over.

Truth be known, his cattle ranch bored him to tears—just as he suspected it would. But he had to make a living without the rodeo. Thankfully, he'd hired a great foreman and hands to run the place for him. Time with Ally was all that kept him sane.

He couldn't take his eyes off her as she helped a little girl hold a rabbit properly while the rest of the kids stood in a circle around her. So patient, so gentle with the children and the animals. Her smile went all the way to her eyes. Her laugh all the way to her heart.

"It's nice seeing her like that, huh?" Caitlyn squeezed his good shoulder. "The old Ally. I see glimmers of her every once in a while. Usually when she's with some critter."

"She used to be so much fun, so lighthearted and carefree. Now she's on edge."

His tone echoed his wistfulness for the old Ally.

"She changed after her dad died. If not for her vet practice, she'd probably be a hermit." Caitlyn brushed her hands down the front of her jeans, removing imaginary fur. "I'm truly amazed she agreed to help with the petting zoo. Usually I can't get her off her farm unless there's an animal needing treatment."

That was probably part of it. But Cody doubted she was tense with everyone the way she was with him. The kiss still hung between them.

"At least she still goes to church."

"Yeah, but something inside Ally died when her dad did."

"I shouldn't have left."

Caitlyn gave him a questioning look.

"I mean, her dad had just died." *Make it sound casual.* If Caitlyn figured out his feelings for Ally, she'd badger him to make a move. A move he had no right to make until he figured out what to do with his aneurysm. "I should have stuck around a little longer, put off my career for a while and supported my friend."

"She didn't want you to and if you had, she'd have pushed you away just like she did everyone else."

"How can we help her?"

"I think you moving in next door already has. You got her here. And no matter what she says, no one can resist your infectious charm for long." Caitlyn shot him a wink, patted his arm. "I better get back to horseback-riding duty. I just wanted to check and make sure you're not overdoing it on that leg."

"Ally ordered me to sit in this chair by the puppies and kittens, so that's what I'm doing. She handles the kids."

"Good." Caitlyn tousled his hair as if he were a child and turned toward the game area.

Ally caught him staring. Her smile died. The light in her eyes dimmed.

"Okay, kids." She clapped her hands to get their attention. "Let's go see the puppies and kittens over by Mr. Cody."

It would take much more than every ounce of charisma Cody could muster to crack the wall Ally had built around herself. And then he'd have to tread carefully on the friends-only path.

Invite the kids in for food, ply them with treats, then make them sit through a mini-sermon. They'd fallen for it both nights.

But Ally had seen through their plan. It was for the children and their parents. Not the workers.

In the church parking lot, dedicated members cleaned the game area, deflated the bouncy houses and picked up trash. She headed for the cattle trailer.

By the time parents and kids streamed out of the church, she'd loaded the horses, ponies and goats and hosed off the corner of the parking lot where the horses had been.

"There you are," Caitlyn called. "Mitch and some of the other guys could have done this."

"I know. But I'm used to it and I'm in charge of the animals."

"I'm glad to get a minute with you alone. Without Cody."

Ally's heart rattled. Caitlyn was on to her. She knew Ally was having a hard time resisting his appeal.

"Do you think he's okay?" Caitlyn asked.

Ally squelched a relieved sigh. This wasn't about her feelings for Cody. "You mean his injuries?"

"No. I mean his heart."

Oh, no. Had he just come off a bad relationship? *Please, Caitlyn, don't tell me about some woman in his life.*

"I know it must be hard for him to not rodeo anymore. He must be heartbroken." Caitlyn folded the chairs and leaned them against a tree.

Huh? So this wasn't about his love life. "I thought he decided not to go back."

"I can't imagine Cody deciding to quit, not as long as he's breathing. Don't you think it's strange that his sudden retirement came on the heels of his bull wreck?"

"You think he's hurt worse than he's letting on?" Ally's heart lodged in her throat.

"He's gotten a lot of concussions over the years."

"Maybe his doctor refused to release him."

"Don't tell him I said anything." Caitlyn rolled her eyes. "He tries to be all tough, you know."

Was Cody here only because he had to be? Grounded permanently? But even if he were banned from rodeo, that didn't mean he had to stay in Aubrey. He was only leasing.

More reason to stay away from him. He'd need a new diversion. Even if by some miracle Cody fell madly in love with her, she refused to be anybody's consolation prize. Especially not a temporary one.

"Speaking of Mr. Tough Guy," Caitlyn whispered.

The hair on the back of Ally's neck prickled.

"Where'd you go?" He limped toward her.

"I figured I'd get a head start out here." Was his limp permanent?

"It could've waited. We had six kids come forward."

"That's great." Her tone fell flat.

"Last night we had nine, for a total of fifteen. I wish some of the parents had gotten the message."

Why? So he could disappoint them, too?

"Are you okay?" Cody touched her arm.

"Fine." She took a step backward. "Just trying to get all these animals back to their homes." *And keep my distance. From you. And from God.*

"Once we get all the animals settled where they came from, all the carnival workers are meeting at Moms on Main for supper." Caitlyn strolled toward her car. "Want to join us, Ally?"

"I better get home."

"Oh, I forgot." Caitlyn checked her watch. "It's almost five and if you stay out past six—you turn into a goat."

"I do smell like one, but goats are cute." Ally folded her arms.

"Come on, Al." Cody sidled between the two women, slung his arms around each of their shoulders.

Ally's breath caught.

"You barely had any lunch." He gave her shoulder a squeeze. "You must be starving."

Why did his touch do things to her insides? Make her want to do his bidding? Her stomach growled.

Cody chuckled. "I'll take that as a yes."

"I guess I am kind of famished." Ally patted her tummy, willing it to silence. "But didn't y'all eat with the kids?"

"I saved my appetite for Moms." Caitlyn brushed off her jeans.

"I did eat a PB&J sandwich." Cody gave her a sheepish grin. "But I consider it an appetizer."

She really should just go home and stay away from Cody. But her mother had book club tonight and Ally didn't relish the concept of heading to an empty house. "I'll get the critters settled and see y'all there."

"We're shooting for seven." Cody finally moved his arm. "That'll give everybody a couple of hours. Caitlyn should have plenty of time to get rid of her horsiness."

"I wouldn't be talking." Caitlyn picked cat fur off his sleeve as her mischievous grin slipped into place.

They separated then, going to their respective vehicles. The three of them—like old times. Ally had missed them. Except her heart couldn't conjure up her past friendly feelings for Cody. It wanted much more.

Chapter Six

W hy had Cody suggested he ride with Ally to Moms? He needed to keep her at a distance. Being in the same truck hadn't helped his resolve. Neither did sitting beside her at the long table.

He polished off his cheeseburger and tried to concentrate on what Pastor Thomas was saying.

"We got names and addresses for the kids who came forward each day?" The pastor squirted another blob of ketchup on his plate.

"We did." Mitch folded his napkin, pushed his plate away. "We'll invite the parents to church or see if the kids want to ride the bus."

"Definitely," Pastor Thomas agreed. "I've been going through our files, too, checking on members we haven't seen in a while."

"Ally used to be a member," Cody said, then popped a fry in his mouth.

Ally set her tea down with a thunk. Her face pinkened. "I'm a member of a church in Denton now."

"As long as you're going somewhere." The pastor gave her a genuine smile.

Something caught her attention and her eyes widened.

Cody followed her gaze toward the end of the long table. Her mom and Dr. Bridges laughing and talking as they searched for a table. Coworkers sharing supper? Maybe, but Diane's hand rested in the crook of Dr. Bridges's arm. On a Saturday night? With him wearing slacks and a button-down and her in a dress? Still could be a coworker thing. He glanced back at Ally. Not from the look of shock on her face.

"Well, this preacher needs to get some sleep if I intend to deliver a lucid sermon in the morning." Pastor Thomas pushed his chair back and laid several bills on the table for their server.

The rest of the gathering contributed to the tip, stood and strolled toward the exit.

Surprise spread over her mom's features as she saw them. "Ally?" Her hand jerked away from Dr. Bridges's arm. Color flushed her cheeks. "Lance—um, Dr. Bridges—and I just decided to stop in for pie and coffee after our dinner."

"They have really good pie here." Cody tried to ease the tension, but it swirled thick around them. "But not as good as Miss Diane's four-layer delight."

"Are you hinting for another?" Her mom smiled. "I'll be home shortly, Al."

"See you then." Ally leveled a look at Dr. Bridges. "Shortly."

Obviously upset. Cody pressed his hand to the small of her back to get her moving, then opened the door for her. Maybe it was a good thing they'd ridden together after all.

"I can't believe my mom is dating." A pent-up wail escaped from Ally as soon as Cody shut his truck door.

"You think it was a date?"

"Hello? It's Saturday night. Did you see what they were wearing? She admitted they'd been out for dinner. And they were all cozy." She let out a world-weary sigh.

"I thought you liked Lance."

"I do. But she's my mom." She started the engine, pulled out of the parking space. "I know it's been twelve years since my dad…and I should be happy for her. Her life basically stopped when Dad's did. But…"

"It's hard seeing your mom with somebody other than your dad." He covered her free hand with his.

"I'm acting like a preteen. How did you know how I'm feeling?" she sputtered.

"Grandpa's seeing someone. I met her when I stayed with him in Medina. It's been almost thirteen years since Grandma died. But seeing him with this new woman—it didn't settle well at first."

"I remember how broken he was when your grand-mother died." Six months before her dad. And her parents had let her go to Medina for the funeral. She'd hugged Cody for the first time. With that hug, a bar-rier between them had slipped away. Or at least it had for her. "You got used to him having someone new?"

"Had to."

"Do you like her?"

"She's a right fine lady. Been good for him. But I had to get past my awkwardness to see that."

"How'd you do that?"

"I consciously listed all the good things I knew about her and then I prayed about it." He turned toward her. "So what do you know about Dr. Lance Bridges?"

"He lives in Denton and started coming to our church after his wife died of cancer about two and a half years ago. They'd attended where they were married and he couldn't bring himself to go there after her death." She pulled into her drive and cut the engine.

Cody got out, came around and opened her door.

She climbed out, leaned against the truck. With him beside her. Familiar and comforting, his arm against hers.

"What about his veterinary practice?"

"It was at their house and his wife helped with the office work. I think the memories got to him, so it was overwhelming after she died. He sold and moved to a smaller house. But he was at loose ends, so I hired him to work for me. He's planning to work a few more years and then retire."

"Nothing bad?"

"Nothing other than he's dating my mom. And I shouldn't see that as a bad thing."

"Pray on it." His hand clasped hers. "I'll pray for you, too."

"Thanks." Warmth threaded through her, along with unease over more than her mom.

He patted his shoulder. "Need this?"

She shouldn't. She really shouldn't. But she did.

"I've really missed you." She turned into him, resting her cheek against his chest. His arms came around her, gentle, soothing. A contented sigh escaped. Cody's embrace was like home. "I mean your friendship. Your nonjudgmental ear."

"Glad to be of use and right back at you." His voice rumbled against her ear. "Dear Lord, help Ally to cope with her mom dating Lance. If they're meant to be, let Lance be the man Diane needs and ease Ally's discomfort over the whole deal. If there's someone else in

Diane's future, You know who he is. Whatever the future holds for Diane and for Ally, give them both peace. Thank You for all the blessings You give us. Amen."

No man had ever prayed for her. Except her dad. Even though she'd quit putting any stock in prayer a long time ago, Cody's sincere gesture liquefied her heart further. He gave her an extra squeeze and Ally was certain she'd never be able to pry herself away from him.

"Hey, I've been thinking." He propped his chin on her head. "We should put together a float for your shelter in the Peanut Festival parade."

"A float?"

"Maybe a Noah's ark theme with animals everywhere. It would be great advertisement. Might get some adoptions out of it."

"Noah's ark with cats and dogs only?" The throb of his heart, strong and steady against her ear. How could he be so calm, when her heart was racing?

"Well, yeah. But it fits the concept. The ark saved Noah's family and the animals. Our ark will save cats and dogs. I'll find a way to make it work."

"That's actually a good idea. But I don't know a thing about floats."

"I can figure it out. Build a cardboard frame shaped like a boat, cut windows for the cages to show through."

"It's only a few weeks away."

"It won't take long." He rubbed calming circles on her back. "I'll do the building. If you help paint in the evenings when you finish work, we can knock it out in no time."

"I don't have a trailer."

"I do."

"I can't ask you to do this. You already help so much with my animals."

"You're not asking. I offered. And to be honest, I'm feeling kind of useless."

If he felt useless was wanderlust taking hold? "What about your ranch?"

"I've figured out ranching isn't really my thing. My foreman and hands do all the work."

Bored already. He probably wouldn't stick around much longer.

"If it doesn't come together as fast as we need, I can put some of my hands to work on it, too."

"There's no need for that."

"Whatever you need, I'll do. I'd do anything for you, Ally—don't you know that by now?"

Anything except stay. Anything except love her.

But she didn't want him to anyway. She didn't.

Her eyes flew open as an engine sounded and headlights panned over them.

"They're back." Ally jerked away from him. "I can't face her right now." She barreled toward the house and scurried inside. Already showered, she didn't even stop to let the dogs out of the mudroom. She went straight to her room and pulled out her jammies. By the time Mom got inside, Ally planned to be in bed. No heart-to-hearts over Mom's new beau. Ally couldn't take it.

As she settled, switched off the lamp, Lance's engine started, then faded away.

Foxy's and Wolf's nails clicked across the living room floor.

Mom's shadow darkened her doorway. "It's not what you think. Lance and I are only friends, coworkers."

"It's fine. I'm just tired from wrangling all the animals at the carnival."

A pause. "Goodnight, then." Mom's silhouette drifted away.

Ally had worked with Lance for two years. All the times Mom had invited him to stay for supper, the times they'd shared a laugh in the clinic, drunk a cup of coffee in the break room or worried over an animal together. Why hadn't Ally seen them growing closer?

Because she hadn't wanted to.

Her stomach churned. But even worse than the upset over Mom and Lance was the disquiet of how good Cody's comfort tonight had felt.

"Ally?" Cody rapped his knuckles against her childhood bedroom window. Had she changed rooms?

A light came on, and the curtain was pushed aside. Her face in the window—squinted eyes. "What are you doing?"

"Your critters are loose again."

"Oh, no." The curtains swooshed closed.

"I called Mitch to help."

"Thanks. I'll be right out," she shouted.

Cody had been consistently using his newly purchased treadmill to strengthen his knee. This time he wouldn't sit back in the barn. This time he'd rustle animals. The barn door was open and by the time she stepped out on her back porch, Cody had a handful of leashes.

"Thanks." She grabbed several from him as headlights pulled into the drive.

A truck door slammed. "Don't touch any doorknobs

or latches," Mitch called. "Maybe I can get some prints this time."

Ally whirled around to face Cody. "You called him in Texas Ranger mode?"

"It's the second time, Ally. I don't think you can handle this on your own." Cody hobbled after a Lab mix, clicking his tongue, baby-talking until the dog came to him. He slipped the collar in place. "Where does this one go? Barn or clinic?"

"Barn." She vaulted toward the open door of the clinic. "This can't get out. It could ruin my business. Get my shelter shut down."

"We use discretion with all our investigations." Mitch's flashlight cut through the darkness as he followed after her. "But if it'll make you feel better, I'll file it under unofficial business. Helping out a friend. I'm even off duty for a couple of days."

"I like that second option. Tell your brother to stay in the barn. I don't want him hurting himself."

"I'm fine." Cody steered the large dog into the barn. He elbowed the door shut and latched it, then shone his beam over the property. A flash of white. "Oreo, is that you?"

The dog bounded toward him, wagging his tail.

"You better not run off, boy." He slid the collar over the dog's head and made another trip to the barn. "We need to know how many."

"I'm on it." Ally jogged toward the clinic.

The back door of her house opened and her mom stepped out on the lit porch. "I called Lance. He should be here any minute."

Ally's heavy sigh echoed through the darkness. Already upset over the situation with her mom and Lance, and now her animals being loose again added more stress. Whoever did this, Cody would gladly ring their neck. But right now he needed to rustle up the critters. And keep Ally safe.

Hours later, with the first rays of daylight, Ally gently set the last kitten in her cage.

"That's all of them?" Cody shuffled into Oreo's pen and settled in a folding chair.

"Yes. Thankfully, it wasn't as bad this time." She swiped her wrist over her temple, pushing sweat-soaked hair away from her face. "Only eight dogs and eleven cats this time."

"But one of 'em was Oreo. That makes this personal."

"Either of you notice anything suspicious lately?" Mitch leaned against the wall.

"I really don't think this is necessary." Ally shook her head. "I'll change the locks. It'll be fine."

"If this was the first time, I might be inclined to let it slide. But twice? Whoever we're dealing with obviously has no concern for your four-legged friends' safety. If somebody wants to shut you down, they might not be above hurting the animals."

Ally gasped. "I hadn't thought about that."

"Or hurting Ally." Cody's low tone sent a shiver over her.

Or Mom. The magnitude of the situation twisted her insides.

"I got several partial latent prints off the barn door latch, the clinic knob and the cage bolts. I got your mom's, Lance's and Cody's prints already. Once I get yours and Derek's, I'll know which ones can be ruled out. Anybody else I need to exclude?"

"About a dozen volunteers from church come each evening, but I need this to stay quiet."

"I'll show up tomorrow and explain there's some new state regulation that requires all volunteers' prints on file."

"Trick them?" Ally's shoulders sagged.

"Either that or come clean. I'll let you decide. Anyone else?"

"My state inspector was here last week." Her eyes squeezed shut. "But you can't contact him for information or prints. If he finds out about this, he'll write me up and could shut me down. And if you're right, whoever is doing this would win."

"I see." Mitch made a note on his pad. "Anybody got a bone to pick with you?"

"Not that I can think of."

"What about your employees, Cody? Any of them complain about the noise level of the shelter getting on their nerves?"

"No." Cody scratched Oreo's neck. With a contented sigh, the dog set his head on Cody's knee. "In fact, they're all animal lovers and most have mentioned what a good program Ally runs."

"Anything odd other than the loose animals?"

"The inspector only comes once a year and he'd already been here back in the spring." Ally sank onto a hay bale. "For him to come again, someone had to file a complaint. But again, you can't contact him and grievances are usually anonymous, so he wouldn't tell you anyway."

"Maybe something will turn up with the prints."

Mitch closed his notepad. "You let me know if anything else happens. I mean it, Ally. I'm on your side. And the most important thing is to keep you and the animals safe."

She nodded, swallowed hard. Could Mitch be right? Could her nemesis be willing to hurt the animals? Or Mom?

"What about patrolling the area at night?" Cody's chair moaned as he stood.

"That wouldn't be a problem, since I'm right down the road anyway." Mitch made another note.

"No, Mitch, I can't let you do that." Ally hung her head. "You've got Caitlyn and your baby girl. I can't drag you away from them every night."

"Actually, I meant me." Cody stepped out of Oreo's pen, paced between the kennels. "I don't have a schedule or a family. I could camp out in the barn at night. Or the clinic."

"Absolutely not." Mitch adjusted his cowboy hat. "What if our interloper is armed? If anybody does any staking out, it'll be an officer. How many nights between incidents?"

"About a week. The first time was on a Saturday morning. This time it's Sunday."

"Maybe a nine-to-fiver who doesn't work weekends or someone who works the evening shift. I'll see what I can arrange with the department and keep you posted." Mitch headed for the door.

"Let me sleep on your couch." Cody hung the last leash back in place and turned to Ally.

"No."

"You and your mom—two women alone in a house— with someone up to no good creeping around outside."

"But nothing's been toward me." She stood, hugged herself. "Just the animals."

"Yes, but letting the animals out hasn't gotten our perp anywhere. Both times we wrangled them all back with no one the wiser. Chaotic and problematic, but not conducive to shutting you down. He might go after you the next time. Or your mom."

No fair bringing her mom into this. Her insides gave another turn. "Those are mighty big words for a cowboy."

"Stop trying to use humor as a cover. I can see it in your eyes—you're scared." He stepped close, his breath fanning her temple.

So close. So tempting. His broad shoulder just waiting for her to snuggle in.

Chapter Seven

Ally buried her face in his chest. A shudder moved through her.

His arms surrounded her. Safety and peril in one muscled package.

"I'm sleeping on your couch. Until this is over. Period. I'd rather have you safe than me be sorry."

Slowly going crazy in his embrace. Having Cody next door was way too close for comfort. Having him on her couch was insane. She wouldn't sleep a wink.

"No." She pulled away from him. "They won't come back tonight and I'll have the locks changed tomorrow."

"Fine, Miss Independent." He ran his hand over the back of his neck. "I'll change the locks for you. First thing."

"I can hire someone."

"I'll do it."

"Okay." Whatever it took to keep him off her couch. At a nice safe distance. "You're way too serious these days. Whatever happened to fun-loving Cody?"

"I'm too worried for fun." He shoved his hands in his pockets.

"But you used to be the one to crack a joke when life got too intense." She shrugged one shoulder. "I miss your sense of humor."

"Really." He ducked his head. "All this time, I've been biting my tongue, trying to act more mature."

"Why?"

"So everyone will take me seriously."

"The world is way too grim as it is. We need more Cody—not less. You're perfect just the way you are." She bit her lip, wishing she could stuff the words back in. "Or the way you were."

"Well, in that case, did you hear about the cowboy adopting the dachshund?"

"No." She grinned, anticipating something corny.

"He wanted to get a long little doggy."

She shook her head, started for her house.

"Hey, I thought you'd like that one, being a vet and all." He fell in stride beside her, exited the barn and checked the latch. "Where are you going? I've got a zillion more packed inside me like tennis balls in a Lab's mouth."

"I said I missed your humor. Not your corny jokes."

"I'm rusty. Just give me a minute."

"Maybe your brain will fire better after you get some sleep." She climbed her porch steps.

"Lock up." All humor died in his eyes. "I've half a mind to stay with you despite your protests."

"We'll be fine. Thanks for your help. Get some rest." *Let me breathe.*

"I'm not leaving until I hear the dead bolt."

She dragged her gaze away from his magnetic pull and stepped inside. With a metallic click, the dead bolt slid into place, and his footfalls descended the porch. She leaned back against the door.

But even with the distance between them, she still couldn't breathe right.

Coffee. Cody inhaled, savoring the rich scent. Whoever came up with the concept of the automatic timer on coffeemakers deserved to be a millionaire. Even though it was decaf. He opened his eyes to the bright sunshine. As he stretched, the previous night came back to him.

Ally's animals loose again. They'd worked a good five hours rounding them up.

After he'd seen Ally safely to her house, he'd showered, and since Jackie's Hardware was closed on Sundays, he'd driven to Denton, then returned and changed the locks on Ally's house, clinic and barn. He'd sorely wanted to go to morning service, but after all that, his eyes wouldn't stay open and he'd conked out in the recliner.

Another stretch and he peered at the clock. Almost twelve thirty. He sat up, rubbed his eyes. When was the last time he'd missed church? He'd definitely go tonight.

Coffee. Even if it was fake. He headed toward the kitchen.

A scream pierced the quiet.

Ally?

Cody bolted outside.

Over in front of her truck, Ally backed away with both hands over her mouth.

"What's wrong?" He ran to her.

Her hand shook as she pointed at the windshield.

DIE! A single word scrawled in soap.

A chill crawled up his spine. He stepped in front of her, scanned the property. "Get inside."

The threat had probably been left last night, but just in case.

"But I have a wedding to go to."

"I think you should sit this one out."

"I can't. I'm a bridesmaid."

His brain cleared enough to take in her long burgundy dress. Her dark hair in waves, loose and cascading around her shoulders.

It did something funny to his breathing. "Whose wedding?"

"My cousin Landry and I can't let her down." She checked her watch. "It's at two at the Ever After Chapel."

"Oh, yeah. I was traveling, but she included me in Mitch's invitation." He shifted his weight from one foot to the other. "I'd feel better about things if you didn't go alone today."

"Well, you're not dressed appropriately." Her gaze skimmed over his typical jeans, Western shirt and boots.

"Go inside and give me five minutes." He fished his phone from his pocket. "I'll call Mitch and we'll take my truck so he can check yours for prints."

"Come on, Cody—I don't need a babysitter." She stamped her foot. "It's a wedding. You think some nut's going to attack me?"

"Mitch said to keep an eye on you. Go back inside. I'll be over in a jiff."

"This is ridiculous," she huffed, but turned back toward her house. "You can't babysit me 24/7."

No. But he could make sure she stayed out of trouble

today. And appreciate her beauty while he was at it. He made his way inside.

If only he could talk Ally out of going to the wedding. But he knew Landry and Ally had always been close—graduating only a few years apart. He wouldn't be able to convince her not to go.

What kind of person skulked around in darkness letting animals loose and wreaking havoc, leaving threatening notes on windshields? With soap? Maybe teens pulling pranks? He hoped so. But his twisting gut said Ally was in danger. And he wouldn't let anything happen to her.

"Do you really think it's a good idea to go to the wedding?" Mom wrung her hands.

"I can't let Landry down." Ally willed her shaking to stop. "I'll be fine. Cody's going with me."

"Oh, good." The lines between Mom's eyebrows relaxed.

"Why don't you come, too? I know you said you wanted to leave a little later, but obviously, I'm not going as early as I planned. Mitch should be here any minute, but until he arrives, I'm not sure I like the idea of you being here alone."

"Lance is taking me to the wedding. But I'm concerned about no one being home with everything going on."

"Oh." Torn. Lance escorting her mom would ease Ally's worries. And worsen them. "I'll ask Cody to get one of his hands to come over and keep an eye on things."

A knock sounded and Ally jumped.

"It's me, Cody."

Breathe in, breathe out. Calm down. She unlocked

the extra dead bolt he'd installed that morning, opened the door.

Handsome in a gray suit with a burgundy shirt and paisley undone tie to match. He pointed at it. "I tried three times. Can you help?"

"Sure." She adjusted the ends to the right length, looped it over. "We're worried about no one being here this afternoon. Do you think one of your hands could keep an eye on things?"

"I already arranged it." His breath fanned her hair.

"Thanks." A tremble inched over her. She chanced a glance at him. His gaze was riveted on hers. Too close. She tugged the tie into place, tightened the knot.

Cody's hands covered hers. "You trying to choke me?"

"Sorry."

"You two look like a couple." Mom clapped her hands.

Heat swept up Ally's neck.

"I thought we should look like we'd planned to attend together all along so if our perp happens to be watching, it doesn't look like he's got Ally running scared."

"Good thinking." Ally checked her watch. "We need to go."

"Mitch was pulling in just as I knocked."

"And Lance will be here any minute." Mom peered out the window. "You two go. Forget all this nonsense. And I'll see you in a bit."

Cody held the door open for her and she stepped out.

Mitch and another officer combed over her truck.

"What happened to off-the-record favor for a friend?" she whispered.

"There's been a threat now, Ally. It has to become

official. But don't worry—they'll keep it quiet." Cody's hand pressed against the small of her back.

Too familiar. Too comforting. She stiffened.

"You're a bundle of nerves."

"I can't help it. I've got a few things on my mind."

He escorted her to the driver's side of his truck. "You'll have to drive. My doc is still being overly cautious with my knee and hasn't released me to drive."

It was no easy task to climb into the truck wearing the dress, but she managed. Cody shut her door, rounded to the passenger's side and eased in.

"Thanks." She could feel his stare as she started the engine and pulled onto the highway. Kept her eyes on the yellow line.

"I don't think I've ever seen you so dressed up."

"Good?" Her skin heated. "Or bad?"

"You look great."

"Really?" She smoothed a shaky hand over her skirt. "It's just so different than what I'm used to wearing. I had to practice how to walk for days in these shoes." The strappy high heels matched her dress perfectly, but they definitely weren't built for comfort.

"Who's Landry marrying?"

"Kyle Billings. He's not from around here."

"Ever wonder if you made the right decision to stay single?"

Only since he came back to town. "No. You?"

"I'm not sure anymore."

Her breath hitched.

"I mean, it might be nice to have somebody to share things with. Triumphs, trials, health issues."

"I share all that with my mom." And it had been enough. Until Cody came back.

"Yeah, but if your mom gets serious with Lance? What then?"

"I'll still share my triumphs and trials with her." And she was hoping her mom and Lance wouldn't get more serious. It might make work uncomfortable if they ended things, but Ally's life would get back to normal. Wasn't that completely selfish. "I'm not thirty yet. Surely I've got lots of time before any health issues kick in."

"You never know. But then, burdening somebody else with your health issues doesn't seem right."

"It's marriage." Ally shrugged, trying to feel as indifferent as she sounded. "I guess if two people love each other enough to commit their lives to one another, they're willing to face anything and everything together."

"Ever wonder if we're missing out on that?"

"Tell you what—stick around in Aubrey and when we get old and decrepit, I'll drive you to doctor's appointments and you can haul me to the hospital when I need to go."

"I may just hold you to that." His hand covered her free one, twining their fingers. And it felt way too good. Way too warm. Way too dizzying.

But she knew he wouldn't hold her to her pledge. Because he'd never stick around that long.

Still breathing odd, Cody escorted Ally into the Ever After Chapel.

"Ally. Bridesmaids in here." Landry's mom pulled her away from him. "Cody, nice to see you."

"You, too, Mrs. Malone."

"See you after the ceremony." Ally waved her fingers at him.

The two women disappeared into a side room. Alone, Cody concentrated on normal breathing. Someone poked him in the ribs and he flinched.

"Did I just see you walk in with Ally?" Raquel, his friend and neighbor from several acres away, was downright giddy.

"Yeah? So?" He looked to her husband for clarification, but Slade only smirked.

"What?"

"You really don't remember, do you?" Raquel's smug smile confused him further.

"Remember what?"

"When you were in the hospital after your bull wreck and I came to visit you, we were talking about that time Mitch tried to fix us up but we were destined to only be friends."

"So?"

"So, you said you wished we could pick who we fall for and then you said you were in love with Ally."

Cody's eyes widened. His heart went into overdrive. "I did not."

"Yes, you did." She rolled her eyes. "That's why I came up with the whole pet visitation program to the rehab center—to get her there to see you." She shrugged. "I mean, I wanted to help patients and help Ally's strays, too, but the idea came to me because of you."

Slade chuckled. "Looks like your devious plan worked. I'm glad Mitch's fix-up didn't and I won the prize." He pulled Raquel against his side.

"Ally and I are friends. That's all." Cody lowered

his voice. "She had another break-in at the clinic. I'm worried someone's out to get her, so I didn't think she should come to this wedding alone."

"Well, I hate to hear about her problems at the clinic. But you want to protect her because you love her." Raquel jabbed a finger at him. "You can deny it all you want, but I heard what I heard."

He couldn't have said he loved Ally all those months ago. He hadn't even known it then. There had to be an explanation. Raquel must have misunderstood him. Or maybe the medication had affected him.

"Was I on pain meds when I supposedly made this confession?"

"Well…yeah." Raquel raised one shoulder. "But I used to be an emergency room nurse. Sometimes medication brings out the truth."

"Just do me a favor—keep my drug-induced declaration to yourself, will ya?"

"Of course." Raquel covered her mouth with her hand and winked. "You should be the one to tell her."

"Come on—leave the man in peace." Slade tugged her toward the door to the chapel.

"You coming?" Raquel called over her shoulder.

"I'll wait on Mitch. He's bachin' it, too, since Caitlyn's in the wedding party. I'll be there in a bit."

The open door gave him a glimpse of more lace and filmy fabric than he'd ever seen flanking the old-fashioned pews.

Had he really said he loved Ally back in the hospital? Had his heart known what his head refused to admit?

Why did he have such horrible timing? Why couldn't he have realized his feelings back when he'd kissed her?

Why couldn't he have stuck around to figure it out instead of running scared to the rodeo?

They could have had a chance. Back when he was healthy. Back when his future was endless. He'd have quit the rodeo for her. Never gotten injured. Never been ruled by a time bomb in his head.

So many regrets. But Ally topped the list.

He let out a harsh breath as Mitch stepped inside.

"Hey, little brother."

"Did you get any prints off Ally's truck?"

"A few partials. We'll have to do a comparison with the ones from the other night."

"Any leads?"

Several guests entered the foyer and Mitch waited until they were out of earshot. "The prints from the barn and clinic doors didn't match anything in our database, so our perp has no prior record."

"What now?"

"Patience. You just concentrate on keeping an eye on Ally. But I did learn something you might be interested in."

"What?"

"Garrett Steele is opening a bull-riding school in Aubrey. Thought you might be interested in applying as an instructor."

Adrenaline rushed through Cody. For the first time since his injuries, he was excited over something other than Ally.

The leather interior of Cody's truck still had that new-car smell. He'd always treated his vehicles like his babies. Probably had it detailed once a week.

"I can't believe this." Ally sniffled as she drove.

"You okay?"

"I just feel so bad for Landry. How could her fiancé leave her at the altar? I mean, if you want to call the wedding off, do it before everybody shows up."

"I'd like to put a burr under his saddle." Cody handed her a tissue.

She dabbed her nose. "I thought stuff like this only happened in movies."

"It's good she found out he wasn't the type to stick around before she married him." Cody adjusted his seat belt looser on his injured shoulder. "Where'd she meet the good-for-nothing?"

"He was a guest at your cousin's dude ranch."

"Wow. I'm surprised she still works there after all these years. She always wanted to own her own ranch. I guess I figured she would by now."

"That's what makes it even worse." Ally swabbed under her eyes with her thumb. Probably looked like a raccoon, but seeing her younger cousin so shattered put an ache in her soul. "She and her fiancé planned to buy a bed-and-breakfast in Denton."

"I'm getting madder by the mile."

"It just proves we're not missing out on a thing by staying single." She gripped the steering wheel tighter, turning her knuckles white, wishing it were her cousin's ex's neck.

"That's a blanket statement. I've never heard of this happening in real life before."

"No. But if the wedding actually happens, so many couples end up divorced. And if they stay married, one up and dies."

"Not always." He placed his hand on hers, gave a squeeze. "Both my folks are still kicking. There are several young couples I know who are still going strong. Widows who remarried like Raquel. Even your mom finally seems to be moving on. And lots of folks are still married into their golden years."

"But the uncertainty of it makes it not worth bothering with."

"You really believe that?"

"More and more every day." Especially when Cody compromised her determination for independence. Time to change the subject. "You and Garrett seemed deep in conversation before we left." She pulled into his drive, parked and faced him.

"I got a job." Enthusiasm sparkled in his eyes.

Something she hadn't seen since he'd been home. "What kind of job?"

"An instructor at Garrett's new bull-riding school."

"What?" A vein in her neck throbbed. "How could you do something so stupid! You're barely walking, you can't drive, it's a wonder you're alive, and you're going right back in the arena."

"I'm—"

"I can't believe you." She jerked the door open and climbed down.

Gravel scattered as Cody scrambled to catch up with her as she stalked toward her house. "Ally, I—"

"That you'd torment your family all over again." She wheeled around toward him. "That you'd put me through worrying about you. You barely survived your last bull wreck. Why do you always have to push the limits?"

"You're concerned about me?" A cocky smile settled into place.

And her arteries went hot lava. "Of course I am, you

idiot. Why wouldn't I be when you insist on cavorting around on the backs of mammoth beasts who'd just as soon kill you as look at you?" She spun away from him and started for her porch.

"Ally, wait." His hand caught her wrist.

"What?" She stopped, rather than dragging him along limp and all, but kept her back to him, terrified the tears forming in her eyes might spill. She'd expected Cody to go back to the rodeo. But she'd never thought about how much his riding again would petrify her.

"I won't be riding."

The dread in her chest eased up. "How can you teach bull riding and not ride?"

"I'll review videos of professional riders with students and explain technique. I'll give advice while they practice on a stationary bull and then graduate to real bulls. But my feet stay outside the arena the entire time."

Relief sucked her lungs empty. She blinked several times and turned around. "Oh. Guess I overreacted."

His smile widened. As if he was onto her.

Had she revealed her feelings?

"It's almost time for evening church." She hurried the rest of the way to her door.

Even if she'd let her feelings show, he wasn't interested.

Even if he were, she had to get a handle on this. She could never take the chance of someone leaving her at the altar. Or cheating on her. Or dying on her. She couldn't allow herself to need Cody. Or anybody else.

Chapter Eight

❧

Barren hay fields surrounded the house and barn. Ally moved her stethoscope over the creamy horse's chest.

A typical Monday. Lots of sick pets. Nothing serious. No loose animals. No strays. No surprise inspections. Finishing up with a house call. All in all, a good day.

"Have you seen poor Landry since the almost wedding?" Raquel's sympathetic tone interrupted the steady *whump whump, whump whump* of the horse's heart.

"No. I called to check on her, but my aunt said she didn't feel like talking."

"Poor girl. Hunter's dad and I stayed at the dude ranch years ago and I've gotten reacquainted with her since moving to Aubrey."

"Landry has lots of people to love her through this." Ally removed her stethoscope and stroked the mare's velvety neck. "This one's strong and healthy as a horse."

"That's what I'm afraid of." Raquel blew out a sigh. "Why couldn't Slade have gotten Hunter a pony for his birthday? I mean, every kid wants a pony. Not a full-grown—way-too-tall—horse."

"You can't tell me—" Ally pointed to the weathered

gray barn behind Raquel's house "—you don't realize that barn and pasture are crying out for a horse. This is Aubrey, Texas. I'm surprised it's even legal to live here and not own a horse."

"But Hunter's only eight."

Ally's humor fell flat in the face of a mother's anxieties.

"She's a nice horse." Ally checked the palomino's teeth. "Gentle and she doesn't spook. She barely even flinched when I vaccinated her."

"She's just so big." Raquel shivered. "It's a long way to the ground from up there."

"Hunter will be fine. Has he ever ridden before?"

"Not alone."

"One of my clients gives riding lessons. I'm sure she could teach Hunter. And maybe you, too." Ally patted the horse's shoulder. "Maybe if you learn to ride, you'll feel better about Hunter riding."

"I already made arrangements for lessons. Wait— how did you know I don't ride?"

"Um…you cringe every time the mare moves."

"Okay, I admit it—I'm afraid of horses." Raquel covered her face with both hands. "And I live in Horse Country, USA. Is there a support group for that?"

"Admitting it is the first step." Ally laughed.

"Thanks for coming over here."

"No problem. When the horse is five minutes away, it just doesn't make sense for y'all to load her in a trailer and bring her over to my place."

"I'm surprised you have time for house calls." Raquel handed her a check. "Are you still doing the hospital and rehab visits with the dogs?"

"I am." Ally stroked the horse's silken muzzle.

"Thanks for coming up with that. I've adopted a dozen or so dogs out and the patients love the visits."

"Now that we've settled into newlywed bliss, I'll volunteer to help again soon."

"That would be great. I've gotten a few volunteers signed up, but the more, the better."

"I noticed you and Cody attended the wedding that wasn't. Together."

"We didn't plan to. It just worked out that way."

"He told me about the second break-in." The horse swatted its tail and Raquel flinched. "Don't worry—I won't say a word. But have you ever thought of dating Cody?"

Ally's breathing stuttered. "I've known him forever. Back in high school, he was the brother I never had."

"Back in high school." Raquel's brows lifted. "But what about now?"

"We're friends. Neighbors. That's all." Ally put her supplies back in her bag.

A truck pulled into the drive at the front of the house.

"Here's Hunter and Slade. They went to buy a saddle." Raquel shook her head. "Who buys a horse when they don't even own a saddle?" But when her smile landed on Slade, Ally could see that all her frustration over the horse melted away.

"Tell them I said hey." Ally waved to the man and boy and headed for her truck. To go home. Alone.

She placed her supplies back in the mobile clinic in her truck bed, then climbed in the cab. The engine purred to life and she backed out of the barn lot onto the highway.

No, she wasn't alone. She had a plethora of stray dogs and cats to keep her company, plus a few furry friends of her own. Though now that Mom's relationship with Lance was out in the open, Mom hadn't been home as much. She was losing the one person she could talk to at home.

Truth be told, she'd been lonely for years. Even living with Mom. But it was even worse with Lance in Mom's picture. Nothing was the same. Ally liked Lance. He was a nice man, a conscientious vet, and he treated her mother well. But he wasn't Dad.

And Raquel's happiness put an ache in Ally's heart. A longing for her own romance. Her own forever after with Cody.

Her road appeared. Almost home and she didn't even remember the drive there.

Stop thinking about him that way. He was already obviously bored playing ranch. How long before he got bored teaching bull riding? It was only a matter of time before he'd be raring to get back on the road. She needed to remind herself often of Landry's attempt at happily-ever-after.

Her phone rang as she exited her truck. She dug it out of her pocket. "Hello?"

Silence. The uncomfortable sensation of someone watching her. She scanned her property.

"Hey." Cody on his side of the fence, holding his phone up. "It was me calling, but I saw you pull up, so I figured we'd talk in person."

"About?" She tried for a casual tone. Didn't quite pull it off.

"If we're gonna build a float, we need to git 'er done. It's almost the middle of September already, less than three weeks away from the parade. I've been researching and figured out the design. Feel like coming over to talk about it?"

How could she not think about Cody if he kept popping up with one idea or another? And now they were going to work on a float together? But her participation in the parade would help her animals.

"Sure. Let me get cleaned up a bit and I'll be right over."

How could she say no? She'd just have to pull up her big-girl boots, concentrate on her strays—not Cody—and get the job done.

Cardboard and two-by-fours surrounded Cody on the hay-strewn floor of his barn. He'd almost tripped once already. Had he bitten off more than he could chew? No. Not for Ally. He'd do anything for her. He'd even told her so. She'd figure him out—his iffy health and how he felt about her—if he didn't keep his guard up better.

Not in all his almost thirty years had he ever built a float. But he'd found help on the internet and managed to cut the cardboard into a pretty convincing ark shape. All he had to do was build a frame, staple the cardboard to it, and work out where to cut windows and how to stack the kennels without endangering any animals. That was where Ally would come in.

"Wow. I thought we were just going to talk about it." Ally. Behind him.

He turned to face her. "We don't have any time to waste."

"How did you come up with all this?"

"YouTube."

"I'm impressed." She held the frame for him as he used his nail gun. "Where did you get such huge sheets of cardboard?"

"There's a manufacturer in Fort Worth. One of my hands was going there anyway for ranch supplies."

"How much do I owe you?"

"Consider it my contribution to your shelter. All I require in return is some work and sweat. I need your brainpower on where to put the windows and how to stabilize the cages in place." He finished securing the cardboard and she stepped away.

Hands on hips, she strolled around the supplies a few times, then tapped her chin with a forefinger. "We can put the smaller animals higher up. Maybe stack hay bales for support and build a shelf between the beams where the cages will sit."

"I knew you'd figure it out." He started the next side of the frame and again she held it for him.

"Did I tell you about my big event this Saturday?"

"I saw a flyer on the bulletin board at church. Something about people getting pictures with their pets and a concert featuring Aubrey's own Garrett Steele and Brant McConnell."

"Kendra came up with it months ago." She waited while he sank three more nails. "When Garrett and Brant heard about it, they offered to do the concert and donate all profits to my shelter. And when Kendra picked up Charcoal last week, she decided not to charge me for her photography services."

"She must have been happy to get her cat back."

"She was. I can't believe he wandered this far."

"There's no telling where tomcats wander."

"Yeah, but he's neutered. Usually that tames them a bit and they stick closer to home. He's never wandered so far before." She frowned. "I'm just glad he ended up here. Her kids were really happy to get him back."

"Sounds like a great opportunity. Getting all those people here will advertise the shelter and maybe drum up adoptions." He drove the final nail into the frame.

"I'm just standing here rattling, while you work. What can I do?"

"No, you weren't. You were helping me hold the frame." He pointed to a bale of hay. "There's a pack of black Magic Markers over there. The float I saw on the net had lines drawn across the cardboard so it looked like slats of wood. Maybe you could make it look like there's wood grain."

"I'll try." She grabbed the markers and an uncut piece of cardboard to use as a guide and got busy. But after a few lines, she set down the marker. "I've got a better idea. Let me run to the house and see if I can find some wood-grain contact paper."

"What's that?"

"It's adhesive shelf liner. Comes in a long roll."

"Who knew?"

"Apparently not bachelors. I donated it for our church's Vacation Bible School last summer and had several rolls left over." She hurried out of the barn, taking her scent with her. "I'll be right back," she called.

An emptiness filled his chest as she disappeared. As if he missed her. And she'd be gone only a few minutes or so.

He was getting way too used to having her around. If only he could tell her how he felt. If only he could plan a future with her. If only he had a future to plan.

Should he have the surgery? Risk ending up in a vegetative state? Or keep living so carefully he wasn't really living?

The sweet hay smell permeated the air. Why were barns so peaceful? Peaceful except when Cody was around, anyway.

"Stop," Ally shouted as a huge wrinkle formed.

"What?" Cody stopped unrolling.

"We've got a wrinkle and it's getting crooked. Just stay put while I fix it." She gritted her teeth as she carefully pulled the paper loose, tugged on each side of the crease until it disappeared, then pressed the paper onto the cardboard again. "Don't take any more backing off until I get this part stuck good." On hands and knees, she crawled around smoothing the paper in place.

"It looks a whole lot better than the one I found on the net." Cody slowly began pulling the back off again as she neared him until they reached the edge of the cardboard. "Now what?"

"Does it look straight?" She stood and surveyed the side of the ark they'd just completed.

"I think so."

"I'll make sure it's all stuck good with no wrinkles and you can trim around the edges. Just leave a couple of inches to fold over so it'll stay securely in place." Back on her knees, she crawled the length of the cardboard until spicy aftershave filled her space. She looked up—right into Cody's aloe-colored eyes. Soothing just like the plant, and for the life of her, she couldn't tug her gaze away.

"Am I leaving enough, you think?" The smell of coffee on his breath sent a shiver over her.

Oh, to get a coffee-flavored kiss from Cody.

"The edge. Am I leaving enough?"

Unwillingly, she looked down at his hands. "Yeah, looks good." But not as good as he did.

She crawled in the other direction. They still had to cut the windows in the contact paper, then line a whole other half of an ark, then attach the cardboard to the frame and stack tons of hay in the trailer. And on their first night of working together, he was already way too hard to resist.

Twelve years and he tempted her heart just as much as he had back then. She needed to put it in high gear, get this float done, stop spending time with Cody and pray for him to move it along. Out of her life again.

"Hey, Ally." Lance stepped in the doorway. "I'm heading out."

"See you tomorrow."

"Could I talk to you a minute?"

"Sure." She stood, brushed off the knees of her jeans. "Did the last patient visit go okay?"

"Fine."

So if it wasn't about the clinic, did he want to talk about Mom? The conversation she'd dreaded since seeing them together at Moms on Main. Which was worse—being alone with Cody or discussing her mom with Lance? A toss-up. Straightening her shoulders, she stepped outside.

"I think we need to talk about your mom and me."

The thwack of the staple gun started up in the barn.

"I don't want to have this conversation." Ally leaned against the wall for support.

"We've always worked together really well, but lately

you've been stiff, conversation stilted. Seems like it all happened about the time you caught us on our date."

"So it was a date?"

"I care very much for your mother."

Ally covered her face with her hands. "I'm not ready for this."

"Do you want me to back off?"

"I don't know." She drew in a long breath, dropped her hands. "I know I'm being childish. My dad's been gone twelve years. I know Mom is lonely. I know I should be glad she's found a good Christian man, someone I know will treat her right."

"But I'm not your dad. And seeing her with someone else is tough. Probably makes you miss your dad all over again, too." He set his hand on her shoulder. "I don't want to cause you pain, Ally, but if you ask me to back off, I'm not sure I can."

"That would be selfish." She swallowed the lump in her throat. "Just don't hurt her."

"I won't. We okay?"

She nodded.

"Can I go have a cup of coffee with your mom without upsetting you?"

"She'd like that." She forced a smile.

"Me, too." He shot her a wink and turned toward the house.

Ally stayed there a minute, breathing in and out, listening to the birds and the rhythmic clunk of the staple gun echoing from the barn. She headed back inside.

Cody had already cut out the windows and folded the contact paper through the openings and was in the process of stapling the cardboard onto the frame. Maybe this project could be wrapped up quickly.

He stopped, caught her gaze. "You okay?"

"Fine." She rolled her eyes. "I think he wanted my blessing to date my mother."

"Did you give it to him?"

"Sort of."

"Need this?" He patted his shoulder.

"No. I'm good." She grabbed the window guide and started tracing on the other side of the ark.

Cody's eyes might be the color of a soothing aloe vera plant. But instead of healing, if she got too close, he could inflict third-degree burns. On her heart.

Chapter Nine

The dachshund's long body stretched out on the operating table. In dreamland, the little dog lay with his tongue lolled to the side and his mouth braced open, the anesthesia tube in place.

"There it is." Ally gripped the bulge in the dachshund's intestine with gloved hands.

"What is it?" Derek dabbed blood near the incision in the dog's abdomen.

"We're about to see." She slit the engorged intestine and fished out a hard oval object. "A peach pit. Silly boy, you're not supposed to eat that part."

Derek handed her a suture. "Will he be okay?"

"He'll be just fine." She stitched the slit, carefully pressed the intestine back in place, then closed the incision. "He'll feel a lot better when he wakes up. And probably ready to eat. Can you lock up tonight?"

"Sure."

"Thanks. I'm doing my pet visitation at the hospital." She pulled off her gloves and gave Derek final instructions for the patient as the lobby bell dinged. "I'll take care of it."

Her inspector waited in the lobby. Her blood went cold. Everything should be fine. She was way under limit. "Hello, Mr. Humphries."

"Ms. Curtis. Whenever there's a problem with a clinic, I make a return visit to make sure things have been ironed out."

"Of course. I just finished a surgery. Let me wash up real quick."

"Do you need to wrap things up with the patient?"

"My vet tech is taking care of him."

"Very well."

"I'll introduce you to Derek and you can inspect the clinic. Then I'll take you out to the barn."

"Lead the way." Mr. Humphries followed her to the back.

Derek had already settled the dachshund in a recovery crate and cleaned the surgical table. They should pass this inspection with flying colors, but Ally still held her breath.

"Derek, this is Mr. Humphries. He's our state inspector."

"Nice to meet you, sir."

"Yes. Likewise." Mr. Humphries peered at Derek's certification on the wall underneath Ally's and Lance's licenses.

"Can you show Mr. Humphries around while I go wash up?"

"Sure."

Ally stepped into the bathroom and leaned back against the door. Was there a mess in any of the rooms? Surely not. Mom or Brandy meticulously cleaned after each patient. But they had been busy today with numerous dog and cat vaccinations and then the emergency surgery. Surely Mr. Humphries understood emergencies.

She pulled off her smock and threw it in the washing machine. If only she could just stay in here. She soaped, rinsed and dried her hands, then sucked in a deep breath and went to face the paws patrol.

As Ally exited the bathroom, Derek and Mr. Humphries stepped out of an exam room. The inspector marked something on his clipboard. "Everything looks good here. As usual. I'm ready to see your shelter, Ms. Curtis."

"Of course." She suppressed a relieved sigh and headed for the barn.

The longest walk of her life. Mind blank, she couldn't think of a thing to say.

"Relax, Ms. Curtis. Remember, I'm on your side. You do good work here."

Tears pricked her eyes. "Thank you."

As they entered the barn, Cody was fastening a collar on the golden retriever mix she'd just gotten in a few days ago, with the spaniel mix she'd had awhile already leashed.

"Perfect timing for their walk. They're exactly the guys I need."

"To visit the hospital. That's why I got them ready." Cody rose up, saw Mr. Humphries. His mouth tightened. "Mr...? I'm sorry—I can't remember your name."

"Humphries."

"Yes. Nice to see you again." Mr. Humphries wrote something on his form. "Tell me about your hospital visits, Ms. Curtis."

"A friend came up with the idea earlier this year. I have several volunteers and we take dogs to visit patients at a hospital and a rehabilitation center. The dogs cheer up the patients, and the program advertises my shelter and the pets I have up for adoption."

"Very creative." The inspector smiled. Actually smiled. "How do you decide which dogs to take with you?"

"Unfortunately, not many fit the guidelines. Cats are too unpredictable and I can't take excitable dogs."

"So only the calm dogs get a chance at adoption through the hospital program."

"Not necessarily." She grabbed her photo album. "When I get a new pet in, I take its picture and put it in this album. When they get adopted, I remove their pictures. So if anyone at the hospital or the rehab center shows interest, I have the album to show them in case they're interested in a different breed or a cat."

"Very impressive." He flipped through the album, then handed it back to her and strolled the long line of pens.

His bushy eyebrows lifted. "Is this all you have? Boarders and shelter pets? I must say I'm impressed. I don't believe I've ever seen so many empty cages."

"Thank you. Cody's been volunteering here and he's had some good ideas for publicity. We adopted out several pets at a church carnival."

"I saw something about a pet photography day and a concert." Mr. Humphries made more notes. Hopefully good ones.

"That was Ally's doing." Cody leaned against a pen. "All proceeds will go to her shelter, and hopefully, more pets will find good homes."

"We're also building a float to advertise my adoption

program at a local festival and parade next month." She couldn't take the credit for that. "It was Cody's idea."

"Sounds like y'all make a good team. Good job, Ms. Curtis." He wrote something on his clipboard. "Very good promotions. I might mention your methods to other shelters."

"Thank you, sir." She couldn't keep the grin off her face.

"You've earned your rating of above satisfactory. Keep up the good work."

"I will, sir." As the barn door shut behind him, she sank onto a hay bale to absorb the compliment. "Above satisfactory."

"That's awesome."

"It really is." All her tension melted away. She could just sit here and cry. But she needed to get on with it. As she stood, Cody raised his hand for a high five.

She slapped her palm against his, then pointed at the two dogs he'd leashed. "How did you know I needed these two for my visitation program tonight?"

"One of your volunteers told me. Could I go with you?"

Cody. In her truck. Visiting patients by her side. Not what she had in mind for a relaxing evening. She'd paused long enough that a frown settled between his brows.

"Sure. But why?"

"Like I said, I'm kind of at loose ends."

"What about your ranch and your new job?"

"My foreman keeps the ranch running like a finely oiled machine, and I teach bull riding only three days a week until we get the word out and get more students. My evenings get long and lonely."

Just like hers. "Okay. We better get going."

"The pets are lucky to have you. And the patients. When I was in rehab after my bull wreck, seeing you walk in my room made my day."

Her breath faltered. Not because of her, she reminded herself—because of the dog. Dogs always cheered people up. "Midnight, the black Lab I had that day, was great with patients. He got adopted pretty quickly after that first visit."

"I don't even remember the dog." His eyes locked on hers.

She concentrated on breathing. In and out.

"I mean, it had been so long since I'd seen you, and then poof, there you were."

Oh. Silly. Of course that was what he meant. "Yeah, well, I'm sorry I didn't come sooner. I tend to get caught up with the clinic and the shelter and let everything else slide. Even friends." But she remembered the night of his wreck. Calls back and forth with Caitlyn, waiting to hear if he'd live. Her stomach took a dive at the memories.

"It didn't matter when you came. Just that you came."

Because they were friends. That was all. "Um, we should go. The hospital administrator is expecting us."

"Lead the way."

Heart, stay under control. It was just Cody beside her. In her truck. Her friend. And only that—all he ever wanted to be. All she could let him be.

Every time Cody got near, Ally startled. Why was she so quiet? And jumpy. He walked backward, slowly pulling the backing off the sticky side of the contact-paper roll as Ally bonded it onto the cardboard.

They'd both gone to Wednesday-night Bible study at their respective churches. Church relaxed him. Maybe it keyed Ally up.

As she smoothed the final foot in place and he peeled off the last of the backing, his ringtone started up—"Amarillo by Morning." He took out his phone.

"It's Natalie. I hit her up to do our publicity for the festival." He pushed the button. "Hey, Nat. You in?"

"In on what?" his publicist asked in confusion.

"On helping with publicity for Ally's shelter for the Peanut Festival."

"Oh, that. Sure, I can help. But not what I called about. I have two offers for you."

"Offers?"

Ally looked up from her project.

"Cowtown Coliseum wants to know if you'd be interested in signing on as a backup announcer at their rodeo and you got an offer to be the spokesperson for a tractor company."

If he kept living, he could be a backup announcer. But he couldn't make that promise.

And the spokesperson thing didn't interest him at all. Would probably involve travel.

"I'm not interested in either offer. I'm happy right where I am, owning my ranch and teaching bull riding." And being close to Ally. He held her gaze.

"All right. I'll let them know, and I'll get with you soon about the parade. Will you ask Ally to keep an eye out for our dog? It's the strangest thing—he knows how to open the gate, so we keep a metal fastener ring in the latch. Only a person can open it, so it's like someone let him out."

"That is strange. I hope your dog turns up. Thanks for calling, Nat."

"What about Natalie's dog?" Ally stood and dusted off her knees.

"She thinks somebody let it out of the pen. What kind of dog does she have? An expensive breed?"

"A chocolate Lab. Rusty. Her husband adopted him from me three or four years ago. He's a great dog. I was shocked the first time he showed up here as a pup because he's full-blood. We don't get many of those. I'll watch for him."

"A pet-napper in Aubrey? What is this world coming to?" She stood the cardboard up and folded the edges of the contact paper through the window cutouts. A long pause stretched between them. "So you turned down offers?"

"To be a backup announcer at Cowtown Coliseum and spokesperson for a tractor company."

"Why'd you say no?"

"I'm content here." *Being near you, for whatever life I have left.*

"Cowtown is only an hour away. And you said your evenings are lonely. That would occupy weekends."

"Maybe I have something else in mind to occupy my time." He shifted his weight from one foot to the other, ventured a glance at her. *Like you.*

"Cody Warren settling down in one place. For good?"

"Things change. People change."

She searched his eyes. Measured him. But he couldn't tell if he measured up.

"By the way, I'm taking Oreo home with me tonight."

"You think you're ready, huh?"

"My knee is a lot more steady since all my exercising on the treadmill. I think Oreo and I are both ready to put down roots."

"He's all yours."

If only she could be all his. A few more days of working on the float and they'd be finished. He needed to find a new excuse to stick close to her.

If he died, who would keep Ally safe from whatever nut was trying to shut her down? Who would keep her from doing stupid things like climbing in pens with cows separated from their babies?

He had to live. But the only way to do that for certain was to have surgery. And the procedure might just finish him off anyway. But maybe he should consider it. A successful operation was his only chance. To stay alive. To plan a future with Ally.

If she'd have anything to do with him.

"Amarillo by Morning"? Ally unwound the leash from around her legs for the fifth time. The poodle she was boarding seemed intent on tripping her up as they rounded the well-worn path around her back field. All her volunteers had left for the evening. And she was about to wrap it up, too. Almost time for the long hot shower she'd dreamed of all day.

Maybe Cody just hadn't gotten around to changing his ringtone. Or maybe he simply liked the song. Or missed the circuit.

But he'd turned down two good offers last night. That had to mean he was thinking about settling down and staying in town. Maybe teaching bull riding would satisfy his adventurous nature. Could he be content in Aubrey? Could he be content with Ally?

The poodle stopped, statue still, looking toward the road. She cowered and scurried behind Ally.

"What's up with you, Trixie?" Ally surveyed the road. A flash of brown. A bark. "Oh, no. Not another stray. Why don't people at least bring y'all to me, instead of dumping?"

She picked the poodle up and headed for the front yard to investigate. A chocolate Lab sniffed her lilac bush.

"Rusty."

The dog wagged his tail and bounded toward her as Trixie quivered in her arms.

"It's okay, Trixie. Rusty won't hurt you." The large dog wagged his entire body as he reached her. Ally sank her fingers into his thick coat, scratching behind his ears. "He's a good boy. What are you doing here, boy? Your family is worried. Let's get you in the barn and call them."

The good-natured dog followed her to the barn. Barks and yips reached a crescendo at the new arrival as Ally settled Trixie back in her kennel.

"Is that Nat's dog?" Cody took a break from cleaning old hay out of one of the larger pens and rested his chin on the pitchfork handle.

"I'm almost certain."

"That's weird." He wiped sweat from his brow with his sleeve. "You've had two pets wander from the other side of Aubrey within a week's time. And Nat said only a person could unlatch Rusty's pen. Someone had to have let him out."

"Maybe they just forgot to put the extra latch in place and he let himself out." She filled a bowl with dog food and another with water, guided Rusty into one of the large boarder kennels and fastened the latch. "You stay in there."

"Or maybe whoever is trying to shut you down is stealing people's pets and bringing them here."

"Why would they do that?"

"Maybe to get you back over limit. Or to make it look like you're the one stealing the pets."

"That's crazy." She perched on a hay bale.

"It is. But I'm beginning to wonder if we're dealing with someone rational."

She face-palmed. "Oh, that makes me feel a lot better."

"I don't want you to feel better. I want you safe. And if you being cautious helps with that, it works for me." Cody returned to his cleaning.

"Did Mitch get anywhere with the prints he found?"

"No. Whoever we're dealing with has no criminal record."

"That's good, isn't it?"

"I guess." Finished with the pen, Cody moved to the next one. "I just wish we could get to the bottom of this. Maybe I'll ask Mitch to check for prints at Kendra's barn and on Nat's gate."

"You really think it's all connected?"

"Have you ever had any pets from the other end of Aubrey show up here?"

"No." Her shoulders slumped. "I just can't imagine anyone going to so much trouble to mess with me."

The barn door opened and Mom stepped inside. "Oh, Cody. I didn't know you were still here."

"Miss Diane." Cody tipped his cowboy hat.

Mom's smile trembled. She clasped and unclasped her hands.

"Is something wrong, Mom?"

"It can wait until you finish."

"You're making me nervous. Just tell me."

"It's nothing really. It's just—Lance and I want you to get to know him better."

"I've worked with the man for two years." Ally tried to keep her tone casual. "I think I know him pretty well."

"We want you to get to know him outside of work—on a personal level." Mom glanced at Cody, then back to Ally. "We were hoping you could join us at his house for lunch after church Sunday. His daughter and her family will be there, too."

Ally's throat closed up. Her desperate gaze went to Cody.

"I know it's a lot, Ally. I know this is hard on you. But it's really important to me. And to Lance. Just think about it. Okay?"

"Sure." The single word was all she could manage.

"Oh, Ally, thank you." Mom gave her a nervous smile and left.

Cody patted his shoulder.

As if drawn by a magnet, Ally rushed into his arms, pressed her face into his muscled chest. "I can't do this."

"Yes. You can." He gave her a squeeze, then rubbed her back in soothing circles. "You're the toughest woman I've ever known."

"I think it's even more serious than I realized. They want me to meet his daughter. Like we're gonna end up being sisters or something."

"It could happen. Might as well prepare yourself for it."

"Will you come with me? To lunch Sunday? Give me strength not to act like a selfish brat?"

"It would be my pleasure."

"Thanks." She should take a step back now. Disentangle herself from Cody. Put distance between them. But she couldn't move.

Drat. Not only did she need Cody—she loved him. Had for years. How had she let this happen? What would she do if he left again?

Chapter Ten

Cody rested his elbows on the top rail of the metal arena fence as hoofbeats and snorts echoed around him. The mid-September sun warmed his back as the early evening cooled off.

The bull lurched to the right, flinging his student in the air. Cody pressed the button on his stopwatch as David landed in a heap in the dust. The young man got up quickly and dashed to the fence as two pickup men headed off the bull and drove him to the gate.

"That's better." Cody checked his time. "Almost three seconds."

David hung his head. "Less than half of what I need."

"We'll get there. It takes time and practice to work up to eight seconds." All Cody had to do was get the twenty-year-old past his fear. If David could relax in the saddle, he'd achieve his dream. "Just be patient."

Gravel crunched in the drive behind him. Cody turned. A white truck neared the exit. It had to be Ally. No one else in Aubrey drove a truck with the distinctive mobile-clinic box in the bed.

"My hour's up." David climbed the fence.

"Don't worry—we'll get it. See you Monday."

"Thanks." The teen headed for his truck.

Cody pulled out his phone and jabbed in Ally's number.

"Hello?"

"Am I watching you pull out of famous singer Garrett Steele's driveway?"

"Where are you? I mean—I have no idea where Garrett Steele lives. And if I did, I wouldn't tell anyone."

"Uh-huh. Well I'll let you in on a little secret. I teach bull riding at his private ranch. Why don't you come over to the big barn to your left and watch me work?"

"I need to get back to the clinic."

He glanced at his watch. "It's six o'clock. Don't tell me you have more patients scheduled."

"No. But I need to work on the float."

"We're not working on it tonight. You said you needed to get ready for your big pet photography day tomorrow."

"You're right. So I better get to it."

"I'll help you prepare if you'll come help me out. My student might perform better with an audience." Not exactly true, since David had already said his goodbyes. But Cody wanted to see her. Again.

Silence ticked past in seconds. "Okay. But I can't stay long."

The line went dead. Cody's heartbeat filled the silence.

David was almost to his truck. The chute boss swapped stories with the two pickup men still on horseback.

"Hey, guys, can you stick around for one more?"

They looked at each other. Then all three nodded.

"Hey, David, want to go one more round?"

"My time's up."

"I won't tell if you won't."

"Sure." A wide grin spread across the young man's face and he jogged back to the arena. He neared the chute as Ally parked in the small lot. "Oh, I see. You need me to help you impress the lady."

"Something like that. Give me your best."

"Yes, sir."

Ally strolled toward him. "Will this give me nightmares?"

"It's about as safe as taking a calf from its mama," he cracked, as the chute boss corralled a fresh bull. Metal clanked against metal as the beast tried to buck in the small space.

Ally reached the fence, stepped onto the first rung beside him and hooked her elbows over the top.

"That's David Morris," Cody whispered. "He took lessons at another school for a year. He should be lasting eight seconds by now. The best he's done so far is almost three in his last ride."

"Why can't he last?"

"He hasn't had me as a teacher for very long." He shot her a cocky grin.

She scoffed.

"Seriously—he's scared."

The bull rammed his horns into the chute. Ally jumped. "I would be, too."

"I have to find a way to get him past the fear."

"Maybe he's right to be afraid. Maybe bull riding isn't what he's supposed to do with his life."

"It's his dream. I have to help him reach his goal. Otherwise he'll have regrets."

"But maybe he has a girlfriend who loves him and he isn't supposed to leave her."

Cody's insides stilled. Was she talking about them?

The chute opened and the bull careened out. Ally's hand clamped on Cody's arm, her nails biting into his biceps.

But David matched the bull's movement, in sync with each buck, each twist. More fluid and rhythmic than he'd ever been.

Cody eyed his stopwatch. Almost five seconds. "I think he's gonna do it."

The bull did a spin that normally would have lost David, but the young man kept his balance. The buzzer went off.

"He did it." Cody let out a whoop. "You did it."

David bailed off the bull and landed on his feet.

The pickup men herded the bull to the gate as David pumped his fists in the air. "Eight seconds? Really?"

"Eight whole seconds. You did it." Cody grabbed Ally around the waist, pulled her off her perch and spun her around with her back nestled against him. "He did it."

Arms and legs flailing, she laughed as he spun her again, then set her down and held her as she wobbled.

"Thanks for the ride. Now I'm dizzy." She leaned back against him.

"I think I figured out how to make David forget his fear."

"How?"

"Get a pretty girl to watch."

"I better get back." She pulled away, practically ran to her truck.

Had she wanted him to stay all those years ago?

Maybe her hypothetical girlfriend for David was just that—hypothetical. Or maybe… But if Ally had wanted him to stay, if she'd had feelings for him, there wasn't a thing he could do about it now.

Not unless he did something about the bubble in his head. And lived to tell about it.

If Cody didn't know better, he'd think Ally was avoiding him. Her volunteers had come, walked and fed the dogs, and left. He'd known she wouldn't take him up on his offer to help her get ready for tomorrow's photography day.

If she wouldn't come to him, he'd go to her. He headed toward the clinic, but his nerve ebbed away as he neared. *Calm down.* Don't let her know how desperate he was to see her. He stepped inside. Orange-scented cleaner heavy in the air.

"May I help you?" Her voice came from the back.

"It's Cody. I meant it when I said I'd lend a hand."

"I figured you'd come over when you got ready." Ally came through the door and stopped behind the counter.

"Hey." His breathing went all funny at the sight of her.

"Derek's wife, Brandy, is helping out tomorrow and several of my volunteers will be here, too."

"What can I do?"

"Maybe just greet people." She wrote something on her schedule. "I was going to have the cat pictures taken in the barn and the dog pictures in the clinic. But the barn is such a better background."

"Can't you have both in the barn?"

"Kendra's bringing her assistant." She swept her thick braid over her shoulder and twirled it around her finger. "With two photographers, things will move more quickly if we set up two clients at a time, one with cats and one with dogs. But I can't have dog pictures taken next to cats. That would be mayhem."

"I see what you're saying." He tapped his chin with his finger. "You could use my barn for the cat pictures."

"I thought of that. But your loft is open. I don't want any of my clients' cats getting spooked from all the barking and escaping out of your loft." She opened a drawer and slid a file into place. "And I can't do the dog pictures in your barn, because that would terrorize your cats."

"I'll board up my loft so we won't have any escapees and the cats can come to my barn."

"That would work. But it's a lot of trouble."

"I don't mind."

"Thank you." She set her hand on his arm, warming him all the way to his booted toes. "Now all I have to do is figure out what to do with the dozen or so families bringing cats and dogs."

"My barn will work for that, too. My cats stay in the loft most of the time. And if the dogs are used to cats, they probably wouldn't bother them anyway."

"You're brilliant." She rubbed her temple. "I think my brain is too tired to think anymore."

"Get some rest. I'll prepare my barn and play greeter tomorrow, and you'll be amazed how smoothly everything goes."

"You may regret that offer. We've had such a great response I probably should have made two days out of it."

"No worries. I'll be here."

"Thank you." She looked at him as if he were a hero.

And he felt like one. Ally's hero. A glow filled his chest. What more could he aspire to?

* * *

With Lance and Derek manning the clinic, Ally was free to oversee pet adoptions.

Once Kendra had set up all her equipment in Cody's escape-proof barn, Ally watched as she took pictures of the first families on their schedule.

It was nice to see her friends and clients without their pets being injured or sick. A fun, relaxing day and she'd already adopted out three cats and six dogs.

Today would slam her with lots of happy families. Something in Ally longed for that.

"Call me if you need anything," she said to Kendra. "I better get back to my barn in case there are any potential adoptive families waiting."

"We're good here." Kendra's flash went off as Ally exited.

Outside in the field behind her house, Garrett Steele and Brant McConnell, superstars of the Christian country music scene, performed a concert.

The event was looking to be a roaring success, and to top things off, the two musicians had pledged to match the proceeds of the concert. She'd have plenty of money for another barn—if she could just buy some of the land Cody was leasing.

The bright sun blinded her as she entered her barn. Cody was cracking jokes as Kendra's assistant got some shots of a family of six with their dog.

Her vision cleared enough for her to make out Caitlyn and Mitch milling about the cages.

"Hey, Caitlyn, I saw y'all on the schedule." But as far as Ally knew, they no longer had any pets.

"We've decided to get a dog."

"Oh, how fun. And thank you so much. I can direct you toward kid-friendly breeds and what to expect, though most of the dogs we have are a mixture. Did you have anything specific in mind?"

"Nothing too big, since Michaela is still small." Mitch held their seven-month-old in his arms.

"House or outside dog?"

"Outside. We have a nice barn and fenced-in area."

"I have a beagle mix and a bulldog mix." She toyed with the end of her braid. "They're great with kids and great with other dogs and other animals."

"I had a beagle when I was a kid. I loved that dog." Mitch's expression went distant, his voice filled with reverence.

"Male or female?" Caitlyn shifted her diaper bag.

"Both. The beagle is female. The bulldog is male. Spayed and neutered and up-to-date on shots."

"Can we see them?"

"Of course. Cody, if you'll get Splotch, I'll get Brutus."

"Brutus?" Caitlyn's eyes widened.

"Don't worry. It has nothing to do with his personality. I call him that because he's so stocky and tough looking, but if you adopt him, you can call him anything you want."

Ally and Cody worked quickly, unlatching the dogs' kennels and leashing them.

"I like the name Brutus." Mitch grinned. "What do you think, Micki?" He set their daughter down with her feet on his, took her hands and walked her toward the dogs.

The little girl squealed. Both dogs wagged their entire bodies.

"Easy." Caitlyn dashed after them.

"Both dogs are very easygoing and patient." Ally laughed. "They love attention."

Mitch guided Michaela's hand, petting the dogs, who sucked up the adoration.

"What do you think?" He caught his wife's eye. "Maybe both—they seem to get along."

"I usually kennel them together for companionship and they've become great friends. The bulldog isn't known for energy, but the beagle gets him going sometimes."

"It'd be a shame to split them up." Caitlyn gave her a hug. "Thanks, Ally. They're perfect."

"I'm so glad." She got the paperwork for both dogs. Minutes later, the family and their new pets were in the middle of a photo session, looking as if they'd been together for years.

As they left, Cody settled on a hay bale. "Why didn't they get the third degree?"

"Because I've known them forever. I know their land is the perfect place for dogs to romp and they both had pets as kids. I already know they'll take excellent care of Splotch and Brutus."

"These animals are very lucky to have you. It's obvious how much you care about finding the perfect home for them."

"They're childlike, incapable of caring for themselves." Her mouth twitched as her eyes welled. "They deserve a good life."

The barn door opened. Her mom stepped inside, her eyes wide. "Um, Ally, you need to come to the clinic."

"What's wrong?" She hurried out with Mom on her heels.

"Lance and Derek haven't arrived yet and all the

pens are open in the clinic." Mom's words tumbled out. "I got the patients still recovering from yesterday's surgeries back in the kennels just fine. But the Lewis' cat is on top of the refrigerator and the Gonzaleses' dog won't let her come down. And he's kind of big and scary, so I wasn't sure how to handle him."

As Ally bolted toward the clinic, the barn door clapped. "Ally, need some help?" Cody.

"Yes."

Chewed up magazines and an overturned chair greeted her in the clinic lobby. At least the clinic didn't open until ten on Saturdays. Though her four-legged clientele often got messy, she tried to keep the building clean and her first appointment was prone to show up early. A rumbling growl echoed from the break room followed by several gruff barks.

Samson had always been a sweet Doberman, but what if she got between him and a cat he wanted to attack?

"What should I do?" Mom twisted her hands together.

Dobermans and pit bulls were the only breeds Mom was nervous around.

"If you'll take care of that—" she pointed to the shredded magazines in the floor "—and check for any other disorder throughout the building, I'll handle Samson."

With a relieved sigh, Mom got the broom and disinfectant spray.

The door opened and Ally held her breath.

Cody stepped inside. "What's going on?"

"I'm so glad it's you instead of my first client. All the patients were out of their kennels. Mom took care of it except for a Doberman who has a cat treed on top of my refrigerator."

"A nice Doberman?"

"Usually. But I've never had to get between him and a cat before."

"Do you have a plan?" He followed her into the surgery/recovery room.

"Maybe if we put a kennel up level with the cat, she'll go in. Usually when felines are frightened, they love their crates."

"We'll give it a shot."

Ally grabbed Cinnamon's kennel and Samson's leash. Cody was right behind her as she opened the break room door.

"Hey, Samson, sweet puppy." Ally baby-talked the sleek canine. "You don't want to hurt that precious little kitty. Just think how sad her people would be."

Cody strolled past the dog to the refrigerator, took the kennel and held it up next to the cat.

"Come on, Cinnamon. Get in your crate, girl. You'll be safe. Here, kitty, kitty, kitty."

Desperate, the cat shot into the kennel as Samson let out a series of deep woofs and looked as if he'd take Cody down. But Ally snapped his leash on and held him back with all her might.

Cody set the kennel on the counter. "Let me have the dog." He took the leash from her. "Where do you want him?"

"In the surgery room." She followed him through the adjoining door and coaxed Samson into his cage. "I'd think after tangling with a copperhead, the last thing on your mind would be a cat, you brute." Ally scolded the dog and he hung his head as she fastened the cage door back in place. Crisis averted, she let out a long exhale.

"I'll get Cinnamon." Cody disappeared for a moment, then came back carrying a still-terrified cat.

"It's okay, sweetie." Ally stuck a finger through a hole in the box and stroked the frightened cat. "I won't let that mean old dog get you. And your mommy will come get you soon. Let me check you over and make sure you didn't rip any stitches." Gently she pulled the cat out of the cage and set her on the examining table. Ally used her body as a shield to block the cat's view of Samson.

"She just had surgery?"

"I spayed her yesterday." Ally inspected the stitches on the cat's belly. "Everything looks okay. I'm so sorry you had such a traumatic night. I wonder how long y'all were out."

"Your nemesis obviously came back."

"I thought surely the new locks would do the trick."

"I'll see if Mitch is still here."

"Not until the pet photography thing is over." Her insides twisted. "Please. I don't want everyone wondering why the Texas Rangers are here. And I'll have patients soon."

"Relax." He leaned against the counter, crossed his arms over his chest, as if reminding her how to settle down. "He'll keep a low profile."

"I guess that'll have to do." She checked her appointments. "Thanks for helping. There's no way I could have gotten the kennel up high enough to reach the cat."

"I just can't believe someone was skulking around here last night and I didn't hear a thing. I promise I've been sleeping with both ears open."

"I didn't hear anything, either. It's not your fault."

"No, but if anyone hurt you, I'd never forgive myself."

Her heart shot into triple rhythm.

But he cared for her only as a friend. He'd be upset if she got hurt on his watch. Not because he loved her.

The door opened and Lance strolled in. His jaw went slack when he saw her. "Morning, Ally."

"You missed the excitement. I'm sure Mom will tell you all about it. We better get back to the barn and make sure things run smoothly."

"Nice seeing you, Lance." Cody followed her out.

Cars lined both their drives. Though her shelter was less occupied these days, the cacophony of usual barks reached a fevered pitch with all the activity and extra pets. Hopefully, her clients wouldn't leave before getting their pictures done just to escape the ruckus.

"So how are things with Lance?" Cody fell in stride beside her. "After the talk."

"I try to act natural." She slowed to accommodate his slight limp. "But I fake it. It doesn't feel like anything will ever be normal again, and I'm dreading tomorrow's dinner. I'm twenty-nine, my mother has a boyfriend I work with every day, and I feel like I'm losing her. How childish is that?"

"I think it's perfectly normal. You'll never lose her. It'll be different. But different can be good."

"I can't imagine living here by myself." Her eyes went skyward.

"You're probably getting a little ahead of yourself."

"I don't think so." She hugged herself. "He was still at the house when I went in last night. They were holding hands and the way they were looking at each other…" She closed her eyes. "If he kisses her, I'm not sure if I'll scream, cry or laugh. Maybe all three. Yet the rational part of me knows Mom has been lonely for so long. I want her to be happy and he's a good man."

"Just give yourself time to get used to the idea. And pray about it."

"Pray about it?" She stopped. "Like for them to suddenly get on each other's nerves?"

"Not exactly." He chuckled. "Pray for God to give you peace about their relationship."

"I like my idea better." But how could she begrudge her mother the love of a decent man?

By the time they got to the barn, another family was in the middle of their photo session.

Another happy family.

She'd give anything for Cody to return her feelings. But if he couldn't love her, she shouldn't love him. Yet her traitorous heart refused to listen to reason.

Lance's doorbell played some song Cody couldn't quite put his finger on as Ally's hand quaked in his.

"Relax." He squeezed her fingers. "At least you know Lance. You sat with him during church this morning. And for a lot of Sundays before that. It's not like he's some random man preying on lonely women."

"Thanks. You just gave me a whole new worry." She shot him a grin, and despite her nerves, her eyes sparkled with something he hadn't seen before.

Something he liked. A lot.

The door swung open. A pretty redhead with a toddler clinging to each leg greeted them. "Hi, you must be Ally. Come on in. I'm Erin. This is Zane and this is Zoey."

Ally seemed rooted to the spot. He squeezed her hand again, propelling her forward.

"I'm Cody."

"I'm so glad you could come." Erin pried the children loose and grabbed each by the hand. "Everyone's in the living room. Follow me."

They made slow toddler progress to a room just off the foyer.

"Ally, you made it." Diane sat next to Lance on a cozy love seat.

A blond man relaxed in a recliner.

Cody gave her fingers another squeeze, but she pulled free of his grasp as if she'd just remembered they were holding hands.

"This is Ally and Cody. My husband, Scott. If he'll keep up with our two cling-ons, I'll put ice in the glasses and we'll be ready."

"Come here, rug rats." Scott stood and wrangled the toddlers. He tickled the children, reducing them to giggles, as everyone trailed Erin to the dining room.

Something tugged inside Cody's gut. A pull he'd been feeling for a while now. Being home, seeing all his friends and family happily married with kids made him feel like he was missing out on something. Something with Ally.

Diane and the men settled at the table while Erin and Ally filled the glasses with ice. Lance and Diane sat at the ends, Scott and the twins on one side, leaving Cody with Erin and Ally. Taking the middle seat would be too obvious. He chose a chair next to Diane's end, praying Erin would leave the chair beside him for Ally.

He couldn't take his eyes off her. Forever with Ally

sounded good. He could imagine spending the rest of his life with her. Her having his babies.

But did she have any feelings for him? She certainly hadn't resisted their long-ago kiss. And since he'd been back, there'd been a few times when she'd seemed drawn to him. Like the other day while they were working on the float. If he didn't know any better, he'd say she'd wanted to kiss him, too.

Finished with the ice, Erin claimed the chair by her dad, leaving Ally to sit beside Cody. Her elbow brushed his. Stole his breath.

"Sorry." That softness was still in her eyes.

That thing that turned him into a puddle at her feet. Could she have feelings for him, too?

But even if she did, Cody didn't know how long his forever would last. He couldn't pursue Ally. Not unless he had the surgery. And lived.

Surgery was his only chance. And Ally was worth giving it a shot.

Grilled steak, roasted potatoes, green beans and yeast rolls. Yum. Ally's mouth watered over the food. But it wasn't enough to distract her from Cody. Since she'd come to terms with her feelings for him, since he seemed like he might stay, she couldn't seem to stop thinking about him.

Lance prayed over the meal, and chatter filled the air as they passed dishes, filling their plates.

Mom seemed so happy. Happier than Ally had seen her since…since Dad. What right did Ally have to let her conflicted feelings put a damper on her mother's happiness?

"So how long have you and Cody been together?" Erin bumped her elbow.

"We're not." Ally gave a decisive shake of her head. "We're neighbors."

"And friends." Cody cleared his throat.

"We've been friends since high school and now we're neighbors." Ally focused on cutting her steak.

"Oops, my bad." Erin offered an innocent shrug. "Y'all seem so close I just assumed…"

"I think—" Scott wiped potatoes off his son's mouth "—my lovely wife was envisioning a double wedding with y'all and Dad and Diane. Guess it'll have to be a single affair."

Erin's eyes widened.

"Ouch." Scott grimaced. "That was my shin."

Ally's gaze pinged from Mom to Lance. Waiting for her response. "A wedding? Isn't that rushing things a bit?"

"Not really." Mom giggled.

Giggled? Mom giggled? "Y'all are talking about getting married already?"

"Since the cat's out of the bag—" a throb started up in Lance's jaw "—I guess I should ask you for your mother's hand in marriage."

Ally's mouth went numb.

Chapter Eleven

❧

"I think Ally's just surprised." Cody's hand closed over hers under the table, gave her a gentle pat. "I mean, you've only been dating a few weeks."

"We've worked together for two years, ate a lot of lunches together and officially started dating six months ago." Mom blushed.

"Six months?" Ally almost swallowed her tongue. "You hid it from me?"

Mom's face went a deeper shade of red. "Um… I haven't exactly been going to book club meetings."

How could she have been so naive? Book clubs didn't meet on Saturday nights.

"Your mother didn't want you to be upset." Lance's tone was cajoling.

"So you hide your relationship from me for six months and then spring a proposal on me out of the blue. What am I? A child?" The high-pitched panic in her voice made her sound like one. She gulped her sweet tea.

Something beeped in the kitchen.

"Ally, let's go check on my pie." Erin scooted her chair back. "I need a second opinion since I'm bad about underbaking the crust and there's nothing worse than doughy pie."

Saved by the buzzer. But the last thing Ally wanted to do was talk about pie. She wanted to grab Mom by the shoulders and shake some sense into her. Instead she pushed her chair back and followed Erin to the kitchen.

"I tried to get them to tell you. From the beginning." Erin opened the oven and slid out the rack. Blueberries bubbled under the golden lattice crust. With mitt-covered hands, Erin pulled the pie from the oven and set it on a hot pad on the counter.

"So you knew they were dating from the beginning?"

"Yes. Dad told me he wanted to ask your mom out and I kind of coached him along."

"Why did they tell you and not me?" Ally folded her arms over her chest as something heavy sank to the pit of her stomach.

"I guess they knew I was ready. I'd been trying to get Dad to date for at least a year."

"But they thought I needed to be treated with kid gloves?"

"I'm married with a family of my own. Your mom didn't want you to feel like she was abandoning you. But it doesn't look like you're alone. Are you sure you and Cody are only friends and neighbors?"

"Yes." Sort of.

Her mom entered the kitchen then wearing a sheepish grin. "How's the pie coming?"

"I think it turned out perfect. For the first time ever." Erin grabbed a knife and the pie and headed for the dining room. "Will you bring the ice cream, Diane? No rush—this'll need time to cool."

"I'm sorry, sweetie." Mom cupped Ally's cheek when

they were alone. "I know this must seem fast to you. And I handled it all wrong. I should have told you from the beginning. Lance tried to get me to."

"Why didn't you?"

"You were so crazy about your dad and I knew it would be hard on you to see me with another man."

"I'm an adult." She swallowed hard. "I'm trying to pull up my big-girl boots."

"We shouldn't have rushed you. Forget about Lance's proposal." Mom patted her arm. "We'll wait until you're more comfortable with everything."

"You really love him?"

"I do. He makes me happy." Mom chuckled. "He makes me laugh. Makes me feel young."

"You're sure enough to marry him?"

"I am." Mom bit her lip. "After your dad died, I didn't think I'd ever love again. But Lance is a very special man. He treats me like a queen."

"You've been alone a long time." Ally drew in a big breath. "You deserve to be happy and Lance is a good man."

"He really is." Mom patted her cheek. "I'm glad you're remembering that you like him."

"We better get back in there with the ice cream."

Mom opened the freezer, fished out the bucket and linked arms with Ally.

They stepped back in the dining room and the conversation went silent.

"Perfect timing." Erin tried to cover the sudden quiet. "I think the pie is cool enough to cut."

"I haven't had blueberry pie in ages." Cody rubbed his hands together.

"It's Mom's favorite." Ally took her seat beside him.

"Before we start dishing up the pie, I have something to say."

Lance's jaw tightened. Scott's eyes went big. Erin sipped her tea. Cody's hand found Ally's under the table again.

"I'd like to give Lance my blessing. Yes, you may marry my mother."

Smiles broke out around the table, followed by excited conversation as Erin served up pie and ice cream. Cody squeezed her fingers.

Drat. She'd probably use his shoulder again on the way home. She really should keep her distance. Even if he stayed in Aubrey, he might not have any feelings for her other than friendship. And she wanted way more where Cody was concerned.

"I'm proud of you." Almost home, but Cody wasn't ready to let Ally go just yet. "I know that must have been hard."

"It was." Ally turned into her drive. "But it was the right thing to do. Mom deserves to be happy. And I don't have any right to stand in her way."

"Lance is a good man. And he has no criminal record."

"What?"

Cody ducked his head. "Mitch checked his background after the first break-in at your clinic. He's clean. Derek, too. Of course, I'm not supposed to know any of that, so if you could forget it, I'd be forever in your debt."

"My lips are sealed." She grinned. "Thanks for letting me know, but I already knew he was okay. You can tell a lot about a person from the way they treat animals. His daughter and her family seem nice, too. I could get real attached to those twins."

"You always worried about never being an aunt. Here's your chance." Practice for being a mom to his children someday?

"I hadn't thought of that. But I hope it's a long engagement. I need time to adjust."

"I'll go with you to your mom's wedding if you'll go with me to my grandpa's."

"He's getting remarried?" She killed her engine.

"This Saturday." A chorus of barks from Ally's barn filled the silence. "He called to tell me last night."

"Wow, our relatives move fast, don't they. At his ranch in Medina?"

"It's a six-hour drive. You up for a road trip?" Six hours in a truck with Ally. Could his heart take that much one-on-one with her?

"I guess so. I'll definitely need support at Mom's." She didn't seem to be in any hurry to go inside.

"If we go it alone, you'll have to drive." *Please say yes.* "Or we can ride with my mom and dad in the mini-van with my niece, Michaela."

"You know I'm all about kids. But the farther back I sit in a vehicle, the more carsick I get. So I guess I better drive us. How long until you can get behind the wheel?"

He'd hoped she wouldn't ask. Hated lying, but he wasn't ready to share his aneurysm with her. "I'm not sure. Just a precaution because of my knee."

"Isn't that a bit extreme?"

"It was a pretty extreme injury. And not my first." At least that part was true.

"All this time, you haven't driven. How do you get groceries?"

"One of my hands takes care of things for me and

takes me where I need to go. And I catch a ride to church with Mitch and Caitlyn."

"That's why you're here, isn't it?" She turned to face him. "Your doctor won't release you to rodeo, either."

"He might eventually. But even if he does, I'm not going back."

"You sure?"

For some reason, his answer seemed to be important to her.

"I'm positive. The rodeo is behind me." It felt good to make plans for the future. Plans with Ally. Monday morning, first thing, he'd call his doctor and schedule his surgery. If he was going to pursue Ally, he needed a guaranteed future.

Sometimes going after what he wanted required a huge risk. Ally was worth the uncertainty.

"Friday?" Ally squeaked. "This Friday?"

"Is it too soon?" Mom winced, set a food bowl in the Rottweiler's cage. "Here you go, girl. You sore, honey?"

Only a day after spaying, the dog looked so forlorn. Ally felt her pain, but give her another day and she'd be feeling better. Maybe Ally would, too. Thankfully the clinic was closed and Ally didn't have any more patients or surgeries after the bomb Mom had just dropped.

"In four days? I just wasn't expecting a wedding quite so soon." Ally went through her closing routine— checking on patients, supplies and her schedule for the next day. But she couldn't focus.

"Well, when you get to be our age, what's the point in waiting?"

"You're fifty-two, Mom. You sound like you're eighty. I just don't understand what the hurry is."

"Lance and I love each other." Mom lifted one shoulder. "We're not silly kids. We want to start our lives together. You're going to Medina Saturday, the Peanut Festival is the week after that, the church is booked the next weekend, and then Erin and her family are going on vacation. It's this Friday or wait a month."

"At least a month would give us a little time to plan— to send out invitations."

"No invitations." Mom held her palms toward Ally. "We both had big weddings the first time. This time we both want small—just our families and closest friends. None of the hoopla."

"Okay." Ally swallowed. "This Friday it is. Tell me what you need me to do."

"Nothing. We're not decorating or having a reception. Just a photographer—I've already booked Kendra—and our families." Mom finished filling bowls and turned to Ally. "The only thing I hate about all of this is you living here alone. With all that's been going on around here."

She hadn't thought of that. After the wedding, Mom would move in with Lance. Ally would be alone.

Mom frowned. "Maybe we should put off the wedding until our mystery is solved here."

Ally wanted to jump on the idea. But more than that, she wanted Mom happy. "No. It could be months before the perp is caught. I'll be fine."

"Maybe Lance should move in with us until things are settled."

"No." Ally's eyes widened. She didn't want to be alone, but she really didn't want to live with Mom and her new husband. "I don't even have to stay here. I can find a new place for my clinic and shelter if you want to sell the house. I need more acreage anyway."

"Nonsense. This is your home." Mom perched on a tall stool. "After all the years I struggled and sold off bits of land to keep this place so you could have it one day, I wouldn't dream of selling it out from under you. But it's yours to do with as you please. If you'd like to sell it and find something with more acreage, you have my blessing."

"I'd like to stay here." It was the only home she'd ever known and her only memories of her dad were here. "As far as the break-ins, Cody's right next door." Though with an excessive number of strays streaming in daily, if the bulk of them didn't turn out to be lost pets, she'd soon be over-limit again.

"Maybe with me out of your hair, you and Cody will get together."

"Mom! We're friends. You know that's all it is."

"I wonder."

"There's nothing to wonder."

"I see the way he looks at you." Mom wagged a finger at her. "The way you look at him."

"We don't look at each other any special way."

"If you say so." Mom hurried toward her desk. "I better get things in order. Lance is taking me out to dinner. Would you like to join us?"

"I'm beat." True. But even if she weren't, she would not be a third wheel. "Y'all have fun."

Mom would live with Lance. And Ally would be alone. Except for her cute cowboy neighbor who rattled her heart.

Ally checked each exam room, wiped down the tables with disinfectant. Where was Cody? She hadn't heard a peep or caught a glimpse of him all day.

Her cell rang and she fished it out. "Hello."

"Hey, Ally." His voice turned her to butter.

"I was just thinking about you." Why had she admitted that?

"Really?"

"I haven't seen you all day."

"Yeah, I was hoping to make it home this evening. But I'm in Dallas. One of my hands and I ran some errands. We couldn't manage everything in one day, so we're getting a hotel room and I won't be home until tomorrow evening."

"Oh." Disappointment loaded her tone.

"I'm having my foreman stay at my house in case there's any trouble."

"Your foreman must be tired of babysitting me."

"Not at all. I'll see you tomorrow evening."

The call ended and she missed him even more.

With Mom gone, would Ally's lonely heart be able to resist Cody?

Aubrey had never looked so good to Cody as Joe drove him through the small town. The leaves hadn't started turning quite yet. Trucks lined Main Street. Suppertime at Moms on Main. His stomach growled, but he wanted to get home.

How had he stayed away for twelve years? After thirty-six hours in Dallas, he was homesick. Mostly for Ally.

But the test his doctor ran yesterday had revealed bad news: the bubble in his head was growing. Finalizing his decision. The week after the Peanut Festival, Cody would go under the knife. His surgeon had explained everything during their consultation that afternoon.

"Lord, get me through this," Cody whispered. "Am I doing the right thing? Just because there's a possible fix for this, am I supposed to try?"

The same peacefulness he'd felt when he first decided to have the surgery flowed through him. For whatever reason, this was the path God wanted for him.

"You say something, boss?" Joe turned onto Cody's road.

"Just praying."

"Didn't mean to interrupt." Joe was still clueless about his health. They'd stayed in a hotel next to the hospital. While Joe had bought ranch supplies, Cody had walked to the hospital.

His doctor and the internet assured him the surgeon was highly recommended and had performed the procedure successfully countless times. If there had been any mishaps, nobody was telling him.

Even though he might not survive, though he might have a stroke and his reasoning processes or motor skills could be affected, he had to try. For Ally's sake. And with the aneurysm growing, he didn't have much choice anyway. It was all up to God now. Cody could rest in that.

Joe pulled in his drive.

"Thanks for letting me tag along."

"Anytime."

Looked like Ally's clinic was already closed for the day—it was well after five. As he got out of his truck, the door to her clinic opened, and she ran toward him. Right into his arms. It was a dream come true.

With a knowing grin, Joe headed for the barn, made himself scarce.

"We gotta stop meeting like this." The corners of his mouth twitched.

"Mom and Lance are getting married Friday." She sniffled.

"As in this Friday? In three days, Friday?"

She shuddered against him. "It's the only time everybody will be in town unoccupied, and the church isn't available again for a month."

"I'll get you through it. And the next day, you can get me through Grandpa's."

"Why didn't you tell me you were leaving? I was kind of worried about you."

His heart did the two-step. Ally was worried about him. "It came up kind of sudden."

"Is everything okay?"

"It will be." His arms tightened around her. "Everything okay here?"

"Just more strays. And two more escaped pets returned to their grateful owners. I hope there aren't any emergencies this weekend. I'll be in Medina with you, and Lance will be on his honeymoon." She groaned. "With my mother."

Cody chuckled. "At least they're getting hitched and doing it the right way. And as far as the clinic goes, you've alerted the vet in Denton."

"But what if my nemesis decides to pull something this weekend?"

"I arranged for one of my hands to house-sit for you."

She relaxed against him. "Thank you."

"Anything else I can do?"

"You're doing it." She burrowed in closer.

Making his heart clip-clop like a Clydesdale. This

surgery had to work. So he could be here for Ally. So he could have the chance to win her heart.

Ally was exhausted. She'd helped her volunteers tend all the animals then had gone to Wednesday-night Bible study.

Though she barely had the energy to put one foot in front of the other after all that, she headed for Cody's barn with a cup of coffee for each of them. She'd have never thought of him as the decaf type.

The usual yaps and barks followed her across the yard. As she neared Cody's barn, something familiar echoed from inside. The nail gun. They'd completed building the frame and contact-papering the cardboard. Only one more night of working together. Tonight they'd assemble the ark, put shelving in place to support a kennel in each window and strategically pile hay bales in the center.

She slid the door open to see Cody holding two sides of the frame together at a right angle.

"Let me help." She set their cups on a hay bale, climbed the ladder next to the trailer and stepped up beside him. As he drove the nail in, she braced her weight against the frame.

"You look tired."

"Thanks. We vaccinated a large ranch today."

"I noticed you were gone all day." He set another nail. "You didn't do anything stupid like get in a pen with a mama cow, did you?"

"Nope. We didn't have any difficult cases. Everyone went right into the chute and took it like a bull."

"I'm glad." He set the final nail.

"Coffee break."

"You speak my language. Decaf?"

"Fake, just for you." She picked up the two cups, handed him his.

They sipped in grateful silence, then set the mugs down and got back to work.

As Cody picked up another piece of the frame and moved it into place, muscles strained against his shirt.

She had to look away as she positioned her foot, hip and hands to hold the frame steady while he sank the nails.

"I did something today."

Like what? Made plans to leave? "What's that?"

"I bought the ranch."

Her breath stilled. "You bought it?"

"I did. And I donated five acres to Ally's Adopt-a-Pet."

His handsome image blurred as hot tears welled in her eyes.

"Now, don't go crying. That's what you wanted, wasn't it? Five acres. I can donate more if you need it. What's five acres or even twenty when I own two hundred fifty?"

"Five is plenty." She blinked several times to clear her vision and braced the frame for him.

He set the last nail, tested the strength of the two curved sides they'd joined together, then stepped back to survey their handiwork.

"Thank you." She flung herself into his arms.

"If I'd have known I was gonna get this kind of thank-you, I'd have bought the land a long time ago." He nuzzled her ear.

Sending a delicious shiver through her. Step back. Better yet, run away. But her boots stayed rooted in place, her body nestled against him. She tipped her head back, looked up at him.

His eyes pledged much more than friendship.

Chapter Twelve

Ally rose up on tiptoe.

His head dipped. Lips met hers. Fireworks went off in her head, heart and veins. Cody filled her senses. The feel of his muscles. The spicy scent of his aftershave mixed with fresh hay. The taste of his fake-coffee-flavored lips. Her hands wound around his neck, fingers curled in his hair.

But then he was pulling away.

She whirled away from him, turned her back to him, tried to get her breathing back on track.

"Ally, we can't—"

"That's twice you've kissed me. Exactly two times too many." Never mind that she'd cuddled up to him like a winter coat on a Labrador Retriever. "Don't let it happen again."

"I was just accepting your thanks." He chuckled.

Her skin went hot. She could only imagine how many shades of red she must be.

"We better get back to work." She closed her eyes, worked at calm and turned to face him. Without looking at him. How could they nonchalantly get on with their day when her whole world had tipped on its axis? Again.

As he held the frame in place and fastened it to the trailer, she braced it for him. He sank nails as if nothing had happened, while she kept her gaze focused on the hay-strewn trailer bed.

"I really appreciate your donation. But you didn't have to do that. I can buy the land from you."

"Nope. It's already done."

He was staying. He'd bought the ranch. So if he was staying, why had he pulled away from her? *"Ally, we can't"* what? Can't kiss? Can't cross the friendship line? Why?

Because he didn't have any feelings for her? Had she misread the message she thought she'd seen in his eyes?

While she was over the moon for him and had laid it all out for him with that kiss. He must know how she felt. And he must feel sorry for her since he didn't feel the same.

Even her toes burned with humiliation.

The dogs were used to his presence. Only the new residents barked their curiosity as Cody finished the pen, tested the latch. Three more pens and he'd feel as if Ally's shelter would be okay if he died.

He'd seen a lawyer after buying the ranch. Arranged for Ally to be his beneficiary. The ranch, his bank accounts, everything. If he didn't make it through the surgery, she'd be able to hire someone to build more pens, another barn, whatever she needed.

But would she have someone to love her the way he did?

Twelve year old memories were hard enough to wrestle with. Revisiting her kiss had kept him up most of the night. He rolled out the fencing and measured for the next pen.

That she had kissed him back must mean she had more than friend feelings for him. But he couldn't do a thing about it. Not until after his surgery. If he survived and still had control of his faculties, then he'd act on it. But not a minute before. His head was fine with that. But his heart was another matter.

Several other volunteers were walking dogs. But no Ally in sight. Maybe she was still at the clinic and he wouldn't run into her. Maybe she was trying to avoid him, too. At this point, space was his best solution. Lots of space between them. And that was doable. They'd finished the float last night.

All he had to do was get through her mom's wedding tomorrow, the road trip to Medina and Grandpa's wedding on Saturday, and the Peanut Festival parade next weekend. Just keep his distance for a little over a week.

The barn door clapped shut and Ally's scent filled the air. "You're building more pens?"

"Now that the float's done, I've got time."

"I'm so excited about the land." She settled on a hay bale beside him. Her knee almost touching his shoulder. "I don't know how I'll ever thank you."

"No need to thank me. I'm just glad to help." His heart skipped a beat. Space. He really needed space.

"I think I'll build another barn with more pens and runs. I have the funds, thanks to the pet photography day and concert."

Chatty. Relaxed. Not afraid to get too close. Not afraid to touch him. Friendly. Like the old Ally.

As if neither of their kisses had ever happened.

Was she on to him? Did she know he was crazy in

love with her? Was she trying to remind him of how their friendship was supposed to be? To let him down easy?

"A couple of my ranch hands are starting a construction business. I'll get you their card." The more he could do to help her, the better he'd feel going into surgery.

"Sounds great."

"Ready for the weddings this weekend? And the road trip on Saturday?"

"I'm more at peace with Mom and Lance. They're really great together. Very compatible and happy." She squeezed his shoulder. "You ready for your grandfather's wedding?"

"I'm getting used to the idea. He's been alone about as long as your mom has. No one should be lonely for that long." His throat closed up.

"Project Weddings on track." She stood. Moved away from him. "I better go walk some dogs so my volunteers won't think I'm a slacker. By the way, Mom's wedding will be semiformal. Wear a suit. What about your grandpa's? What should I wear?"

That awesome burgundy dress she'd worn to Landry's almost wedding. Wouldn't mind seeing her in that again. "Casual. Jeans will do."

"That sounds fun. And comfortable."

"Yep." But driving six hours with Ally wouldn't be. How many weddings could he attend with her and keep his distance?

Just get me through ten more days until surgery, Lord. Then with Your help, I'll be a healthy man. And I can eventually see Ally walk the aisle for our own wedding.

All he had to do was survive the surgery with his head, heart and body intact.

* * *

The church was pretty as usual. Mom had said no decorations and she'd stuck with it. No extra flowers, no ribbons on the pews, tulle, candelabra or arbors. Just Mom wearing a cream-colored satin jacket and skirt and Lance in a suit, with Pastor William, Erin and her family, Ally and Cody.

The twins were adorable—Zane wearing a miniature suit just like his grandfather's and Zoey in pink ruffles. These two had Ally wrapped around their little fingers within a mere week.

As her mom pledged her heart to a man who wasn't her father, Ally teared up. Mom was happy and Lance obviously loved her. He'd be good to Mom and she wouldn't be lonely anymore. This was a day for celebrating—even Dad would approve.

"By the power vested in me by the state of Texas, I pronounce you husband and wife. What God hath joined together, let no man put asunder. Lance, you may kiss your bride."

The couple exchanged a chaste kiss, then hugged.

Ally's gaze strayed to Cody and he shot her a wink. Her cheeks went hot. She'd worked at acting natural with him. As if their kiss weren't seared into her memory. As if she had only friend feelings for him. The false front was wearing her out. And tomorrow she had six hours with him in a truck to look forward to.

The gathering took turns congratulating the happy couple and Kendra snapped several pictures of the newlyweds.

"Okay, let's do families, Mom and Ally first." Kendra waved them in front of the altar and took several shots, then some with Lance, too. "Cody, you get in one, too."

"I'm not family."

"No, but you're Ally's date."

"No," Ally squeaked. "We're just friends. Lifelong friends."

"Well, last time I checked, friends can have their picture taken together on special days."

Cody stepped into the shot with Mom and Lance in the middle.

"Now let's do one with the friends, just for fun."

"Good idea." Mom tugged Lance away.

Ally didn't move. Cody didn't, either. Standing there awkwardly with a gap between them where Mom and Lance had been.

"You'll have to move in closer than that. What? Are y'all afraid of each other?"

They took two steps closer, still not touching.

"Okay." Kendra lowered her camera. "You're friends. So you like each other, right? Act like it! Maybe hold hands. Something not so stiff."

Cody's hand clasped hers.

"That's better." Kendra snapped another shot.

"Will you remember me in a year?" Cody whispered.

What was he getting at? Trying to tell her he was leaving?

"Will you?" He squeezed her hand.

"Yes."

"Will you remember me in a month?"

"I sure hope my memory is that good." She frowned, looked up at him.

"Will you remember me in a week?"

"Duh."

"Knock knock."

Oh. A joke. A relieved grin teased her mouth. "Who's there?"

"See? You forgot me already."

"That's so corny." She giggled, all the tension of the day seeping away. He hugged her close and her hand settled on his chest as they laughed.

"Finally. Now, those were some good shots. Let's get some with everyone. Then we'll do Lance's family."

She'd forgotten all about the camera. The rest of the gathering closed in on them.

"Bride and groom in the middle. Respective families on each side."

After a few pictures, the twins got fidgety. Ally picked Zoey up and the little girl curled into her. Zane eyed Cody and stretched his arms up, and Cody scooped him up.

Ally bit her lip. He looked good holding a child. Too good. She could imagine marrying Cody. Could imagine them with kids. Could he?

"Very good. Okay, now let's get Lance's family and we'll be done."

Ally and Cody handed the kids over to their parents and settled on a pew to wait. Several minutes later, Kendra wrapped the photo session.

"Thanks so much, Kendra." Ally jumped up to help with her equipment.

"You know how I knew I loved Stetson?" Kendra whispered.

"How?" Why did Kendra feel the need to share this?

"I was all awkward around him. And he made me laugh."

Her gaze cut to Cody talking to Lance. As if sensing her interest, he looked her way. And sent her another wink.

Her cheeks scalded. "We're not—"

"Uh-huh." Kendra slung her bag over her shoulder. "I'll have the pet pictures ready soon. And I hope you'll let me do your wedding photos."

"We're really just friends. Cody makes everybody laugh."

"You just keep telling yourself that." Kendra grinned. "Bye, everyone. I'll get with you about the pictures in a few weeks." She waved and exited the church.

"You sure you'll be all right?" Mom gave Ally a lingering hug.

"I'll be fine. Don't worry about me."

"Comes with the territory." Mom pulled away. "Watch out for my girl, Cody."

"You can count on me."

Then, hand in hand, Mom and her new husband walked out of the church. Leaving Ally behind. Alone.

"You okay?" Cody's calloused hand closed over hers.

She nodded, not trusting herself with words.

"No cleanup. I reckon we can go if you're ready. Best rest up for the trip tomorrow."

"Feel like working on the pens?"

"Sure." His smile lit his eyes as if building pens were his favorite thing to do.

What had she done without him for twelve years? He was such a good guy. Such a good *friend*.

"I need to keep busy." If she went home, with nothing to do, she'd ramble around the empty house missing Mom and drowning in loneliness.

"How 'bout we stop at Moms on Main and get supper."

"Sounds good." She needed Cody today. Not to get too close. But to keep her company. Keep her from being alone. She was almost looking forward to their trip tomorrow.

When had she allowed herself to need him so much?

Once they got on the road, Cody reached for her free hand. Her slender fingers entwined in his. "You're quiet."

"I miss my mommy." Her put-on childlike voice melted his insides.

"Have you heard from her?"

"She called last night—let me know their flight went okay. They're in Florida and the weather is lovely."

"You sleep okay?"

"I cried like a big baby and let both dogs sleep in my bed. I needed cuddling."

He squeezed her hand. "Sorry."

"I'm okay. I'm a big girl. An adult. It just happened so fast. And I never saw it coming."

"It was fast. 'Bout gave me whiplash trying to keep up. I've still got that shoulder if you need it."

"I think I've taken advantage of your shoulder enough as it is. Besides, I'm driving."

Even if he didn't touch her any more than this for the entire trip, he could spend the rest of his days like this. Just being with her was better than any bull ride. Who knew a road trip with Ally would be the highlight of his year? Except for the kiss.

He needed to quit thinking about that or he'd mess up and do it again.

"I just hope none of my clients have emergencies and whoever is out to sabotage me doesn't pull anything."

"You left the vet in Denton's number on your machine. My foreman's staying at my place and Derek and his wife at yours. Besides that, Mitch is keeping an eye on things. And I doubt your nemesis knows we're all gone. Relax."

"I'm trying." She blew out a big breath.

"Why do you always wear your hair like that?" He let go of her fingers, caught the end of her braid and gave it a light tug.

"My hair's so thick and heavy it gets in the way when I'm working."

"But you're not working."

"Habit, I guess."

"Take it down."

"Um, I'm driving. And what, you don't like my braid?"

"I do. But I really like to see it down sometimes. You look more relaxed when it is." He slipped his fingers under the band at the end. "May I?"

"I guess." She rolled her eyes.

He pulled the band free and gently unwound each strand. Fruity shampoo tackled him as wavy tendrils escaped.

"So tell me about the woman marrying your grandpa."

"She's very nice. And she loves him."

"That's all?"

"It's enough." He could barely concentrate. The longing to run his fingers through her silky mane plagued him. He fisted his hand. Stop looking at her. But he couldn't seem to pull his gaze away. Especially with her hair down. "I don't know if you remember or not, but Grandma made quilts."

"I do remember. There were beautiful quilts all over their house when I went to her funeral with you."

"They're still there. When Grandpa asked Vivian to marry him and she agreed, he put all the quilts away so she wouldn't feel like she was moving into another woman's house. But Vivian had a hissy fit. Said such lovely quilts shouldn't be hidden and she wanted to help him keep Grandma's memory alive."

"She sounds great."

"He's been lonely a long time." He really had to stop looking at Ally's delicate profile. He turned away, facing front, leaned back on the headrest. "Like your mom. But we're not losing them. We're gaining new people in our families. New people to love. Speaking of which, you were great with the twins. They sure latched on to you quick."

"It's funny. I've always been better with animals than kids. But those two charmed my boots off."

"I can't imagine having twins." Except maybe with her. With Ally by his side, he could handle anything.

"Definitely double the work." She got quiet again. "But maybe it wouldn't seem like work with the right person at your side."

A comfortable silence settled between them.

Could he be that person for her? Cody relaxed. Content just being with her. How had she woven herself so deeply into his heart?

Chapter Thirteen

❧

Cody snored like a bulldog.

"Wake up. We're here," she said, shaking him a little.

His eyelids fluttered and slowly opened. "We're here? In Medina? You mean I slept the whole way?"

"From the way you were snoring, guess you didn't sleep good last night. Or do you always do that?" She smoothed her hands over her hair, glanced around.

"I don't snore." He looked insulted.

"Got proof." She tapped her phone. A sucking sound echoed from the speaker, then a loud rumble.

"Wow. Are you planning to blackmail me with that?"

"It could come in handy." The homey farmhouse looked the same as it had almost thirteen years ago. Would his family think it odd she was here? Would they assume she and Cody were dating? She'd have to be on guard with her feelings. Especially around Caitlyn. "Did you tell your grandpa I was coming?"

"I mentioned I was bringing a friend. Didn't tell him who." He got out. "I'll get the cases later. Not sure where we'll be sleeping. We may end up in Mitch's cabin."

"You think your grandfather will even remember

me?" She climbed down from the truck. "I mean, he met me during the worst time of his life."

"He liked you. He's even asked about you over the years."

"Really?"

"You're hard to forget."

Her pulse spiked.

The front door opened and Caitlyn stepped out with Michaela snuggled against her shoulder. "Ally. I didn't know you were coming. How did you pry her away from her clinic, Cody?"

"I reckon it was my charm."

"You know, come to think of it, you always could handle her better than anyone else." Caitlyn's suspicious gaze moved from Cody to Ally.

"You make me sound like a donkey or something." Ally hurried to the porch.

"If the hoof fits. But I'm so glad you're here. We'll have so much fun. Just like old times with the three of us back together."

"Let me see that baby girl."

Caitlyn handed Michaela over.

"She's getting so big." Downy coal-colored hair and eyes a vivid blue like her mother's. "And she gets prettier every time I see her."

"Thanks." Caitlyn grinned. "Going on eight months."

"Just wait, punkin." Cody climbed the steps and blew a zerbert on the little girl's fist. "I'm gonna teach you all kinds of things when you get a bit more mobile."

"Don't do us any favors." Caitlyn whacked his shoulder.

"Just a little horseback riding, swimming and fishing. We'll save mountain climbing, hang gliding and bull riding for when she gets older."

"We'll pass on the last three." Caitlyn clutched a hand to her heart.

"Don't even try it." Ally leveled a glare at him.

"Guess I'll tuck my tail and head for the house." He winked at Michaela. "For now."

"Don't worry, baby. Your daddy carries a gun. He'll keep you safe from Uncle Cody's shenanigans." Caitlyn swatted him again as he opened the door for them. "Everyone's gathered in the family room."

The house had changed little from what she remembered of the one time she'd been there.

The scent of the cedar walls gave off a cozy feel as they strolled to the back of the house. In the huge gathering room, Mitch and Grandpa occupied recliners, with Cody's parents, his aunt and his uncle lining the taupe leather sectional.

Tara and a sandy-haired man cuddled in the window seat, and Cody's cousin, his wife and their daughter worked on a puzzle at an oak pedestal table. Three quilts brightened the room.

"Do you know everyone?"

Cody's hand rested at the small of her back. Making it hard for her to think. "I haven't officially met Tara's husband."

"This is Jared. Ally was in the same class as Cody and Caitlyn and owns the shelter where I got Buttercup."

"Nice meeting you," he said.

"You, too. How is Buttercup?"

"We just love her," Tara gushed. "We brought her with us. She's out in the back right now."

"Oh, good. I get to see her."

"Cody didn't tell me his friend was female." Grandpa stood, grasped Ally's hand. "Or have y'all become more than friends?"

"No, Grandpa." Cody's tone was stiff. "We're just friends."

Ally's heart took a nosedive.

Though she had clarified their relationship to others, it hurt to hear it coming from Cody.

"You young people and your issues," Grandpa scoffed. "Silly boy. This girl's much too pretty to be just friends with."

Heat washed over her face. "It's nice to see you again, Mr. Warren."

"Call me Tex."

"Sorry for the teasing, Ally." Mitch chuckled. "It means he likes you."

"I reckon you'll get to meet my bride at the church. I don't get to see her until she walks the aisle." Tex grimaced. "I don't believe in superstition, especially at our age, but Vivian insisted we follow tradition."

"Can I help with decorations or prep?"

"It's done." Audra, Cody's mom, curled her legs up on the couch. "Our crew of ladies was able to come a few days ago."

"What time's the wedding?"

"Seven." Cody checked his watch. "We've got three hours. How 'bout we go for a walk?"

"Look at you raring to go after you slept the whole way while I drove."

"Car rides always knock me out like a light." Cody gave her a sheepish grin. "Maybe a horseback ride would be more relaxing. I can show you the ranch. Unless you're too tired."

"Sounds fun. Lead the way."

As they stepped outside, the late-September afternoon was perfect, the sun warm and bright, with a breeze rustling through brittle leaves. Live oaks with twisted, knobby limbs reached toward the trail on each side of them.

The path beside the ranch house opened into a pasture where a dozen palominos grazed. In the distance, a cabin nestled beside a pond.

"It's beautiful."

"It is. It was hard to leave behind."

"Why didn't you stay here? Why did you come back to Aubrey?"

He shrugged. "Aubrey's home. The bulk of my family is there. And I felt like I was cramping Grandpa's love life here."

So it had nothing to do with her. Not because she'd stumbled upon him in the rehab center with her dog program and he'd realized he couldn't live without her.

"I hope you brought boots."

"They're in my suitcase."

"My kind of gal. Never travel without boots."

If only she could really be his gal.

Cody scanned the church. He'd attended here during childhood visits and his recovery after his bull wreck. Knew several faces but couldn't connect most of them with names. He'd met Vivian's son and daughter and their spouses and kids before the wedding. They all seemed nice. Good Christian people.

This was a positive thing. Grandpa had to be lonely in Medina with the rest of his family in Aubrey. With Vivian, he'd have companionship and he'd still be home.

Ally patted his hand. "You okay?"

Drowning in her coffee-colored eyes, he nodded. How much longer could he resist her? Just another week. Then if he was still alive and still had a brain, wild horses couldn't drag him away.

"I really like Vivian."

"Yeah, me, too. Her husband died five years ago. She and Grandpa have a lot in common."

"I think your grandmother would approve."

"Me, too."

"How come your grandpa lives here and not in Aubrey?"

"This is where the Warrens were originally from. But my uncle Ty traveled the rodeo circuit and met my aunt in Aubrey. After he retired, they settled there and Dad wanted to get into horse ranching. With Aubrey being Horse Country USA, he and Mom decided to make the move."

If they hadn't, he'd have never met Ally. A sinking sensation grew in his gut at the mere thought of not knowing her.

He cleared his throat, kept rambling. "I think they all planned on moving back to Medina, but some of us kids grew up and married locals and Aubrey became home. We tried to get Grandpa to move over the years, but Medina is home to him just as much as Aubrey is home to the rest of us."

Music began and the chatter quieted as the wedding march rang through the church. Grandpa entered from beside the stage and the doors behind them opened as the crowd stood.

Escorted by her son, Vivian wore a denim skirt and

red flannel blouse that matched Grandpa's jeans and shirt.

They made it to the altar and her son handed her over to Grandpa. The pastor said a prayer and the congregation sat down. As the vows began, Cody couldn't stop thinking about Ally.

If he lived, complication-free, would she be interested at all? What if he survived surgery and revealed his love for her, and she didn't feel the same? Just because they kissed once—twice—it didn't mean she loved him. Did it?

With a clean bill of health, he could always go back to the circuit. But how empty would that be? Nothing would be the same without Ally. If he made it through the operation and she didn't love him, what would he do? Live next door, humiliated and heartbroken?

He watched her out of the corner of his eye. She dabbed her nose with a tissue—crying over his grandfather's wedding. He had to try.

If she didn't love him, he had to convince her to. For him, there'd been a thin line between the love of a friend and the love of a lifetime. He had to convince Ally to make the leap over the line with him.

Three weddings he'd escorted her to now, and by doggies, the next one would be theirs.

Bleary-eyed, Ally scuffled to the kitchen of Mitch's cabin, drawn by the aroma of freshly brewed coffee. No movement. Someone must have set a timer on the pot last night.

As she neared the couch, she tried to ignore the still form covered in blankets lying there. But as if pulled by a magnet, her gaze darted there.

One socked foot stuck out at the far end. Cody's face was visible. Her steps stalled. He looked vulnerable and a little boyish in sleep. And so handsome.

She could happily wake up to that face every morning for the rest of her life. Stop thinking like that. She shook her head and got moving again.

Focus on something else. The coffee was already made and waiting. She quietly found a cup in the cabinet, poured the fragrant brew and stirred in cream and sugar—careful not to clink her spoon against the porcelain.

Mitch's cabin was all man cave. Unfortunate trophy animals on the walls, antlers everywhere, camouflage galore. A few lavender camo pillows announced Caitlyn's touch.

Quiet. Such a peaceful Sunday morning. Everyone still asleep except her. Mitch, Caitlyn and Michaela in the master bedroom. Though the guest room was cozy, it had taken Ally half the night to relax enough to fall asleep with Cody under the same roof.

"I can't believe it took me this long to catch on," Caitlyn whispered.

Ally jumped, whirled around. "You just took five years off me."

"You're in love with Cody."

Ally's insides stilled. "I am not."

"You are. Don't even try to deny it. I saw the way you looked at him just now."

"I just thought he looked cute. Like a little boy."

"Uh-huh. How long has this been going on?"

"There's nothing going on. We're—"

"Just friends. Yeah, right. Not only are you in love with Cody, but he's in love with you."

"No." Ally pressed a finger to her lips. "He's right there."

"If there's no truth to it, why are you afraid he'll hear? Friends don't get all googly-eyed over each other."

"I've never been googly-eyed in my life and I don't plan on starting now."

"Why fight it?" Caitlyn studied her as if she were a puzzle missing a piece. "I don't understand. You love him. He loves you. Go for it."

"I don't know what you think you saw." Ally tried not to wilt under the scrutiny. "But Cody and I are friends. That's all."

"Mitch and I were high school sweethearts. Everybody expected us to marry after graduation. Do you know why we didn't?"

"No."

"I let fear get the best of me. I don't mean to bring up painful memories, but I was there when you found out your dad had died in the line of duty."

"I remember." Ally tried to swallow the lump in her throat, but it wouldn't budge.

"And Mitch was bound and determined to be a Texas Ranger. I decided I couldn't take the possibility of losing him the way your mom lost your dad."

"I had no idea."

"I let fear keep us apart for ten years." Caitlyn crossed her arms under her chest. "Whatever's holding you back from admitting your feelings for Cody, get over it. Life is short and should be spent with the man you love."

If Caitlyn could see her feelings for Cody, could he? And why did Caitlyn think he loved her back?

"When I meet the man I love, I'll go for it. I promise." The lie tasted bitter. "I better get ready to hit the road." She grabbed her cup and headed for the sanctuary of her room.

"Better get your shower before everyone wakes up. We'll leave for church at ten thirty or so."

"Church?"

"We're all going to Grandpa's church before we leave."

"Oh. I thought we'd head back to Aubrey this morning. But that sounds good." Another lie tumbled right out. Getting entirely too good at this. "I'll be ready."

With Mom not on watch, she'd looked forward to skipping. And now she wanted to escape Caitlyn's perceptiveness as soon as possible.

Besides, she wanted to get home. Back to the safety of sleeping in a whole different house than Cody. The only problem was that getting home would trap her in a truck with him for six hours. Would it be possible to hitch a ride with someone else without raising suspicions? Not with Caitlyn already on to her.

If only Cody could drive. That way she could sleep the whole ride home, since she'd barely slept last night. Maybe he'd sleep most of the trip again.

Movement from the couch.

"Coffee," Cody growled, then sat up, squinted at them and stood. Stiff-legged, he stuck his arms out in front of him like a zombie and lurched to the kitchen.

"Here you go." Caitlyn poured him a cup and handed it to him.

"Mmm." He tilted the mug to his mouth, then jerked away, sloshing the hot liquid over the rim. "Sorry. Is this decaf?"

"One cup of the real stuff won't kill you. And you obviously need it."

He set the mug on the counter, grabbed a soapy dish-cloth and wiped the mess from the floor. "Is there an-other pot? I'll make my own."

Caitlyn sighed. "Go for it, health freak."

How long had he been awake? Had he heard Caitlyn's observations and Ally's denial? And more important, if he'd heard, did he believe Ally's denial?

With her cheeks scalding, she scurried the rest of the way to her room.

As the pastor began to plea for nonbelievers, those struggling with faith issues, or anyone wanting to pray to come forward to the altar call, Ally's breathing con-stricted. His eyes rested solely on her, as if he could read the struggle inside her.

Pressure in her chest built. Finally, the pastor's atten-tion shifted to another victim. Had Cody or Caitlyn told him she was at an all-time low in the faith department?

No. No one knew. Not even her mom. She was a dedicated pew warmer, there every time the doors were open. And disillusioned every time.

"No, God," she whispered under her breath as the pianist started up. "I do not need You. I let myself need You once and You let me down. Let my dad down. Let my mom down. I don't need You. I don't need anyone. Not even Cody."

Several people went to the altar—including Cody, Caitlyn and Mitch. The faithful, certain God would an-swer their prayers, thanking Him for the blessings He'd supposedly sent. But Ally wasn't falling for any of it. Not even if her chest exploded.

After four torturous verses, the music faded away and the pastor thanked everyone for coming and called on a man to say the closing prayer.

It was long and flowery and by the time it ended, Ally's teeth were on edge. The amen finally came and she opened her eyes. The congregation moseyed into the aisles, most seemingly in no hurry to get out the doors.

"You okay?" Cody's frown dripped concern.

"Fine. I'm just anxious to get home. Even though Derek assures me everything is fine, with me gone over twenty-four hours, I'm figuring there will be at least fifteen strays and six escaped pets."

"Stop worrying, Suzie Rain Cloud."

"It's the way things have been going lately."

"Can we at least stop and get a bite to eat?" His stomach promptly growled.

Her shoulders slumped. "Sure."

Would this trip never end?

Home for a day. Cody had slept all the way back from Medina even though he'd wanted to enjoy every moment with Ally. But car rides had always made him sleepy unless he drove. Especially without caffeine. Since they'd gotten back, he hadn't seen hide nor hair of Ally.

The float was ready. The weddings were done. What could Cody do now to keep her near once he finished building the pens? He rolled the fencing into place along the frame he'd built. It immediately rolled back up before he could sink a single staple.

It was way after hours. Her volunteers had come and gone. Even though she was shorthanded at the clinic, surely she was finished by now. He dug out his cell, punched in her number.

"*Ally's Veterinary Clinic and Adopt-a-Pet*. May I help you?"

"I'm in your barn slaving over pens for your critters and I could use a pair of extra hands."

Silence. For several seconds. "I'll be right there."

The dial tone started up. Maybe she'd had a rough day without Lance and was just tired.

He had to watch his step with her. Stop giving off mixed signals. Kissing her one minute, keeping her at a distance the next, but not too far. Seven more days.

He'd already come up with an excuse for his impending absence—tests on his shoulder and knee along with ranch errands that could keep him in Dallas for several days. If he woke up in his right mind a week from today, he'd tell her exactly how he felt. And hope she loved him, too.

The barn door opened and she stepped inside, looking defeated.

"Rough day?"

"I'll be glad when Lance gets back. I need him here and I miss my mom."

"You can come over to my house anytime if you need company."

"What do I need to do?" She settled on her knees beside him, dismissing his invitation.

"Just hold the fencing in place while I staple."

"That I can do. Have you heard from your grandpa?"

"They're having the time of their life in Hawaii. I never imagined my grandpa going there."

"We should be glad our loved ones are happy—that they're feeling young and adventurous again." As she crawled on her hands and knees holding the fencing up, her thick braid nearly dragged in the hay on the floor. Her scent and proximity almost overwhelmed him.

He had to refocus on their topic. Oh yeah, being happy for Grandpa and her mom. "I am. It just makes me miss Grandma."

"I know what you mean. I miss my dad. It's like Mom moving on makes me miss him more."

He finished the frame and they went to work on another. Sometimes chatting, sometimes in comfortable silence. Ally was the only woman he'd ever felt completely at ease with without talking. Soon they had the base of the pen and three sides finished. She held them in place while he fired nails with the gun.

"I'll put the door in tomorrow. Want to watch a movie or something?"

"No. I'm tired. Think I'll turn in early."

"Thanks for helping."

"Thanks for building pens for me." She stood. "By the way, they're coming to start the construction of my new barn tomorrow. Garrett Steele and Brant McConnell matched the proceeds from the pet photo day, so I've got funding to cover the entire cost, plus a nice sum left over for pet care and repairs."

Good news. But would she need him anymore? Panic gnawed at his insides. "Once the barn is up, I can build more pens."

"Thanks. But you've done so much. And there's enough to pay for pens, too."

"But I build them for free. Then you'll have more funds left over for care."

"True." She shrugged. "If you insist."

"See you tomorrow?" He tried not to sound desperate.

"Probably."

One more week. Just one more week.

With Mom gone, Foxy and Wolf vied even more for Ally's attention. Technically, Wolf was Mom's dog. When she came back from her honeymoon, would she take the gray Pomeranian to live with her and Lance? Then Foxy would be as lonely as her person.

A mere three days since Mom's wedding. How would she survive the rest of her life by herself?

She set the dogs off her lap and wandered around the empty house. Both Poms trailed her. Cody's light was on next door. Like a beacon. They'd worked on pens again tonight and again he'd asked her to come over and watch a movie. So tempting. Him and his company.

It was a temptation she could no longer resist. Not after the day she'd had. She hurried to the kitchen, snagged a packet of her favorite microwave butter popcorn and headed for the back door.

"Sorry, guys." She latched the dog gate in place, locking the Poms in the mudroom, and tossed them each a treat. "But I won't be gone long." She grabbed the flashlight and stepped outside.

Barks started up as the door shut. A creepy feeling as if she was being watched washed over her. She shone the light around. Nothing. But all the same, she doubled her speed across the yard and ran up Cody's steps. She'd barely knocked when his door opened.

"Is everything okay?" His hair was wet. Fresh from the shower. Irish Spring soap. Handsome and smelling good.

"I decided to take you up on that movie offer." Maybe this wasn't such a good idea after all. "I brought popcorn."

A wide grin spread over his face. "I'm glad." He took the bag from her. "Have a seat and I'll have this ready in a jiff."

She scanned the room. A dark couch with a recliner at each end. Oreo occupied the one on the right near the remote and a glass of sweet tea sat on the end table.

"Look at you, boy." The dog jumped down to greet her and she scratched behind his ears. "From homeless to a barn, and now you're a bona fide house dog." She settled in the recliner on the left and Oreo hopped up and sat in her lap.

"Traitor." Cody set the bowl of popcorn between them and handed her a glass of sweet tea. "Want me to take him?"

"He's fine."

"You should have brought yours with you." His gaze searched hers. "You sure everything's okay? You were awfully quiet earlier and you just don't seem right."

How did he do that? He'd always known when something was wrong. Her eyes singed. "I had to put a family pet down this afternoon."

He winced, knelt in front of her. "I'm so sorry."

"Me, too." She sniffled. "I never get used to that part of my job."

"Want to talk about it?"

"No." She gave a decisive shake of her head. "I'll turn into a blubbering ninny and that could get messy."

"I can handle it." He patted his shoulder.

"Can we just watch a movie? Please."

He squeezed her hand, then stood, handed her a tissue and crouched in front of the TV. "What movie do you want?" He named off several.

"Nothing where the dog dies." She dabbed her eyes.

"Trust me, I don't have any of those."

Finally, they settled on *Flywheel*. Not only clean but Christian.

"We can have a marathon this week and watch *Facing the Giants*, *Fireproof* and *Courageous*." He sat down in his recliner and looked across at her.

A movie marathon with Cody. Like a married couple, she in her recliner, he in his.

She couldn't think of anything better than this.

When Cody got home from Bible study on Wednesday night, Ally was waiting on his porch with her Pomeranians. Had she even gone? Not unless her church had changed service times.

"Hey. I took them for a walk and came on over since I knew you wouldn't be gone long."

"You didn't go to church tonight?"

She flushed bright red. "My last appointment went late and I couldn't get there in time."

"Come on in." He unlocked the door. "I'll go make the popcorn."

Again they sat on each end of his couch, with her two dogs in her lap and Oreo in his. He'd rather move to the middle. But that would freak her out. And he couldn't let her get that close. Not yet. Maybe tomorrow night he'd go to her house. Fill her empty home with conversation. Get just a bit closer.

"I love these movies." He reached for a handful of popcorn. "They're family friendly and I could watch them over and over."

"I thought I saw a few tears last night," she teased.

"Gets me every time when people turn their lives over to Christ. Even in movies."

She bit her lip, sipped her tea. "Did you see how fast the barn is going up?"

"They'll probably have the frame finished by Saturday." Why didn't she want to talk about Jesus? He knew she went to church, had been a Christian since her youth. But lately she seemed uncomfortable with anything to do with the subject. "So what's the church you attend in Denton like?"

"A lot like the one in Aubrey."

"Do you like it?"

"Sure. The people are nice."

"Okay, but what about the preaching, the worship service?"

She shrugged. "I hadn't really thought about it. I just go with Mom."

"I was wondering since your mom's married now and living in Denton—you'd have to drive to church by yourself. Might be a good time to start coming to Aubrey again."

"We'll see. It's only fifteen minutes." Her gaze never left the TV screen even though he hadn't started the movie yet.

Was Ally in a crisis of faith? Why? And what could he do to help her?

"Better start the movie so we'll have time to watch it all."

He scrutinized her profile a moment longer, then pressed Play. Maybe the Christian movies they were watching would touch a chord with her.

* * *

"Popcorn break." Ally pushed Pause and hurried to the kitchen. For some reason, Cody had suggested they watch *Fireproof* at her house tonight.

"I can't believe how this house looks exactly the same as it did when we were kids." Cody kept his seat on the couch.

"New furniture." She refilled their bowl from the still-warm bag in the microwave.

"Same hardwood floors."

"New walls and paint. A couple of years ago, I decided I couldn't take that old dark, dingy paneling anymore." Back in the living room, she settled on the couch. Put some space between them. "I tore into it with plans for drywall but found this lovely wood underneath."

But Cody scooted her way. "Trying to hog the popcorn?"

Sitting way too close.

Ally's couch didn't have a recliner at each end. She should scoot away, but she pushed Play instead.

As the husband and wife in the movie found their way back to each other, the romance of it moved her. When the main character came to terms with God, a large knot formed in Ally's throat. She closed her eyes, tried to think of something else. Her mind drifted and she yawned.

She'd just rest her eyes and mind. That way God couldn't use the movie to hammer at her.

Mom had forced her to watch the movie before, so she knew how it ended anyway.

Something solid under Ally's head. Solid and it smelled wonderful. Manly cologne.

Huh? She opened her eyes.

Her cheek rested against Cody's shoulder, his head leaning heavily against hers. Level breathing. He was asleep. How could she move away from him without waking him up? Without letting him realize they were basically cuddling on her couch.

Maybe nice and slow. If she supported his head with her hand, put a pillow in her place.

The TV screen was dark. Dogs barking outside. Please, not her intruder again. But something flickered on the dark screen. A reflection. Like fire. And another scent. Acrid and smoky. Something burning.

She jerked away from Cody.

"What! What's going on?" He blinked several times.

"I think there's a fire." She turned to the window behind them, pushed the curtains aside.

Chapter Fourteen

A huge glow. "The new barn's on fire!" *Please God, no.* It was perilously close to the barn housing her strays and boarder pets.

"Call 911." Cody dashed toward the door. "I'll hose down the shelter barn, so it doesn't ignite too."

Ally jabbed the numbers on the phone.

"911. What is your emergency?"

"This is Ally Curtis. My barn is on fire." The operator confirmed the address and Ally hung up, then ran out to help Cody.

He was dousing the front of her stray barn. She grabbed another hose and joined him, though the heat was intense behind them.

Howls and yowls filled the night air. Even if they could keep the second barn from going up, the animals inside were still in danger of inhaling smoke. Though it was completely enclosed, there were pet doors out to the fenced dog runs along each side.

Sirens in the distance. The most glorious sound she'd ever heard. Her throat hurt and she rasped a choking cough.

"Ally, get back. They're almost here and you're taking in smoke." Cody hacked out the last few words.

"I'll go if you will."

He threw down his hose, grabbed her hand. She tugged him toward the barn with the animals as the fire truck with its siren blaring roared into her drive.

"They'll be fine until the fire is under control. If we go in now, we'll only let a bunch of smoke in." He coughed, covered his mouth.

Firefighters spilled from the truck, swarming like ants.

"Anyone inside the structure?" a fireman shouted.

"No. But there's an animal shelter chock-full of dogs and cats in the other barn. We hosed down the side closest to the fire."

They stood back, out of the way as the firefighters rolled out their hose, blasted the fire. An ambulance arrived and soon a paramedic led Ally and Cody to the back, insisting on giving them oxygen.

With the mask strapped in place, Ally breathed deeply. It did feel good. Her lungs eased and the tightness in her throat let up. Within minutes, the fire started to die down.

The paramedic checked them out, removed their oxygen masks.

"Thank you. For saving my animals." Ally flung herself into Cody's arms and soaked his shoulder as all the sobs she'd held back hit her all at once. "Do you think they're okay?"

"I'm sure they are. Don't you hear all that racket? And look—the wind's blowing the smoke away from them. Besides, if any critters inhaled a bit of smoke, I know a great vet who'll fix them right up."

As the flames sizzled into billowing smoke, the fire chief ambled in their direction. "I just called the police in. I'm afraid this fire smacks of arson."

Ally's knees went weak.

But Cody held her up. "Let's get you inside."

"No." She mustered all her strength. "I have to check on the animals."

"Then I'll help you." His arm around her shoulders. "Let's enter through the back door, away from the smoke." He turned to the fire chief. "We'll be in the other barn if anyone needs us."

They rounded the structure. She should move away from him. But she didn't want to.

"I can't believe this," Cody growled.

"You think it's connected with the break-ins?"

"It's too much to be coincidence. This is getting too dangerous." Cody let go of her long enough for her to dig out the key and unlock the door.

Inside, there was only the faint smell of smoke. Thankfully all of the animals seemed fine. Just rattled.

They split up, working each side, strolling along in front of the pens, soothing the boarders and strays.

"Ally." Mitch entered the back door. "You in here?"

"Hi, Mitch." She stopped, turned toward him, slid her hands into her jean pockets.

"Cody, y'all okay?"

"Fine. Just shaken up."

"Did either of you see anything? Hear anything?"

"No." Ally shook her head. "We watched a movie at my house and fell asleep sitting on the couch. I woke up, heard the dogs howling and saw the reflection of the fire in the TV."

"Well, it looks like we've got arson to add to our

list." Mitch scribbled something on his pad. "Along with breaking and entering and criminal mischief."

"Great. But it won't do much good until y'all catch this creep." Cody raked a hand through his hair.

"I know it's frustrating, little brother. But we'll get whoever is doing this."

"Thanks for coming, Mitch." She tried to keep her voice even, though her insides quivered.

"I hope you have insurance."

"I do." She hugged herself.

"Good. You'll have to cease construction for a while. It's important the structure stay as is until the arson investigator checks it out."

"She can't afford this setback." Cody grimaced. "After the arson investigator, she'll have to wait for an insurance adjuster before she can get back to barn building."

"Afraid so." Mitch's mouth settled in a firm line. "Unfortunately, it can be a lengthy process."

"Since I can't tell you anything, the fire's out and my animals are okay, I'd love to go to bed." Not to sleep. But to have a good cry before she made a fool of herself on Cody's shoulder again.

"Sure." Mitch gave her an encouraging grin. "You get some rest."

"I'll walk you to your door." Cody fell in stride beside her.

"It's really not necessary." She had to avoid his shoulder and keep herself together.

"It is to me." As they stepped outside, his arm settled around her waist. "Sure you're okay?"

She nodded. "I'm starting to get scared, though. Thank goodness whoever we're dealing with has some semblance of a heart. I'm so thankful it wasn't my shelter barn they set on fire."

"I won't let anything happen to you. Or your animals. If I have to start sleeping during the day and staying awake all night, I will."

"Thanks."

They made it to her door and she couldn't resist one more hug. She turned into his chest and he wrapped his arms around her.

"Don't worry. I'll keep you out of harm's way."

She did feel safe with him near. Bodily protected. But her heart was a whole other matter.

"I've been thinking." Cody tried to sound nonchalant as he set a kennel in place on a shelf inside the float.

"What's that?" Ally tested the cage for stability and strapped it down.

The sweet smell of hay and peaceful sounds of kittens clambering in his loft couldn't help him. Ally would go into orbit over his idea. "Maybe we shouldn't enter the float in the parade."

"What?"

"Maybe it's too dangerous."

"So you think my nemesis will shoot me off the float in broad daylight?"

Cody's stomach twisted at the thought. "I hadn't really thought that graphically. But I don't think we should risk your well-being."

"The parade is tomorrow. It's a bit late to pull out." She set a larger kennel on a hay bale. "It will give my shelter publicity. And we've worked so hard. We can't let some coward make us quit."

"What makes you think we're dealing with a coward?"

"Someone who creeps around in the wee hours tormenting animals, dumping them and starting fires is a coward in my book." Her tone sounded casual, as if she wasn't worried in the slightest. "Whoever is doing this won't pull anything in public with a crowd."

"What if I ride the float and you stay home?" Maybe he was worried enough for both of them. He'd barely slept last night, jumping at every sound and peering out his window toward her place at least a dozen times.

"I'm going." She checked the stability of the kennel on the hay bale.

"Figured you'd say that."

They worked in silence, setting crates in place. Each kennel had bricks inside to simulate its animal's weight. They'd have to go through the whole routine again tomorrow with actual dogs and cats in the cages. But tonight would ensure there were no mishaps during the parade.

The barn door opened and Mitch stepped inside. "Evening."

Ally jumped, spun around, clasped her hand to her heart. "You just about gave me a heart attack."

So she was shook up. But determined. *Lord, keep her safe.*

"I need to ask you some questions, Ally."

"Sure."

"I know I've asked before, but do you have any enemies?"

"Yeah, whoever's causing mayhem around here."

"Think concrete. Any neighbors complain about your animals? Or clients? Anybody whose pet died in your care?"

"I don't have any neighbors other than Cody. If any

of my clients are disgruntled, they haven't told me." Her hand shook as she tested another cage on a high shelf. "And usually they just move on to another vet, not burn my barn down. As far as pets dying in my care, it's part of the job." Sadness tinged her words. "I wish I could save them all, but I'm only human."

"I need you to go through your files." Mitch took down a few notes. "List any clients who haven't brought their pets to you in a while. And any whose pets died in your care."

"My clients are my friends. I can't think of anyone who would pull this nonsense."

"We have to get to the bottom of this." Cody set his hands on her shoulders, forcing her to face him. "Each episode has escalated. We can't sit around and wait until this nut strikes again."

"All right." She sighed. "Once we finish with the float, I'll go through my records."

"I'll be by to get them first thing in the morning." Mitch tipped his hat. "In plenty of time for you to get to the parade."

"Do you think she'll be safe tomorrow?" Cody caught Mitch's gaze, sending him mental pleas to make her stay home. "Should she ride the float?"

"So far our perp has skulked around in the middle of the night. I don't think we'll have any trouble in broad daylight with half the town and countless tourists in attendance."

Mitch didn't play fair.

"That's what I said." Ally quirked an "I told you so" eyebrow at Cody.

"I'm just looking out for you."

His surgery was scheduled for Monday—a mere

three days away. He needed Ally safe for completely selfish reasons. So he could tell her how he felt about her.

If he lived. And could still form words.

So far three dog-loaded kennels had snapped into place easily. Now for a cat.

The early-morning sun streaked through the cracks in the old barn as Cody picked up the feline and woofs and yowls reached a fever pitch.

"I know it, boy." Ally soothed a terrier mix as she tested the stability of the kennels he'd already placed— even more carefully than last night since there was live cargo involved. "We'll get moving soon and maybe someone will fall in love with you and take you home."

He wasn't sure about the dog, but Cody was head over heels for Ally. And longed to be her protector until the end of time. Unfortunately, his end of time could come Monday.

For now, he just had to get through the parade. He set the cat's carrier on its designated shelf.

Apparently satisfied with his work, she strapped it down. Her hand grazed his, firing excess wattage straight to his heart. She gave him more of a jolt than any caffeine ever had.

The barn door opened again. "We're home," her mom squealed.

"When did y'all get back?" Ally scrambled down the ladder and Cody hurried to steady it for her.

As Lance entered, the two women hugged.

"Late last night." Diane's smile seemed lit from within.

Happiness was very becoming on her. Cody had

never really noticed her beauty before. A lovely older version of Ally.

"I thought you were meeting us at the parade." Ally disentangled herself from her mom.

"We wanted to help with setup." Lance stood awkwardly by. "You don't have to hug me. Unless you want to. I'm just Lance—you don't have to refer to me as your stepdad or anything like that. Unless you want to."

"Welcome home, Lance." Ally gave him a genuine hug, nothing stiff or uncomfortable about it. "I'm glad y'all are back."

"Us, too." He patted her back, obviously grateful for the lack of tension between them. "What can we do to help?"

"Cody will show you while I show Mom. With your help, we'll get this knocked out in no time."

As the foursome worked, yips and yowls intensified while Ally and her mom tried to soothe the disoriented critters. It was refreshing to see Ally so relaxed, in her element and content with her mom's new life.

But he'd rather work with Ally than Lance. Chance bumping elbows with her instead.

Two more days. If everything went well Monday morning, maybe he could arrange to bump elbows with Ally for the rest of his life.

It was so nice to have Mom back. Even though Ally barely had time for a hug before it was time for Lance to drive the truck to the parade with Mom sitting by his side.

The lineup trailed in front of Aubrey Middle School. The Noah's ark float looked great, especially with all the adorable critters peeking through the windows. Barks, yips and meows echoed through the air.

"Wouldn't it be great if you left here today with no animals?" Cody sat on a hay bale between the kennels, not visible from outside the float.

"Let's hope."

A huge banner down the side proclaimed Ally's Adopt-a-Pet—A Noah's Ark of Hope for Homeless Dogs and Cats, along with the phone number. Caitlyn was manning Ally's booth in the field by the old peanut dryer. After the parade, she and Cody would transport the animals to the booth and hope for adoptive families.

He checked his watch. "It's almost time to begin. Guess we should climb up to our perch."

And it hit her. She and Cody would be in close quarters in the elevated platform his ranch hands had built over the gooseneck hitch at the front of the trailer. Putting her above the animals to wave at the crowd seemed like a good idea at the time. But the platform was four by four feet—built for one.

"Ladies first." Cody bowed low.

She turned toward the ladder and he held it steady as she climbed. The platform was nice and sturdy as she stepped up onto it, with railing around the sides except for the entry opening. Attached to the railing, Cody had insisted on two safety harnesses. Side by side, she and Cody would wave at the crowd. As Cody stepped up beside her, the platform seemed to shrink to two by two.

"Buckle up for safety." He wrapped the harness around her waist.

Her breath stopped as he clasped it into place. His hands moved away to his own harness and she started breathing again. Maybe the platform was more like one by one.

Since they were toward the back of the lineup, only a few other floats trailed them, and the horses and horse-drawn buggies brought up the rear. With the slow-moving procession, it would take forever to get to the end of the parade. Stuck on this tiny stage with Cody.

"I think we're starting to move." Cody peered toward the front of the parade.

Several floats ahead of them, she saw movement.

"Be sure and hold on tight when we start rolling."

She gripped the railing, white-knuckled.

"Once you find your balance, then you can wave."

"That's right—you're an authority. You used to ride your horse every year. But I don't remember you riding a float."

"I did once. I happened to be home for a visit and rode the church float a few years back. I didn't hold on good enough, lost my balance and landed in Mrs. Thornbury's lap."

Ally giggled as the vision of him in the ninety-year-old spinster's lap filled her imagination.

The float in front of them inched forward. Seconds later, theirs followed.

"So you must have been glad to see your mom this morning."

"They're ridiculously happy."

"You seem more comfortable with things."

"I'm glad Mom's content and Lance is obviously crazy about her." She shrugged. "How's your grandpa?"

"On cloud nine."

The procession sped up a bit and Ally turned to inspect the kennels below them, making sure none of the animals shifted. The dogs had quieted once they started moving. Probably with their noses sniffing ninety miles an hour at new smells. The cats kept yowling their discontent.

"I know, babies," she called out. "But this bit of discomfort might just find y'all forever homes."

An eternity later, they were finally at the junction to Main Street. As they made the turn, Ally lost her footing.

"Whoa." Cody's arms came around her waist, steadied her, then lingered for a moment.

"It's amazing how wobbly I feel when we're going five miles an hour." She giggled, trying to cover the emotions moving through her.

"You okay?"

She nodded.

"Don't try waving until you're certain you're steady." His hands settled back onto the railing.

And Ally had to concentrate on something else.

Throngs of people lined Aubrey's Main Street. Booths lined the field in front of the old peanut dryer—with people selling crafts, quilts, peanut-themed food and hand-carved items. Every first Saturday in October, the town held the Peanut Festival to celebrate Aubrey's heritage of peanut farms.

Ally let go of the railing with one hand and waved at the crowd. Lots of people she knew and lots of kids saucer eyed over her dogs and cats.

Her arm bumped Cody's and awareness coursed through her. Oh, would this parade never end?

"I can't believe we adopted them all out already." Cody held his hand up for a high five as Ally drove.

"I know." Excitement sparkled in her voice. "We always get lots of out of towners for the festival. I'm just glad so many wanted pets."

His hand tingled at her brief touch. "Do you ever miss them?"

"I do." Her mouth tilted down a bit. "That's the only part I hate. If I had the time and space, I'd probably keep them all. But it wouldn't be fair to them. Pets need a focused person. Not some crazy lady trying to take care of twenty-five-plus. But knowing they're going to good homes makes it easier."

"You do good work." He found her hand on the console, threaded his fingers through hers. A few more tingles wouldn't hurt. "A lot of those pets are still alive because of you."

"I just wish I could save them all."

"I know." He squeezed her hand as she pulled into his drive.

Movement near her barn caught his attention. The arson inspector?

A man bolted from the barn toward the woods.

"I think we just caught your nemesis." Cody flung the door open.

"You can't go after him." She clutched his hand. "Call Mitch."

"I can't let him get away. You call Mitch."

"What if he has a gun?"

"I'll be careful." He jerked away from her and vaulted out of the truck after the man.

"*Careful* doesn't stop bullets."

Cody's knee throbbed as he ran. But he didn't care. This menace would not get another chance to hurt Ally.

Chapter Fifteen

The man's gait was slow. Cody could take him. Even with his bum knee.

By the time the intruder entered the woods at the back of Ally's property, Cody was almost on him. If he had a weapon, he'd have threatened to use it by now. "Stop. Or I'll take you down."

The man stopped, put his hands up—weapon-free—and turned to face Cody. Gray hair, wrinkled face, kind blue eyes filled with fear.

"Mr. Peters?"

"I didn't do anything. Why are you chasing me?"

Herbert Peters, the man who'd sold Cody his land, wouldn't hurt a fly. "You were at Ally's barn. Were you looking for me?"

"Ally who? I don't know you or any Ally."

"Cody?" Mitch called from a distance.

"Over here. I'm with Herbert Peters."

Footfalls through the woods, and after a bit, he caught sight of Mitch.

"What's going on, Mr. Peters?"

"I don't know. Why are you chasing me? I want to go

home." He pressed a shaky hand to his mouth. "I think I left my four-wheeler around here somewhere. But I can't remember where."

"It's okay, Mr. Peters. We'll help you get home." Mitch finally reached them. "You remember me, Mitch Warren?"

"Don't know any Mitch or Warren."

"We all go to the same church. Your wife, Ms. Georgia, was my Sunday-school teacher when I was a kid."

"Mitch. Mitch. Mitch." Herbert tapped his chin with his index finger. "Oh yes, now I remember. You're a policeman."

"Yes, sir, a Texas Ranger."

"I didn't mean to hurt anyone." Herbert shook his head. "I just wanted her to leave. I never could sell my land because of her dogs. Every time I had somebody interested, they'd bail because of those yapping hounds."

"But I bought your land, Mr. Peters." Cody softened his tone, as if he were talking to a child. "Remember? Just a few weeks ago. The dogs don't bother me."

"I don't know you or what you're talking about, son. I just wanted to sell my land, that's all. You understand, don't you?" The old man's gaze went from Cody to Mitch. "Don't you?"

"Of course." Mitch offered his arm to Mr. Peters. "How about I take you home? Your son's probably worried about you."

"I'd be much obliged." Mr. Peters slipped his hand into the crook of Mitch's elbow. "What'd you say your name was again?"

"Mitch Warren."

"Ah, yes. There used to be some Warrens around these parts. You related to them?"

"Wayne and Audra are my parents." Mitch walked the old man out of the woods as Cody followed.

Alzheimer's? Dementia?

"Now, where did you say you're taking me?"

"Home. To your son's house."

"Ah, yes. But what about my four-wheeler?"

"After I get you home, I'll find it and bring it to you."

"That's nice." Mr. Peters patted Mitch's arm. "Such a nice young man. You say I have a son?"

The old man's confusion cracked Cody's heart open. But at least now Ally would be safe.

"I can't believe it was Mr. Peters." Ally held the Noah's ark frame steady as Cody pulled it apart with a pry bar. "But it makes so much sense. He used to be a locksmith."

"Apparently, he still has lucid moments. He had a few tonight."

"He seemed okay when I talked to him about buying the land." She stared up at the loft window of Cody's barn. The sunset painted lavender, pink and peach streaks across the sky. "Stubborn. But okay."

"He seemed fine when I originally leased the land and then bought it." One side of the frame came loose and Cody set it down on the floor beside the trailer. "His son, Gil, had to sign the paperwork, too—I guess as a precaution."

"I wonder how long he's had Alzheimer's."

"He was diagnosed last year, but I don't think Gil realized how fast it had progressed."

"It's so sad. I wonder what will happen to him."

"He might have to go to court."

She took in a sharp breath. "But I'm not pressing charges."

"You don't have to, since he kind of committed crimes during his nonlucid moments." Cody tore the cardboard off the frame and threw it in a heap by the wall. "But I'm certain a judge will rule him incompetent to stand trial and he'll probably end up in a nursing home."

"I guess he'll be safer that way. It's a wonder he didn't catch himself on fire the other night." She shook her head. "What if my shelter pushed him over the edge?"

"It's not your fault, Ally. He's sick."

She nodded and they worked in silence a few minutes.

They'd already dismantled the platform where they'd stood for the parade and removed all the hay bales. With the frame in four pieces now, Cody got busy prying two-by-fours off the floor of his trailer. His muscles flexed as he worked and she had to look away.

At least they were almost finished.

Minutes later, he threw the wood aside and climbed down the ladder. Taking her hand, he helped her down until her feet touched the barn floor. But he didn't step away.

"I can't tell you how worried I've been about you. I'm glad the mystery is over and you're safe."

"It is a relief. I just wish it hadn't turned out like this."

His tender gaze captured hers and he dipped his head. Their lips met. Her insides curled.

If only Cody had never left Aubrey. Would they have ended up married back then? A lifetime spent with him.

But he had left. Even after their first kiss. He'd left her. And she couldn't let him do it again.

She pulled away, bumped into the ladder behind her.

"Ally, I—"

"Don't." She kept her eyes on the third button of his shirt. "Let me go."

"Ally." His hands fell to his sides and he took a step back.

"If not for your injury, you'd still be on the road refusing to grow up."

"Maybe." He swallowed hard. "But because of my injury, I came back. And I've realized some things."

"Well, bully for you but I won't give up my independence to be your second choice or some sort of temporary detour until you go back on the circuit." She bolted for the door and ran all the way home.

Even though he kept calling her name.

What had he been thinking last night? Cody exited the back door of his barn and strolled toward the feeding troughs, the morning sun warm on his shoulders.

Clearly he hadn't been thinking or he wouldn't have kissed Ally again. He'd gone over and over this. He couldn't pursue her until he survived his surgery. Not a minute before.

Oh, how he'd wanted to follow her home last night. To tell her how he felt. But he couldn't.

Besides, he needed to get to the bottom of her spiritual issues before they could have a relationship. But he'd been so relieved she wasn't in danger. And she'd been so close when he helped her down the ladder. His brain had stalled just long enough for him to kiss her.

He had to concentrate. Feed the calves, take a quick shower, get ready for church, leave Ally alone. Surgery was tomorrow. If he woke up after that, he'd find out where Ally was with God, then tell her everything. Until then, he had to stay away.

"Give me strength, Lord. Strength to stay away from Ally. And give her the wits to draw close to You." He looked up at the clear sky dotted with cotton-ball clouds.

But his head swam. His ears buzzed. Then his vision tunneled. Almost went black. He fell, strewing grain all around him. As his left side hit the ground, all he could think about was how much feed he was wasting. That and Ally.

Had the aneurysm burst? Was this the end? His vision cleared, but he was afraid to move. No pain. So far.

Oreo licked his hand.

"Hey, boy, I think I need help." Where was his cell phone? On the coffee table where he'd left it. "Go get Ally, boy."

The dog kept licking his hand. Guess that only worked with Lassie.

A door shut. Ally. Probably leaving for church in Denton.

"Help! Ally, help!"

Nothing. She'd likely never hear him.

"Help! I'm behind the barn!" *I've fallen and I can't get up.* But it wasn't funny like in that old much-mimicked commercial.

A truck door slammed, followed by an engine starting up. Gravel crunched beneath tires and the engine faded away. She wouldn't be back for at least two and a half hours.

Maybe if he just lay here a minute, the aneurysm wouldn't burst. Maybe then he could make it inside and call for help. But the sky got fuzzy again. His vision tunneled and went black.

* * *

As Ally killed her engine, a dog's frantic barking caught her attention. Along with the attention of every dog boarding in her shelter. She jumped out of her truck and bolted toward the barn. But it wasn't coming from there. It sounded like it was behind Cody's barn.

Surely Mr. Peters hadn't evaded his son again. She unlocked the barn and scanned all the kennels. No missing boarders. She darted to her clinic and checked her patients. None missing there either. It must be Oreo.

But he was barking like something was wrong. Maybe he had a loose cow or a snake or a stray cat. She did not want to go over there. After yesterday's kiss, she could never look at Cody again. His truck was in the drive. He ought to be able to hear Oreo and know something was wrong.

Blast, she had him in her contact list. She punched it in. The rings multiplied, then went to voice mail.

She really did not want to go over there. But she couldn't risk Oreo getting snake bitten because she wouldn't swallow her pride and go see about him. She took in a deep breath and trudged toward Cody's barn. As she rounded the back, she could see Oreo barking at something at the other corner. Something wearing jeans and cowboy boots.

Her feet went into high gear. "Cody?"

It was him. Lying on his side.

She reached him and knelt. He was unconscious. She shook him. No response.

"Cody!" His skin was hot. How long had he been here in the dry Texas heat? Thankfully the barn shaded him from direct sunlight.

She jabbed in the numbers on her phone.

"911. What is your emergency?"

"This is Ally Curtis. My neighbor is unconscious."

The operator confirmed her address. "Are you certain he's breathing, ma'am?"

"Yes. I'm a vet." She checked his pulse and respirations, then gave the operator his numbers.

"We'll have an ambulance there as soon as possible. Where are you exactly?"

"We're behind his barn. He lives right next door and we're the only two houses out here."

"Approximately how old is your neighbor, ma'am?"

"Twenty-nine." *Please, God, let him be okay.*

"Does he have any visible wounds or any swelling?"

She scanned his face, arms, hands. "No. He looks fine. I just can't wake him up."

"Does he have any health issues?"

"Not that I know of." A siren whined in the distance. "He did have a bull wreck last spring and his doctor hasn't released him to drive. Because of a knee injury—I think."

"A bull wreck?"

"He was a bull rider in the rodeo. I think he's had several concussions."

"I see."

The siren wailed closer. "The ambulance is almost here. There are two barns here, so I'll go direct them to the right one. Thank you." She hung up.

Hating to leave Cody, she patted Oreo's head. "Good job, boy. You stay with him. I'll get help."

She ran around the barn as the ambulance pulled into her drive. As her heart tried to beat out of her chest, she directed them around to the back of Cody's barn.

The ambulance reversed to him and two paramedics bailed out. "You don't know what happened to him, ma'am?"

"No. I just found him like this. I was gone over two hours, so I'm not sure how long he's been here." Her voice broke. She clamped a hand over her mouth, swallowed hard. "He's hot, so I think he's been here a while. I wouldn't have found him, but his dog wouldn't stop barking. He probably needs fluids."

"Yes ma'am, he does." The paramedics inserted an IV into his hand. "You have medical training?"

"I'm a vet."

"Are you a family member?"

"Um, no. Just a friend. We're neighbors." *And I've been in love with him since I was eighteen years old.* "I need to call his family. What do I tell them?"

"His vitals are stable. Can you do something with the dog?"

"Oreo." She whistled and patted her thighs. "They're helping him. We have to stay out of the way. Come here, boy."

As if he felt guilty for leaving Cody, the dog crept toward her. She wrapped her arms around him.

The paramedics lifted Cody onto a stretcher. "We'll know more when we get to the hospital."

"Where are you taking him?"

"Baylor Emergency. Here in Aubrey."

As they loaded him into the ambulance, Cody's eyes fluttered open.

"Cody! What happened?"

He stared at her a moment, then looked up at the paramedics tending him. "Just got dizzy. I'm okay. Where are y'all taking me?"

"The ER. Just to get you checked over. Now relax, Mr. Warren."

Maybe heatstroke? But it was only in the mid-eighties.

"I'm fine. There's no need for that."

"You were unconscious for quite some time, Mr. Warren. Just enjoy the ride."

She managed a reassuring smile. "Should I call Mitch?"

"No." The word ripped from Cody, his eyes panicky. "I mean, don't worry them."

"I'll follow you."

"I'm fine. It's really not necessary."

Oreo strained against her as if he might leap right into the ambulance.

"I'm okay, boy. I'll be home as soon as they'll let me loose."

The dog settled a bit at the sound of Cody's voice. But as the doors of the ambulance closed and they drove away, Oreo broke free of her grip.

"Here, boy. You can't go with him." She managed to coax the dog to her side. "Let's put you in the barn so you don't get any ideas, and then I'll go check on him."

Oreo watched the ambulance until it turned onto the street, then followed Ally to her barn.

"I'm sorry to bring back memories for you, but hopefully Cody will be home soon." She put him in his old kennel and poured food in his dish. "Cody will be just fine."

He had to be. If anything happened to him, a piece of her heart would die.

Chapter Sixteen

"We've talked with your surgeon in Dallas, Mr. Warren. We're transporting you there this evening." The doctor checked something on his chart.

"You mean I can't go home?"

"Your surgeon wants to stay on the safe side and keep you in the hospital until your surgery tomorrow."

Cody closed his eyes. "Is my friend still here? Ally Curtis?"

"There was a lady asking about you."

"Can you send her in?"

Something kind and understanding settled in the doctor's knowing gaze. "For a few minutes. Then I need you to rest."

"I promise."

The doctor exited and Cody stared at the ceiling. This was bad. He'd planned to have surgery with no one the wiser. Not Ally. Not his family. He'd written them all letters and left them in envelopes on his kitchen counter—explaining everything—in case he didn't survive tomorrow's surgery. Or in case his brain didn't compute afterward.

But now Ally knew something was wrong. Could he pass it off as heatstroke? Maybe if they'd release him, but not if they were transporting him to Dallas. Besides, Ally was like a bloodhound. She wouldn't rest until she got to the bottom of this.

A knock.

"Come in."

The door opened. She stepped inside, her brows pinched with worry. "How are you feeling?"

"Much better. Like I might live."

"Don't joke. I want the truth. And remember I'm a vet. If I have the slightest inkling you're not telling me everything, I'll call Mitch."

He blew out a big sigh. "Sit down."

She pulled a chair close to his bedside and he clasped her hand in his.

"I have a brain aneurysm."

"What?" Her jaw dropped.

"Probably from too many concussions. After my last bull wreck, rehab and physical therapy, my doctor in Dallas ran a battery of tests and found it. He's not sure how long it's been there."

"What are you thinking? Running a ranch, teaching bull riding?"

"Sometimes they burst. Sometimes they don't. I had a list of triggers to avoid, including caffeine."

Her eyes closed. "The fake coffee makes sense now."

"I couldn't just lie around on my backside and not live because I was afraid of dying."

"So have you had other symptoms?"

"No. Just the dizziness and passing out."

"Aneurysms can cause stroke or death." Her eyes shimmered. "What are they going to do about it?"

"I'm having surgery tomorrow. I set it up a few weeks ago. They're transporting me to Dallas tonight."

"Tell me about the surgery."

"I could die on the table, I could survive with brain damage, I could have a stroke, or I could live and have a normal life."

"I don't want you to die." She laid her forehead against his bed rail. "Or be sick. I can't believe you kept this from me."

"I kept it from everyone." He stroked her hair, savoring the silky feel of it against his calloused fingers. "My family doesn't even know."

She raised her head and her tear-brightened gaze met his. "Why?"

"Because I knew they'd push for me to have the surgery."

"They love you."

"And I love them. But this is my aneurysm, my brain, my life. I wanted to pray and make the decision in peace and on my own."

"Then I'll be there by your side." Her chin trembled. "You can't go through this alone."

"Weren't you steamed at me less than twenty-four hours ago?"

Her cheeks pinkened. "A brain aneurysm puts things in perspective. You have to tell your family."

"Why not just let them be in peaceful ignorance until it's over?"

"And what if you die?" Her voice cracked. "You can't let them be oblivious and then out of the blue die during surgery they don't know you're having."

"Thanks for your confidence in my surgeon." He grinned. When all else failed, crack a joke.

But she didn't smile or laugh. "I'm praying for you to live. But your family needs to know what's going on."

"I left letters for them at my house. If anything happens, you can—"

"Do you want me to call Caitlyn or will you call Mitch?"

She was right. "Can I borrow your phone?" They deserved to know.

"How could he not tell us?" Cody's mom dabbed her eyes with a tissue and his dad gave her a hug.

"He didn't want to worry you." Ally set down the magazine she'd picked up just to keep her hands busy.

"I can't believe he planned to go through this surgery alone." Mitch paced the waiting room.

"If he hadn't passed out and I hadn't found him—" she clasped her hands together to stop their trembling "—he probably wouldn't have told any of us."

"He's so stubborn." Tara leaned into her husband's shoulder. "Always thought he had to do everything on his own."

"Not on his own." Wayne squeezed Audra's hand. "With God. But he still should have told us. I'll give our boy what-for once this is over."

A nurse stopped in the doorway. "Mr. Warren is prepped for surgery, if y'all would like to see him before they take him back."

Everyone stood. Except Ally. She wanted to see him more than anything. But she wasn't family.

"Come on, Ally." Audra touched her arm.

"You sure? I don't want to get in the way."

"Cody thinks the world of you. There was a time

when I thought you might end up being my daughter-in-law."

Her cheeks flushed. "We're just friends."

"Uh-huh." Caitlyn linked arms with Ally and whispered, "Not buying it anymore."

The nurse led them down a long hall, then directed them to a cubicle with the curtain pulled aside. Cody was a bit pale, but other than that, he looked like the picture of health. How could he be so sick and look so great?

"Hey, y'all." He grinned.

Was his perkiness an act for his family?

Audra dabbed her eyes. "I don't know how you can be so upbeat. If you weren't about to go into surgery, I'd box your ears."

"Get in line." Tara sniffled.

"I'll be fine. It's gonna take more than a little blood vessel to take me out." But his eyes weren't quite as lively. He was just as scared as they were. The over-confident bluster was a front.

"I'm glad you're here, Ally." He reached toward her.

She stepped forward, took his hand.

"At least they're not shaving my head."

"Just get well." Her free hand went to his hair as if she had no control and her fingers wound through his waves. "Oreo needs you."

And so do I. Oh, to kiss him. She settled for grazing her lips against his cheek.

"Don't worry." He squeezed her hand. "God's got this."

"He better have." She pulled away and managed a smile. "But I think I'll have a talk with Him just to make sure."

His eyes lit up. "I'm relieved to hear you say that. I was worried you weren't on speaking terms with Him anymore."

"We're good." Or they would be once she did some apologizing. "I'll give you time with your family."

One foot in front of the other, she hurried away before she did something stupid. Like plastering herself against him, begging him to live and love her back.

"I'm going to the chapel." Caitlyn, right behind her. "Want to come with me?"

"Yes." She slowed to let Caitlyn lead.

Just outside the waiting room, she noticed stained-glass windows in paneled doors. She followed Caitlyn inside, where pews lined the large space facing a lit cross.

Caitlyn knelt at the front near the cross. Ally joined her friend there.

Okay, God, I'm sorry for turning my back on You. For pretending I don't need You. When I found Cody unconscious, what did I do? I called out to You—proving that I do need You.

I need You to bless Cody's surgeon's hands. I need You to bless the procedure. I need You to heal Cody. And let him still be Cody. Warped sense of humor and all. Please, let him be healthy and whole.

Waiting for the orderly to roll him into surgery, Cody lay still. If only his brain would stop spinning. What if he had a stroke? What if he couldn't talk or walk? What if he ended up a vegetable?

His parents had gone, along with Tara and Jared, Caitlyn and Ally.

But Mitch stayed by his side. "You okay?"

"So far, so good. I'm kind of hungry, though." Cody patted his empty stomach.

"That's a good sign." Mitch chuckled, but his eyes turned serious. "You should have told us."

"I saved you some worry and myself some pressure while I decided what to do."

"You're right there. Mom wouldn't have let you rest until you scheduled surgery. You scared?"

"Not of dying." His hand shook as he tugged his sheet up against the frigid hospital air-conditioning set on deep freeze as usual. "But living and not being myself, that terrifies me."

"I guess that's why you took so long to decide."

"That and Ally."

"What's Ally got to do with it?"

"I'm head over heels in love with her."

Mitch's mouth twitched. "Tell me something I don't know."

"How?"

"You get all sappy-eyed when you look at her."

"Really?" Cody's grin widened. "Think she knows?"

"Probably not. Women are clueless when it comes to love. You pretty much have to spell it out for them. Put it into words. So you haven't told her?"

"Not yet." Cody closed his eyes. "I decided to have the surgery for a chance with her. But I won't tie her to a vegetable. If everything goes well, I don't have a stroke, I don't have brain damage and I live, I'll tell her."

"What if you have some mild side effect?"

"We'll see. But if I end up half-paralyzed or not knowing who I am or how to speak, I can't saddle her with that."

"Way to think positive, little brother." The seriousness of the situation weighed heavy in Mitch's tone.

"I mean it. If anything bad goes down, I don't want her to know how I feel. Promise me you won't tell her."

"I promise." Mitch patted his knee. "But you'll be fine. We've got all of Aubrey praying for you."

"So much for privacy." Cody rolled his eyes.

The orderly strolled toward them. "They're ready for you, Mr. Warren."

Mitch hugged him. "See you in a few hours, bro."

"I hope so."

Please, Lord, heal me or take me home.

They'd been told the surgery would last three hours. Ally glanced at the clock. Time was almost up. Why wouldn't someone tell them something?

Rubber-soled shoes squeaked on the shiny tile as medical personnel rushed back and forth past the nurses' station.

Mitch paced. Caitlyn flipped through a magazine. Audra and Tara sniffled. Wayne and Jared talked horses, though both were distracted. While Ally slowly went insane.

A nurse stepped in the doorway. Everyone stood.

"Mr. Warren is in recovery. The doctor will be right with you."

What did that mean? In her clinic, it meant everything had gone well and her patient was resting. Ally sank back to her chair. One by one, the others followed. Except Mitch, who continued to pace.

"That means everything's okay? Right?" Audra wiped her nose.

Wayne stroked her hand.

A man wearing blue-green scrubs stepped in the room. "The procedure went well. Everything looks good."

"No brain damage?" Wayne looked like he might fall over.

"There wasn't any bleeding." The doctor's soft tone comforted. "The repair went off without a hitch. We'll know more tomorrow. We'll just have to wait until Cody wakes up."

More waiting. This was torturous.

"How long will that be?" Audra's voice quavered.

"He should be coming out of it soon. He'll probably drift in and out of sleep until tomorrow. We'll see how lucid he is then and run tests. At this point, only time will tell."

But he'd made it through the surgery. With no bleeds. That was a good sign. Every surgery she'd ever done with no bleeds resulted in the pet making a full recovery.

Ally covered her face with her hands. *Thank You, Lord, for letting Cody make it through surgery.*

"Can we see him?" Hope filled Audra's voice.

"Once he's out of recovery, he'll be in ICU. We'll allow two visitors at a time for a few hours and then he'll need to rest. The nurse will let you know as soon as he's in a room."

"When can we take him home?" Ever-optimistic Audra.

"As well as the surgery went, barring complications, usually one to three days."

Meaning Cody could be fine tomorrow. Or he could be a different man.

But he was alive. That was the important part. If he was a different man, they could become friends all over again. If he was a different man, maybe he'd fall in love with her.

Whatever the future held, having Cody alive and well was all that mattered.

Chapter Seventeen

Light. And voices. Cody tried to open his eyes, but they wouldn't seem to budge. Heavy. Heavy eyelids.

He wiggled his toes.

"Hey, I think he's coming around." Mitch's voice.

Surgery. He'd had surgery. And he remembered that. That was good. He smiled.

"What are you dreaming about, bro? It must be good."

He willed himself to open his eyes. It worked this time. Faces came into focus. Mitch and Catherine. No, that wasn't her name. But what was it?

"Hey." She rested her hand on his arm. "How are you feeling?"

"Hungry." His throat was dry, voice croaky. "I want a peanut butter and grape sandwich."

Catherine frowned. But that wasn't her name. "You mean peanut butter and jelly?"

"That's it." Why weren't his words coming out right? Why couldn't he remember his sister-in-law's name? She'd been his friend in school and their youth group long before she'd ever dated his brother. What was her name?

"Lunch should arrive soon. You slept right through breakfast." She picked up a plastic mug of water with a straw, held it to his parched lips. "How about water for now?"

"Thanks." He drank, the iced liquid soothing and cold on his throat. "Am I okay?"

"You seem okay to me."

He focused on her, searching for the right name. "I can't remember your name. I'm coming up with Catherine. But I know that's not right."

Her smile faded. "It's Caitlyn." Sadness tinged her voice.

"That's it. Sorry."

She squeezed his forearm. "They just played around in your brain. I'm sure a little confusion is normal."

"What day is it?"

"Tuesday."

What day had his surgery been? He couldn't remember. "How many days since the surgery?"

"One." Mitch opened the blinds. "You've been in and out. This is the first time you've really been lucid. Must have been some good drugs."

"They got the appendix out of my head?"

Caitlyn giggled. "The aneurysm is gone. They'll run more tests, but your surgeon said everything went textbook perfect and you should get out of here tomorrow or the next day."

Of course. His appendix was in his chest and he hadn't had it since he was fifteen. Why could he remember that, but he couldn't say the right words? Or think them, for that matter. His appendix hadn't been in his chest, but where had it been?

"Only two people can visit you at a time and there are several waiting." Mitch's boots clicked on the floor as he stepped back. "We'll get out of here so you can see Mom and Dad. They've been worried sick."

Was he okay? He had to think really hard. Say the right things. Not worry Mom and Dad.

He had to be okay. Had to have a chance with Ally. Was she one of the visitors waiting?

The nurse checked his monitors.

"Ma'am, can I ask you an answer?"

She cocked her head to the side. "Sure."

"I'm having a hard time coming up with the right talking. Am I okay?"

"I'll have your surgeon speak with you."

Was that a good thing? Would the surgeon tell him his brain was toast?

Ally waited. Everyone had seen Cody. Except her. It was only right. They were family and she wasn't. But impatience gnawed at her stomach. What if the doctor put a halt to visitors before she got to see him?

And she was worried. She'd heard murmurs about Cody saying odd things. Had he had a stroke? His doctor was evaluating him now, then would consult with the family. After that, it was her turn. But what would she find? He hadn't been able to think of Caitlyn's name. Would he even remember her?

Silence reigned among his anxious family members.

Rubber-soled shoes squeaked toward them. Cody's surgeon. He smiled as he stepped in the room. "All of

Mr. Warren's tests look excellent. He should be able to go home tomorrow."

"But what about his speech?" The muscle along Wayne's jaw flexed.

"Some confusion in speech is a normal side effect of the procedure Mr. Warren had."

"So he didn't have a stroke?" Audra put into words Ally's greatest fear.

"No. He's doing quite well. His speech should improve over time. It might frustrate him, but he should get back to normal soon."

"So he doesn't have any other side effects?" Mitch sank into his chair. "He's fine. Normal."

"His fine motor skills, mobility and balance are good. All his tests look great. He'll need to take it easy for the next two weeks and no driving. We'll run another MRI and MRA after that and if everything still looks good, he can return to his regular activities. He can even ride bulls if he must."

"Please don't tell him that last bit." Caitlyn squeezed her eyes closed.

The doctor chuckled, then hurried toward the hallway.

Cody was okay. The speech thing was temporary. He could live a normal life.

And go back on the circuit.

"It's your turn to see him, Ally." Caitlyn checked the clock. "Better hurry. Before the doctor decides it's time for Cody to rest."

"I'll wait. He's probably tired."

"I think he'd like to see you." Mitch squeezed her elbow. "I'll show you the way."

How could she say no?

Mitch propelled her down the long corridor. Some sort of alarm started up, sending doctors and nurses scurrying. *Please not Cody.* Her legs noodled.

The staff sprinted into a room. Mitch led her past the turmoil. It wasn't Cody. She started breathing again, said a prayer for the patient in jeopardy. It felt good to pray again.

"He's right here." Mitch gestured to an open doorway, then turned away.

"Aren't you staying?" Did she sound as panicked as she felt?

"I've already seen him. I think he'd like to see you alone."

Ally sucked in a deep breath, slowly let it out and hesitated in his doorway, afraid to enter.

Because she was here only to say goodbye.

"Bye." He waved her inside.

So quick? Her chin wobbled. "You want me to leave?"

"No. Why would you think that?" He stretched his hand toward her. "Please come in."

"You just said bye." She frowned.

He let out a growl. "Don't pay much attention to what I say. I can't seem to get things out right."

"Oh, you meant hello?"

"No. Like what horses eat."

"Hay." She giggled. "Oh, you meant to say hey."

"Even though you seem to think my frustration is funny, you're a sight for sore ears."

Sore eyes? She stifled another laugh. "The doctor talked to you about it. He said it's temporary."

"Yes. But it's very annoying."

"You just got several sentences right." She nibbled

on her lip, trying to hold back a grin, but it couldn't be contained and her vision blurred. Only hours ago, she'd thought she might never hear his voice again. So what if he bungled a few words? "And you probably get to go home tomorrow."

"Remember when we were old and we used to hold hands and each waltz a side of the railroad track?"

She chuckled at his slip.

"What did I say?" He rolled his eyes.

"You said when we were old and we waltzed the tracks, but I think you meant when we were young and we walked, unless we've been to Narnia and I don't remember." She flipped her thick braid over her shoulder, twirled the end around her finger. "And I don't know how to waltz."

"Very funny." He reached for her hand.

She shouldn't, but she did. His fingers linked with hers. Warm and strong.

"Anyway, I want to walk the tracks again. And remember how we used to jump from hay bale to hay bale?"

"We had a lot of fun."

"I want to live death to the fullest." He growled. "That wasn't right. But don't tell me. I want to life... life. I want to live life to the fullest. You have no idea how frustrating this is."

"It's temporary, it keeps me on my toes trying to figure out what you're trying to say, and it's kind of cute."

"Cute?" His grin melted her insides.

"I better let you rest."

"I'm too hungry to rest." He held on to her hand. "All they let me have was soup juice and that orange jiggly stuff. I'm dying for a peanut butter and grape sandwich.

But they said they didn't have them. And I said it wrong again. Peanut butter and…jelly."

"Very good."

"Ally. There's so much I want to tell you." His tone was thick with whatever was on his mind.

Her heart skipped a beat. "Like what?"

"After I get out of here. When I get better with my talking."

"Okay. We'll talk then." The way he looked at her curled her toes. Had they wiggled something in his brain? Made him have feelings for her?

"I came here not knowing if I'd ever wake up. Now they tell me to take it easy for two weeks and then I can ride buffaloes again."

His slip wasn't funny this time.

She pulled out of his grasp. "How about I go tell them you're still hungry?"

"Stay with me." He reached for her again.

But she couldn't stay a minute longer. "You need food and rest. So you can get well." She backed away, out of the room, and hurried down the hall.

A clean bill of health. And he was already planning to leave.

Thankfully Ally had critters to tend to. A good excuse not to go next door for Cody's homecoming. His family had all left hours ago, except for his mom, who was spending the next few nights with him. There was no reason to go over there. No reason to see Cody for his two weeks of rest. Best to wean herself from his intoxicating presence.

She checked on her patients in recovery one more time, then tested the front door lock and left out the back.

Straight to the barn. She had only four boarders and two strays. The emptiest her barn had been since she started her shelter. And her volunteers had already walked, fed and watered them. She made sure all the runs were open and locked up, then hurried toward her house.

"Ally?"

Cody? What was he doing outside? She turned around.

He stood on his side of the wood rail fence separating their properties.

"Should you be out here?"

"I'm already going stir-crazy. Surely walking twenty feet won't kill me."

"Don't tease like that." Her eyes stung at the memory of finding him unconscious.

"Sorry. Poor word choice." He dug an envelope out of his shirt pocket. "Remember I told you, before I went in the hospital, I wrote each of my family members a letter in case I lived?"

"Why not just tell them what you want to say?"

"I did it again." Cody stomped his foot. "What's the opposite?"

"Oh. You wrote letters in case you—" her throat closed up "—died." Something hard sank to the pit of her stomach at the mere thought of it.

"Yes. I wrote you one, too." He handed her the envelope.

Her gaze stayed locked on his.

"Read it."

"Now?" At his nod, she opened the envelope and pulled a single page out.

"Read it out silent."

"Out loud?"

"Isn't that what I said?"

She dragged her eyes from his and concentrated on deciphering his chicken scratch. "'Ally, you've been the best friend I've ever had. I love you and I've arranged for you to inherit my land if I die.'" She clutched her heart. "This is very sweet. But I'm so glad I'm not inheriting your ranch."

"But I've been thinking." He patted the top rail of the fence. "Do you like this wood?"

"Looks like perfectly good wood to me. It's not rotten or anything."

"Not the wood, the hurdle." He gestured at the length of fence between them.

"The fence?"

"That's it. So frustrating." He gritted his teeth. "Do you like this fence?"

"Sure. Are you thinking of building a new one?"

"I think we should tear it down."

"But the fence marks our property lines except for the acreage you donated for my shelter."

He stared up at the sky. "I wanted to wait. To make sure I get the words right. But I can't wait anymore."

"What is it? Are you regretting giving me the five acres? You can have it back."

"I don't want it. The only regret I have is you."

"I'm not following." Did he regret the time they'd spent together in the last month?

"I regret leaving after your dad died. I shouldn't have left you."

"It wasn't your job to stay here and babysit me." She shrugged, swallowed the knot lodged in her throat. "It was hard, but I survived."

"I can't change the past. But what do you think about a corporate takeover?"

"You want to buy me out?"

"No, I want you to be my...partner."

"Oh. A merger." Business partners with Cody? When her heart longed for so much more. "You want to go into business together?"

"Warren Veterinary Clinic/Adopt-a-Pet/Longhorn Ranch."

"You want me to oversee your ranch when you go back on the circuit." Her eyes singed. "My plate's pretty full already. But I'm sure you can find a good manager."

"No." Cody took off his hat and sailed it through the air like a Frisbee. "That's not what I meant. I have no desire to ride buffaloes again. That page of my death is over."

"You're not going back on the circuit?"

"I want you to do the loop with me."

"Do the loop?" Do the loop? Tie the knot? No, he couldn't mean that. Her heart went into overdrive.

"To marry you, Ally. I want to marry you."

His handsome face blurred. "Why?"

"Because." He closed his eyes, concentration apparent in the taut lines of his face. "I love you."

"You do?" Her hand flew to her heart as it tried to beat out of her chest.

"Didn't I say that in my email?" He pointed at the letter she still held.

"I thought you meant as a friend."

"Nothing friendly about it. I've been in love with you since our first kiss."

Tears threatened to spill. "Really?" The word came out barely a whisper.

"If you'd have given me any idea you had the slightest feelings for me, I'd have never left to ride buffaloes. You were never my second choice. Always first. You're my…" His jaw clenched as he searched for the right word. "You're my forever. I hope."

She traced the tense muscles along his cheek with her fingertips. "I love you. I'd love to be your forever. And I'd really love to do the loop with you."

"Really?" His eyes lit up.

"Please tell me this isn't just your scrambled brain talking."

"Nothing scrambled about my feelings for you. How about we seal the deal?" He claimed her lips with a tender kiss.

All rational thought faded away until there was nothing but Cody and the pounding of her heart. She forgot to breathe.

He dragged his mouth away from hers, then leaned his forehead against hers, pulling her as close as he could with the fence between them. "I told you this hurdle was in the way."

Epilogue

Cody's hand shook in Ally's grasp under her mom and Lance's kitchen table. Why was he so nervous? Her mom loved him and he and Lance had built a solid relationship. Though Cody's brain-to-speech issue had completely cleared up in the two months since his surgery, there was no telling what he'd say in his nervousness. He hadn't even touched the four-layer delight her mom had fixed.

It was so old-fashioned anyway. Her mom didn't expect it. Ally should have insisted they skip this step.

Mom popped the last bite of dessert in her mouth, her gaze darting from Ally to Cody and back.

Obviously aware something was up, Lance cleared his throat.

Ally squeezed Cody's trembling hand and he set his tea glass down with a thunk.

"I'm a traditional kind of guy." Cody swallowed hard. "Since Ally's dad can't be here, I need to ask you something, Diane."

"That's what's got you so nervous?" Mom smiled. "I hope it's what I think it is."

"Me, too." Cody drew in a big breath, let it out slow and deliberate. "I'd like permission to marry your daughter."

"That's exactly what I was hoping for." Mom clapped her hands, then stood and rounded the table to Cody's side. "I couldn't ask for a better son-in-law."

"I'm so glad you think so." His hand stopped shaking as he let go of hers. Then he rose and hugged Mom. "I'll take good care of her."

"I know you will." Mom patted his cheek.

"You're not surprised?" Ally couldn't stop smiling.

"Me?" Mom reclaimed her seat. "It's hard to fool a mom."

"Your mother's been onto you since Cody first arrived back in town." Lance smirked.

"How did you know?" Cody took Ally's hand, gently pulled her to her feet and into his arms.

"I knew there was something up between y'all way back." Mom's eyes went to Cody. "But then you left and nothing came of it. As soon as I learned you were our new neighbor, I knew."

"Knew what?" Ally frowned, so certain she'd hidden her feelings.

"I knew there'd be a reunion and sparks would fly." Mom shot her a satisfied wink.

"You hear that?" Cody nestled her close, cheek to cheek. "We got your mom's blessing. We get to tie the knot."

"I can't wait." A contented sigh escaped her. "But I think I'd rather do the loop, if it's all the same to you."

He chuckled, a deep, happy and healthy rumble as his arms tightened around her.

Reuniting with the cowboy of her dreams. She couldn't ask for a better dream come true.

* * * * *

ROCKY MOUNTAIN COWBOY

Tina Radcliffe

This book is dedicated to the heroes in my life,
my husband, Tom, and my dad, Joe.

Acknowledgments

Many thanks to beta readers
Nancy Connally and Vince Mooney.
They took the time to help me saddle the horse
and get this story off on the right path.

Thank you to the people who assisted me with the
research on this story. All errors are wholly mine.

To real-life Nebraska rancher Ivan Connealy
and his author wife, Mary Connealy, thank you
for your time, insights and information on cattle
and hay. Thanks to Missy Tippens
for that calf-roping assistance!

Thank you to Rob Dodson, CPO, FAAOP clinical
manager with Advanced Arm Dynamics, who
connected me with the amazing Barry Landry.
Barry, who has a transradial amputation, utilizes
the Michelangelo myoelectric prosthesis and
happens to be an amateur rodeo cowboy. Not only
does Barry ride horses, but he ropes cattle.
Thank you, Barry, for taking time to answer
all my questions. You can find out more about
Advanced Arm Dynamics and the Michelangelo
at www.armdynamics.com.

A final thank-you to my editor, Giselle Regus,
for her endless patience with a slow writer
and insightful editing on this book.

Do not remember the former things, nor consider the things of old. Behold, I will do a new thing, now it shall spring forth; shall you not know it? I will even make a road in the wilderness and rivers in the desert.
—*Isaiah* 43:18–19

Chapter One

It had been a good many years since Rebecca Anshaw Simpson had inhaled the earthy combination of cattle, horse and hay that was home. As the scents wove their way in through the vents of her car, it seemed like only yesterday that she was a kid, riding like a swift rush of wind through the valley of Paradise, Colorado. Life was simple then. So blessedly simple.

Rebecca yawned and rolled down her window to fully appreciate the enticing perfume of home. As she stretched, her aching neck protested. The muscles were stiff because she'd fallen asleep inside the ancient compact Honda.

When an almost icy spring breeze moved through the car, Rebecca pulled her down-filled vest closer.

A horse and rider appeared in the distance. Silhouetted against the horizon and the rising sun's orange glow, the man in the dark Stetson approached at a rapid clip, with two dogs racing alongside.

She'd know that profile anywhere.

Joe Gallagher.

Tension crept along her shoulders. She'd had serious reservations about taking this job because of Joe. They'd dated all through high school, even though she was two years younger than him. Joe was her first love. Until she'd dumped him.

Young and naive, she'd been swept off her feet at the end of her sophomore year of college, and eloped with Nick Simpson.

What a trusting fool she'd been. For a lingering moment, Rebecca allowed herself to contemplate what life would have been like if she'd stuck with the homeboy.

"It doesn't matter," she whispered.

None of it did. All that mattered was today. Life as she'd known it had been stolen from her two years ago. She had returned to Paradise to begin again.

What irony that she should be returning home to the man she had scorned. Forced to face him again, after so many years. The Lord surely had a sense of humor opening the door to this assignment. OrthoBorne Technology had not only given her a job, but it had dangled a huge bonus, like a proverbial carrot on a stick. She'd taken the bait and was determined to make the most of this chance.

When the man on the horse was close enough for her to see his midnight-black hair peeking out from under his hat and the shadow of a beard on his face, Rebecca inhaled a sharp breath. Joe Gallagher had changed. He'd become ruggedly handsome in the years since they'd parted.

"Becca?" Joe slid off his horse and approached the gate. His deep voice reflected stunned surprise, and the underlying tone was anything but welcoming.

Tired of craning her neck, she opened the car door and stepped out, stretching her stiff legs while discreetly pulling down the sleeves of her sweater. She still had to look up to meet his gaze. Joe was taller than she remembered, with that same dangerous loner aura.

He rested his gloved left hand on the top of the gate, while his other hand, the prosthetic one, according to her notes, remained tucked away inside the pocket of his fleece-lined denim jacket. For a long minute he simply stared. It was as though he was looking through her, to the past.

The lean black-and-white cattle dogs at his feet barked and raced in energetic circles, eager to be part of the conversation.

"Sit," Joe commanded, his voice steely.

The animals instantly obeyed.

"Been a long time," he finally said, his gaze returning to hers.

Rebecca tried to gauge what he was thinking, but his expression was unreadable. Apparently he still held everything deep inside.

"It has been, hasn't it? A very long time," she murmured. "I heard you joined the army after college."

"Yeah. When my dad died, I went ahead and took an early discharge."

"I'm so sorry about your father," she said, immediately regretting her words. "I, um, I know how close you two were."

He gave a quick nod of acknowledgment. "What about you?" he asked. "Home for a visit? Is your husband with you?"

At Joe's question, everything around Rebecca slowed down and began to blur. The world came to a stunning halt as the words slipped from her mouth.

"Nick is dead."

Joe jerked back slightly, eyes widening a fraction. "I didn't know. I'm sorry for your loss."

Unmoving, she stared at him. The surprise on his face seemed genuine enough. Could Joe Gallagher be the only person in Paradise, in Colorado for that matter, who didn't know about the accident? The trial? Hadn't it been splashed in every newspaper? The grandson of one of the founding families of Paradise Valley had been taken from this world far too soon.

Apparently Joe didn't know her life had been on hold for the last twenty-four months as she awaited the results of the jury trial.

"You okay?" Joe asked when she didn't answer.

"Yes. Yes. Sorry." Rebecca leaned against the Honda and massaged her arm. Glancing down, she realized what she was doing and stopped. "Long drive from Denver. I started out Friday afternoon. It was so late that I just slept in the car."

His eyes rounded. "You spent the night in your car? Why didn't you drive to your mom's house?"

"No. That's not what I meant. I didn't spend the night in the car. Two hours. A nap."

Joe raised a brow.

Rebecca shrugged. "There was a huge accident on I-25 outside the Springs, and then I ran into issues with the starter when I hit Alamosa."

"Why are you parked here?"

She nodded to the sign on the gate. "I thought this was still the main entrance to the ranch. Until I saw the sign."

Joe grimaced as he, too, glanced at the sign.

"Do not cross this pasture unless you can do it in

nine seconds, because the bull can do it in ten. Please close the gate."

"That would be my mother's handiwork."

"Why not put a padlock on the gate?"

"It's the ingress for emergency vehicles. If I put a padlock on it, then I have to remember where the key is." He paused and looked at her, eyes narrowed. "Wait a minute. Why are you at Gallagher Ranch?"

"Since I have to drive out here to see you anyhow, I thought I'd do a dry run. By the time I finally arrived, I was a little more tired than I realized." She lifted a hand. "Thus the nap."

"Whoa. Whoa. Whoa." When he suddenly straightened and raised a hand, the black horse behind him whinnied and stepped back several paces, causing the dogs to bark.

Joe laid a comforting hand on the animal and silenced the dogs again. "Let's start over here. Did you say you're here to see me?"

Rebecca glanced at her watch. "Yes. Our meeting is scheduled for Monday morning."

"Things have been pretty hectic around here, but I don't forget appointments. And I'm even less likely to have forgotten an appointment with…"

Rebecca swallowed when his words trailed off. What had he been about to say? With someone who had treated him so callously? The girl who dumped him.

Joe pulled the glove off his right hand and then tugged the matching one off his left hand using his teeth, before taking out his phone. The skin tone silicone cover of the myoelectric prosthesis made his right hand appear nearly identical to his left. She couldn't help assess that he really didn't use the prosthesis, apparently utilizing the device simply as a placeholder.

After fiddling with the phone for a moment, he paused and slowly met her gaze. Complete shock was reflected in his eyes. "Are you…"

"I'm the therapist who's been assigned to complete the certification for your prosthesis."

"You're a therapist?"

She nodded.

"I thought they were sending someone from Denver. They told me it was someone who would help with those media people who are coming, as well."

His voice was edged with irritation, and Rebecca held her breath and stepped back from him.

"They are. They did. I am."

Joe Gallagher's face looked like he'd just been struck with a cattle prod.

She crossed her arms and stated the obvious. "This is going to be a problem."

He took off his Stetson and then slapped it back on so that it rested at the back of his head, revealing more of his jet-black hair. She could clearly see that his moss-green eyes were troubled.

"Joe?"

"I guess it better not be, because the way I see things, I don't have much choice. Do I?"

"You tell me." She looked him straight in the eye. "Is our history going to get in the way?"

"History? Is that the politically correct term these days?" He offered a bitter chuckle.

She studied him once again. His face was a mask, his gaze shuttered.

"No, Becca," he finally continued. "You don't have

to worry. Even this Colorado cowboy realizes that was a long time ago. We were kids. This is business. More important, the future of Gallagher Ranch depends on me completing the requirements of my contract with OrthoBorne. I cut a deal to pay off this fourteen-karat-gold myoelectric arm." His eyes pinned her. "And I always keep my word."

Joe turned his head to glance out at the land, and she realized she'd been dismissed. The knowledge burned.

"So Monday, then?" she asked quietly.

"That's fine. I'm past the main house. A bit farther up the road. Two-story log cabin."

She nodded.

He turned to her. "When do your friends arrive?"

"They aren't my friends." Rebecca bristled. "I don't even know who was contracted for this job, except that there's a videographer and a copywriter."

"When will they finish?"

"That is wholly dependent upon you and the weather."

He offered a slow shake of his head that said her answer wasn't nearly satisfactory enough. "What about certification? How long do you think that will take?"

"Once again, everything depends on you. I don't anticipate more than four weeks reviewing your ADLs."

He straightened, jaw tense, and his face was almost thunderous. "Four weeks! Four weeks? I have a ranch to run."

"Joe, that's exactly why it will take that long. In fact, knowing how a ranch runs, I asked for extra time so our sessions don't interfere with what you have to do at the ranch or with the media crew."

"And what's an ADL?"

"Activities of daily living."

He sucked in a breath but said nothing.

"Look, that doesn't mean we can't get everything done earlier than scheduled. I'll accompany you on your routine chores, schedule one-on-one sessions related to your ranch work. Then I'll assist you to incorporate the prosthesis into your daily life that isn't ranch related."

"Can you still ride?"

"What?" She shook her head, certain she'd heard the terse question incorrectly.

"Ride. Do you ride?"

Rebecca frowned. "I was born in a saddle, like you were. Cowgirls don't forget how to ride."

The tension in Joe's shoulders eased a bit. "That'll help, because, no offense, Becca, but I plan to graduate way ahead of schedule."

"While it's my job to treat you the same as all my clients, there is no doubt in my mind that you'll beat all records getting this done. Then I'll be gone, and you can go back to your life."

Rebecca looked up at him, standing tall and proud, profiled against the land. For a brief moment she imagined she saw a glimpse of something familiar from years ago and the closeness they once shared.

That was crazy because yesterday was long gone. Once again Rebecca reminded herself that it was high time to start looking forward instead of behind.

"I'm sorry, Mrs. Simpson, but it's no longer available."

"How can that be? I called before I left Denver to make sure everything was set."

Joe turned at the sound of Becca's voice.

He'd sidestepped the woman for twelve years, and now he managed to run into her twice in the space of a few hours?

She stood on the sidewalk of downtown Paradise, and was obviously doing her best to get her point across to a wiry guy as they stood outside the real-estate office.

How little the years had changed her. He'd been stunned to see her at the fence this morning. The years had tumbled back, and he realized with painful clarity that the tall, lean beauty who'd stolen his heart at sixteen apparently could still tie him in knots.

The difference was that this time he had a strong rope anchored to his heart, holding down those once generous emotions of his. *Only a fool gets burned twice.*

He'd made more than his share of mistakes in his life, and he liked to believe he'd learned from every single one of them. Joe glanced down at his prosthesis, remembering the farm accident that had taken his limb. He pushed the memory away and focused on the here and now.

Joe glanced back down the street. From a distance, he could feel the tension in the air. He tucked himself back into the doorway of a shop, grateful he stood well behind Becca's line of sight.

She pushed strands of dark hair away from her face as she dug in her purse to pull out neatly folded papers. "You took my deposit and my credit-card information. Why, you even mailed me a receipt. I have the paperwork right here."

Confusion laced Becca's voice. To her credit, she maintained her composure, though her hands were clenched tightly around her purse.

The Realtor adjusted his tie, swallowed and

shrugged, obviously avoiding eye contact with her. "I've reversed the charges, ma'am. No worries."

"No worries?" She blinked and began to gesture with her hands. "No worries?"

Joe found himself unable to resist listening to the conversation, and at the same time fighting the urge to come to her defense. Why should he? Becca had made it clear a long time ago that she didn't want him in her life. No, he reminded himself, her return to Paradise and whatever was going on here was none of his business.

"Are you kidding me?" Becca continued, her voice louder and tight with frustration. "Couldn't you go inside and check your files again?"

"No need," the man returned, his voice low and upbeat in an effort to defuse the situation. "That's why I stepped outside. I saw you coming, and I thought I'd save you some time."

"Okay, so if that rental isn't available, do you mind telling me what is?"

"Ma'am, I don't have anything for you right at the moment. Maybe you could try some of those new condos down by Paradise Lake."

"I can't afford those."

"I'm real sorry, Mrs. Simpson. It's just one of those things."

"One of *what* things?"

The young man squirmed while gesturing helplessly.

"Look, I rented the house a month ago. Not only that, but your ad today in the *Paradise Gazette* says you have at least five summer rentals still available in the area. Now you're claiming that you have none?"

"Ma'am, I'm real sorry."

Shoulders slumped, Becca shook her head. "This is unbelievable," she murmured.

An ache he couldn't explain gnawed at Joe. Without thinking, he strode down the sidewalk, zigzagging around people, oblivious to a sudden flurry of shoppers creating obstacles in his path, and stepped up to Becca and the real-estate agent.

"Everything okay here, Becca?"

Startled, her brown eyes popped open and she looked up at him. "I… I have this under control, Joe."

"Doesn't sound like it to me," he returned, purposely shooting the other man a scowl.

"*Joe.*"

He met Becca's gaze.

"You need to stay out of this. Besides, my business is done here." She turned on her heel and walked away, her face shielded by a curtain of chocolate-brown waves.

Behind him, Joe heard the sound of bells as the real-estate agent disappeared into the storefront.

Joe quickly yanked open the door, setting the bells into a wicked frenzy. The guy behind the desk had a solicitous smile on his face when he turned around.

Then he saw Joe.

He straightened and inched back farther behind the desk. "May I help you?"

"I sure hope so…" Joe glanced at the man's name tag. "Jason."

Jason came out from behind the desk and thrust a hand in greeting. Apparently his plan was to pretend that the incident outside moments before had never happened. "Have we met?" he asked.

"No, we haven't. Joe Gallagher. Gallagher Ranch."

Joe looked the other man up and down before offering his prosthetic hand.

Jason's eyes widened, and he dropped his own hand.

"New to town?" Joe asked.

"Yes, I am. How may I help you, sir?"

"I want to rent a house."

"I'm sure we can fix you up. Anything in particular you're looking for?"

"I'd like the one that you were supposed to lease to Rebecca Simpson."

Jason's face paled and he stepped backward, once again effectively putting the desk between him and Joe. "Sir, I don't recommend that you get involved in that situation." Tiny beads of perspiration popped out along his upper lip.

"What situation is that, Jason?"

The man swallowed hard before darting to the front door and switching the sign from Open to Closed. "Sir, if you'll excuse me, I'm closed for the day."

Joe followed him, getting squarely in the man's personal space, towering over him with as much intimidation as he could muster. "Off the record, Jason, tell me what's going on."

Jason swallowed again as if he was desperate for a glass of water and a way to get rid of Joe.

"Can you tell me why you just turned down a paying customer?"

"I… I…"

Joe shook his head and growled, "I don't like this, Jason."

"I don't much like it either, but I have a wife and a new baby to think about."

Joe turned on his boot heel and left the office.

Though he did his best not to slam the door, the bells were once again ringing a dissonant tune behind him as he put distance between himself and a sour situation.

It was time for a little chat with the sheriff of Paradise. Joe started toward his truck and then changed his mind. Walking was just what he needed. He headed in the other direction, cutting through the park in the center of town and past the gazebo toward the office of Sam Lawson, where he pulled open the heavy wooden door.

This wasn't about Becca, he reassured himself. It was the principle of the thing. No one should be treated unfairly. Especially in Paradise.

Bitsy Harmony MacLaughlin, the administrative assistant, sat at a huge battered desk, guarding the entrance to Sam's office like a geriatric bouncer.

"Sam available?" he asked.

Bitsy stood and realigned the silver braided knot on the top of her head. "The sheriff is on the phone. Give him five minutes."

Joe nodded. He wasn't eager to lose the momentum of his purpose by chitchatting with Bitsy, so he turned to examine the bulletin board.

"Cup of coffee, Joe? It's fresh."

He eyed the pot and sniffed the air. "What do you have brewing?"

"Vanilla caramel pecan."

He did his best not to grimace. "Um, no. I'm going to pass. Thank you very much, ma'am."

Bitsy poured herself a mugful from the carafe, all the while shooting him inquisitive glances. "I heard you've got some Hollywood people coming out to your ranch next week to film a movie."

His eyes widened with surprise. "Hollywood? A movie? Where did you hear that?"

"Here and there."

Joe met her gaze. "I never told anyone they were coming."

"They did." Bitsy's blue eyes were unwavering. "Made reservations at the Paradise Bed and Breakfast and chatted with the clerk. She mentioned it to me."

"I see." He nodded. "Except your source got it wrong. It's not a movie. They're coming out to film ranch life and take a few pictures. In and out. No big deal."

"They don't need any extras?"

"Extra? Extra what?"

"You know. Like actors. Walk-on parts." She offered him a knowing smile. "I had high hopes of becoming an actress myself, once upon a time."

Joe ran a hand over his face. "Bitsy, I'm telling you, it's not a movie."

"If you say so, Joe." She glanced down at the lights on the desk phone. "He's done. Let me buzz him." She picked up the receiver. "Joe Gallagher here to see you, boss."

Moments later, Sam Lawson came out of his office and crossed his arms over his chest. "I thought we agreed you wouldn't call me 'boss' anymore."

Bitsy shrugged. "Coffee's fresh."

The sheriff's expression made no effort to conceal what he thought about the coffee. Joe nearly burst out laughing.

"No, thanks," Sam finally said. He looked to Joe. "Come on in."

The two men walked into his office. Sam shut the door and took a deep breath. "The woman would try a saint. No doubt she's listening at the door right now," he muttered.

"I figured as much."

Sam turned on the tower fan in the corner.

"You're warm?" Joe asked.

"White noise. She can't hear us when the fan is on."

"Ever thought about replacing her?"

"Only about three dozen times a day, for the last four years." His eyes narrowed. "But that's for cowards. I am no coward. My plan is to wait her out. She has to retire eventually." Sam sat down behind his desk and took a deep breath. "What can I do for you?"

"Rebecca Simpson is back in town," Joe said as he eased into the banged-up oak chair.

"The woman who was in all the newspapers? I heard she was found innocent."

Joe's head jerked up. "What are you talking about?"

"Rebecca Simpson. Isn't that who we're discussing? I've never met her, but I read about it in the *Denver Post*."

"Read about what?" Joe asked, becoming as agitated as he was confused.

"The accident."

"What accident?"

"Are you telling me you don't know?" Sam rubbed his chin. "Rebecca Simpson was arrested for vehicular manslaughter. She was driving in the rain when the vehicle skidded, ran off the road and overturned. Her husband Nick wasn't wearing a seat belt. The news said he was killed on impact."

The air whooshed from Joe's lungs and he froze, unable to speak for moments. Finally he cleared his throat. "That doesn't sound like vehicular manslaughter to me."

"Exactly what the jury decided. Her father-in-law, Judge Nicholas Brown, was the one who insisted she be charged."

He shook his head. "How did I miss this?"

"Two-and-a-half years ago, you were in Afghanistan. Then your dad died." He nodded toward Joe's prosthesis. "Your arm. I don't suppose reading the Denver paper was on your radar, although by then they were probably onto something else."

"Hard to believe my mother didn't mention anything."

"Maybe she thought you had enough on your plate."

Joe released a breath. "I guess."

"Did you know Nick Simpson?" Sam asked.

"No. Though it was hard to avoid the gossip when he and Becca eloped. His parents have a summer home near Four Forks. He went to boarding school out East. I hear he spent most of his summers doing whatever it is that rich kids do in the summer. Never saw him in Paradise."

"How'd she meet him?"

"College. Becca had a full ride to Colorado College. I went local. We ranch boys like to stay close to home, so we can smell the loam in our own backyard."

"Is that how it works? Didn't someone tell me you two used to be an item?"

"We were kids. Too long ago to even remember." Joe shifted in his seat. "So what do you think about the accident?"

"I don't know what to think, Joe. Why wasn't a smart guy like that wearing his seat belt was my first question."

Joe shook his head, thinking.

Sam shrugged. "Truth is, I can't tell you anything that wasn't in the news or on the television. I remember thinking at the time that the whole situation seemed sensationalized to sell more papers."

The only sound for moments was the hum of the fan as Joe considered the information Sam had shared, while trying to piece it all together.

"Funny how one moment can define the course of your entire life," Sam finally said.

"Tell me about it." Joe stood. "Thanks for your time."

"Sure. I can't say I've told you anything everyone else doesn't already know. You can probably read the newspaper account at the library." Sam stood as well and came around his desk.

Joe nodded.

"Any idea if she's here to stay?" Sam asked.

"To stay? No idea. She's doing the certification on my prosthesis. That's all I know."

"Is there a problem?"

"I thought there was. The real-estate agent refused to rent her a house."

"You think Judge Brown could be behind that?"

"I'm not sure."

"Do you want me to investigate?" Sam asked.

"No. But thanks, Sam. After what you told me, I'm sort of looking forward to figuring this one out myself."

Chapter Two

"Momma!" Casey Simpson raced across the lawn, her dark braids bouncing as she moved. When she got close, she launched herself into her mother's arms.

Rebecca buried her face in her daughter's neck, breathing in the sweet scent.

"I've missed you so much, Momma."

"I've missed you, too, baby."

"Grandma's in the house. I'll get her."

A moment later, the front screen creaked open, then closed with a bang, causing Rebecca to look up. Joan Anshaw stood on the front porch of the gray clapboard house. "I thought you'd never get here."

"I was starting to feel the same way. That old Honda is on its last legs."

Her mother pushed back a strand of her short dark bob, and took off her glasses to wipe the moisture from her eyes. "Oh, Mom, don't cry." Rebecca moved quickly to the porch, wrapping her mother in a warm embrace.

"I'm not crying."

"You're not?" Rebecca peered down into the face of

the woman who had been her rock for the last twenty-four months.

"No. Cowgirls don't cry. Remember? Your daddy always said that."

Ah, her father. Rebecca smiled at the memory. Her dad, Jackson Anshaw, had spent most of his life as foreman for Hollis Elliott Ranch Holdings.

"Daddy only said that so I'd stop whining about all the chores he gave me."

Joan laughed. "It worked, didn't it?" She sniffed before slipping her glasses back on.

"Yes, it did." She pressed a kiss to her mother's cheek. "We're in the homestretch now, Mom. Let's not forget that." She smiled. "I am so grateful for OrthoBorne Technology for giving me my job back and this opportunity. Just the fact that we don't live four hours from each other is a blessing."

"Does that mean you're here in Paradise to stay?"

"One step at a time. I have custody of my daughter again. I have a job, and I'm here until Joe Gallagher finishes certification." Rebecca smiled, savoring the thought of being in the same place as her mother and her daughter for a while.

"What then?" her mother asked.

"Then the company will decide if I can be promoted to full-time senior case manager. With that position, I can work from home. I'd touch base with the Denver offices once a week."

"Oh, Bec, that would be wonderful. Casey wouldn't have to change schools again."

"I know. There's a lot riding on this assignment, not to mention a fat bonus check."

Joan sank onto one of the rocking chairs on the

porch. She tucked her slim, denim-clad legs beneath her. "So what's the plan?"

Rebecca leaned back against the porch railing. "I start at Gallagher Ranch on Monday."

"Wonderful."

"Yes. And I'm still looking for a place for the summer."

"I thought you had a rental."

"That fell through."

"Fell through? That's odd. You don't think Nick's grandfather had something to do with it, do you?"

"Let's not go there." Rebecca shook her head. She refused to let Judge Brown put a cloud on all the good things that were happening. "I'll be making a few calls on Monday. Something will open up."

"You know you can stay with me," her mother said. "Casey will be here after school and during the day in the summer anyhow."

"I appreciate all you're doing, but it's really important for me to establish a home for myself and Casey." She pushed her hair back. "You've raised her the last two years while we've been waiting for the case to go to trial."

"I was glad to be able to help."

"And I'm grateful, but I don't want her to forget I'm her mother. Besides, you deserve a little time for yourself. You've given up everything for me, and the least I can do is give you your life back. It's time for you to just enjoy being a grandmother."

"Grandma?"

Rebecca and her mother turned to see Casey standing inside the house, her face pressed against the door screen looking out at them. "May I go next door to see if the twins can come out to play?"

Joan opened her mouth and then paused. She looked to Rebecca. "Honey, you need to ask your mother."

Casey looked back and forth between the two adults, her brows knit. "Momma?"

"Who are the twins?"

"My best friends. We go to school together."

"Well, then, sure. Go ahead," Rebecca said.

"Thank you, Momma." Casey pushed open the door and then raced down the stairs.

Rebecca turned to her mother. "Thank you."

"I suppose it is confusing for her. I hadn't considered that."

"It's all going to work out."

Her mother met her gaze. "Rebecca, do you really think this is finally behind you?"

She stepped forward and knelt next to her mother's chair, reaching out to wrap her hands around her mom's. "I have made a commitment to the Lord to stop looking at how far I have to go. I need focus on how far I've come instead."

Joan nodded slowly. "You're absolutely right."

"I want you to do the same. Promise me, Mom."

"I will, but you know it's hard. Casey is your baby, and you'll always be mine. I hurt when you hurt." She reached up to gently place her hands on either side of her daughter's face. "Even though you were far away in Denver, don't think I haven't read between the lines these past years. I always suspected there was a problem. I should have pushed harder, even when you denied anything was wrong."

Rebecca bit her lip, her eyes shuttering closed for a

brief moment, all the while rhythmically rubbing her right arm, as her mother continued. Yes, she could re-call the too many times that she visited her mother, all the while disguising the bruises and scars on her arm with long sleeves. Or answering a phone call while hold-ing back tears and pretending everything was perfectly fine when it wasn't.

"All I knew to do was to get down on my knees and pray," Joan continued.

"Oh, Mom." Rebecca's voice cracked, and she paused to swallow hard. "I thank God every single day that I have a mother like you."

Joe glanced at the clock. Nearly nine a.m. He'd fin-ished his Monday morning chores in record time before heading back to the house to shower and wait for Becca.

Reaching in his drawer for a clean white undershirt, his hand touched a box in the back of the bureau. Joe pulled it out. *The ring.* Twelve years ago he'd with-drawn everything out of savings to purchase the silver band with the solitaire diamond. His plan was to pro-pose after college graduation, in the spring, his favor-ite time of year. He'd be working full-time at the ranch again, and he'd hoped Becca would transfer to a col-lege close by.

Yeah, that was the idea.

Only Becca had married Nick Simpson.

He should have sold the ring right then and there. Bought a car maybe. Except he couldn't do it. Instead he kept it to remind himself that he didn't know a thing about women back then, and he sure hadn't learned anything since.

Shoving the box out of sight, Joe yanked an undershirt and a sweatshirt from the open drawer.

A glance in the mirror confirmed that he wore a permanent frown on his face, but there wasn't a thing he could do at the moment to change that. It wasn't just the weather souring his disposition. He'd hardly slept last night knowing that Becca would be back today. That meant that he'd have to show her his arm.

Why was he nervous? No big deal, right? After all, she worked for the prosthesis company. Seeing amputees and amputations was part of her job on a daily basis. Only this wasn't just another day in Paradise for him. His stomach churned at the thought of being fully exposed, figuratively, as well as literally. No one had seen his arm since the accident, except medical professionals. He'd made sure of that. Yeah, she was a medical professional, except this was different. It was Becca.

Would she be as repulsed as he was at the sight of his misshapen flesh? The residual limb was a shameful, daily reminder of his mistake and all he'd lost.

Joe groaned as he rubbed the taut muscles at the base of his neck. He needed coffee. Lots of coffee and he needed it now. Java might soothe the beast rumbling inside him. He headed to the kitchen where the coffeepot's spitting noises indicated the brew was nearly ready.

The doorbell rang. Without thinking, he reached for the glass carafe with his left hand. He fumbled, causing the hot, dark liquid to slosh over the lip of the container onto the counter. In seconds it became a moving stream that raced to the tile floor.

It took an effort to bite back angry words. Shoving the carafe back into place, Joe tossed a towel onto the dark puddle on the floor and headed out of the room, nearly tripping over his brother's black lab, Millie, on the way.

He swung open the front door. As his gaze met Becca's through the screen, the building irritation that stalked him diffused. She wore a crisp blue shirt with *OrthoBorne* stitched on the pocket, and dark slacks, with a rolling briefcase at her side. Her long hair had been pulled back into a ponytail. Dressed like a professional, and she was bright-eyed and chipper to boot.

"Hey, Becca."

"Joe."

"Find the place all right?" He folded his arms across his chest. The residual limb remained hidden in the folds of his long-sleeve shirt, just the way he liked.

Becca cleared her throat and nodded. "Yes. I did. Thank you."

Joe held open the door and nodded an invitation into the house. He was grateful the cleaning lady had been by on Friday. Everything still sparkled. High oak-beamed ceilings and polished oak floors made the interior appear huge. The décor had a Southwest theme, but the place was minimalist, like him.

"Beautiful room."

"Thanks," he muttered.

She turned her head and smiled. "Who do we have here?"

Joe followed her gaze. Dan's dog padded into the room. The animal looked at them with baleful eyes.

"This is Millie."

Millie whined, nudging Becca's leg until she reached down to rub her ears. "Oh, goodness, isn't she sweet?"

"She's neurotic."

"Excuse me?"

"Separation anxiety. She's been like this since Dan and my mother left. The dog is driving me crazy."

Becca tilted her head, and her ponytail swayed with the movement as she assessed Joe. "You do seem a little out of sorts. Do you want to reschedule?"

"No. Let's get this over with." He nodded toward the kitchen. "This way."

Becca grabbed her briefcase handle and followed him down a short hall to a spacious kitchen, the wheels clicking on the tile floor.

"Coffee?" he asked.

"No, thank you." She stopped, her gaze drawn to the mess on the floor. "What happened?"

"I got into a little argument with the coffeemaker."

"I hate when that happens."

Before he realized it, she had reached for a roll of paper towels on the counter. Joe insinuated himself between her and the spilled coffee.

"I don't need help."

"Sorry," she murmured.

Joe carefully mopped up the counter, then the floor before pouring coffee into his travel mug and sealing the lid. "Would it be okay to work at the kitchen table? I have the prosthesis charging there."

"Sure." Becca glanced at the table and then the room.

Joe glanced around, as well. He was proud of the place. The same oak beams overhead dominated the room and held an oak ceiling fan with rows of recessed lights. The kitchen itself was oak, with stainless-steel appliances and black granite countertops. The room lacked clutter, and that was exactly the way he liked things.

"You built this place?"

Joe shrugged. "Can't say I built anything. My job was to nod a lot. Somehow I ended up with this." He walked to the table and set down his mug. When he lifted his gaze, Becca was intently watching him. "What?"

"Nothing. I didn't expect…"

"Didn't expect a poor cowboy to have a place like this?"

"That's not what I meant, Joe." She took a deep breath, then opened her briefcase and placed a thick file on the table along with her tablet computer. "Do you mind if I take a look at your residual limb?"

"Have at it." Joe pulled off his sweatshirt and offered her his right upper extremity. He held his breath for moments, but she didn't flinch or grimace as he'd expected.

Becca's hands were soft and cool upon his skin as she examined first the biceps, then the triceps of the limb before moving to the slightly puckered, scarred incision line and the skin on either side of the amputation. She dappled her fingers along the entire surface, her gaze intent. Finally she looked up.

"Sensitivity?"

Joe shook his head in denial because he'd been just fine a minute ago. Until she touched him.

When she began to type notes in her tablet, Joe was unable to look away. He found himself assessing her concentrated effort as she worked. The ponytail shifted, exposing her neck and the curve of her face.

Becca raised her eyes, and her pupils widened as she caught him staring. With a flip of her fingers, she moved a wayward lock of hair behind her ear, then cleared her throat.

"Pain or phantom pain?"

"Nothing a couple ibuprofen won't fix."

"You've been doing your exercises and taking very good care of the area. The muscles are in excellent shape, and the skin tone and the incision line are very healthy. All in all, it looks beautiful."

"Beautiful?" The tension in him eased. "Is that a medical term?"

"Would you prefer, 'incision line healed, edges well approximated, clean and free of exudate, swelling or edema'?"

"Beautiful it is."

"Obviously you followed your surgeon's instructions to a T."

"I'm pretty good at following orders. The army will do that to you."

"The army? Right. I forgot about the army. Though, your upper body strength is indicative of more than following instructions."

"I have a small gym set up in one of the bedrooms. I can't afford any further setbacks."

"Any other learning-curve issues with the left hand?"

"Yeah. A few. Roping cows. Brushing my teeth. Shaving with a razor remains an interesting experience. I had a beard for a long time, just to keep me from bleeding all over the place."

"Too bad I didn't come out here sooner. I could have saved you a couple pints of blood." She smiled. "Anything else?"

"Still have the occasional clumsy episode, as you can see." He nodded toward the spilled coffee.

"We all have the occasional clumsy episode in the morning, Joe." She picked up the two pieces of his prosthesis he had ready on the table and inspected them. "Do you want to go ahead and don this?"

He massaged antiseptic lubricant into the area and examined the cosmetic silicone glove for damage. Then he disconnected the charger from his myoelectric prosthesis, snapped together the hand and forearm and applied the device to what remained of his right arm.

He held it up for her review. "There you go. Bionic man reporting for duty."

"Are you always this hard on yourself?" she murmured.

"I deserve to be hard on myself. I messed up. I should have asked for help, as everyone keeps reminding me. If I had, I wouldn't have this. I'd be normal. A normal rancher."

Her jaw sagged slightly as she stared at him. "I don't know what to say to that."

"What's there to say? I'm not the guy I used to be."

"That's not true, and believe me, normal is highly overrated."

"Becca, I'm sure most people appreciate platitudes, but I deal in reality and I'm sorry, but you don't know what you're talking about."

She stiffened. "Joe, your arm doesn't define you."

"Sure it does."

"You're wrong. You're a person who happens to be an amputee. That integral person inside is what people imprint in their minds when they define who you are." She stared past him. "No matter how hard something else tries to change a person's core, it generally doesn't change."

"What exactly is my core, Becca?"

When she met his gaze, she reached out to lay a hand on his arm.

Joe moved from her touch.

The rebuff only seemed to make her more determined to make her point, and she leaned closer.

"You're an intelligent, kind, godly man."

"Are you sure you're not confusing me with someone else? God and I haven't been buddies for some time, and I'm not as kind as you like to think." He shook his head. "Sometimes our mind blocks out the not-so-memorable things about people we haven't seen in a long time. We tend to remember people in a skewed positive light. I'm not that boy from high school."

"Trust me. I don't have that problem. I'm cynical enough to remember everything from the past." Becca chuckled softly. "I'm absolutely certain you haven't changed as much as you'd like to believe." She refused to give him eye contact; instead, she reached for her tablet, her fingers sliding across the keys on the screen once again.

"It's been over a year since your accident. You began prosthesis fittings and training six months ago. Why didn't you complete certification then?"

"It's taken me a while to actually commit to the whole prosthesis thing. After the accident and a couple of surgeries and rehab and all, I'd already been going back and forth to Denver so many times for preprosthetic therapy, and interim prosthetic therapy, that my head was spinning. I admit I didn't adhere to the usual patient guidelines."

"You aren't exactly the usual patient," she said.

"Bingo." He took a deep breath. "Dan ran the ranch and my mother helped. I needed to take that load from them as soon as possible."

"Is your mother still living in the main house?"

"Yeah. She and my niece just left for California.

They've gone to visit my sisters, then meet up with Dan and his wife."

"Dan's married?"

"Yeah. Sort of a newlywed, too. He postponed his honeymoon for me."

"That's a great brother." She paused, thinking. "Family is everything, isn't it?"

"Yeah. Sometimes it's the only thing that gets me through the day."

"And faith," she said softly, her eyes averted.

"Truthfully, I'm not sure what faith is anymore." Joe cleared his throat. "No disrespect. I know you've been through a lot, and if your faith is what helped you, then good for you."

"Good for me?" She offered a scoffing laugh. When she met his gaze, her eyes were hard and unflinching. "But we're not here to talk about me, are we?"

He nodded. "Understood."

"I need you to fill out this paperwork."

Joe groaned. "More paperwork? OrthoBorne is big on it, aren't they?" He glanced at the clock. "Could we save that for another session? I'm getting behind on my day."

"I promise this is the last of it."

He looked her in the eye. "You know what's been the most difficult part of this transition?"

"What's that?"

"Learning to write with my left hand. I'll do anything to get out of paper shuffling."

Becca paused. "We are in the field. I'm willing to compromise. We can skip that and go straight to shadowing. However, don't be surprised if I come up with some unique teaching sessions while I'm shadowing you."

"Deal." He looked at her. "What do you mean by shadowing?"

"That means that I show up tomorrow and follow you around for a couple of days, asking you the questions. I basically need to document the tasks that make up the majority of your workday so I can create a plan of care for your specific occupational therapy."

"I get up at four thirty, and I'm ready to start the day at five.

"Seriously?"

"Too early for you?"

"No. I meant you're okay with me following you around from dawn to dusk for a few days?"

"I'll do anything to avoid wasting my time—" he glanced with distaste at the paperwork "—checking little boxes and writing answers to inane questions. But five seems a little early for someone who isn't punching a clock."

"I understand my job, thank you. This is all about getting to know your world. So if you start your day at five, so do I, at least to start with."

"Fair enough. I'll meet you at the barn." He glanced at her outfit. "You do have boots, right?"

"Yes. Several pairs, in fact."

"Ranch boots. We're not talking city girl, fancy boots."

"Yes, ranch boots. You seem to forget that I worked on a ranch with my father practically my whole life."

"I didn't forget." He paused. "But people change."

"I'm still the same ranch girl I was twelve years ago."

"I guess we'll see," Joe murmured.

"I guess we will," Becca answered without missing a beat. She closed the cover on her tablet.

"What time does your crew arrive?"

"Nine thirty."

"They're late," he observed with a glance at the big stainless-steel clock on the wall.

"I don't want to keep you from your chores." She began to pack up her briefcase. "I'll wait outside for them."

"You're welcome to wait in the house."

"Oh, no. I'll wait outside."

"Your call." He reached for his keys, with his left hand, and fumbled. The keys clattered to the oak floor.

An awkward silence ensued as they both stared at the ground between them.

"I got 'em." Joe scooped up the keys with his other hand and shoved them in his pocket.

"Do you mind if I give you a little impromptu lesson?" Becca asked.

"Okay," he said slowly.

"You're using the myoelectric hand statically."

"Pardon me?"

"Static. Like a placeholder. I've observed your hand mostly in the relaxed position. You have quite a few positions available. Utilize them. The more you do, the more it will be automatic. Like the lateral pinch. You could have picked up the keys that way." She demonstrated, putting her own keys on the table. "See how much more accurate?"

He nodded. "I'll, ah, give it a try."

"I hope you will. Why not maximize the technology? After all, it's yours, and the photographer will want to see you taking advantage of their product."

Becca was right. He might not be paying for the prosthesis in cash, but he was paying for it by agreeing to

OrthoBorne's offer. And he had been pretty much ignoring the technology, thinking maybe if he did, maybe he could ignore the fact that he was an amputee.

All he'd really wanted was for life to go back to the way it was before the accident. It suddenly occurred to him that maybe his way wasn't working. Maybe the Lord had other plans despite the fact that he'd been ignoring Him, as well.

But was he ready for what was in store?

Chapter Three

Rebecca leaned against her Honda. She checked her watch and then focused her gaze on the main road. Late was an understatement. Joe had been gone two hours. Her stomach growled, and she wondered what the day's special was at Patti Jo's Café and Bakery in downtown Paradise.

Things with Joe had gone better than she expected. He wasn't nearly as surly this morning as he'd been on Saturday at their unexpected reunion. She pushed away the worrisome thoughts that hovered nearby. This was going to work out. It had to.

That was, if the team would show up. She pulled her cell from her pocket to call the OrthoBorne offices in Denver. When she looked up, a big white pickup truck, with rooftop bar lights and the logo of the Paradise Sheriff's Department, appeared on the road to the ranch, moving to the arched entrance. Behind it was a black SUV, kicking up a cloud of dust on the gravel road.

A police escort to the ranch?

She hurried to the drive and met the sheriff's vehicle as it pulled up.

The uniformed officer unfolded his tall form and stepped out and placed a tan Stetson on his head. "I'm Sam Lawson." He reached out to grasp her hand in a strong handshake. "You must be Rebecca Simpson." His eyes were warm with welcome.

"Yes. How did you know?"

"Joe mentioned you." He nodded toward the car pulling in behind his truck. "These folks say they're from OrthoBorne Technology in Denver. Sound right to you?"

"Yes. They're Joe's media team."

"I found them driving through town. After the third pass through, I decided to take pity on them. According to the driver, they were here an hour ago, at another gate, but couldn't find the road."

"Thanks for bringing them here, Sheriff."

"Better not thank me. This crew is greener than the grass, and I'm feeling guilty for delivering them to the ranch. In fact, maybe you could not mention to Joe that I brought them."

She laughed.

"Oh, sure, you're laughing now, but you won't be when you figure out that I'm right." He waved as he left.

A tall man in his midforties got out of the SUV. He shook his head and released a breath. "Gallagher Ranch, I hope."

"It is, and I'm Rebecca Simpson."

"Our liaison, right?"

"Yes. I'm also doing the certification."

"Great. I'm Rod, photographer and videographer." He stepped forward to offer a grin of relief, along with a brisk handshake.

She took his hand while returning the smile.

"Looks like we're all in the family. OrthoBorne family, that is. Sorry we're so late. The GPS on the rental went wacky once we hit the outskirts of town. We thought we were here once, but there was no road beyond the gate. For all I know, we were on another ranch somewhere around here."

"No worries," Rebecca said. "The good news is after the first time, you won't forget your way to the ranch. It's pretty easy. There's only one paved road in and out of Paradise. Take it until you come to the arched entrance." She pointed to the wrought-iron archway with the large entwined letters *G* and *R*.

"Easy. Yeah, that's what I said until the third or fourth time we passed Patti Jo's Café and Bakery, and I realized I was driving in circles." He turned to the vehicle, giving a wave for the other occupants to join him. "I brought Julian, our intern, and Abigail, one of our staff copywriters."

"Mr. Gallagher didn't mention three of you."

"Julian was a last-minute addition," Rod said. "He'll assist with shoots."

The front passenger door of the vehicle swung open, and a tall, thin, young man with long shaggy hair, a minuscule beard and wire-rim glasses rolled out. Earphones were propped on his head. When he glanced around, enthusiasm brightened his eyes. "Wow. This is great. I've never been west of the mountains."

The only female of the group came around the truck to assess the situation. With one hand, she shoved back her shoulder-length cascade of strawberry-blond hair and with the other she pushed an oversized black leather tote over her shoulder.

"I knew we were in Paradise the minute I laid eyes on

the good sheriff." The woman smiled and stepped forward, offering a handshake in greeting. Her nails were short and unpolished, no-nonsense like the woman herself, who was dressed in tan khakis and a taupe sweater. "Abigail Warren. Call me Abi."

"Rebecca Simpson."

"Yes," Abi said quietly. "I've read about you."

"Don't believe everything you read," Rebecca murmured in response.

"Never. I'm a writer. I recognize fiction when I see it."

When Abi winked, Rebecca knew she'd found an ally.

Overhead the sky rumbled. "Uh-oh." Julian tugged the earphones from his head to listen closely. "Thunder? That can't be good."

"Let's move over to the horse barn. It's the closest shelter." Rebecca pointed to the large red building. "The log cabin to your left is Mr. Gallagher's, and that two-story colonial on your right is the main house."

When the sky thundered again, the crew picked up their pace, following Rebecca. Along the way, their curious gazes took in the details of the Gallagher ranch, the barn, the fenced-in corral and the utility garage.

"Is that a windmill?" Abi asked, pointing to the teetering, metal structure standing out in the distance.

"It is."

"What do they use them for?" she asked.

"They used to be utilized to bring water from the aquifers to the cattle. Most ranches use pump irrigation now."

"When will we meet our client?" Rod asked.

"That depends on when he comes back from the pasture."

"Horses," Julian said when Rebecca pulled open one of the large barn doors. Wonderment laced his voice. He turned around to observe the stalls.

"That's probably why she called it a horse barn," Abi noted.

"This is Julian's first big on-location assignment," Rod said. "His life is usually spent working with computer software in the office. Generally his idea of nature is the Denver Zoo."

Julian shrugged. "I'd deny it, except it's absolutely true."

"Great, then you'll appreciate that we're going to tour the ranch first thing tomorrow."

"It's starting to rain." Julian observed the fat drops beginning to touch the ground.

"Rain doesn't stop life on the ranch," Rebecca said.

She scrutinized their clothing, from Abi's open-toe sandals to Julian's flip-flops and realized that it was actually a very good thing that Joe wasn't here.

"Let's talk about your schedule, and then I'll let you get back to town to check in at the Paradise Bed and Breakfast and do some shopping."

"Shopping?" Abi perked up.

"Yes." Rebecca smiled. "First, I'd like to take this opportunity to make a few safety recommendations." She stared pointedly at Julian. "Leave your earphones and earbuds in your suitcase. While you are working on the ranch, it's important to listen and be in tune with your surroundings. You'll want to hear the nuances of the land, including the weather. There are potential dangers, as well."

"Dangers?" Julian asked.

"Dangerous wildlife, or even a ranch animal in distress."

Rod nodded as the others focused on her words.

"You need boots. Cowboy boots, hiking boots or sturdy rubber boots with safety toes. Whatever you prefer. They'll protect your feet and ankles from things like horse hooves, cow patties, insects, or even snakebites. Besides boots, you'll want to dress in layers. It's cold in the morning, warm in the afternoon."

"I'd really like a cowboy hat," Abi said.

Rebecca chuckled. "You do need some sort of hat. A cowboy hat is perfect. Gloves, sunscreen. All a necessity. Our altitude is higher than Denver's. You can get burned faster here than in the city."

"Anything else?" Rod asked.

"Tomorrow we'll start by driving around the ranch, so bring your gear and water bottles. Keep in mind that there are no restrooms out in the pasture."

"Any place to charge a cell phone?" Julian asked as he held his phone aloft in various positions, searching for reception.

Rebecca blinked. "I imagine we'll be using a ranch truck, or utility vehicle, and usually ranch vehicles are of the ancient variety. It probably doesn't have an adapter." She paused. "I can't even guarantee one bar out here. Most days in the warm months, yes. But you never know. It all depends on Mother Nature and where you happen to be standing."

"You're on the wild prairie," Rod said with a chuckle.

"Your priority needs to be hydration. We're at nearly nine thousand feet above sea level, which beats the 5,280 of the Mile-High City. If you aren't sufficiently hydrated, you'll get headaches, feel faint and possibly pass out. You're Coloradans. You know the drill."

Julian took another swig from his water bottle.

"Try not to get between Mr. Gallagher and his chores. I can't emphasize that enough. This is a working ranch. One that he manages pretty much solo."

"We're going to want to follow Gallagher around for at least a full day," Rod said. "Then we can go back later to set up some specific shoots."

"I figured you'd want to shadow him."

"What time should we be out here?" Rod asked.

"Five a.m. is the time he gave me. Sunrise is at five thirty."

"In the morning?" Julian squeaked.

"The last time I was up at five in the morning I was pulling all-nighters in college," Abi murmured.

"Yeah, but think of the sunrise shots we can get. I imagine the sky is endless out here that time of day."

"Yes. You're right, Rod. Though tomorrow you get a break. I'll be shadowing Mr. Gallagher until eight a.m. I'll meet you in front of the barn at eight thirty, and we can do our tour of the ranch. Keep in mind that it's another twenty minutes from town to the ranch. You'll actually have to be up earlier to get here in time."

"I'm exhausted just thinking about our schedule," Julian said.

Rebecca chuckled. "Welcome to Paradise, folks."

Thunder cracked, and they all jumped, turning in time to see the darkened sky light up with a brilliant flash.

"This cannot be a good sign," Julian murmured.

"They have rain slickers at the tack shop in town," Rebecca offered.

Abi's eyes rounded and she looked past Rebecca, mesmerized. "Who's that?"

Rebecca turned around. From the west, a lone figure rode toward them. A black Stetson on his head, he sat tall and formidable in the saddle.

"That would be Joe Gallagher?" Abi asked.

"My model?" Rod asked with a wide grin on his face.

"It is," Rebecca said.

"And here I thought I was going to be photographing a grizzled old rancher."

"Well done, OrthoBorne," Abi said.

Two dogs appeared, not far behind, racing toward the corrals. As Joe got closer, he raised his left hand to tip the Stetson to the back of his head and narrowed his eyes to assess the strangers on his ranch.

"Uh-oh. Your model doesn't look happy," Abi murmured.

Joe reined in the horse a short distance away and dismounted easily from the saddle. Steely-eyed, he crossed his arms on his broad chest and faced them.

"We have a problem," he said to Rebecca. The words were a slow accusation delivered with a tone that brooked no argument.

"A problem?" She swallowed.

"The paddock and north gate were left open."

"Oops," Julian murmured.

Rod and Abi turned to glare at Julian.

"So it *was* your ranch," Abi said.

"We took a few cow pictures when we were lost," Rod said.

"Bull."

Rod jerked back, his eyes rounding. "Excuse me?"

"That's a bull, not a cow," Joe returned.

"Yes, sir," Rod said with a nod.

Joe narrowed his gaze and looked slowly from Julian, to Rod and then Abi. "You know the first rule of the ranch?"

"Do no harm?" Julian asked.

"That's doctors," Rod said drily.

"Leave everything the way you find it." Joe moved into the barn with his horse.

"Seriously?" Julian said. "I would have never guessed that in a million years."

"Pay attention, Julian. I suspect Mr. Gallagher is trying to tell us something," Rod muttered.

Rebecca raised a hand, indicating for the crew to stay put as she followed Joe into the barn. "Your bull is loose?"

"*Was.* Rowdy crossed the road and knocked down my neighbor's garden fence and trampled his wife's tomato plants. It would have been worse except he's old, and all that exercise wore him out."

"What are you going to do?"

"Already done. Gil and Wishbone helped me herd him back, which put me an hour behind on my chores, not including the fence I still need to repair." He ran a hand over his face. "I'll need to go into town for tomato plants. Oh, and I'll need to add those fancy frost guards to my list. Good old Rowdy smashed those, as well." He let out a weary breath.

"Joe, I'm sorry. I'll have the crew go into town for the plants if that will help."

"This is my ranch. I'll handle it." He met her gaze. "I can tell you what will help. Getting them in and out fast. The longer they're on Gallagher Ranch, the greater the chances are I'm going to lose my temper."

"Yes. Yes. Of course. I'll monitor them more closely and we'll get this done quickly."

"The clock starts ticking now, Becca."

Rebecca offered a solemn nod. He was absolutely right, and she was completely certain that she was going to need some serious prayer time in order to pull off this assignment.

"I'll be back in the morning."

"What?" At the sound of Becca's voice, Joe turned from brushing his horse and stared at her. She stood in the doorway of the barn, hesitation on her face.

"To shadow you." She rubbed her right arm for a moment, then stopped, as if realizing what she was doing, and slipped her hands into the pockets of her jeans.

Joe put the curry comb on the shelf. He glanced at his watch, a decision already made in his mind. "Come on, then. I only have a few minutes."

"A few minutes?"

"Lunch and a trip into town are next on my list."

Becca followed him as he left the barn. Overhead the sky continued to spit, and dark clouds rumbled. He moved to the gravel drive.

"I don't follow. A few minutes for what?"

"The truck." Joe nodded toward the used-to-be-black, muddy farm truck. He unlocked and opened the passenger door for her before getting in on his side.

"Yes. But where are we going?"

He didn't answer but continued down a well-worn dirt road to the south, right behind the barn. Less than two minutes later, he pulled up in front of a small cottage with a simple rail porch. Large weathered terra-cotta pots had been placed along the brick walkway that led to the porch steps. They were ready for planting.

"What's this?" Becca asked.

Joe played with the leather cover on the steering wheel, avoiding her eyes. "It'll be easier to monitor what's going on if you stay at the ranch."

"What?" She looked from the house and back to him.

He gave a nod of affirmation.

"Oh, no, I could never impose." The words came quickly as she shook her head.

He focused straight ahead at the mud-spattered windshield, now blurred with drops of rain. "You wouldn't be imposing. No one is using this place. It's been empty since last September."

"Whose house is it?"

"Dan lived here with his daughter before he got married. The place is furnished, too."

"But—"

"This is strictly a business agreement. I need to complete certification, and having you close by will ensure that will happen as quickly as you've promised. Especially since you have to babysit greenhorns, who seem to have a knack for stepping in cow patties everywhere they go."

She paused, considering his words. "What about Casey?"

"Who's Casey?"

"My daughter."

Joe's jaw sagged. "You have a daughter?"

"I do. She's six."

"Yeah. Of course your daughter is welcome."

Becca stared at him for moments, confusion on her face. Then her eyes widened. "Is this about the rental deal falling through?" She released a small gasp. "You overheard the entire conversation, didn't you?"

"I heard enough. Doesn't change the facts."

She turned away. "Of course it does."

"Why? I told you, this is business."

When she didn't say anything, he muttered a short expression under his breath. *Stubborn.* He'd forgotten how stubborn the woman could be when her back was against the wall.

"Becca, don't let your pride stand in the way."

"It's not my pride. I'm used to that being shredded." She met his gaze for a moment, then shifted her attention out the window. "I...don't think you understand what's going on here, Joe."

"Going on? What do you mean?"

"Letting me stay on your ranch may put you right in the center of the bull's-eye." She gestured with her hands.

"You aren't making any sense."

"Why do you think I didn't get that rental house?" Rebecca asked.

"I have a few ideas."

"So do I. Nick's grandfather. I'm sure of it. Judge Nicholas Brown used his considerable influence to sway the courts to bring what was simply a horrible car accident to a jury trial."

Joe opened his mouth and closed it again, his lips forming a thin line.

"My bail was set so high that my mother was left scrambling to raise the money. I sat in jail for two weeks. *Two weeks.* Do you know what it's like to be in jail, Joe?" She swallowed. "Do you have any idea?"

Hands tightening on the steering wheel, Joe's head jerked back as though he'd been hit.

She took a steadying breath. "When Hollis Elliott heard about it, he put up the bond money."

"I don't get it. You were found innocent."

"Judge Brown continues to punish me for Nick's death."

"Why, if it was an accident?"

"Not in his mind." She twisted her hands in her lap. "I think he's aiming for custody of my daughter."

"He has no grounds for that."

"Rich people live in a different world than you and me. He's a prominent citizen in the valley. He owns a lot of property in Four Forks. He'll claim he can better provide for Casey." She released a breath. "The truth is that he can."

"You're her mother. You're employed, and now you have a place to call home."

Rebecca shook her head as she gazed with longing at the little house. "You don't know the judge," she murmured. Her hands trembled as she met his gaze yet again. "If I stay here, he might very well retaliate against you. Against Gallagher Ranch, as well. You need to know that up front."

"I'm not concerned about Judge Brown."

"You also need to know that I'm not looking for someone to rescue me. The Lord and I have been working together for some time now."

He shook his head. "Not applying for the job. This offer is all about me. I've given a crew of city slickers carte blanche to roam my ranch. All I'm trying to do is protect my interests. I can't do that without your help. Living closer makes sense."

"Just so we know where we stand."

He held out the keys to the little cottage with his left hand. "I know where I stand. Do you?"

She nodded, then slowly, ever so slowly, reached up and took the keys, her fingers brushing his.

Joe let out the breath he didn't realize he'd been holding.

Chapter Four

Rebecca turned when she heard the front door of Joe's two-story log-cabin house open behind her.

It was the man himself. Joe placed his black Stetson on his head and slid his arms into the sleeves of a fleece-lined denim jacket as he stepped outside.

The dark angles of his face were illuminated by the porch light, creating a fierce image of the indomitable rancher. He yawned and rubbed a hand over the stubble on his face before raising his head. Joe's eyes rounded when he saw her. "What are you doing out here?"

She ignored the harsh note of surprise in his voice. "I'm here to do a job."

"Why didn't you knock on the door? How long have you been waiting?"

Rebecca shrugged. "There was no need to bother you. I've only been here a few minutes."

"When are you moving into the cottage?"

"Friday. After Casey's school lets out for the summer break."

"What will your daughter do while you're working?" Joe asked.

"My mother will keep her during the week and I will have Casey here on the weekends. That will be less disruptive while the crew is filming or photographing you."

"You're sure that's going to work?"

"Yes. This is far better than when I lived in Denver and she lived here with my mother all of the time."

He shook his head and frowned as though he waged a mental battle.

"Everything okay?" she asked.

"Yeah. Perfect." He strode to the end of the cobblestone walk and paused to take a deep breath. "Smell that?" he asked.

"What?"

"That heavy, dank odor in the air. The smell of cow manure and pond water are magnified when a low pressure system moves in." He took another deep breath. "Oh, yeah, that's some strong manure on the wind. It won't be just dry lightning like last night, either. No, we have a real storm front on its way."

"I guess I've been gone too long. Nothing smells different to me."

"Give it a few more weeks. We'll have your smeller sensitized in no time."

"Sensitize my smeller?" Rebecca smiled at the terminology.

She pulled a pair of worn, soft leather gloves from her back pocket. When she looked up, he was watching her.

"Those look like expensive gloves. Do you want a pair of old ranch gloves?"

"I'm good."

"And you're going to be warm enough in that vest?"

Rebecca assessed her black, down-filled vest. "You bet. I've got several layers on beneath this."

"Hat?"

"I've got a ball cap in my pocket," she said.

"You need a proper Western hat to protect you from the elements."

"This isn't my first rodeo. I'll be fine."

"Your call," Joe replied.

He turned away and she followed, stretching her stride to keep up with his long legs as he headed past the circular gravel drive, across the yard toward the horse barn.

The morning was silent. The only sound was the sizzle of a halogen light overhead as it came to life, casting a pink glow on the yard. Rebecca glanced up and stared at the endless black carpet of night sky, illuminated only by the scattering blanket of glittering stars.

"Everything okay?" Joe called out.

"Yes, yes. Sorry." Rebecca doubled her pace in his direction. "I forgot what it was like."

He shot her a questioning glance. "New moon, you mean?"

"That, too. But I'd forgotten how amazing a ranch is before dawn."

"I don't even notice anymore. This is all I've ever known. It's a real life, that's for sure. You make me realize how much I take it for granted."

Memories of following her father around Elliott Ranch swirled through Rebecca's mind. She missed her father with a deep ache, but she never thought she'd miss ranch life once she left.

Then again, she'd been wrong about so many things. *Like Nick.* Why should she be surprised?

Joe slid open the barn door and whistled. Two dogs raced to his side. "Meet Gil and Wishbone."

She laughed, offering a bow at the waist. "Gentlemen. Pleased to meet you."

From a corner of the barn a squawking radio sound cut through the silence. Startled, Rebecca jumped. She looked around. "Dispatch radio. I'd forgotten about them."

"Technology moves on, but some things don't change in Paradise. It's still the best backup communication in the agricultural community. Cell phones can't be relied on, and phone lines are iffy with a heavy snow or rainfall."

He strode to a row of stalls.

"Normally I take the truck around the ranch in the morning. That won't be nearly as much fun for you, I imagine."

"I don't want you to deter from your regular schedule."

"The horses could use a good workout, and you'd be doing me a favor. How about if you ride my sister-in-law's horse? She's spirited but not headstrong."

"Your sister-in-law?"

He coughed, biting back a laugh. "The horse."

"Ah." Rebecca offered a short nod while maintaining a poker face. "Whatever you think. You're the boss."

"Need any help with your tack?"

"I'm pretty sure I can handle tacking up my horse. I started doing it when I was five."

"How long since you've ridden?"

"Twelve years," she murmured.

"You'll be sore tomorrow." Joe shook his head. "Tack room is over here."

She glanced around as they entered the small area. Saddles, felt pads and ropes hung neatly on the walls. "This is very nice." She inhaled deeply, attempting to identify the smells. "Leather, castile soap and neatsfoot oil," she said aloud.

"You forgot sweat."

"Yes. That, as well."

Joe handed her a comb and brush and led her to a far stall, where he opened the door and gently nudged a chestnut mare out into the main area of the barn. "This is Princess."

The horse snorted at the interruption.

"Oh, isn't she a beauty?"

"Sure is, and Beth will appreciate you exercising her mare."

Joe opened another stall and offered the horse inside his palm to sniff, before gently running his hand along the animal's flank and then rubbing him between the ears. "This is Blackie."

"Hi, Blackie."

They worked quietly, cleaning their horses for minutes. When Rebecca looked up, Joe was leaning over the stall rail observing her.

"Why are you smiling?" he asked.

She looked up from where she was bent over Princess's front hoof. "A simple thing like picking hooves. I haven't done it in years, and yet it feels right." Rebecca shook her head. "How did I leave this behind?"

"You tell me." The words were as hard as his expression.

"I don't know," she murmured. Yet she did know. She had stopped listening to her heart and the whispered words from the Lord when she met Nick Simpson. His money and charm had turned her head. He'd offered her a life she thought she'd always wanted. Shame and regret filled Rebecca, and she concentrated on the task once again before finally dusting off her hands.

"All done?" Joe asked minutes later.

"I am, and if you don't mind, since we have the opportunity, I'd like to see how you get that saddle in position with your prosthesis."

"No big deal, now that I've worked on my upper body strength. Though in truth, it was difficult when I first got home without any prosthesis. I sure wasn't going to wait around for the incision to heal before I rode again."

Of course not. She held back the words. Joe Gallagher hadn't changed that much. He was still stubborn and determined to do things his way.

"Actually I wasn't sure if I would ever ride without assistance, until Dan came up with the idea for a ramp. It has wheels that lock into place with the toes of my boots. It did the job until both my horse and I adjusted to my new situation. Now—" he raised a shoulder in gesture "—I don't need it. It's pretty much business as usual."

He grabbed a saddle pad and carefully placed it on the horse before adding the saddle, positioning them both and tightening the cinch and turning to Becca again.

"Piece of cake," he said.

She followed suit and dropped Princess's stirrups into position. "Now let's see you get yourself in the saddle."

"It's not pretty, but it works."

Joe firmly adjusted the Stetson on his head before he moved to stand on the left side of Blackie. He snugged up on the reins and grabbed the mane with his left hand. Once his left foot was in the stirrup, using his prosthesis, he reached for the saddle horn and then smoothly swung his leg over the horse. The movement was fluid and fast.

"Seriously? You get on your horse slicker than someone with two hands. Best utilization of your prosthesis I've seen yet."

He offered a nod of acknowledgment at the compliment.

"Now what?" Rebecca grabbed Princess's reins and walked the mare outside, right behind him.

Around them the sun had kissed the landscape in a rosy light, illuminating the ranch.

"Look at that." She knew her voice was laced with the awe of a girl who'd lived too long in the city. "'Red sky at morning. Sailors take warning.' Right?"

"That's right," Joe said. "That's not an old wives' tale, either. Red sky at morning is indicative of low stratus clouds, and dust close to the Earth's atmosphere. Another sign a storm is coming."

"I meant that it was beautiful."

He shrugged. "Yeah, that, too."

Rebecca looked out at the land, her gaze moving straight west. "What's the plan? I have two and a half hours before the crew arrives."

"That reminds me." Joe pulled a key from his pocket. He inched his horse close to hers. "Spare key to the farm truck. So you can show them around."

"Thanks."

"I trust you'll read them the ten commandments of ranch life while you're at it?"

"If you mean no repeats of yesterday? Then yes. Absolutely. Along with a couple of rounds of sage cowboy wisdom."

"Cowboy wisdom?" Joe asked.

"Oh, you know. The usual. Look before you step. Don't stand behind a coughing cow."

"That wasn't quite what I meant, but they probably need to hear that, as well."

"Where will you be? I mean in case we need you."

"I've got at least a couple hours of spring pasture maintenance ahead of me before I move the cattle."

"Clearing out the rocks and sticks." She made a face.

"Exactly. Then I'm going into town yet again. I reviewed my contract for this publicity thing last night. They expect me to get a haircut. I don't know how I missed that detail. I could have done it yesterday." He removed his hat and ran a hand over shaggy black hair that skimmed his collar. "Ridiculous. Nothing wrong with my hair."

A smile escaped, as she recalled the time in high school when he'd trusted her to give him a trim. She'd been so tongue-tied and red-faced once she'd run her fingers through his thick hair that she'd given up on the task.

Joe glanced at her and his eyes widened. Was he remembering, as well?

"We better get going," he said gruffly. "We're going to ride the entire fence line before your people show up." He picked up his reins and clicked his tongue. Blackie began to trot forward through the yard.

When he released a long, low whistle for the dogs, Gil and Wishbone came running. "Now I'll get to see if you can still ride," he said, as he adjusted his Stetson. "I'll meet you at the fence."

"Which fence?" Rebecca called after him as she mounted Princess and looked around. "Gallagher Ranch is surrounded by fences."

"We'll start at the one that separates Gallagher Ranch from Elliott Ranch, to the southeast. I know you're familiar with that border. It's the easiest to check because Hollis Elliott has the money to keep up his fences."

"Slow down," she called out. "You started before me."

He turned in the saddle and narrowed his eyes. "Are you telling me you want the handicapped guy to give you a handicap? Doesn't sound like an experienced cowgirl to me."

She blinked, outrage simmering just below the surface. "Careful what you say, Mr. Gallagher. You may have to eat those words."

"I've eaten worse. And this meal is guaranteed to be tasty." Joe Gallagher's deep laughter filled the morning air.

Rebecca froze at the sound. His spontaneous laughter had lit up a dark room inside her. She hadn't realized before this very moment that the lights had been off.

Joe pulled the collar up on his fleece-lined jacket and adjusted his Stetson as the chilled air hit his neck. He turned his head and took in the silhouette of the Sangre de Cristo Mountains, then spared a quick glance over his shoulder.

"I'm still here," Becca called out.

He held back a chuckle and waited for her to catch up. Who would have thought he'd be riding his ranch with Becca? Now wasn't the time to analyze the confusion he felt around her. For the moment, he was simply going to appreciate that it was spring and he was alive.

Yeah, being alive was good. There was a time in Afghanistan when he wondered if he'd ever be back in the saddle. After he'd dropped the tractor on his arm, he wasn't sure if he ever wanted to be. Life as a one-armed rancher was more challenging than he cared to admit. He'd like to be able to say he'd moved on. But that wouldn't happen until the prosthesis was paid for and he proved he could run his own ranch by himself again. And that meant Becca would be gone.

He wasn't ready to consider why that should give him pause. After all, leaving was probably the only thing he could count on for certain with Becca.

A breeze brushed against his face, teasing him with the scent of spring wildflowers. This was his favorite time of year. The time when the valley woke from winter's slumber and all sorts of surprises peeked out from the soil. The hundreds of spring and late-spring bulbs his mother had planted around the ranch, when she thought he wasn't looking, were blooming. The scent of daffodil, freesia, iris and anemone rode the morning air.

Joe led Blackie along the perimeter of the ranch, keeping to the fence line until they reached the pasture where the cattle currently grazed.

"How many head?" Becca asked.

"About two hundred."

Joe slid from his horse to the ground. He tied the reins to a tree with a slipknot and headed to the water troughs. The dogs dutifully followed him.

"Do you want help?" she asked.

"Nah. They're set to autofill. I'm just checking

for contamination." Finding everything in order he mounted Blackie again.

Sunrise continued a steady appearance behind them, as they headed the horses toward the hay fields. Riding slowly near the crop, he began to check the stalks.

"How do you know when it's ready to harvest?" Becca asked.

"Didn't your daddy teach you about hay?"

"No. My father was a cowboy, not a farmer."

"We run a small operation. You have to be both around here." He nodded toward the crop. "Timing is everything. It's as much a fine art as it is a science. We want the young, tender stalks."

"Looks to me like it's about ready, isn't it?"

"Yeah. Almost. This will be the first cutting of the year. That means the highest quality alfalfa hay. The question is, will the hay mature and Mother Nature cooperate at the same time?"

"The hay will make or break your operation?"

"Probably not. We're fortunate to have water rights on the property that bring in a little extra income, though not everyone in Paradise is happy about that situation. But with the high cost of hay, cutting and baling our own is one less expense. Sometimes we even have enough to sell. That would be a very good year."

"So it's all a gamble," she observed.

"You said it. Basically the only thing I can control is the machines. So I'm getting the windrower, rake and bale wagon ready to go."

"What will happen if it rains?" Becca asked.

"If the weather doesn't hold, we'll have to do it sooner than planned, and OrthoBorne will have to wait its turn. All we need is a couple of sunshine days strung together to get the job done."

"Does 'we' mean you?"

"Usually Dan is here. Even then, sometimes we bring in a contractor with his own machine to assist, or an extra ranch hand. It will all depend on the budget. When the weather is fickle, I'm likely to let anyone help."

Sliding off Blackie, he tossed the reins over the saddle and pointed to a four-wire fence. "Need to fix this barbed wire, as it's a little loose. Then we're done."

"I can do that. I've fixed many a fence in my day."

Joe nearly laughed aloud. "In your day, huh? How old are you?"

"Thirty-one." She frowned as she dismounted. "Are you making fun of me?"

"Not at all." He offered her the fence pliers. "I'll let you take care of this, then. I'm going to have a look at that downed tree over there. Probably come back later with the truck and chain saw."

Joe led his horse to the creek, where indeed a tall cottonwood had been struck by lightning. Its twisted trunk was split and lay between the grass and the creek. The dogs followed, running through the long grass that grew near the water, chasing each other.

"Come on, boys. Let's go see if that old cowgirl is done."

Becca was in the saddle and waiting for him as they moved down the fence line. Joe inspected the barbed wire with exaggerated care. "Nicely done," he finally pronounced.

"Thank you." She handed him the pliers.

"Let's get you back before your city slickers show up and get into trouble again."

"I can go back alone," she said.

"No. We ride in pairs around here."

"You're the only one here most of the time."

"Except for me. I'm the boss."

"Overall, how did I do?" Becca asked once they returned to the barn.

"You did two hours of good riding. I imagine that answer will be obvious tomorrow after your city muscles start complaining."

"Faint praise?"

"Not at all. You did fine."

"Fine?" She uttered a noise of displeasure, and as if to agree, Princess snorted. Joe hid his smile. Becca had done more than fine, keeping up with him as he moved along the perimeter of the ranch making note of work that would need to be done later. A tedious chore, but necessary.

"Fine is a good thing. I noticed you didn't mention how I did. You were, after all, observing my daily activities."

"As a horseman, you're far exceeding my expectations. As a rancher, well, that remains to be seen. You still favor your left hand."

"Fair enough," Joe replied. "So I guess I did fine, as well."

Becca shook her head, but said nothing more.

Silence stretched as he rubbed down his horse.

He closed the stall behind Blackie and turned in time to see Becca pull off her gloves and wince.

"You all right?"

"Yes." She tucked the palm of her left hand under her arm. "I cut my hand on the fence wire. It was fine until

I yanked my glove off and it started bleeding again. No big deal."

"Those fancy gloves. Why didn't you say something?" he muttered.

"No big deal," she insisted.

"Let me see your hand."

"I'm fine, Joe."

"I need to see your hand." He sucked in a breath when she offered the palm for his inspection. Jaw clamped tight, all he could do was stare at the ragged cut, oozing blood, that marred her smooth skin. His gaze went from her hand to her face as irritation began to build.

"The glove has a cotton liner that clotted the cut. I didn't realize—"

"Your tetanus shot up-to-date?" he fairly snapped.

"Yes."

"First-aid kit is over here." Joe moved to the other side of the barn where he'd built counters for working on paperwork. He pulled open a cabinet and yanked out the large first-aid kit.

"That's some kit," she murmured.

"My brother is a pharmacist and my sister-in-law is a doctor. They keep it well stocked." He tucked a bottle of sterile water under his arm and opened it with his left hand. "Here, slosh this over the cut. Use the whole bottle."

While she complied, he tore open sterile gauze packs with his teeth.

"You can use your prosthetic fingers to hold the gauze squares while you tear the package open."

Joe slowly lifted his head to meet her gaze. "Seriously? You're going to give me a lesson...*now*?"

"I said we'd being doing teaching in the field. The more you make yourself use the prosthesis, the more second nature it will become. If you keep accommodating and ignoring the device, then your myoelectric prosthesis is really just an expensive toy."

He took a deep breath. "Duly noted."

She nodded and took the gauze from him.

"Let me get the antibiotic ointment," Joe said. He pulled the tube from the kit and looked from her to the cap. Determined to use his right hand, he focused on utilizing his muscles to generate the movement that allowed him to grasp the tube. Then, using his left hand, he removed the lid.

"Nicely done," Becca murmured with her eyes on the tube and his prosthesis. She took the tube from him and applied a blob of clear ointment to her laceration line before topping it with the gauze. "Tape?" she asked.

"I've got wrapping gauze. That'll work better with your glove."

Joe held the small roll of gauze with his prosthetic hand and tore off the paper before handing it to her.

"Um, you'll have to hold it in place while I wrap," Becca said. Her lips curved in a small smile at the irony of the situation.

Yeah. He got it. *They both were handicapped now.*

Stepping closer, Joe held the end of the gauze against her skin. He averted his gaze, refusing to consider how soft her skin was or how long it had been they'd been this close. A lifetime ago, and the memories were as vivid today as then.

His gaze traveled from her jaunty ponytail sticking out of the back of the ball cap to the curve of her jaw as she concentrated.

Becca wrapped the roll around her palm several times, tucking the ends under. When she finished, she raised her head and their eyes met. She froze and licked her lips. "I… I…"

"All set?" Joe asked, stepping back into his safety zone.

"Yes. Thank you."

He could only grunt a response.

"Joe?" Becca said his name softly. Barely a whisper as it slid over him.

He raised his brows in question.

"I'm so sorry." Her eyes were sincere as she pleaded with him.

Sorry? She was twelve years too late for sorry. He turned and headed out of the barn, cautioning himself. He had vowed not to make the same mistake again. If he did, he'd be twice the fool.

Chapter Five

Rebecca poured coffee into a to-go cup and rummaged around in the darkened kitchen for a lid. When the lights suddenly came on, she was blinded and nearly stumbled over a chair.

"Mom? I sure hope that's you."

She heard a familiar chuckle and turned to see her mother tighten the belt on her old, blue chenille robe.

"Yes. Of course it's me. Sorry. Did I startle you?"

"That you did. It's four in the morning. What are you doing up?"

"I've hardly seen you this week. Goodness, you've put in long hours at the Gallagher Ranch."

"Oh, Mom. I'm sorry. You shouldn't have to get up at four to see your daughter. Things will slow down soon."

"All the same, this is what mothers do when they're looking for an opportunity to say they're extremely proud of their children."

"Aw, thank you." Rebecca popped two slices of oat nut bread into the toaster. "But here I proclaim my independence and then turn around only to ask you more favors. I appreciate you helping with Casey during the week."

"She's my granddaughter. I'm happy to. We'll manage around Casey's summer vacation." Joan opened the cupboard and grabbed a large container of peanut butter. She slid the jar across the laminate countertop to Rebecca.

"I only wish I could tell you what time I'll be home today."

"No worries. This brings back memories of you and your father putting in sixteen-hour days on Elliott Ranch."

"Yes. You are so right." Rebecca grinned. "Those are wonderful memories, too. I loved working with Dad."

"Did you ever think you'd be on a ranch again?"

"No. I thought my ranch days were long gone once we lost Dad."

Joan shook her head. "Well, just like the good old days, you have to go out even in lousy weather. Take my rain slicker, will you? It's pouring out there."

"Thanks, Mom." Rebecca pulled a butter knife from the drawer.

"When are you moving into the cottage?"

"Casey's last day of school is today, so maybe tonight. Maybe tomorrow. Are you sure you're okay with watching Casey while I'm working?"

"I'm happy to. It means less disruption in her life. We'll all work around your crazy schedule."

"Thank you." Rebecca smiled, her gaze fixed on the glowing grates of the toaster. Her chest ached with joy, just thinking about the little house. "I keep pinching myself because it's so perfect. Two bedrooms. A small, but modern kitchen with all the amenities. The house is furnished, too. Did I mention that?"

"No. That's wonderful."

The browned bread popped up, and she plucked the slices from the toaster. "Oh, and there are clay pots outside that are begging for summer flowers."

"Casey is going to love helping you plant."

"That's exactly what I thought." Rebecca unscrewed the lid of the peanut butter jar. "I know it's only for a short time, but living a normal life again is all I ever dreamed about when the trial was going on."

"Oh, Becca." Her mother closed the distance between them, wrapping her in a hug. Releasing Rebecca, she hesitated for a moment before taking a deep breath. "Honey, there was something else I wanted to discuss with you before you leave."

Rebecca stiffened, sensing the uneasy tone in her mother's voice. "Is everything okay?"

She nodded. "I, um, I got an email from Casey's other grandmother."

"Virginia emailed you?"

"Apparently the family is back in Four Forks for the summer. Nick's sister is graduating from college. On Sunday. They want Casey to attend a party. Though it is short notice."

"Jana graduating. Oh my. It seems like just yesterday that she was the youngest bridesmaid at my wedding."

"Yes. Time does race by, doesn't it?" her mother mused.

Rebecca nodded. "You were worried about telling me about this?"

"Not worried. I've tried to banish that word from my vocabulary and turn things over to God. Yet try as

I might, I can't help but be concerned. You know Judge Brown will be there."

"The judge and I may have our issues, but Casey should still have the advantage of growing up with her extended family."

"You aren't concerned about the judge?"

"Of course I am, but I'm still going to try to do the right thing. I'm believing Virginia has my back this time, as well."

"Then why didn't she do something when you were arrested? All those ridiculous accusations that she knew weren't true."

"Mom, I've told you before. Virginia Simpson isn't like you or me. She's been taken care of all her life. That doesn't make her a bad person." She sighed and shook her head. "Besides, it wasn't her job to defend me against her father. In the end it was God's job."

"You're a much nicer person than I am, Rebecca."

"Don't give me too much credit."

"You're going to let Casey attend?"

"If that's what she wants."

"I could drop her off, if that will help you. I have plans, and it's right on my way. Virginia did mention she'd be happy to bring Casey home."

"That's probably the best arrangement. Thank you for offering, Mom."

"Thank you for reminding me to be more charitable."

Rebecca glanced at the wall clock. "Uh-oh, I have to shower and get dressed."

"You didn't eat your toast."

Rebecca reached for a small plate. "I'll eat while I'm getting ready."

"Some things never change."

"You're remembering high school, right? Always on the run."

"Exactly." Her mother paused for a moment. "Rebecca?"

"Mmm."

"Isn't it awkward working with Joe Gallagher?"

"Challenging. That's what it is."

"Do you ever wonder...?"

Rebecca's head jerked up in time to meet her mother's wistful gaze. "No. Let's not go there."

"Does that mean you *do* wonder?" her mother murmured with a small smile.

"Mom, to tell you the truth, I can't allow myself to think about anything. I've made wrong choices in my life. I don't know if I trust my judgment anymore."

"Don't blame yourself because you believed in the good in people."

"I do blame myself." She took a deep breath. "I'm grateful the Lord kept his hand on Casey the entire time."

"We're only human, Rebecca. Sometimes all you can do is ask for forgiveness before moving on."

"I'm grateful He forgives."

"That doesn't mean you should shut yourself off from the possibility of finding happiness."

"I'm not. I'm just not looking for anything beyond what the Lord has given me today. One step at a time is about all I can handle."

"Rain." Joe grimaced and stared out the kitchen window at the gray world outside. Fat drops plopped onto the gravel drive and the yard, creating muddy puddles. Overhead, thunder cracked, promising continued rain.

Another dismal and bleak day, guaranteed to leave him soaking wet and chilled to the core.

He lifted a mug to his lips. Even the aroma of strong, rich coffee and Patti Jo's muffins waiting on a platter couldn't lift his sour mood.

Truth be told, he'd like to have words with that smiley-faced meteorologist on television. The man was obviously not familiar with ranches. If he were, he'd use caution before sharing his weather promises for Paradise and the valley.

Scattered rain showers? Twenty-four hours of solid rain, hammering down, was what he should have announced.

Joe shook his head. Nothing to be done about the situation. Becca's smile was pretty much the only thing positive about the last few days, though he sure wasn't going to tell her that.

She'd been upbeat despite the weather, taking the crew to town yesterday for a tour of the historic landmarks in downtown Paradise, which took all of fifteen minutes. They'd stopped for lunch, and Becca brought him back a box of his favorite muffins from Patti Jo's. A gruff thank you was all he could muster at the time. Fact was, he was floored she remembered that he preferred blueberry muffins.

If she was trying to test him, she was doing a good job.

He kept reminding himself that there wasn't a single reason to strike up anything but a business relationship with the woman. It may have been twelve years ago, but he had nothing more to offer her now than he did then. It was more than apparent in hindsight that back then his future on Gallagher Ranch wasn't enough to keep her in Paradise.

Not a thing had changed in the years since. He remained a rancher who was getting by. Not a rich successful lawyer like her husband had been.

Besides, she'd sign off on his certification and be gone again in a month or so. No, he'd continue to keep her at a distance. It was better for everyone.

Joe checked the fit on his hook prosthesis. The myoelectric version wasn't waterproof, and rain or no rain, he had work that couldn't wait another day.

When he opened the front door, once again, Becca stood outside. This time she wore a cheery yellow hooded rain slicker over blue jeans. Her head was turned up toward the sky like a kid, letting the drops kiss her face.

"What are you doing?" he growled.

"I like rain. Don't you?" Drops of moisture clung to her long black lashes. She pushed a wayward lock of dark hair into the hood of the slicker, waiting for his response.

Joe stared, entranced, as the rain moved leisurely down her face, landing on her lips.

"Joe?"

He blinked. "Yeah. I like rain, too. In moderation. I like everything in moderation," he muttered. "I keep whispering that word into Mother Nature's ear, except she's deaf." Slapping on his Stetson, he tucked his face into the collar of his coat and strode across the yard. Today he was headed to the equipment garage.

"What will you do if it keeps raining?"

"Watch and wait. Just another day in Paradise." He dodged a puddle and turned to her. "What are you doing here so early, anyhow? Not much for you or your crew to do today."

"I need to talk to you about the photo shoot."

"What photo shoot? It's raining."

She grimaced. "Yes. It's been raining for twenty-four hours. This is Friday, and the crew is getting antsy. Rod suggested, um well, they, ah… They want to do some filming in the barn with the horses and the dogs and hay and such."

He pulled open the big door to the garage and held it for her.

Becca nodded her thanks. "They've been very patient, and I…that is… I think they've acclimated to the ranch well, don't you?"

"You mean that guy who keeps complaining about a rash?"

"Poison oak. Yes. That would be Julian. Even he's adjusting well, since I got him some cortisone cream. I bet you hardly noticed them following you around the stalls yesterday morning, right?"

Joe snickered. Unable to hold back, he began to belly laugh.

"What's so funny?"

"Becca, it's a little hard not to notice three city folks stumbling around in the dark at five in the morning, crinkling food wrappers and whispering. They spooked Blackie when the alarm clock on somebody's cell phone went off, and then one of them stepped on Wishbone's tail."

"That was an accident. It could have happened to anyone."

"It never happened to you."

"Be fair. I was raised on a ranch. These are people whose idea of roughing it would be coffee in a foam cup."

Joe offered only a snort to that. He flipped on the over-head lights. "I don't even understand why they were there yesterday. Nothing for them to do when it's raining."

"They need to get to know you and your routine. That's what will make this project a success." She paused. "Rod spent yesterday afternoon sketching plans for the shoot and checking lighting and set design with Julian."

Joe pulled back the riding lawn mower and un-screwed the oil cap. Today would be a fine day to check on the mowers and replace that part that came in on the baler, he thought. Pulling out the dipstick, he wiped it off on a clean rag.

Becca stepped closer, her muddy boots inches away from his. He kept his focus on the dipstick measure-ment and inched back from her.

"Are you listening to me?"

He looked up. "Sure am. Hard not to when you're in my face."

She ignored his remark and continued. "Abi's fitting in pretty well, isn't she?" she asked.

"Yeah, okay, yes. Abi has been the least obnoxious of the group." Joe released what he hoped was a long-suffering sigh. "What do you have in mind for the photo shoot?"

"Rod asked for a couple of hours. Maybe this after-noon after lunch?"

"I've got a few calls to make. How about two?"

"Sure. He wants you to bring a few of your Western dress shirts. Pearl button. And maybe a bolo tie. Oh, and wear your Tony Llamas, not work boots. He'd like you to bring both your tan and your black Stetsons and your straw Resistol."

"How does he know I have a straw Resistol?" He crouched a bit lower to examine the blade on the mower.

She cleared her throat. "I might have mentioned that I saw it on a coatrack at your house."

"Anything else?"

"Yes, Abi needs to do a one-on-one interview with you. This might be a good opportunity," she said with a hopeful tone.

"Fine," he said through gritted teeth. "Point me in the right direction at the right time, and I'll do whatever we need to do to get them out of here quickly."

"Two it is. I'll have them set up and meet you in the barn."

"Fine. Whatever." He reached for a can of oil. "What are you going to do until then?"

"I'll drive back to town," she said. "Unless you'd like to squeeze in a therapy session while you work on the equipment."

"What?" The wrench slipped from his fingers and clanged as it hit the mower and tumbled to the ground. He scowled, his gaze on the tool. "No. I really need to get some work done today."

"Fine. Then I'll see you after lunch. Oh, and I appreciate your cheerful attitude, Mr. Gallagher. It makes my job so much easier."

Joe tipped his hat back, his gaze following her as she offered him a two-fingered salute and then turned on her heel, making it clear that her determination to get the job done would outlast his bad attitude.

"Rod, you're amazing." Rebecca glanced around the main area of the barn. Round bales of hay had been strategically stacked and placed in the center. A seating area had been created from single hay bundles. Lights hung from the ceiling on a rope of orange industrial extension cords, and reflector boards were propped and ready for use.

"What time did you get here?" she asked.

"Two hours ago," Julian said. "He wouldn't even let me order a second piece of caramel apple pie at Patti Jo's."

Rod held a fancy camera in the air as he took an exaggerated bow in response to her compliment.

"Too bad we can't do something about that smell," Julian commented.

"What smell?" Rebecca asked.

"That horse manure." Julian shivered and shook his head. "Ugh, it's thick today."

Rebecca laughed. "This is a barn. I should warn you two that there's no guarantee the horses won't decide to mess up your shoot, if you know what I mean."

"Terrific," Rod said drily. He looked to Julian. "Let's save the horses for our outdoor shoot. We'll use the dogs instead."

Abi stepped into the barn, peeled off her wet jacket and evaluated the area. "Nice work, guys!" She leaned close to Rebecca. "I'm guessing your cowboy isn't going to be real happy about doing this in the middle of his workday."

"He isn't my cowboy."

The smiling journalist shrugged. "I call 'em as I see 'em. When you're in the vicinity, Mr. Gallagher only has eyes for you."

"That's because he's looking for another opportunity to bite off my head."

"I don't think so," Abi said in a singsongy voice.

From behind them, Joe Gallagher cleared his throat. Rebecca whirled around.

Looking handsome enough to take her breath away, the rancher stood in the doorway of the barn, closing a huge black umbrella. He wore creased Levi's and a crisp white pearl-button Western shirt. His black hair was damp and curled slightly over his ears. And he'd shaved. Rebecca couldn't even remember the last time she'd seen the man clean shaven. She examined the smooth planes of his angular face and found no evidence that he'd nicked himself.

"What are you looking at?" Joe asked.

"You mentioned losing a pint of blood when you shave," Rebecca murmured.

"I've been practicing," he returned.

"So I see."

He held a white straw Resistol and his Stetsons stacked in one hand. A spare shirt on a hanger dangled from his prosthetic fingers as his gaze swept across the impromptu photography setup.

"You certainly clean up nicely," Abi drawled, as she took the shirt and hats from Joe.

He responded with a wink and a wide, winning smile that made even the sassy journalist blush.

It was clear to everyone in the room why this particular cowboy had been chosen for the advertising campaign. He was definitely the perfect poster boy for OrthoBorne, despite his numerous protests.

It was also obvious that Abi had been plain wrong in her summation of where Joe's interests were. It had been a good twelve years since Joe had offered a smile like that to Rebecca.

"Julian," Rod called out. "We're ready for makeup."

"Makeup?" Joe stepped back and held up a palm. "Whoa."

"It's a loose powder that absorbs oil. We apply it with a sponge to keep your skin from shining under the lights."

"Makeup." Joe repeated the word on a sour note.

Julian inched nervously toward his model. "Could you sit down?"

Joe averted his gaze, as though wishing himself elsewhere, and eased down to a bale of hay.

"Close your eyes, please."

The cowboy tightened his jaw when Julian dabbed the powder on his face.

All Rebecca could do was cringe, praying Julian would finish quickly.

"Now let's get you comfortable," Rod said. "Go ahead and lean back against the hay." He moved in to position Joe's arm.

Not a thing about Joe looked comfortable. Rebecca started nibbling on her thumbnail.

"Julian, get that light over here. Abi, do you mind holding the silver reflector board for me?" Rod nodded and pulled out a light meter. "Higher please."

"Chin up, Joe. Give us a smile, like the love of your life walked into the room."

Joe's eyes widened and his gaze locked with Rebecca's. His lips curled dangerously. She met his eyes, straight on and worked hard not to flinch. No, she wouldn't back down.

"Rebecca. Your phone," Abi whispered.

"I'm sorry. Excuse me. I'll step outside." She pulled up the hood on her slicker and ducked out to the yard to check the number. *Unidentified.*

"Hello?"

The call disconnected, and she stood staring at the device. Could it have been her mother from an outside number? She scrolled through and found the familiar number. "Hey, Mom. Just checking to be sure you weren't trying to reach me… Okay, great. I'll talk to you later. I should be done here early." She stepped into the barn in time to hear Joe arguing with Julian.

"Touch my hat, and I might have to relocate your fingers."

Julian jumped back. "But Rod said to adjust the brim."

"Do you have a mirror?" Rebecca asked, intervening.

"Sure," Rod said. He rummaged in a large duffel and passed a hand mirror to her.

"Okay, Rod," Rebecca said. "Can you tell Mr. Gallagher how you want the Resistol?"

"Push back those curls in front and put the hat on the back of your head. Sort of rakish."

"Rakish?" Joe repeated.

"Yeah. Like a bad boy."

"A bad boy," Joe muttered the words and adjusted the hat.

"Perfect. Now turn slightly to the left, chin up."

Joe stiffly complied.

"You don't happen to have a guitar, do you?" Rod asked.

This time Joe's brows rose.

"I guess that's a no." Rod glanced around. "Becca, can you get that rope from the tack room? The one that was hanging from the horse."

She raced to grab the coiled lasso rope from the wall.

"Perfect. Okay, try this. Hold that rope with your prosthesis. Let it rest against your leg."

Again Joe complied, his green eyes dark and annoyed.

"Stretch your legs out in front of you and cross them at the ankles, so we get the boots in the picture." Rod kept circling around Joe and the bales of hay, snapping dozens of pictures. Finally he paused to evaluate. "Nice."

"Does that mean we're done?" Joe began to rise.

"No. Sit. Head down. Turn right, and tip the brim of your hat over your face. Let your prosthesis rest on your bent knee."

The tension in the barn was palpable as Rod continued to call out orders and snap digital pictures.

"*Julian.* He's shiny on the right side."

Julian stepped hesitantly toward Joe with a powder sponge.

"Rebecca," Rod called out. "We need a saddle. And the dogs. Where are the dogs?"

Joe whistled for Gil and Wishbone, while Rebecca strode back to the tack room and grabbed a saddle from the wall.

"Toss it over that high bale of hay behind Mr. Gallagher."

She slung the saddle awkwardly and missed, nearly hitting the dogs. Joe stood and easily scooped the leather from her hands and lifted it into place.

"Thank you."

"I'm about two hands shy of fed up," he murmured, his breath warm against her ear.

Startled, she met his gaze. "We're almost done."

Joe dutifully returned to his position against the hay, and Rod began adjusting the reflector board.

"Can you make the dogs sit still?" Rod asked.

"Sit." Joe bellowed the command. The dogs sat, as did Julian.

"What's that smell?" Abi whispered to Rebecca.

Rebecca glanced around. "It does smell funny, doesn't it?"

Rod looked at Joe. "Do you mind changing into another shirt and grabbing the black Stetson?

A cell phone began to ring.

Joe pulled it from his back pocket. "Yeah, Jake. Sure. I'll be there in a bit. Thanks."

"Everything okay?" Rebecca asked.

"The other piece for the windrower is in. I'll need to get to town."

"We're almost done here," Rod said.

"Jake closes early on Friday," Joe stated.

Rod looked from Joe to Rebecca. She nodded her agreement with Joe.

"Okay," Rod said. "I'll look over today's shots. Hopefully we have something to work with."

"What about my interview?" Abi asked.

"Talk to Becca," Joe said. Pausing, he glanced around the barn. "Something is burning."

He strode to the wall and grabbed the fire extinguisher before searching the barn, stall by stall. Rebecca followed.

Joe stopped suddenly at a wall outlet. His wide shoulders heaved, and he let out a frustrated breath before yanking out two heavy-duty extension cords piggybacked into the wall outlet.

The overhead lights went dark.

"They could have burned down my barn," Joe fairly growled. He whipped around. Face thunderous, he pinned her with an icy glare. "They could have burned down my barn, Becca."

"I'm sorry, Joe. This is my fault. Rod and Julian got here before me and set up."

"You're right, it is your fault. I'm trying to save my ranch, and this is the second time they've fouled things up."

"It won't happen again."

"It can't happen again." He took a deep breath as if willing himself to calm down. Then he met her gaze. "Becca, life as a one-armed rancher is more challenging than I'd ever admit to anyone. Except maybe you. All I want to do is move on. But that can't happen until the prosthesis is paid for and life returns to normal. I'm willing to do whatever it takes, but my patience is running thin."

She bit her lip and nodded. "I'm sorry, Joe. It seems that all I can offer is another apology, and I realize that doesn't cut it."

Joe massaged his forehead with his fingers. "When are you moving into the cottage?"

"Tomorrow."

"Good. This isn't going to work unless you can ride herd on this team."

"You have my word."

"I'm counting on you, Becca. Gallagher Ranch is counting on you."

Rebecca swallowed. The man certainly knew how to hit her right where her guilt was located. He was right. So far her attempts to get this project on track were failing miserably. If Joe failed, she failed, as well. It was time to step up her game. Both their futures were on the line.

Chapter Six

"Who's that?" Casey asked.

Rebecca pulled on the Honda's parking brake. She looked from her daughter in the passenger seat, staring glumly out the car window, to Joe Gallagher, who stood in front of their new home. The cowboy's arms were crossed, his prosthesis visible in a black short-sleeve T-shirt. His face was unreadable as he watched the packed Honda edge up the circular gravel drive.

Why was Joe here? He should be off doing whatever it was he did on Saturday afternoons.

"That's Mr. Gallagher. Remember, I told you that this is his ranch."

"Why is he mad?"

Rebecca sucked in a breath. "He's not mad."

"He looks mad to me."

"No. He's just frowning. Joe, I mean, Mr. Gallagher, does that when he's nervous."

"Why is he nervous?"

"You know what? I think he might be a little scared to meet you, sweetie."

Casey unbuckled her seat belt and turned, her gaze

meeting her mother's. Her brown eyes rounded beneath the fringe of chocolate-brown bangs. "Me?"

Rebecca nodded. "I told him how awesome you are. Come to think of it, he may be a little scared you won't like him."

Her daughter's small mouth formed a perfect little circle of astonishment.

"We better get moving, Case. We have a lot of work to do." Rebecca glanced at the backseat. "Why don't you start by grabbing your suitcase? Then you can work on those smaller boxes with your name on them. Take them right to your room. Okay?"

"Okay, Momma, but, how do I know which room is mine?"

"Yours is the pink one, of course."

"I have a pink room?" She beamed, pleasure lighting up her face.

"That's what Mr. Gallagher told me." Rebecca opened her car door and popped the trunk. "We can move all the boxes in before we begin to unpack."

Joe moved down the steps toward them. "I thought you might need some help."

"How did you know we were here?"

"I was on my way over to make sure everything was turned on."

"Thank you. We don't want to take you away from your work."

"Paperwork today. It can wait."

She nodded and narrowed her eyes at him. "I don't suppose you happen to know how to smile?"

"Excuse me?"

She narrowed her eyes. "Casey thinks you're mad at her."

"Me?" He blinked with surprise. "You can't be serious."

"I'm very serious. You look a little intimidating with that expression on your face and that black getup."

"What are you talking about?" He glanced down at his black jeans and black shirt.

"You're making a six-year-old nervous."

"Are you messing with me?" He took off his black ball cap and slapped it back on. "I have a niece, and she's not afraid of me. Kids usually like me."

"Casey isn't like most kids."

He hesitated for a moment. "Did you tell her about my arm? Maybe that's what's scaring her."

Rebecca glanced at his arm. "Why would I?" she returned. "And she distinctly asked why you were mad. She doesn't care about your prosthesis."

"I don't know…" His chin was set as he uttered the words.

"Joe, you are not defined by your residual limb. No one cares. It's not as big a deal to everyone else as it is to you."

He gave a slow nod as though considering her words. Then he strode over to the car and held the back door for Casey, who struggled with a suitcase.

"May I help you with that, ma'am?"

Startled, Casey jumped. She looked him up and down. "Okay," she said softly.

"I'm Joe."

"I'm Casey."

"Nice to meet you," he said.

She glanced from his face to his prosthesis and then nodded. "Cool arm."

"Uh, thanks."

Rebecca passed by him with a box tucked under her chin. "Told you so," she murmured.

Joe put the suitcase on the front walk, shook his head and went back to the trunk for another box.

"Is this all you have?" he asked as he followed Rebecca into the house.

"There's two more boxes in the front seat."

"That's not much. Where's all your other stuff? No U-Haul or anything?"

"There is no other stuff." She chuckled. "I am probably the only woman you will ever meet with a lot of baggage but without a lot of stuff."

He opened his mouth, then pressed his lips together, brows knit.

"What?" she asked.

"Not a thing." He raised a palm in defense.

"You know you want to ask, so I may as well tell you." She glanced around to be sure Casey was out of earshot. "I sold pretty much everything I owned to pay for the attorney fees and court costs, and to keep us solvent when I wasn't employed."

"You were fired, too?"

"Not at all. OrthoBorne held my job when I took a leave of absence. It was difficult to work when the accident and the trial were regularly in the news. Of course, it didn't take long to burn through my vacation and sick time, either."

"Didn't Nick have a life insurance policy or savings account or something?"

"He sure did. Life insurance policy, as well as a hefty savings account. I was unable to access either of them until I was cleared of all charges."

Rebecca put her box down on the floor in the living room, and Joe followed suit.

"The legal system frowns on handing out money to murderers. By the time I had access to any resources, it was much too late. I used those funds to pay my attorney and the staggering list of bills I had accumulated. The leftover is in the bank for Casey's college education."

Joe ran a hand over his face. "I'm sorry you had to go through all that, Becca. You lost everything, even though you were innocent."

She shrugged. "God's taking care of us."

"How can you be so blasé about what they did to you?"

"Not they. Judge Brown. Yet I am certain that holding on to bitter feelings would only make me exactly like him, so I take it to the Lord when I'm tempted to be resentful. Which, on a bad day, can be often. He said he'd never leave me. He hasn't."

"You think not?" Joe asked.

"I know not." She cocked her head and looked at him. "The old Joe Gallagher wouldn't have doubted Him."

"The old Joe Gallagher. I have no idea who he is, let alone how God fits into things," Joe muttered.

"You'll find Him again, eventually. When you least expect it." She glanced around. "So are you going to give me the tour?" Rebecca asked, glad to change the subject.

"Sure. Sure. Of course."

He moved into the cozy living room where a leather sofa and two leather chairs were positioned in front of a stone fireplace.

Rebecca ran a hand over the back of the couch, imagining a relaxing evening with the fire blazing in the hearth, a quilt on her lap and a book in her hand.

"There are two fireplaces," Joe said. "The other one is in the master bedroom. Firewood is on the back porch. As you may remember, we never know what the weather is going to do in the valley, no matter what month the calendar says it is. We have to be prepared."

"Why did Dan leave this lovely place?"

"Dan and Beth want a big family. They built a larger house near town. She works at the Paradise Hospital, and he's either at the pharmacy in town or at the clinic. It only made sense to live closer to downtown."

Joe moved through the kitchen. "Furnace is in this closet. Instructions are taped on the wall inside." He kept walking and tapped his knuckles on the entrance to a small room near the back of the house. "Washing machine, dryer and hot-water tank are in here." Then he pulled open the back door to reveal a screened-in porch with two red rocking chairs, parked beside a stack of empty terra-cotta planters.

Rebecca released a small gasp as she took in the view. "I can see straight to the mountains."

Joe turned to follow her gaze to the west. "Pretty spectacular. I guess I take it for granted. It's good to see my world through someone else eyes."

"There's still snow on the Sangre de Christos."

"Yeah, it's been a chilly spring."

"A garden patch." She peered through the screen into the yard. The grass was freshly mowed, the garden recently tilled. Neat rows of soil begged for planting. Beyond the garden, the lawn stretched to a grouping of conifers on the right, and behind them, a fence indicated the border of Gallagher Ranch.

"Yeah, I guess so. Small one. Beth, Dan's wife, grew vegetables. I forgot about that."

Rebecca lowered herself to one of the rocking chairs and set it to a slow rhythmic motion with her foot. Planting a garden would be like setting down roots. But where would she be when it was harvest time? It seemed almost cruel to tempt her with the thought. She probably wasn't even going to have time to plant the flowers in those big pots and planters, the way things were moving along.

Suddenly realization hit her. She stopped the movement of the rocker and looked up at Joe. "I need to give you a deposit."

"Huh?"

"A deposit. On the cottage."

"No."

"Let me know what day you prefer that I turn in the rent. I know we haven't discussed this, but I'm hoping you charge about the same as the house I was going to lease. I'm happy to pay you weekly, since I don't know how long I'll be here."

"I'm not charging rent." The words were flat, laced with the usual Joe Gallagher high and mighty annoyance.

Rebecca stood. "Give me a good reason why not."

Joe leaned against the doorjamb, his arms crossed in a take-no-prisoners stance. "First of all, my mother would kill me if she found out. Second, you're going to help me with the media crew. And third, it's not my house. When Dan gave me the keys, he told me to use it if I get a ranch hand."

"Then I shouldn't be staying here." She shook her head. "And you shouldn't be offering the place."

"*If I get a ranch hand*, it'll only be for a week or so during the hay harvest. He can stay at my place. That's the way we've always done things in the past."

"I don't do charity." She met his gaze. "Period."

"This isn't charity. Charity is what they do down at the Paradise Valley Church. If you want to throw money at me, well, I suggest that you put it in the offering plate instead."

Rebecca rubbed the bridge of her nose. Clearly the man was even more stubborn than she was.

"Wednesday evening service is at six," he continued. "Sunday morning services are at eight, nine thirty and eleven. Bit of advice. Avoid the eleven o'clock service. While it is the shortest service of the three since Pastor likes to be out for lunch so he can watch the Broncos games, it's also the one Judge Brown attends."

"You sure know a lot about church services for a man who's turned his back on God."

"I'm pretty sure you're only here to handle my prosthesis, not my soul," he shot back.

"Whatever, Joe. I don't want to argue."

Silence stretched for a moment, until Rebecca couldn't stifle a yawn.

"Tired, huh? Good news is you made it through the week."

"And no one was more surprised than you, right?"

"I didn't say that." His words were a little less sharp this time. "But since you mentioned it, you did surprise me. There's no hiding the fact that you were born to ranch life. Your daddy would be proud."

"Thank you." Embarrassed by his praise, Rebecca shifted to professional mode. "Now that I've got a complete understanding of your ADLs, we're going to have to carve out time to work on some techniques I think may help you fully utilize your prosthesis on the ranch."

"Does that mean I might graduate early?"

"I didn't say that."

"A guy can dream."

"I'll be out of your hair before you know it, Joe. I promise."

"I wasn't trying to get rid of you," he said.

"No?" She glanced up at him.

"No. I think you and I work well together."

Rebecca opened her mouth and then closed it again. Before she could answer, he had turned and walked away. She stared at his retreating form, confused and a little terrified. Joe had every reason to be hard and unforgiving with her, given their past. However, this unexpected crack in the formidable cowboy, well, it was much more than she was ready to handle.

"Don't be nice to me, Joe," she whispered. "I don't deserve it."

Joe walked past Casey's room on his way out of the cottage. He stopped and paused in the doorway, giving a small knock on the door frame.

"Is the bedroom okay?" he asked.

Casey whirled around, her dark braids flying. "Oh, yes. I can't believe it's really mine." Her eyes were bright with pleasure as she assessed the canopy bed and small vanity with its matching mirror and chair.

"Glad to hear it."

"Are there…are there any kids around here?" Casey asked, her voice so soft that Joe had to move closer to hear.

"My niece Amy is on the ranch quite a bit of the time, with her grandmother. Right now she's in California."

When Joe reached for the cord and pulled open the blinds, Casey quickly crossed the room. With her nose nearly pressed against the glass, she anxiously peered out.

"See that big house?" Joe asked.

"Uh-huh."

"That's Amy's grandma's house."

"Is Amy's last name the same as yours?" she asked.

"Yes. That's right. Amy Gallagher. Do you know her?"

"She's in my Sunday-school class. Amy is a year older than me."

"I see."

Casey was silent for moments as she continued to take in the view.

"I like the ranch. It's nice here," she finally breathed.

Joe followed her gaze, once again seeing his home through different eyes. The horses grazed in the yard outside their pavilion, tails swishing back and forth, the slight breeze lifting their manes. Gil and Wishbone slept on the grass, bellies up toward the late-afternoon sun.

"Yeah, it is," he answered.

"Can I ride a horse?"

His eyes widened at the question. "Sure. If your mom says it's okay."

"She will. She rides horses, too, you know."

"Yeah. I heard that."

Casey smiled up at him. "Thanks for letting us stay in your house."

"You're welcome."

"I prayed for you."

"Excuse me?" Joe cocked his head. She had his full attention now.

"I prayed for God to bring a friend for my momma. Someone nice, like you, to make her smile again."

Joe swallowed. He was more than touched by Casey's honest admission. There were no words to say in response to the pureness of heart that shone in her dark eyes.

"Do you have anything else in the car?" he asked.

"Two boxes. Kind of small ones."

"Come on. Let's grab them and get you unpacked, so we can see about a horse."

When Casey took his prosthetic hand in her small one and led him out of the pink bedroom, he found himself speechless yet again.

Minutes later, Joe located Becca in the kitchen putting away the few groceries she'd brought with her.

She turned at the sound of his boots on the hardwood floor. A grin lit up her face. "The first thing I'm going to do is bake a chocolate cake."

"Okay." He said the word slowly, his mind tripping back in time. Chocolate cake and blue ribbons from the fair. He used to drive her to the fair in Monte Vista and Alamosa every year.

"I'm sorry." Her face reddened as though she was remembering the same thing.

The moment was awkward, and he found himself irritated for no good reason. "You apologize a lot," Joe said, more gruffly than he intended.

"The way I see it, I have a lot to be sorry for." The words tripped from her tongue easily and without guile. She cleared her throat. "Was there something you need?"

"Your daughter would like to ride a horse."

"What?" Her head jerked back, and her brown eyes rounded. "Really?" Her voice rose with a tremor of excitement. "Did she tell you that she wants to ride? My Casey wants to ride?"

"Hold on a minute there." He stopped her, confused by what he was hearing. "Are you telling me that Casey has never ridden...*at all*?"

"No. Never."

"Why, that's plain shameful, especially when she's the granddaughter of a ranch man."

"I have no excuse. You're completely right," Becca murmured, her eyes downcast. "Casey's been shuttled back and forth so much between Paradise and Denver. Sometimes I feel like her entire childhood has been on hold since the accident."

"Well, we can sure take care of that. Right now, in fact."

"Now?"

"Sure. How about if she rides double with you? We can take a short ride down to where the cows are grazing."

"I don't want to inconvenience you. I'm sure you have things to do."

"Not at the moment."

Becca clasped her hands together and grinned. "Thank you, then. Casey will love that."

"I'll meet you at the barn."

"Yes. Yes. I'll get Casey into some blue jeans."

Joe nodded. He turned and tucked his head away from her, before she could see him smiling. Why would it be that making Becca and Casey happy warmed his heart? Maybe he shouldn't overthink this, but simply enjoy the moment.

Chapter Seven

"I'm going to ride a real horse," Casey repeated the words for the umpteenth time as she twirled around the living room.

"Come on, little cowgirl," Rebecca called as she held open the door.

"I'm going to ride a real horse."

"You're going to ride with me," Rebecca said.

"When can I ride by myself?"

"I don't know. These are Mr. Gallagher's horses and—"

"Joe. He said to call him Joe."

"Joe. Yes. Okay. Well, Case, these are Joe's horses and we are here on his ranch. My job comes before riding horses." Rebecca pointed to the barn. "This way."

"Are you doing therapy with Joe?"

"Yes, I am, but remember what I told you. That's confidential. We do not discuss Momma's clients. Ever."

Casey gave a solemn nod. Suddenly her little six-year-old legs picked up speed, the pink sneakers kicking dust into the air as she moved. "There he is. There's Joe. He has the horses."

Rebecca looked straight ahead to where Joe stood in front of the barn, holding the reins to the gelding and the mare. They were saddled and ready to go.

"Are these ponies?" Casey asked him.

"Ponies?" he scoffed. "These are horses."

"They look like ponies," Casey said.

"Nope." He gave a slow shake of his head. "We measure horses by hands, and these are not ponies."

When Casey screwed up her face, Rebecca nearly laughed out loud.

"I'm serious here," Joe said. "One hand is four inches. We measure from the ground to the top of the withers."

Casey started giggling. "A wither? Wither what?"

Joe chuckled at her response. "This bony part." He ran a hand over Blackie's spine. "This is the wither."

"Can I touch the wither?"

"Sure." Joe scooped her up with his left arm and held her next to the gelding. "Right. There."

"Oh, it is bony," Casey declared with awe as her small hand patted the horse's neck.

"Yep." He let her down again. "Blackie here is sixty-three inches tall or almost sixteen hands. Ponies are anything under fourteen hands and two inches. No ponies on Gallagher Ranch. Not a one."

"Wait until I tell my math teacher about that."

"Higher mathematics," Joe said with a grin for Casey.

It was a killer smile, one that reached his eyes and made Rebecca wish that she had such an easy relationship with the cowboy. She used to. A long time ago.

"Why does he keep moving his tail?" Casey asked.

"That's his flyswatter."

Casey whooped with laughter.

Rebecca stood amazed as the two of them chatted back and forth. He wasn't kidding. Kids did like him.

"Ready?" Joe asked.

"Hmm?" Rebecca returned, her gaze meeting his.

"Casey is ready to ride. How about you?"

"Yes. Of course." Her phone began to ring. When she pulled it out of her back pocket, the unidentified caller hung up. Rebecca shook her head.

"What's wrong?"

"I'm getting hang-up calls," she said quietly, for his ears only.

"Can you tell who it's from?"

"No. I tried that callback method. But whoever it is either has the wrong number or a poor sense of humor."

"How many times have they called?" Joe asked, genuine concern on his face.

"Six times in the last two days."

"*Six*? That's harassment. I can ask Sam what he suggests."

"No. Please don't. I'll contact the sheriff myself if it becomes necessary."

"I don't like it, Becca."

"Neither do I." She turned to Casey. "Ready, sweetie?"

With her daughter's enthusiastic nod of approval, she lifted herself to the saddle and nodded to Joe, who lifted Casey to Rebecca's waiting arms.

"Okay, sit back against me and you hold the reins," Rebecca said.

"Reins?"

Rebecca raised the leather leads. "These help us direct the horse."

"The horse doesn't know his left hand from his right," Joe added as he mounted Blackie.

"Horses have hoofs, not hands." Casey's laughter bubbled over at the words, her gaze upon Joe in a gesture Rebecca recognized as pure hero worship. Mixed emotions settled on Rebecca. It was wonderful for her daughter to have a male role model in her life, but what would happen when the assignment was over and Joe Gallagher no longer welcomed them in his world?

They rode in silence for several minutes until they reached a pasture filled with cows, to the east of the barn.

"Whose cows are those?" Casey asked.

"All mine," Joe returned. "They're eating the grass here until early next week, then I'll move them to another pasture."

"How many head did you say you have?" Rebecca asked.

"Close to two hundred."

"You're going to move two hundred head by yourself?"

"Naw. Gil and Wishbone will help me."

"You can't be serious?"

"Dan usually helps, or my mother."

"Your mother?" Rebecca looked to see if it was a joke. "Elsie really helps you herd cattle?"

"Are you kidding? It was just her and my dad when they started this operation. She'd put Dan and me and my sisters in the pickup truck, which was new back then, and ride along with my father, getting out every now and again when the cows went astray."

"That's amazing."

"That's ranch life," Joe said. "You lived on Elliott

Ranch, where the deer and the antelope play and the cash is in abundance."

"It wasn't easy street. We worked sixteen-hour days there, too."

"If you say so."

She cleared her throat, swallowing a lump of hesitation since he was in such a good mood. "Um, I'm happy to help you herd the cattle."

"You?" He turned his head and adjusted his Stetson.

"Yes, me. I've done it before. Many times."

"Who's going to watch the greenhorns if you help me?"

"Couldn't they use the truck and shoot video? We'd be taking care of two things at once." She smiled, pleased at her solution. It was a brilliant plan.

"Might work. Let me think on it."

Rebecca nodded. "Of course." She led Princess away from the fence and followed Blackie as Joe led the horse back toward the ranch.

"What's that?" Casey asked as they neared the corral once more.

Joe and Rebecca both turned to follow Casey's pointing finger. A plastic cow head, complete with horns, was fastened to a round bale of hay, the size of a small heifer.

"Why, that's a dummy steer," Joe said.

"What do you use a dummy for?" Casey's face was bright with amusement, and she seemed about to burst into laughter again.

"I'm learning to rope again with my prosthetic hand. Roping is when you take your rope and twirl it in the air and it lands around the cow. The dummy is how I practice."

"Are you really roping again?" Rebecca asked. "And using your right hand or your left hand?"

"A little of both, and learning is the key word here. I don't have a lot of time right now, but yeah. That's the plan."

"I used to rope," Rebecca mused.

"Give it a shot," Joe said.

"Give what a shot?"

He inclined his head toward the dummy steer.

"Yes, Momma. Do it," Casey urged.

"I don't know."

"Sounds to me like you're changing your story," Joe said.

She turned to him. "It's been a long time."

"You're riding just fine, and you said you can herd cattle." He shrugged. "Try roping on the ground."

"Oh, no. If I'm going to do it, I'm going to do it in the saddle."

"That might be a little ambitious until you develop a feel for the rope again. Those muscles get rusty after..." He cleared his throat. "Twelve years."

"Are you challenging me?"

"That would be foolish. While I have been known to be foolish upon occasion, I would never do anything that might endanger the animals."

"Endanger the animals?" Rebecca huffed. "Casey, honey, I'm going to ease you to the ground. You go sit against the corral fence, and cheer for Momma." As Casey's sneakers hit the dusty earth, Rebecca turned and narrowed her eyes at Joe. "I trust I can borrow your rope."

Joe slowly released the long rope from the pommel and stepped forward with Blackie, handing it over.

"Is it soft enough for you?" Joe asked.

"Just fine."

"You want my gloves? Don't want to burn those pretty hands."

With a death glare shot toward the cowboy, Rebecca yanked her own gloves from her vest pocket. Pretty hands? They were a mess. Torn cuticles and red knuckles along with a healing wire cut in her palm. She tucked her hands into the leather gloves.

Rebecca checked the coils, the loop and the knot. Then she eyed the dummy and began to roll her loop, leading with her thumb and index finger. Yes. She could do this. It was all coming back to her now. Time to throw her catch. The rope sailed underneath the right horn and missed the left horn. Caught off guard, the rope slipped from her hands to the dirt.

"If you did that on the ground, you wouldn't have to keep dismounting," Joe observed.

"I appreciate your insight." She picked up the rope, pulled herself onto Princess yet again and leaned close to the mare, rubbing her gently. "Cowboys think they know everything," she whispered. The horse whinnied in agreement.

Once again she prepared the rope, refining her loop and coil, stepping Princess in a bit tighter.

This time the rope sailed clear past the dummy.

"Momma, can we have lunch now?"

"Lunch? Yes." She smiled at Casey as she slid from the horse and retrieved the rope. "You go on in the house and wash up. I'll be in as soon as I rub down Princess."

"You know, that was pretty good considering you haven't held a rope in a dozen years," he said.

Rebecca coiled the rope and handed it to him. He dismounted and stood close without touching the offered rope.

"I mean it, Becca. That was a compliment. I don't hand them out on a regular basis."

She met his gaze. "Thank you."

"About that chocolate cake."

"What?" She blinked, confused.

"As I recall, you used to make blue-ribbon chocolate cakes. You said you're going to make one soon. I'm looking forward to a piece."

"My cake-baking skills are likely to be as rusty as my roping."

The corners of Joe's lips curved. "I'm guessing you haven't forgotten.

"I'll make a deal with you. Stop by tonight for a therapy session and I'll have chocolate cake ready."

"Therapy?"

"Take it or leave it."

"You drive a hard bargain."

She nodded, hiding a smile. "That I do."

"That's another kid's toy," Joe said.

"No. It's another therapy tool." Rebecca pushed the puzzle across the kitchen table to him, ignoring his irritation.

He glanced around. "Where's Casey?"

"She's getting ready for bed."

Joe released a breath. "Good, because I feel pretty silly."

"We use this one for manual dexterity. You aren't the first patient to utilize this tool. Simply pick up the shapes and place them in the right slot using your prosthetic hand. It's a repetition exercise to get you accustomed to using those muscles again."

"What muscles? I'm missing half my arm."

"You know what I mean. Your nerves still transmit the same signals as if the limb was there. All we're doing is reminding them again. The goal is to increase your control. The strength and speed of your response will increase as well, the more you practice."

"Whatever. Seems like a lot of work for chocolate cake."

"As you said, my cakes were blue ribbon winners." She glanced over at the counter, where the cake was cooling and waiting to be frosted.

"It better be for this," he muttered.

"You're doing an awful lot of complaining, considering you're whizzing right through all these exercises. I don't think you really appreciate all you have going for you."

"How so?"

"You have great range of motion. No medical problems. Your phantom limb pain is minimal. You have great skin integrity and muscle development. You're like a model patient."

"Except for my crummy attitude, right?"

"I didn't say that."

"No, I did."

Rebecca focused on documenting his activity in her tablet.

"Maybe I wouldn't have such a bad attitude if I wasn't responsible for all of this," he muttered.

"It was an accident. Accidents happen."

He met her eyes, his fingers poised in midair. "Do you know what happened?"

"I've not wanted to pry, though of course I've read your medical records."

"The fact is, I should have asked for help. I didn't. Simple as that." He shrugged. "I was repairing a tractor. The tractor fell on me."

"Oh, Joe." It was one thing to read a report, another to hear the words from his mouth. Pain cut through her, and she raised her hands to cover her mouth.

"I did it to myself. My mistake could have cost me the ranch. If Dan hadn't stepped in, I don't know what I would have done. He'd cashed out of his share years ago. Yet not only was he the first responder on the scene that day, but he was responsible for keeping the ranch running when I was in the hospital. I owe my brother plenty."

"I had no idea."

Joe nodded. "Family really is everything, Becca. Took me a while to fully appreciate that." He dropped the last piece in the slot. "Done."

"Actually, you have to do it twice more. I'll frost the cake while you finish."

"Maybe I should frost the cake," he said.

"Yes. Great idea. We'll let you bake a cake and frost it next time. That will really facilitate more bilateral limb usage."

"Oh, brother," he muttered.

She moved to the counter and pulled out a stainless-steel spatula and quickly frosted the sides and then the top of the cake, swirling the chocolate whipped frosting into little peaks. How long since she'd done this? Years. At least well before the trial.

"What do you want with your cake?"

"Milk would be good. Thanks."

She poured a glass of milk and brought it along with a hefty slice of cake to the table.

Joe snickered.

"Are you laughing at me?"

"I'm laughing at the frosting you planted on your face."

Rebecca turned to examine her reflection in the toaster and swiped at her face with a towel. She straightened. "All good?"

"Nice try. Almost as good as your roping."

"I got it all." She frowned. "Didn't I?"

He bit back a chuckle. "Not hardly."

"Fine," she huffed, tossing the towel to him.

Joe stood. "Hold still." He dabbed at her nose and then her cheek. "You've even got some on your ear. How do you frost a cake and get chocolate everywhere?"

"It takes a certain amount of skill, I admit. But I was rushing before you barked at me."

"I don't bark," Joe murmured. His face was intent as he leaned down to carefully wipe the frosting from her ear with gentle strokes of the terry-cloth towel. Rebecca peeked up at him from beneath her lashes. She shivered when she realized his lips hovered inches from hers.

Suddenly he sucked in a breath and stepped away.

"All done."

"Thanks," she said a little too brightly.

"Aren't you going to get Casey for cake?"

"Yes. Right away." Rebecca nodded and moved down the hallway to the pink bedroom. Right about now she could certainly use a buffer between herself and the handsome cowboy in her kitchen.

Chapter Eight

Joe glanced up at the Sunday afternoon sky as he rounded the corner of the barn. Becca was in the drive with her head beneath the hood of the battered Honda. He was feeling inordinately good today, and he supposed Casey and Becca had a lot to do with that.

Go figure. He seemed unable to resist her and her little girl yesterday. It was a good day, even if he didn't get all the calls he needed to make completed. It didn't escape him that he and Becca could have had a child if things had worked out.

That was probably a road he'd best avoid going down. So he didn't. Instead, he shoved his hands in his pockets as he approached her, making as much noise as possible in an effort to keep from startling her. He inched closer, clearing his throat, yet Becca still didn't turn to acknowledge his presence. Finally he moved to the side of the car and put a gentle hand on her shoulder. That did it. She jumped, coming in immediate contact with the hood.

"Ouch." Her hand moved to her head. She pushed hair out of her face, neatly spreading grease across her cheek.

Earbuds.

That was why she hadn't heard him.

"I'm sorry." He mouthed the words.

"What?" Rebecca pulled the buds from her ears. "What did you say?"

"Sorry. I was actually trying not to startle you. You sure are jumpy."

"I guess I was concentrating." She rubbed her head one more time and pulled down the sleeves of her T-shirt.

"You okay? Maybe I should check your scalp, be sure you didn't do any serious damage."

"I'm fine." She waved him away with a hand. "By the way, I have a bone to pick with you."

"Fire away."

"You didn't tell me you have a rooster."

"Chickens, too. My mother's department." He rolled his eyes. "Woke you up?"

"Not me. I sleep through anything." Becca shook her head. "Casey woke me, determined to go find the rooster."

"So much for sleeping in, huh?"

"Exactly!" she said.

"Add that to your list of things that make ranch life so very special."

"Who takes care of the chickens while your mom is out of town?"

Joe grunted. "I don't do chickens. She hired a local high school student from the 4-H." He shoved his hands back in his pockets. "Other than the rooster, how's the house working out for you?"

"It's perfect, although that empty garden is a little depressing, and I wish I had time to put flowers in those pots."

"Pick up a few plants."

"Maybe. Though I'm not sure it would be worth the time and energy."

"It is if it matters to you."

"Yes. I suppose you're right." She looked him up and down. "You're awfully cheerful."

"Don't look so surprised."

"I am. You've been like a grizzly with a burr in his paw since I arrived."

"No, I haven't."

"Yes, you have."

He looked at the sky. "Maybe I am feeling good. Extended forecast says there might be a long window of sunshine coming up. I'm not holding my breath, but it could be enough time to get my hay harvested. That's enough to put anyone in a good mood." Joe paused. "Do you hear that?"

"Yes. It's coming from these." She lifted one of the earbuds that dangled around her neck.

"What is that you're listening to anyhow?"

She bit her lip and hesitated. "Italian opera."

"Why?"

"My father got me hooked on the stuff. He was a closet tenor. What a voice."

Joe shook his head. "A cowboy Pavarotti. That makes for an interesting visual."

She wiped her hands on a rag and offered a musing smile. "Yes, trust me, my father in a black Stetson singing Verdi's 'Celeste Aida' is a memory I will never forget."

"You're very fortunate to have such a relationship with your father."

"I always thought you and your father were close."

"We were. Most of the time. After all, we were Big Joe and Little Joe." He hesitated, choosing his words carefully as he met her gaze.

"When Dan left, my father was afraid I'd bolt, too. We're a fourth-generation ranching family, and I suppose he saw it all slipping away. I was a kid back then, but I was suffocating. So I joined the army."

"You eventually came back."

"Don't give me too much credit. I came back because he was dying."

"I'm sorry," she murmured.

"The thing is, I don't know if I would have done anything differently. That's what eats at me. I should feel more remorse. I don't. I know that I had to leave, so I could return." He took a deep breath. "Does that make any sense?"

"Yes. It does. More than you realize."

"It's like the life cycle of a ranch kid. You have to leave to appreciate what you left behind."

She stared at him. "I know this is a long time coming, but that's exactly how it was for me."

Joe stared at her. Suddenly his mood began a slow descent south. "What are you saying?" He asked the question that he wasn't sure he really wanted the answer to.

"I'm apologizing for how I treated you. Back then. I don't want to make excuses, but that's exactly how it was for me."

He narrowed his eyes and clamped his jaw.

"My father died. I certainly didn't have the legacy of a ranch like you did. In fact I felt as though I had nothing. No home anymore. No future here in Paradise." She released a sigh. "Nick offered me a chance to escape, a promising future with a man who cared for me. I took it."

Joe stepped back, creating even more distance between them.

"I'm not expecting your forgiveness. All I want to do is explain and apologize for how poorly I treated you."

"Duly noted."

An awkward silence stretched for moments. Becca turned to focus her attention inside the hood of the car.

"Having problems with the Honda?" Joe asked.

"It almost didn't make it out of the church parking lot this morning, which makes no sense. I had the alternator and the starter replaced in Alamosa."

"Battery?"

"Could be. My guess is it's as old as the car. Anyhow, I finished the oil change and was about to check."

"You change your own oil?"

"I do. Much less expensive that way."

"I guess you're a lot handier than I realized."

"Yes. I believe that was the point. Dad always thought he'd stay on Elliott Ranch as foreman until he retired, with me as his shotgun, but his ticker had other plans."

"I don't mean to keep bringing up sad memories."

"Not at all. I only have happy memories when it comes to my father." Becca stopped, her neck craning toward a sound overhead. "What is that?"

Joe shaded his eyes, turning his attention to the sky. A chocolate-brown bird with broad, rounded wings and a short, wide, red tail soared in a large circle, its wings barely moving. "Red-tailed hawk."

"Beautiful," she said. "Hey, and look at that sky. I'm guessing the threat of rain has passed."

"Yeah, I was plenty relieved to get up this morning to find that the storm had moved quickly to the north."

"I imagine so."

"I'm not going to bank on the rain holding off forever. We're at the end of June, which means precipitation is to be expected. In fact, there are a whole lot of folk in the valley praying for moisture."

"Anyone lined up to help with the hay?"

"I have calls to make today."

She cocked her head, listening. "Is that your phone?"

"No. I left mine in the house."

"Must be mine."

Becca patted her pockets before reaching into the car for the cell phone on the dash.

"Missed it." She pressed redial. "Mom?" Becca shook her head. "I had my earbuds in… Oh, my goodness. I better go get her." Seemingly annoyed, she shoved the phone into the back pocket of her jeans.

"What kind of mother am I?" she muttered. "My mom called twice. Apparently I also missed a call from Casey's other grandmother."

"Talk about being hard on yourself. That could have happened to anyone."

"Maybe, but I don't need to look any more incompetent than I already do in front of the Simpsons." Tools clanged as she haphazardly tossed them into the trunk.

"So what's going on?" Joe asked.

"Casey doesn't feel well. My mother is three hours away. I need to pick her up."

"Where is Casey?"

"The Simpson summer home in Four Forks. My mother dropped her off. They've got a huge graduation party going on. Virginia, that's Nick's mom, she was supposed to take Casey home, but she can't very well leave her guests."

"I can do Four Forks."

She bit her lip. "Oh, no. I couldn't ask you to drive all the way up there."

"The last thing you need is to drive to Four Forks and have your car quit."

"Your plan is to drive the farm truck?"

"No. I have a perfectly reputable new truck."

"That would be great. Thank you."

"Um, Becca?"

"Yes?"

"You've still got grease on your face. Maybe you should go clean up real quick."

"Yes. Yes. Of course." She glanced down at her clothes. "I better change, too. I don't want to stand out any more than necessary. I'll be fast."

"I'll get my truck and pull it around."

Becca started toward the cottage, then stopped. She turned back a few steps. "Joe?"

"Yeah?"

"I mean it. Thank you."

He nodded and watched her disappear into the house. She wouldn't be pleased to know that everything inside him was hollering to step up and protect her, shield her from a world that had treated her so badly. No, Becca Anshaw Simpson wouldn't be pleased at all. For now he was simply grateful that this one time she had allowed him to help. He wouldn't spend time wondering exactly why he felt the need to do it.

* * *

Rebecca quickly showered and slipped into slacks and a blouse. With a glance at the ugly, puckered vertical scar inside her right arm, she grabbed a long-sleeve white, cotton sweater before she met Joe outside.

The drive to Four Forks was silent. The scenery passed in a blur as her thoughts raced, anticipating a possible confrontation with Nick's family.

Joe slowed as they approached a sign indicating they were on the outskirts of Four Forks, and Rebecca began to reminisce about happier times navigating this same route.

The little town, twenty-five minutes north, had much less than half the population of Paradise. The standing joke was that Four Forks was a third the size of a postage stamp. The town thrived as a haven for crafters and artisans, bringing tourists in from all over the country.

"Which way?" he asked when they entered the center of the quaint town.

"Veer right when you hit the light. The road is a little hidden."

"Which light?"

She turned to him, brows raised. "There's only one intersection in Four Forks."

"I know. Lighten up. It was a joke. You're as tense as a cow heading to a branding party."

Rebecca relaxed for a moment before quickly leaning forward to point to the turnoff. "There it is. Do you see it?"

"Got it."

"The bad news is that it's a winding two-lane road up that hill."

Joe nodded, his gaze concentrated on the road.

"There's deer in the woods on either side of the road, and, of course, the shoulders are barely there, or nonexistent."

"The good news would be what?" Joe asked.

"The Simpsons own the only house up there, so there's very little traffic."

"I can imagine this is fun in the winter," Joe observed as he navigated cautiously.

"Winters are spent in Palm Springs."

"Sure they are. What was I thinking?"

After a quarter of a mile, the bumpy gravel road became a smoothly paved drive. Joe continued to steer the truck past a long row of conifers and a succession of cars parked bumper-to-bumper. As they drove around a curve, a home came into view, set back behind a huge wrought-iron security gate that was spread across the massive drive.

Camelot. That was what she used to call the sprawling, ranch-style mansion with the impressive columns. As Nick Simpson's wife, she used to be among the royal family that claimed seasonal residency here.

Joe gave a low whistle. "So this is how the other half lives."

"Gallagher Ranch isn't exactly low-rent. Why, you have three houses on that land."

He nodded. "Yeah, and they could all fit inside this one. Who did you say calls this home?"

"My former mother-in-law, Virginia Simpson."

"Her husband?"

"Nicholas Sr. died when the children were young."

Joe didn't ask, and she wasn't going to divulge that Nick's father had shared the family disease. Alcoholism.

"How do we get through the gate?"

"They have a guard on duty during events. He'll have my name." Rebecca glanced around. "You can park wherever there's an open spot. I can walk from here."

Joe eased the car along the side and unbuckled his seat belt.

"Um, Joe, it's best if you stay in the truck," she stated. "I may run into Judge Brown, and he certainly won't make it easy."

"I was going to stay in the truck until you said that."

She leaned back against the seat. "I'm giving you sound advice, and you're ignoring me."

He winked, offering an exaggerated squaring of his shoulders. "I think maybe I can handle myself, and I have no intention of letting you into the corral with a bull all by yourself."

"Fine. Fine. But don't say anything. Your presence alone will be intimidating." She unbuckled her seat belt. "This is Nick's sister's party. College graduation. My plan is to get in and out without a family argument."

"Sounds like an excellent idea to me." He narrowed his eyes in thought. "We go up to the house to get Casey. My job is to look intimidating without opening my mouth. Do I have that straight?"

She released a breath. "That wasn't quite what I said."

"No?" Joe pushed his ball cap to the back of his head.

"No. We'll pass that security guard together. Then you can stand a discreet distance back in case I need help with Casey."

He opened the door of the truck. "That's what I said."

Rebecca took a last look at her appearance in the visor mirror before flipping it back into place. By the time she had opened her door, Joe was there to offer her a hand down to the grassy ground on her side of the vehicle. She met his gaze.

"Thank you," she breathed.

"You know, I could go up there and get Casey for you," he said. "Save you all this anxiety."

She stepped down, gathering her confidence as she straightened the collar of her blouse. "No. I have to do this. I'm sure I'm making more out of this situation than it deserves—however, I haven't talked to any of Nick's family since court."

Two months ago, she mused. Two months since she'd been found innocent. She'd moved the mountain with God's help then, and she would do it again if necessary. It wasn't Joe Gallagher's job to fight her battles for her.

They walked through the gate with a wordless nod from the guard, whose eyes voiced disapproval in one sweeping glance.

"Talkative guy." Joe shaded his eyes and glanced up at the house. "Only five more miles to the front door," he muttered.

In the distance Rebecca could hear music. No doubt a live band or a small orchestra. The Simpsons didn't do anything on a small scale. The closer she got to the house, the louder the buzz of voices and partying from behind the house became.

Rebecca remembered being part of the festivities once. She'd had her wedding reception here. Tents had been set up on the endless lush lawn behind the house. Flowers had been flown in. Expensive catering ordered. They'd pulled out all the stops for Judge Brown's grandson.

Her engagement ring alone had been embarrassingly huge. She'd worn a dress of flowing lace and a simple tiara with a net veil that day, along with Nick's promise of a future together.

Tall, fair and utterly charming, Nick Simpson had provided the complete package. He'd served up every girl's dream come true on a glass platter.

Except that dream had ultimately turned into a nightmare that crashed into a million cutting pieces, and her prince became someone she barely recognized.

As they approached the house, Rebecca wrapped her arms around herself and shivered. She quickened her pace, leaving Joe behind to wait near the large water fountain in the center of the drive as she moved up the walk and up the steps to the front door.

Moments after she rang the bell, the massive oak door opened and she was face-to-face with Judge Nicholas Brown.

Rebecca swallowed hard. When her heart began to beat a furious tempo, she stepped back several paces.

"You." The word was fairly spat in her direction as his probing black eyes seared her with a nameless though oh-so-familiar accusation.

Yet something was different about the judge. Rebecca met the piercing gaze. Refusing to look away, she assessed the older man. She hadn't seen Nick's grandfather since their day in court. At that time, she'd barely had the courage to look him in the eye.

He'd changed. Not only was his color off, the skin sallow, but he seemed smaller than she remembered a mere few months ago. Suddenly realization hit her. Rebecca had lost Nick slowly, painfully over several years. By the time she'd buried her husband, he was a stranger. But Judge Brown had lost his grandson in one tragic split-second accident. She should have been praying for this poor man.

"Sir, I'm here to pick up my daughter."

Judge Brown looked past her to where Joe stood a few feet away, watching.

"I see you brought your bodyguard with you."

Rebecca turned in time to see Joe's jaw clench. She gave a quick shake of her head to keep him from jumping to her defense.

A moment later, Virginia appeared. A grimace of embarrassment crossed her face when she glanced from her father to Rebecca. She placed a gentle hand on her father's shoulder.

"Judge, why don't you go back to the party? Jana was asking about you."

Rebecca released the breath she'd been holding, her attention fixed on the judge as he disappeared into the house.

"Won't you come in?" Virginia offered. "I'm sure Jana would love to see you."

"I'm fine here. Thank you. Casey?"

"I think she overindulged. She's been resting. My assistant has gone to get her."

Virginia clasped her palms together. She glanced down the drive at Joe, her eyes registering confusion before her gaze returned to Rebecca.

"Please excuse my father," Virginia said. The words were soft and apologetic.

"I don't blame you for his actions, Virginia."

"Maybe you should. He's my father and I… Well, it wasn't until that last day in court that I realized what my inability to stand up to him had ultimately done to

Nick—" she hesitated "—as well as to you and Casey, and your family."

"It's not easy. I understand."

"No. You shouldn't understand." Virginia waved a hand in a gesture of frustration. "I knew the accident wasn't your fault. I should have stopped him. I should have asked for your forgiveness long before today, too."

Rebecca reached out and laid a hand on Virginia's arm. "I turned this over to God a long, long time ago. Maybe you should, as well."

"Yes. Yes. You're right," Virginia whispered. Her blue eyes were filled with pain and unshed tears. She turned as a young woman approached with Casey by her side.

Rebecca's heart clutched. The party dress Casey wore was rumpled, as though she'd been sleeping. "Oh, baby, are you okay?"

Her daughter nodded all the while rubbing her stomach with a hand. "My tummy hurts."

Rebecca gently pushed Casey's bangs aside and laid her hand on her daughter's forehead. The damp skin burned with heat. There was more than a stomachache going on here.

"Let's go home," she said, with a nod of thanks to Virginia.

As they headed down the drive, Joe walked up to meet them.

"Look, Joe's here," Casey murmured, a small smile brightening her wan features.

"Yes. Joe's here," Rebecca said.

Joe met Rebecca's gaze. "You handled that nicely."

"Thank you," she returned.

He knelt in front of her little girl. "How about if I carry you to the truck?"

"Yes. Please," Casey said.

Joe walked down the long drive past the guard to the truck with Casey cradled in his arms.

Rebecca knew it was a memory she wouldn't soon forget. "Oh, dear Lord," she whispered. "Thank you for a friend like Joe Gallagher."

Chapter Nine

"Gentlemen. We need to talk." Joe stood in the doorway and crossed his arms.

Rod and Julian both froze and slowly turned to look at him. They stood at attention beside the long metal table set up in the equipment garage. Laptops, cameras and video equipment littered the makeshift work space where they reviewed each day's footage.

Neither man uttered a word in response to his announcement.

"Becca suggested I let you film moving the cows to the fresh pasture."

Rod let out a breath. "I thought we were in trouble again."

Julian paled. "How are we going to do that?" He fiddled with his glasses.

"You two can ride the farm truck and film."

Becca walked into the garage, excitement in her eyes at his words. "You're going to let me help herd?"

"What are you doing here? What about Casey?"

"I took her to the doctor. Whatever she had has disappeared. My mother took her to Pueblo, to the zoo."

"Are you sure you don't want to take the day off? You could go with them."

"I've already missed the entire morning."

"You don't punch a clock. Besides, I moved most of the herd already."

"You did?"

Joe nodded. "There's still a slight chance of rain until the end of the week. I had to. I've got about fifty or so stragglers left, if that makes you feel better. The plan is to gently encourage them back to the pasture. I'll ride Blackie and pull up the rear with the dogs." He met Becca's gaze. "Would you be willing to ride outside the herd?"

"Sure," she said.

"The dogs and I will be zigzagging back and forth." He looked pointedly at Rod and Julian. "Keep the truck away from the cows."

"What about me?" Abi asked as she joined them.

"You can come along, as long as you promise not to put any videos on YouTube," Joe said.

"That hardly seems fair," she murmured with feigned indignation.

Joe only chuckled as they all exited the garage. He slowed his pace to match Becca's stride as they crossed the yard to the horses together.

"Sorry I couldn't wait for you. Eighty percent chance of precipitation predicted for later this afternoon. I'm watching for a four-day stretch of sunshine before I hit full harvest mode. We may have it toward the end of the week."

"Have you had any confirmations from your contacts?"

"Funny thing about that," Joe said. "Suddenly everyone is previously committed."

Rebecca gasped. *"Judge Brown."*

"Not necessarily, but, yeah, that was my initial thought, as well."

"It's because of me. I feel terrible about this, Joe. What are you going to do?"

"We'll find a way. Always do."

They saddled up the horses and headed out toward the pasture.

Joe whistled for the dogs and picked up his pace, trotting Blackie in the other direction. "There they are," he called out. Straight ahead the last of the herd had gathered near the water trough, with a few stragglers near the creek.

"The dogs and I will rustle along those near the creek, then I'll head to the front to turn them around. You're okay working the outside?"

"Of course," she answered. "I've got things covered. Don't worry."

"But I do worry," Joe muttered. "I worry plenty."

"Where's the truck?" Becca called to Joe.

"Here it comes." He pointed a gloved hand behind them. The truck slowly approached with Rod seated in the flatbed with his camera as Julian drove and Abi rode shotgun.

Becca called out to Rod and Julian. "Joe is going to turn the cows and start the forward movement. Stay back from the herd. I'll be moving toward them once he gets things turned around."

"Why would you move toward them?" Rod asked.

"Cattle will move in the opposite direction of a perceived threat or predator." She turned in the saddle. "Julian, stay back so we don't spook them or the horses. And don't get out of the truck. You'll be crushed if you're in the wrong place and they get agitated."

"Crushed? There's a chance of getting crushed? I'm not too sure this is in my job description," Julian returned.

"Follow Becca's instructions and you'll be fine," Joe said. We just don't want you to find yourself between a cow and her calf."

"No worries. We're all staying in the truck," Rod said. "Those cows look pretty big to me."

"They may be big, but they aren't all that smart. Try to remember that cowboys have been doing this for a very long time."

"You'd have thought they'd come up with a better plan than this after two or three hundred years," Rod observed.

Joe chuckled at the comment as he and the dogs pushed past the cows to the front. Gil and Wishbone nipped at the heels of the animals, encouraging them along and turning them around. Joe gave a nod of satisfaction. Finally something was going right.

As the first of the herd plodded along, moving along the trail to the new pasture, Julian called out from the truck. *"Rawhide."* His face was bright with excitement.

Rod offered a hearty thumbs-up to Joe as he filmed.

This was good. They'd get their footage, and he'd get his herd moved.

Becca continued to encourage the herd along, riding Princess on the outside, right where they could see her and out of the cattle's blind spot. "Come on," she encouraged the cows "You've done this before. Let's move nice and steady. We'll be done real quick."

"You talking to yourself?" Joe hollered.

"Yes. I am. You talk to the dogs."

"That's true," he returned with a smile of satisfaction.

Moments later, Julian hollered from the truck window and waved his arms. His panicked voice rang out. "Joe, behind you. Those cows are headed off in the wrong direction. What should I do?"

"Easy, there Julian," Joe called back. "We don't worry about stragglers. Relax, buddy. The dogs and I will catch them later."

The blare of the truck's horn blasted into the air.

"No," Joe yelled. "Don't use the horn. You'll spook the…"

Becca's horse was closest to the truck. At the sound Princess reared with panic, nostrils flaring. Eyes wild, the mare snorted and galloped in a circle with Becca struggling desperately to soothe the animal and rein her in. Princess circled one more time before taking off with Becca clinging to the reins.

"Get the truck away from the herd," Joe called to Julian, his full attention on Becca.

The rumble of hooves on the ground drowned his voice as the remaining cows began to stampede. He wasn't concerned about the small herd. It was Becca who had his full attention. His heart thundered as he raced Blackie after them.

"No. No. No," he whispered. "Not Becca. Not now."

Princess and Becca continued their wild ride. When the horse and rider approached a thicket of trees, the mare suddenly stopped, the action tossing Becca into the air as though she were weightless. She landed against a fallen tree branch.

Joe slid off his horse and raced to where she lay on her side, sprawled on the ground still muddy from last week's rain. He skidded to a stop in the mud, kneeling next to her. Her hat and phone were scattered on the ground, and her body was twisted awkwardly. He was terrified to move her.

He tore off his gloves using his teeth and felt her neck for a pulse. "Oh, Lord," he murmured. "Please, please don't let her die on me."

"I am not dead."

"Becca?" Joe blinked.

When her lashes fluttered, relief pounded through him.

She moaned and rolled to her back. "Ouch."

"What hurts?" he asked.

"What doesn't?"

With a gentle motion, he elevated her shoulder to release the limb that was still twisted behind her.

"Much better. Thank you." She tried to sit up and groaned, easing back down. "Oh, man, I'm dizzy. This is definitely not how I planned to spend my day."

"Stay still," Joe said. He carefully patted her down from head to foot. The back of her head boasted a lump, though the skin remained intact.

"Can you move your legs?"

Eyes closed, she wiggled her boots.

"Thank you, God," Joe said aloud.

"I see you two are talking again," Becca murmured.

"This isn't funny," he ground out. For once, he was grateful for the rain. With the exception of a few jagged rocks from the gravel and dirt road, the ground was cushioned with soft grass and thick mud where she'd landed.

He checked her extremities. All intact except her right arm. Red seeped through a long-sleeve shirt. Joe swallowed hard, fear rising within him. He grasped the fabric with both hands until the cotton tore, allowing him to push the material out of the way enough to evaluate the injury.

A gash at least six inches long bled steadily, but didn't appear to have severed any major blood vessels. Beside the cut, a long, disfiguring scar trailed the inside of Becca's arm. She'd injured herself before?

"Here." A cotton gauze pad was thrust at him.

Joe looked up. Abi stood over them. "Where'd you get this?"

"First-aid kit in the truck."

"Thanks." He applied the pad to Becca's arm and then pulled a cotton handkerchief from his pocket, securing the gauze in place.

"Will she be all right?" Abi asked on a near sob.

"There doesn't seem to be anything broken. I'm not a doctor, and that was some fall she took. No doubt she has a concussion."

"It's not nice to talk about me like I'm not here," Becca whispered, her eyes still closed.

"Oh, Rebecca," Abi said, kneeling down. "That was quite a scare."

Becca reached out a hand, and Abi took it.

"I'm going to be fine," Becca said.

"I'm counting on it," Abi returned.

"Is Rod okay?" Joe asked. "Did Julian get the truck out of the way?"

"Rod's fine. Shaken up, but fine. He nearly fell out of the flatbed once Julian hit the gas pedal."

"And Julian?"

"Julian is a mess, blubbering that he killed Rebecca."

"Oh, brother."

Abi released Becca's hand and stood. "Yeah, tell me about it. What do you want me to do, Joe?"

"Call 9-1-1. Tell them Gallagher Ranch. North access road. Then park the truck there so you can direct them. The north access is the gate Rod stumbled on the first day. Think you can find it?"

"I've got it."

"Thanks, Abi. Oh, and get Rod and Julian back to the house, as well."

"No problem."

An agitated whinny indicated that Princess had returned. Joe stood and pulled the dragging reins from the mud, tying the leather to a tree. "Easy, girl. Easy. It's all over now." He murmured more soothing words as he stroked the mare.

A phone rang and Joe scrambled around on the ground until he found the device. Mud covered the screen. He could let it go to voice mail, but what if it was important? What if it was her mother? Becca would want him to take the call if it was about something important.

"My phone?" she murmured.

"I found it, Becca." He held it to his ear. "Hello?"

"*You need to get out of Paradise. You aren't wanted here.*"

"Who is this?" Joe demanded.

The call disconnected.

There was no doubt in his mind that the voice on the other end of the unidentified call was Judge Brown. He stared at the phone. Did that call mean that the Judge had threatened Becca before? He was going to find out, and right away.

In the distance, the wailing siren of the Paradise Valley ambulance echoed. Moments later, another siren sounded as well, indicating that someone from the sheriff's department was also on his way.

"Becca, open your eyes."

"No need to yell. I'm right here," she said.

"Can you see me?"

She opened her eyes and blinked. "Yes. It hurts to look, but I can see you very clearly." Her eyes closed again. "Stop frowning."

"I called an ambulance, Becca."

"No. I can't afford an ambulance. I'm perfectly capable of getting up."

He put a gentle, yet firm hand on her shoulder when she attempted to rise to a seated position. "Don't move."

"Yes, sir."

"We're not taking any chances. That was quite a fall."

She nodded slowly, her eyes wide open now.

Joe looked deep into her brown eyes. Today they were the color of the pecans harvested on the ranch in the autumn. His hands stopped shaking long enough for him to gently push the hair away from her face, and wipe a dab of mud from her chin. A bruise was starting to color her forehead.

"I'm a real mess, huh?"

"You look beautiful," Joe whispered as he untangled a mass of her dark hair.

He froze, and his breath hitched. The words "and I love you," had nearly slipped from his lips.

In that moment, he realized that he had never stopped loving Rebecca Anshaw. Twelve long years and he loved her as much as when he was a kid.

Joe sighed and shook his head.

"What's wrong?" Becca murmured.

"Nothing at all."

Nothing at all, except now he had one more thing to keep him awake at night.

"Why do I need an IV?" Rebecca asked the nurse.

"That cowboy who brought you in indicated you lost a lot of blood, so the doctor wanted to be safe. Besides, a little normal saline makes everything better, don't you think?"

"I'll take your word for it." Rebecca sat quietly on the gurney as the fluid dripped into the tubing.

"Don't you want to lie down?" the nurse asked.

"No. I feel fine. My vision is back to normal. When can I go home?"

"Your arm isn't sutured yet, but I imagine Dr. Rogers will release you once she has the X-ray and CT scan results."

"Dr. Rogers? What happened to the doctor who examined me when I came in? The one who did that neuro exam."

"Oh, you know. Shift change. Dr. Rogers is taking over. She says she's a friend of yours."

"Dr. Rogers?"

"Sara Elliott Rogers."

"Oh, Sara Elliott." Rebecca smiled. "Yes. We practically grew up together on her father's ranch."

"Well, then. That's good news. She'll be here in a moment."

On cue, the door opened and her old friend walked in. Sara Elliott Rogers looked exactly the same as Rebecca remembered. Petite with a smattering of freckles on her face, and black hair pulled back into a French braid.

"Marta, thanks for cleaning up that wound. I'll finish up." She turned to Rebecca. "This is a terrible way to catch up with an old friend."

"Sara!"

"Easy. Stay on that gurney." Sara moved over to offer her a hearty hug. "I've missed you, cowgirl." She moved back to assess Rebecca and frowned. "That's going to be some bruise in the middle of your forehead. Sort of like old times, right? We certainly got a lot of scrapes and shiners on the ranch, didn't we?"

"Yes. We did. What's this I hear about you having twins? Is that right?" Rebecca asked.

"Yes. They're almost two now. I'm going a little crazy trying to keep up with them. I've cut back to working part-time here and at the Paradise Clinic."

"We'll have to plan to get together. I'd love to see them."

"Absolutely." Sara donned a pair of gloves. "So the nurse cleaned up your wound. All we have to do is stitch you up." She turned to assess the suture kit laid out and ready. "Why don't you lay back and get comfortable."

Rebecca rested against the small gurney pillow.

"Any dizziness when you reclined?"

"No, that seems to have gone away."

"Good. The CT appears normal. However, you'll want to restrict your activity for the next week. No horseback riding until you're cleared. We'll give you a checklist of symptoms that might indicate you need to come back in to the emergency room or the clinic immediately."

"No horseback riding?"

"No. I know that seems restrictive, but we certainly don't want another concussion before this one heals. We'll reevaluate when you come in for a follow-up in the clinic."

Rebecca was silent as Sara's gentle fingers probed the length of the wound.

"I think we're looking at about twelve stitches. First you're going to feel a little needle prick as I administer the anesthetic.

"Doing okay?" Sara asked a moment later.

"I'm good."

"This is going to be to the left of this scar you already have."

Rebecca tensed as Sara inspected the ugly vertical line.

"Who did that last suture job?"

"It was a teaching hospital in Denver. I believe the physician was a student."

"Oh, goodness, let's hope he didn't decide to go into surgery. You might want to consider having a plastic surgeon evaluate the other incision line for revision. We can do much better that that."

"It's no big deal," Rebecca murmured. She was silent as Sara worked, praying against all odds that she wouldn't mention the ugly mark on her arm again.

"Tying off the sutures now. I promise you this one will be pretty. I crochet in my spare time."

Rebecca couldn't resist a smile.

"All done. Let me help you sit up." Sara removed her gloves and assisted her to a sitting position.

"Looks great," Rebecca said, as she inspected the thin, flat line of sutures.

"Thank you. Keep it clean and dry. You can cover it

loosely to protect the area. I'll give you some ointment and extra gauze pads and tape. Apply the ointment to the area once a day, sparingly. Then, as I said, I'll see you in a week in the clinic for follow-up."

"Okay," Rebecca said quietly.

Sara washed and dried her hands at the sink. She grabbed the clipboard chart. "I want to talk to you about the X-ray results."

"My X-rays?"

"You have no new fractures."

"That's good, right?"

Sara met her gaze. "Rebecca, your X-ray shows indications that the right arm has been broken several times. In at least one of those events, the bone was not properly set."

Rebecca began to tremble "Yes. A few accidents."

"The scar on your arm?"

Rebecca turned her head away and closed her eyes tightly, waiting for what she knew would come next.

"I'm required by law to report suspected cases of abuse."

"Why?" she whispered. "Nick is dead."

Sara inhaled sharply and put her hand on Rebecca's shoulder. "Oh, honey. I'm so sorry."

Shame washed over Becca as she stared at the pattern on the hospital gown. "Please, please, don't tell anyone."

"There's no need for me to. The threat is gone. There are laws that protect your health-care privacy. However, I am going to give you a card. I want you to get counseling."

"I've had counseling. With God's help I'm healing."

"Take the card. You never know. If there's anything I can do…"

"Thank you, Sara."

Rebecca hid her face as Sara finished writing on the chart.

"Rebecca, I am looking forward to getting together. Will I see you at the Fourth of July barbecue?"

"I guess I forgot about that."

"You have been gone awhile. No one forgets about my father's barbecue. I'll look for you."

She nodded, waiting for shame to engulf her again as the door quietly closed behind Sara.

Yet this time words of scripture bubbled up from inside.

Do not remember the former things, nor consider the things of old.

"Oh, Lord," she prayed. "I'm ready."

Joe paced the emergency department waiting room of Paradise Valley Hospital. He glanced one more time at his watch.

Sure the place was busy, but it had been an hour since the last update from the nurse. He'd called Joan Anshaw, and she was on her way home. He'd also stepped outside and had a long conversation with God. Basically he'd negotiated what he considered a real good deal. If He'd take care of Becca, Joe would plant himself in church on Sundays.

Desperate times predicated he stoop lower than usual. And he was definitely desperate.

Joe ran a hand over his face. When he raised his head, he noticed a door open in the examination area. Hopeful, he stepped closer.

Finally a nurse appeared. When she turned around,

he could see that Becca was the patient in the wheel-chair she was pushing.

Becca's gaze met his, and she offered him a small pitiful smile. Her hair was a tangled mess, and her clothes were covered with mud. The bruise on her fore-head was now a purple beacon. Joe released his breath in a whoosh and shook his head, saying a silent prayer of thanks.

It only took a minute to pull his truck around.

"Maybe I should lift you," he said as he opened the passenger door.

"No. I can get in by myself."

"I won't bite," Joe murmured.

"Says who?"

"I know lots of people who will vouch…" He paused. "Okay, maybe only one or two." Joe smiled as he care-fully closed the door behind her before jogging to the driver side.

"I can't believe they released you," he said, as he backed out of the drop-off zone.

"Joe, I'm fine. They wouldn't have discharged me if I wasn't ready to go home."

"Okay, but you're going to rest."

"Now you sound like my mother," she said as she fastened her seat belt.

"I happen to recall that your mom is a pretty terrific person, so you can try to insult me all you want. You're still going to rest."

Becca began to laugh. "That wasn't an insult. Sim-ply a commentary. And yes, my mom is still amazing."

"Finally we agree on something." He paused. "How many stitches?"

"Twelve."

"Twelve! You won't be doing ranch work anytime soon," he growled.

"Someone a little grumpy?"

"Maybe so. I tend to get grumpy when I'm irritated."

"Why are you irritated?"

He glanced at her and frowned, shaking his head. *Because my heart was ripped out of my chest when you flew off that horse. That's why.*

They were silent as his truck smoothly headed toward Gallagher Ranch.

"Are you cold?" he finally asked, his voice gruff.

"Maybe a little."

"I brought your sweater. Abi's idea," he said. "Don't want you to think I'm going all thoughtful on you." He reached in the backseat and handed it to her.

"No, of course not," she murmured.

"I'll turn on the heat, too."

"Thank you, Joe." She awkwardly pulled the sweater over her shoulders. "Have you heard from my mom? Is Casey all right? They aren't worried, are they?"

"Joan will meet us at the ranch. I've been calling her with updates. Told her you landed on your head. She agreed with me that fortunately, since you're extremely hardheaded, there's no doubt you're going to be fine."

Becca chuckled and turned to him. "Thank you, again."

"My pleasure. I do it for all my hardheaded friends."

"Do you have many hardheaded friends?"

"You'd be surprised." He shot her a wink, feeling some of the anger subside. "Oh, and I have Julian tied up in the barn until I get back to the ranch, as a precautionary measure.

"Tell me you're kidding."

"I'll let you decide."

"Do you happen to know where my phone is?"

"Yeah, I've got it in a plastic bag in the backseat. The thing is covered with mud."

"Does it still work?"

"Oh, yeah." Joe cleared his throat. "Ah, Becca?"

"Yes?"

"What happened to your arm?"

"You know what happened to my arm."

"I'm talking about the other scar."

Becca tugged the sweater even closer. "That was a long time ago."

"I didn't ask you when it happened," he said slowly and softly. "I asked you what happened."

"Joe, do we have to discuss this now?"

He gripped the steering wheel tightly, struggling to hold back his anger. "Nick did it, didn't he?"

"It was an accident." The words were flat. Rote. Like she'd said them a dozen times before.

"What kind of accident gives you a scar like that, I wonder?"

"Glass. Shards of glass. I tripped and landed on a glass-topped table."

She didn't even stumble over the explanation. That more than anything caused a cold rage to start inside him.

Joe hit the brakes, automatically stretching out his prosthetic arm to keep Becca from pitching forward. Then he carefully eased the truck off the road.

His pent-up frustration was back, and it echoed in the truck, as he released a loud groan of pain. "Am I the only one who's figured out that your husband was hurting you?"

"No. No. No." The words were barely a whisper. A slow tear wound its way over her check and landed on her shirt collar.

It was Joe's undoing. He unbuckled his seat belt and wrapped his arms around her, resting her head against his chest.

The only sound was of the occasional vehicle passing by on the road.

"Casey must never know," Becca whispered against his chest.

"Why haven't you told Nick's grandfather? Surely that would get him off your case."

She eased back in her seat and fiddled with the buttons on her sweater. "Judge Brown would never believe me."

"He still should be told the truth."

"No, Joe."

"If you don't, then I will."

"Why? What good can possibly come of breaking an old man's heart?"

"That old man needs to stop harassing you. That's why. I accidently picked up a call he made to you on your phone. Becca, he's called you at least a dozen times. That's plain crazy. He's making your life miserable, and you don't deserve this."

"Please. Please. Promise me you won't tell him."

He shook his head. "I can't make that kind of promise. What kind of friend would I be if I agreed to that?"

"Joe, promise me you will not tell the judge."

He slammed a hand on the steering wheel, and she jumped.

"Look what he's done to you. You're jumpy as all getout these days. You never used to be like this."

"I've done it to myself. Besides, I'm not the same 'me' that you remember so well. That 'me' disappeared a long time ago."

"*A long time ago.* Yeah, I remember saying the same thing the day you showed up on the ranch. But you know what, Becca? I'm starting to realize that it's not so long ago after all. And really, deep down inside, we haven't changed as much as we'd like to believe."

She stared at him, her brown eyes round, her jaw set. "Joe?" she pleaded.

"All I can say is that I'm not too happy to find out you think you need to have all these secrets. You and I will revisit this conversation again. After you're feeling better and those greenhorns are on their way back to wherever it is they came from."

He started the truck and checked over his shoulder for oncoming vehicles. "Tonight, that's pretty much all I'm willing to guarantee."

Chapter Ten

Joe strode into Sheriff Sam Lawson's office, turned on the fan and checked to be sure the door was shut tight.

"Whoa. What's going on?" Sam asked.

"Becca is being harassed by Judge Brown."

"Are you sure?"

"I have proof," Joe returned.

"The man has to be seventy-five, eighty years old. Do you really think he's got the energy to do that?"

Joe shook his head and sank into a chair. "Yeah, I do. I'd probably be on the mark if I were to say revenge is the fuel that's keeping that man alive."

Sam's grimaced. "He's probably found six dozen Bible verses to support his actions. The thing about bitterness is that it's a disease that kills you by eating you from the inside out."

"You sound familiar with it."

"Saw it firsthand with my stepfather." He gave a shake of his head. "What a waste of a life."

"I'm sorry, Sam. I didn't realize."

The other man shrugged. "I don't talk about him much because I'm a little scared that after living with the guy for seventeen years, I might have the propensity to be like him."

"Not you, Sam. Never."

"I don't know.

"Trouble with this situation is that Judge Brown isn't about to give up until he breaks Becca."

"That's sad because his focus is on revenge, which means the other people in his life are ignored."

"No doubt." Joe took off his Stetson, ran his fingers along the crown crease and put it back on. "I've got another issue needling at me, as well. I have reason to believe Nick Simpson was physically abusing his wife."

"Joe, that's a pretty strong accusation." Sam took a deep breath. "Not one that you can get much traction out of, either, since the man is dead."

"I know. It galls me that I know I'm right and Becca refuses to tell anyone. I'm certain that one look at her medical records would show a pattern of abuse. Typically they're in and out of a variety of emergency rooms and urgent-care facilities. Women in that situation don't like to seek treatment at the same place twice."

"How'd you get so knowledgeable on the topic?"

"I called a counselor friend today. Same person I spoke with when I lost my arm."

"I didn't realize you went to therapy."

"Yeah, my doctor basically delivered an ultimatum."

"Smart doc, if he realizes that's the only way to get you to do anything."

"Thanks for the vote of confidence."

Sam narrowed his eyes, and his mouth formed a grim line.

"What are you thinking?" Joe asked his friend.

"I hate to even go down this road, but ninety to nothing this would explain the accident that killed Nick Simpson."

"You mean the abuse?"

Sam nodded. "Something just isn't right about how that all went down."

"Yeah, I've been thinking about that, too. Every time I do, it makes me so angry I can barely see straight. I have to do something." He met Sam's gaze. "What would you do about Judge Brown if you were in my position?"

"There's nothing we can do inside the law, unless Rebecca is willing to file a complaint."

"Which she won't do." Joe stood and paced across the office. "Isn't what he's doing considered criminal mischief or something?"

"No, that would be if he actually did damage."

"He's doing damage all right."

"Physical damage, I mean. Keying a car. Graffiti. Tire slashing. That generally falls under criminal mischief. While I would tend to agree with you, Joe, my hands are tied."

"Then I'm between a rock and a hard place." He clenched his left hand. "There has to be a way around this."

"Go talk to him."

"She won't let me. Arm wrestled me with tears."

"That'll do it every time."

Joe nodded. "She's not willing to open the door to her past again. Trouble is, it's not going to go away on its own."

"Could you go talk to the daughter? Nick's mother. Maybe talk around the topic until it's clear she understands your point. That wouldn't be breaking your promise, would it?"

"That might work. I'm going to have to pray on it. There's a lot of gray around this whole mess. Either way, I owe you one. Thanks for letting me talk this through."

"Naw, I owe you one. I should have gotten those city people lost instead of taking them to your ranch. What was I thinking? They'd still be driving around in circles if I wasn't so hospitable. I've got to stop that. Being nice is my downfall."

Joe raised a brow as he slid back down into the chair. "What about that strawberry-blond writer who's crushing on you?"

"Well, I might make an exception for Miss Warren." When Sam smiled, a glint of amusement shone in his eyes.

"I suspected as much. What do you think about Abi?"

"What I think is that I've got enough going on in my life. I don't need a city girl. To that end, I'm doing my best to stay out of her way. The woman is smart, beautiful, yields a killer smile and, to make it worse, she's nice. That's a dangerously potent combination."

"Yeah, I heard you've been doing a lot of fishing lately."

Sam leaned forward in his chair and folded his hands on his desk. "I call that self-preservation. Fishing preserves my way of life. Besides, I like being single."

"Do you?"

"Sure I do," Sam said. "Don't you?"

"I don't know anymore. Maybe my brother, Dan, has it right. Either way, sure is a lot of that stuff going around lately. You notice?"

"You mean love and marriage?" Sam laughed. "There ought to be a vaccination for what causes that. Don't you think?"

"Too late for most of the men in town. Look at Jake MacLaughlin. Bitsy is not only his stepmother, but her machinations got him and his wife together."

"Bitsy didn't have to do much. That man fell pretty hard."

"Doesn't look too unhappy about it, either," Joe observed.

"There's only a few of us left. You, me, Deke Andrews, Duffy McKenna. We're a dying breed."

"Ever occur to you that maybe we're just dinosaurs, Sam?"

"No. I like my life the way it is. Content. That's what I am."

"Content my boots! If you're content, it's because the sorry life you have is less frightening than taking a chance on you-know-what."

Sam cocked his head and nodded. "I won't rule out the possibility that you're right. Then again, I'll deny it if you tell anyone we even had this conversation." He pointed to the door. "And don't even let Bitsy get wind of it."

All Joe could do was laugh.

Joe pulled up the ten-day forecast on his laptop and released the breath he was holding. Finally things were looking good. Sunshine promised for the Fourth of July holiday and into all of next week.

"Thank You, Lord. If I don't say it enough times, thank You."

The hay would dry out, and then he'd be able to move

the windrower through. A few days of drying, raking and he'd be able to bale.

Joe pulled up the number of Shady Malone, a friend who had helped him and Dan in the past. Shady and a couple of his friends did extra work on the local ranches in the Four Corners area.

"Shady, it's Joe Gallagher."

"Joe! How's it going?"

"Fine. Fine. I haven't heard back from you. Did you get my messages? Can I count on you this year? I'm looking at next week. The weather looks like it's finally going to cooperate."

"I'd like to help you Joe, 'cept me and the boys have contracted elsewhere."

"Really? You usually manage to juggle a couple of jobs at once, what with the time between cutting and baling."

The line was silent. "Joe, I like you. Gallagher Ranch has treated me well over the years. I'm not going to play games. The honest truth is that I'm being paid not to help you. Good money, too. Real good money."

Joe sat up in his chair, not believing what he was hearing. "Whoa. Whoa. You're kidding, right?"

"I wish I was. If I don't play ball, I'm going to be blackballed in the valley."

"Judge Brown?"

"Don't know about that. I was contacted by an attorney. All legal and such. Made me sign papers. I'm not actually sure where the money is coming from. I may not be the brightest cowboy in the saddle, but I'm smart enough not to ask."

The line was silent for a moment.

"I'm sorry, Joe. Real sorry. You can see the position this puts me in. I've got a family to consider, as well."

"Sure, I get it, Shady. Don't like it much, but I get it."

Joe stared at the screen. *Money and power.* This was what you could do with enough of each. If that was the case, he'd rather remain a struggling rancher. Maybe it was time to talk to Virginia Simpson.

When the front doorbell rang, Joe realized he'd been sitting and staring at the screen saver on his monitor for almost ten minutes. Nothing to be accomplished by that.

Yep, he had a problem. That was the beauty of ranch life. No day was ever the same. Pray, then put one foot in front of the other. Deal with it and move on. He closed the laptop and got up to answer the door.

Becca was on his front step with a smile on her face. She'd taken care to conceal her scar and her sutures with a long-sleeve T-shirt.

"Well, look at you," Joe said. "If you didn't have that purple bruise in the middle of your forehead, no one would even guess you got tossed from a horse and scared the life out of me."

"That wasn't exactly my plan for Monday."

"Good to know. So, how do you feel?"

"Oh, I have the expected aches and pains. But I finally figured out how to cover my stitches well enough to wash my hair. I feel one hundred percent better."

"You look good," he said. And she did. Joe itched to reach out and touch the dark hair that flowed around her shoulders.

"Thank you."

"You're not having any headaches or blurred vision?"

"None."

Joe held up his residual limb. The sleeve was folded

up and empty. He'd taken off the prosthesis when he came in from the pasture and showered. "How many fingers am I holding up?"

"That's not funny," she said with a frown. "Not one bit."

"Oh, sure it is. If I can't laugh at my own expense, then what's the point? I keep telling you to lighten up, Becca."

"Moving right along." She shook her head. "Abi said you stopped by to talk to me?"

"Yeah. Do you have a minute?"

"Considering that I've done nothing at all but rest today, I've got more than a minute."

"I hate to break it to you," he said with a glance at his watch, "but it's only barely nine a.m. You've only been resting a couple of hours."

"Really? Seems like all day to me. I guess that's because even though you grounded me, I still wake up at three a.m."

Joe chuckled. "Come on in."

"You're all cleaned up on a workday," she noted.

"I had to run some errands in town."

He closed the front door. "Come on down to my office."

"Wait. Let me take off my boots first."

"You don't have to do that."

"I'm not messing up your shiny hardwood floors." She glanced down at the floor and stepped carefully to the side of the entry rug. "Goodness, who cleans this place? You?"

"Hardly. Someone comes in once a week. When I come home it's clean. I write a check and say thank you."

Suddenly Becca's arm flailed in an effort to steady

herself. Joe grabbed her hand. The skin was soft to his touch, and an intoxicating whiff of lavender drifted to him.

"Um, thanks," Becca said as she pulled off first one and then the other boot.

He nodded and released her hand.

"Did you get the rest of the cows moved?" she asked as she padded behind him in her stocking feet.

"Cows are safe and sound and grazing happily."

"Good. Good. Oh, and thank you for all you did Monday. Contacting my mother and everything." She hesitated. "I, um, I hope that our talk about, you know… I hope it can remain confidential."

"You don't have to worry. That conversation is on the back burner." He turned and met her gaze. Her brown eyes pleaded with him.

"For the moment," he added.

"Thank you." She breathed the words softly, but there was no mistaking the relief in her voice.

Joe led her into his bookshelf-lined office. He pulled out a chair from the set of sturdy oak chairs that sat on the other side of the desk. "Have a seat."

"It's so tidy in here. It even smells like furniture polish." Her gaze took in the bookshelves that lined several walls, his massive desk and the view of the pasture from the bay window.

"My father's desk used to be piled high with paperwork. I was nearly afraid to go in there."

He tapped his laptop. "It's all in here. If the place seems clean, well, that's because I'm never in here." He pointed out the window. "I'm always out there."

Joe moved to his desk chair. The more distance from Becca the better.

"You wear glasses?" She smiled, her gaze landing on the black frames on his desk.

"Um, yeah." He picked up the glasses and put them away in his drawer. "Paperwork. It makes my eyes cross."

"Sort of Clark Kent, aren't they?"

"Not if you're calling me Superman."

She smiled again, as though the thought amused her.

Joe wished she wouldn't be so perky and bright. Like a candle, she lit up every room she entered.

And here he was, about to throw water on her flame.

She folded her hands in her lap and gave him her full attention. "So what did you want to talk about? You seem a little tense. Is everything all right?"

"No, it's not. I've been doing a lot of thinking."

"Oh, is something wrong?" Becca swallowed nervously, sat up straight and scooted to the edge of the chair.

"I've decided to send them back to Denver," he announced.

Becca blinked. "Send who? Wh-what?" she sputtered.

"The team from OrthoBorne. This was a crazy idea to start with. One that I take full responsibility for. After all, I'm the one who said yes to this whole thing."

When Becca said nothing, he continued. "You have to admit that it's been nothing short of a domino of disasters. One after another. You getting hurt, well, that was the end of the line for me. I was awake most of last night thinking about this."

"What about certification?" she finally blurted out, her hands gripping the arms of the chair. "You have a contract."

"I'll break it. It's not worth the headache."

"You can't do that. Your prosthesis, you've come so far. Joe, you've actually taught me a few things about using the myoelectric arm. You're going to give up? Now?"

"No. Not at all. I'm not giving up on the arm. You're right. OrthoBorne has given me back much of my freedom, and I'm selfish enough to want to keep it."

"If I can be so bold as to ask, how will you finance the prosthesis?"

"Hollis Elliott," he answered.

"Excuse me?"

"Hollis is interested in a parcel of land that borders his ranch. The man has been nagging me about it for years. I'm going to sell the land to him."

"Gallagher land? Land that's been in your family for, what? Four generations? What will your mother say?"

"My mother only owns a fourth of the ranch. I'm the majority shareholder. I make the decisions, handle the books, and I have since Dad died. She'll see things my way."

Becca shook her head, obviously stunned by the news. "Apparently you've made your decision. I guess there's nothing more to discuss, is there?"

"Not really."

Becca looked past him, her brown eyes glassy. Her gaze was somewhere out the window, far away from the room where they were sitting.

She wiped her palms on her jeans and gave a resigned nod. "I'll break it to the team right away, and we'll clear out. Casey and I will be out of the cottage this weekend."

This time it was Joe who was speechless. "Whoa.

No," he finally said. "You and Casey don't have to leave."

"Yes, Joe. We do. I'm part of the certification process, and if you are letting Rod, Julian and Abi go, then naturally, I'll be leaving with the team."

His mind raced. This was not going the way he'd planned. The saddle was definitely being yanked from under him, and he was about to land boots up. It wasn't going to be a pretty sight, either.

"Where will you go?"

"That's not your problem," she said. The words were a slap to his face.

"Call OrthoBorne and see if you can stay."

"Joe, it doesn't work like that. I'm managing your case, and if you are dismissing OrthoBorne, then you are dismissing me, as well."

"I guess I didn't realize…"

"I don't think you've thought any of this through," she said. Becca took a deep breath. Her eyes sparked with unspoken frustration. "You're giving up your land…a couple hundred years of Gallagher land, when you could have everything finished up in a few days if we all worked together. Why, pretty much all that's left is for Abi to do her interview. The guys probably have almost enough to finish, as well."

He stared at her. He'd blinked, and the tables had turned.

"It's Thursday night. The sun was shining all day today. That should help your precious hay, right?"

Joe offered a cautious nod, not sure where she was going with the conversation, and he was in too deep to stop now.

"Tomorrow is the Elliott Ranch's Fourth of July barbecue. I'll get them an invitation and send the team to the party. It will keep them off your ranch. They'll have the weekend in town. Come Monday, I'll ride herd on them and get things finished up. They'll be done in twenty-four hours. You have my guarantee."

"I don't know..." Joe hesitated.

"Please, all I'm asking for is the chance to fix this. I've never in my entire life walked away without finishing what I started."

"This isn't about you, Becca."

"Maybe you don't understand what I'm saying. This is very much about me. My reputation is on the line here. I let you down. I let OrthoBorne down. I'm asking... I'm begging for a second chance."

"If I say yes, what about you? What about certification?" he asked.

"I'm sorry, but you know that it will take a bit more time for us to finish. Not much more. You have a DVD to watch and more paperwork. But really, I think we've covered most of the things in the program. I've been going slowly as a courtesy, but I can see that was the wrong approach. I'll speed things up, though I can promise you that I won't disrupt your work. You won't even know I'm around."

"Becca—"

"Hear me out, Joe. You've been angry since I arrived. I understand why. I treated you very badly by walking away without taking the time to talk to you. I was young and so immature. I'm sorry. This is the second time I've apologized, and I won't do it again. I've paid dearly for my choices. Believe me."

"Becca, I keep telling you that you are not the problem."

"Still, I recognize that what you really want is for things to go back to the way they were before. You want normal again."

"Is that what I want?" he murmured, shaking his head.

"Yes, Joe. You've made that abundantly clear in all you say and do. I hardly blame you. It's been disruption after disruption since we arrived. You're right." She nodded. "All I can do is apologize. My job was to liaise, and I've failed miserably."

"No, you haven't." He rubbed his jaw and met her gaze.

"Yes. I have."

"Look, I don't want to argue."

"We aren't arguing. We're discussing," she said.

"Either way. Looks like you have a deal."

"I do?" She turned to meet his gaze, eyes wide.

"Yeah. Let's see where we stand on Monday."

"Thank you," she breathed.

He nodded, more confused than ever.

When Becca stood and walked to the door of his office, he got up from his chair.

She raised a hand and offered him a quick tight smile. "No, don't get up. I can see myself out." Her gaze met his. "You won't regret this. I promise."

So the team would finish up and life would return to normal by as early as Monday night. And that's what he wanted, right?

All along, that was exactly what he'd been saying.

He wanted things to go back to the way they were before the accident.

Joe stared down at his empty sleeve.

Maybe life hadn't been so great before the accident.

Maybe the Lord had turned the tragedy of his accident into a blessing. It had brought Becca back into his life, hadn't it?

Joe sat down and leaned back in his chair. Becca back in his life was truly nothing short of a blessing. He liked seeing her smile, especially at four a.m. when he didn't have to share her with anyone but Gil and Wishbone, and the rising sun. He'd grown used to doing chores around the ranch and having someone to talk to besides Blackie. Someone who really understood ranch life. Understood that being a cowboy was only part of it. Being a good stockman and farmer, that was the whole picture.

And what about those snacks? She made something every night since she moved into the cottage—muffins, cookies, whatever—and they'd mysteriously appear in her saddlebag, ready to eat in the middle of the morning when his stomach was rumbling and they were too far from the barn to go back.

Suddenly the way things used to be wasn't half as appealing as the way they were now.

In fact, it was pretty alarming when he thought about it. Life without Becca wasn't much of a life at all.

Chapter Eleven

Abi lifted her fingers from her laptop. Both she and Rod turned from the makeshift worktable in the utility garage to look at Rebecca.

"Did you say we have the rest of the day off?" Rod asked.

"After all the time we lost with the rain, your concussion and the whole Julian cattle fiasco, you're giving us the day off?" Abi asked.

Rebecca smiled. "No, I said you have the rest of the day off *and* you've been invited to the Elliott Ranch annual Fourth of July barbecue."

"Well, that's different. That means sleeping in tomorrow." Rod offered a thumbs-up.

"Must be nice," Rebecca said. "There's a rooster in this part of town. No one sleeps in around here."

"I'm sorry," Abi said.

"Tell us about this barbecue, Rebecca," Rod said as he cleaned his camera lens.

"Sounds like one of those fun small-town events," Abi added.

"Actually," Rebecca said, "it's a pretty big deal

around here. Hollis Elliott isn't called the Bison King of Paradise Valley for nothing. Pretty much everyone is on the invitation list, including his cattle and bison cronies. He's been putting on this event at his ranch for as long as I can remember."

"Really?" Abi said.

"Yes. There's always a small country band and all sorts of things to do. They even have rodeo events in the one of the corrals."

"You know," Rod said. "I do some freelance work on the side. This might be a good opportunity to make some connections and add photos to my portfolio."

"There you go. Besides, if nothing else, I can guarantee Mr. Elliott will cater in the best food in the entire valley. Patti Jo's Café and Bakery supplies all the desserts."

"I am so in." Abi grinned.

"Me, too," Rod said. "It was awfully nice of you to get us included. We haven't exactly been candidates for employees of the month since we arrived. I'm pretty sure we've made your life much more challenging."

"He's right. Thank you, Rebecca," Abi added.

"You're welcome. Rod, you were right when you said we're all in the same family. As for Julian, well, I was an intern myself once."

"Please, no one in the history of interns was ever as wet behind the ears as Julian." Rod chuckled. "However, I have to admit. The kid does kind of grow on you after a while."

"He does," Abi admitted. "Like moss."

"The thing is, he means well. You only have a few more days to enjoy his company," Rebecca said. "Monday will be your last day on the ranch. The weather forecast is for sunny skies, with no chance of precipitation. I've promised Mr. Gallagher you will be done by end of day, Monday. So let me know how I can facilitate what you need to complete the project. I intend to keep my word. That means everything must go smoothly on Monday."

Rod shot her a mock salute. "Understood."

"I've got all the background material necessary for my copy. All I need is around thirty minutes with Joe for the actual interview questions," Abi said. "Everything else is gravy. Not that I'm not all about the gravy."

"Rebecca, if you don't mind my asking," Rod said, "why aren't we working today?"

"Um, well, Mr. Gallagher grounded me, due to the concussion. That means the three of you are grounded, too. Sorry about that."

"Certainly not your fault," Abi said.

"Speaking of Julian," Rebecca said glancing around. "Where is our favorite tenderfoot?"

"I sent him to town to get reinforcements from Patti Jo's," Abi said. "We were out of cookies."

"Was that wise? Setting him loose on a defenseless town?" Rod asked.

"He'll be fine," Abi returned with a wave of her hand. "I'd like to stress that I really needed a Patti Jo fix."

Rebecca smiled at the exchange as she started toward the cottage.

"Hey, wait up," Abi asked, jogging to catching up to her. "What about you?"

"Me?"

"You're going to the barbecue?" Abi asked.

"Sure. I'm excited. I haven't been in over a dozen

years. It'll be fun to show Casey the Elliott Ranch. I was pretty much raised there."

"Is your mom going?"

"Mr. Elliott sent her a personal invitation."

"Ooh! What's going on there?"

Rebecca shook her head. "I'm not sure."

"That sounds like a romance-tell to me."

"What do you mean? Romance-tell?"

"You know, those little gestures a guy makes that show he cares when he doesn't have the courage to actually say something. Like Joe does around you."

"I'm going to ignore that. But I think you might be right about Hollis Elliott. Except that it's my mother, so maybe I really don't want to know."

Abi stopped walking and her eyes rounded.

"What?" Rebecca asked.

"I just realized you said pretty much everyone will be there. Does that mean my favorite sheriff will be in attendance?"

"Eventually. He's got his hands full on the fourth. There's a big parade in downtown Paradise in the morning. The Paradise Sheriff's Department consists of one full-time sheriff and deputy, and a few part-timers, plus the administrative assistant. They'll be stretched pretty thin."

"I imagine Casey would like to go to the parade. I'd be more than happy to take her. Of course you'd have to lend me your car."

Rebecca chuckled. "We can all go."

They both made their way back to the cottage. Rebecca peeked in the door to check on her mother and Casey before taking a seat on one of the wide steps outside.

They were silent for moments before Abi turned to her. "I assume the boss found you?"

"Yes." Rebecca shook her head, remembering her conversation with Joe.

"You've got a lot riding on this whole project, don't you?" Abi said quietly.

"I do."

"I don't mean just the bonus," Abi said.

Rebecca's head jerked back, and she met Abi's gaze. "How do you know about the bonus?"

"I'm a writer. It's my job to be a fly on the wall. I pay very close attention to details. Though in reality, I have to admit that I heard it around the office before I left."

"You haven't told anyone, have you?"

"Do I look indiscreet?"

She raised her brows. "I don't know you well enough to make that call."

"We all have our secrets, and I've learned the hard way that God gave us two ears and one mouth for a very good reason. If you'll recall, when I first arrived I said that I'd read about you, yet I've never mentioned it."

"That's true and I appreciate that."

"You can trust me, Rebecca—however, I'm guessing that if I know, Rod and Julian do, as well."

"Really?"

She nodded. "But what does that matter? You deserve the bonus. OrthoBorne really wants Gallagher for this campaign, and you're delivering the goods. It's a no-brainer that you've earned it. You're up before all of us. You finesse everyone's needs before your own. This project will be a success because of you. Good grief, taming the lion alone deserves a bonus."

"What lion?"

Abi chuckled. "You know. Grumpy Gallagher."

"Is that what you call him?" Rebecca released a small gasp. "Oh, he's not—"

"Oh, yes, he is. Though things have sort of changed. He hardly ever growls around you since you were thrown by that horse."

"I'm not sure what you mean."

"Surely you are aware that Joe Gallagher cares a great deal about you."

"We have history. We were friends for a long time, Abi."

Abi shook her head. "Rebecca, this is much more than friendship."

Rebecca froze at the words. She glanced around, concerned someone might overhear. "What on earth makes you think that?" she whispered.

"You didn't see his face when you were thrown from Princess. Anguish. It was as though a part of him was dying." Abi nodded. "I'd like someone to get that worked up over me." She sighed, resting her chin on her hand.

"I think you're looking at the world through a writer's glasses."

"I admit that can be a side effect of my job. Except not in this case. No." She shook her head. "Gallagher wears his heart on his sleeve. It's obvious to everyone, with the exception of Julian. Big surprise there."

"How can it be obvious to everyone, when it seems quite the opposite to me?" Rebecca paused, remembering how Joe had shied away the one time she thought he might kiss her.

"Maybe because, as you said, you've known him

a long time. So you haven't noticed how things have shifted."

"It's true we go way back. The fact is, I sort of, well…" Rebecca grimaced. "I dumped him a long time ago."

"Not one of your better decisions, I imagine."

Rebecca turned her head slowly and stared at Abi. She'd certainly nailed it. "I was young and naive like Julian. I was swept off my feet by Nick, and no, dumping Joe wasn't one of my finer moments. Except that now I have Casey, who's the best thing I've done with my life so far."

"If I'm right and Joe does have feelings for you, are you telling me that you don't have any for him?"

"I haven't spent a lot of time thinking about it." Rebecca looked away. "We're working together long hours. That's part of the job. Don't get me wrong, I like Joe, but the timing couldn't be more wrong."

"Life is like that, I hear. It happens at the most inconvenient times."

Rebecca pondered the truth of Abi's blithe response.

"Why is it you do so much ranch work?" Abi asked as she leaned back on her elbows.

"I like doing ranch work." Rebecca frowned at the random question.

"You don't have to get up every day and help Joe with the chores. He's been doing them without you for years."

"His certification."

Abi leveled her with a look that said "try again."

"I said I like ranch work."

"Do you like ranch work, or do you like ranch work with Joe?"

"You're really pushing my buttons here, aren't you, Ms. Reporter?" Rebecca huffed.

"Well?" Abi prodded.

"Good question. I'll have to get back to you."

"You might want to think long and hard before you ignore what's right in front of you."

"Spoken like someone who's been there?"

Abi chuckled and stretched out her hands, examining her nails with a frown. "Sure. Everyone has a story. But the truth is, I really like you, Rebecca. I don't want you to make the same mistake I did."

Rebecca sighed. "I've made so many, what's one more?"

"Is Joe going to the barbecue?"

"I forgot to ask. I was too busy trying to save our project."

"What do you mean?" Abi sat up straight.

"Joe was ready to throw in the towel."

"Is that why he was looking for you?"

Rebecca nodded.

"Why didn't you tell us it was this serious?"

"I didn't want to worry you."

Abi took a deep breath. "You've got a lot riding on Monday. Bringing this project in will make us all look good. We're in the homestretch now, thanks to you. Don't worry. I'll do my part to make sure the guys stay on task."

"Thank you. No need to mention any of this to Rod and Julian."

"I won't. Of course they're going to wonder why I suddenly show up with a cattle prod Monday morning."

Rebecca laughed. "I wish I'd thought of that."

A horn double tooted, announcing a car's arrival, and Rebecca and Abi looked up.

"Julian is back," Abi drawled with a hint of pain in her voice.

"We're going to have to discuss the top ten reasons why you don't lay on the horn when you live on a ranch."

"You can take the kid out of the city…" Abi said.

Rebecca just shook her head.

"Look, Momma. I can see the flags." Casey jumped up and down in her seat, barely restrained by the car's seat belt.

A morning at the Fourth of July parade in downtown Paradise hadn't dimmed her enthusiasm or her energy.

Rebecca followed her daughter's gaze out the car window to the Elliott Ranch. Banners with the ranch logo, and red, white and blue flags all waved in the afternoon breeze. Neighbors from the valley were moving through the huge black iron *E* archway of the ranch to the festivities. The peppy twang of a country band could be heard playing a familiar Western tune in the distance. Rebecca could hardly resist toe tapping.

"Okay, Casey, here's the rules. This is a huge ranch. I must know where you are at all times, and you must always be with an adult. Either me, or Grandma or Abi. Got it?"

Casey nodded.

"Are Julian and Rod riding out together?" Rebecca asked Abi who was in the passenger seat.

"Yes. And if we're really lucky they'll get lost."

"Abi."

"Please, Julian could single-handedly ruin this

shindig," Abi said as she slathered sunscreen on her bare arms.

"Be kind."

"I can deny I know him," Abi said. "Would that be implausible deniability?" She laughed at her own joke as she straightened the skirt of her sundress.

"Cute dress," Rebecca said, noting Abi's outfit with its little shrug sweater.

"If I had one of those pretty embroidered, yoked Western shirts like yours, I would have gone cowgirl, too. Must remedy that."

"Momma, is Joe here yet? He told me he'd take me on a pony ride. Does he count as an adult?"

Abi stifled a laugh with a hand over her mouth.

"Yes. He does." She looked at her daughter. "Joe told you he was coming?"

Casey nodded.

"Oh, look, Casey, they're painting faces over there. Rebecca, do you mind if I take her over?"

"Sure, go ahead, I'm going to look for Sara, Mr. Elliott's daughter. I can't wait to see her twins. Come and find me when you two are done."

Abi took Casey's hand. "We will, but you might not recognize us, right, Casey?"

Casey giggled.

Rebecca took her time strolling across the grass, nodding at the few people she did know, most of them friends of her mother's. There was a time when she knew every single person in Paradise, along with every inch of this ranch, just like her father. But those days were long gone. She often wondered what would have happened if her father was still here?

How strange it seemed to be back. Ten years ago

she'd just graduated from high school. She and Joe had gone to that summer's barbecue together. It was her first year to attend without her father. Joe had been so caring. Moving to town after her father's death had been tough. Coming back to the ranch, her home for most of her life, as an outsider for the first time had been even more difficult.

Yet Joe had been there when she needed a friend. Then a mere two years later their worlds had parted.

"Whoa, careful there, Becca, you almost ran me over."

He looked good—too good to be loose at a party where there was a thirty-to-one ratio of women to men. He wore a crisp white fancy yoked Western shirt with pearl buttons and red embroidery, along with well-worn creased Levi's and his tan Stetson.

"Joe. Casey said you were coming today."

"Good opportunity to chat with Hollis," Joe said.

"I thought you were going to give us until Monday night."

"I am."

In the silence that followed, the tension between them became palpable.

"I don't like this," Joe said, his jaw set. "Not one bit."

"What do you mean?"

"This." When he gestured with both of his hands, instead of just one, Rebecca was so happy to see she'd finally made significant progress with his therapy.

She smiled.

"Hey, where'd you go? Did you hear what I said?" Joe said.

"Yes. I was smiling at your bilateral use of your hands. We therapists call that significant progress."

"You therapists are a strange bunch."

"Perhaps. What was it you were grumbling about?"

He put on his Joe scowl and shoved a hand in his pocket. "I was about to apologize for being testy lately."

"I thought that was normal."

"Are you being funny?"

"No, I'm simply agreeing that you've been rather cranky since the team and I arrived."

His head jerked back slightly. "Well, don't hold back. Why did you suddenly decide to tell me this?"

"I was agreeing with you. I'm glad you brought it up, though. You and I should clear the air since my time at the ranch is almost over."

"I'd like it if we could be friends," Joe admitted.

"Me, too."

"Good." He gave a satisfied nod. "Wow. Smell that?" Joe took a deep breath, inhaling the savory barbecue aroma that hung in the summer air. "I've got to get some of that. Have you eaten?"

"No. I was waiting for Casey and Abi. They're face painting."

"How about we grab a little something while you're waiting?"

"Yes, sure." She smiled up at him, and it occurred to her that there was nothing else she'd rather do right now. She couldn't change the past, but creating a future with Joe as her friend would be a very nice thing.

"Perfect day, isn't it?" Joe asked.

"It is," Rebecca returned, trying to match her strides with his.

He stopped. "Hold it. What am I doing? I clean forgot."

"Forgot what?" She turned around when she realized he was no longer next to her.

"I ordered something for you, and it showed up yesterday."

"You did?" She glanced up at him. "Why?"

"Because you need it, and after the week you've had, you've earned it." He did an about-face and took off in the other direction.

"Wait," Rebecca called as she struggled to keep up.

"Come on." He stopped and reached for her hand. Rebecca held on tight.

"I'm parked right over there."

She followed, weaving around the sea of pickup trucks that left no doubt that this was an agricultural community.

"Here it is." Joe reached into his flatbed and pulled out a hat can.

"You got me a hat?"

"Yeah. I told you that you need one. This beauty is a Stetson with a pinch-front crown." He unclipped the can and opened it.

Rebecca gasped. "It's the prettiest hat I've ever seen." She ran a hand over the smooth fur felt.

"I figured you can get your own band when you have time." He gently lifted it from the box.

"How did you know what size?"

"They still have you on file in the store."

"Wow, after all these years. I don't even know where my old hats are. Maybe in my mother's attic."

"Well, aren't you going to try it on?"

"Yes. Of course." She rubbed her hand over the taupe material. "I love the color."

"Thought this color wouldn't show the dirt in case you, um, fall again."

"That wasn't my fault."

"I'm just saying."

"Your hat matches mine." Delighted with the hat, she placed it on her head and adjusted the brim.

"Does it?"

Rebecca glanced at him and he winked.

"How's it look?" she asked, moving to the side-view mirror of the truck."

"Careful."

Too late, Rebecca tripped on an orange plastic traffic cone lying on its side in the grass.

Joe grabbed her around the waist, alarm in his eyes.

"You almost fell. Do you have any idea how dangerous a concussion is? Everything from dazed and confused, to full-on memory loss. Hitting your head when you already have a concussion is even more dangerous. You've got to be more cautious, Becca."

She narrowed her eyes, assessing him. "When did you get a medical degree?"

Joe gave a sheepish smile and shrugged. "I looked it up on WebMD."

"You looked up my concussion?"

"Yeah, about midnight, when I couldn't sleep. I was worried about you."

Rebecca stood still in the warm circle of his arms as he stared at her. His gaze moved from her eyes to her lips. Then ever so slowly, Joe's head lowered. He hesitated and stepped back, releasing her.

"Sorry," he murmured. "I shouldn't start what I can't finish. We only just became friends again, five minutes ago. I don't want to make it any more difficult than it is."

"Difficult? What's difficult?"

"I'm doing my best to maintain a professional relationship, but you sure aren't making it easy."

"Me!"

"It would help if you could ugly yourself up or something."

Rebecca snickered. "Doesn't this black-and-blue knot in the middle of my forehead work for you?"

"Not hardly," he scoffed. "Besides, you're assigned to certify me. It would be wrong to attempt to unduly sway your opinion."

Though she did her best, Rebecca couldn't help but laugh. Repeatedly. "Are you saying you think I might go ahead and certify you because you're a good kisser?"

Joe's face registered shock. "No. That is not what I'm saying."

She shook her head. "I'm kidding, Joe. Let's just go get something to eat, shall we?"

"Sure. Okay. But take it easy today, would you?"

"I'll try," she said. "Slowing down doesn't come naturally for me."

"Where have you two been?" Abi murmured to Rebecca as they approached the root beer table. She looked her up and down. "Nice hat."

"Mr. Gallagher decided that I need one." She looked at Joe. "Or maybe he buys one for every greenhorn who gets thrown by a horse on his ranch."

Abi laughed, and Joe shot the reporter a menacing stare.

"How do you like my face, Joe?" Casey asked.

"Red, white and blue with stars. I like it. Maybe I should get a few stars, too."

"Casey, you are beautiful," Rebecca said.

"How about if we go check out those ponies, Casey?" Joe asked.

"I thought you were hungry," Rebecca said.

"Yeah, not anymore," he mumbled.

"Are Momma and Abi coming, too?"

He shook his head. "Nope. Just you and me. That okay?"

Casey's face lit up. "Yes, please."

Joe took her hand, and they headed off to find the ponies.

"Oh, my. Look at them," Abi said, her gaze following the tall cowboy and the little girl. "That's enough to make even my cynical heart a little mushy around the edges."

Rebecca chuckled. "He's a good man."

"Ditto that.

"So you and Joe looked cozy." Abi raised her brows. "I am going to make a wild guess that he's forgiven you for bringing us out to the ranch?"

"Yes. At least for today. Monday will be the real test."

"Rebecca. Good to see you," a voice behind her said.

She turned and smiled, delighted to see Hollis Elliott. He wore a black Western shirt and a black hat angled on the back of his head. The outfit offset his thick white shock of hair. "Mr. Elliott! How wonderful to see you." She gave him a quick hug.

"Sir, this is Abigail Warren, she's here as part of the OrthoBorne Technology team, doing a big write-up on Mr. Gallagher."

"Pleased to meet you."

"You as well, sir. This is an amazing community event. Thank you for allowing us to attend."

"Glad you're here. Paradise gives me so much. This is my way of giving back. Enjoy yourself."

He turned to Rebecca. "Do you mind if I steal you away from your friend for a few moments?"

"Abi?"

"Of course. As it happens, I have a sheriff I'd like to have a word with." She grinned.

"What happened to your forehead?" he asked, peering at her face.

"Thrown from a horse, like I was a rookie. So embarrassing."

Hollis chuckled. "Well, you know what they say. 'If you climb in the saddle, be ready for the ride.' Not that I haven't been tossed a couple times. It's all about how you land, right?"

"Yes, sir." Rebecca smiled, recalling that her father had said those same words.

"Let me get down to business, so you can get back to having fun. I wanted to apologize to you, Rebecca. I found out too late what Judge Brown was trying to do to you with that trial. Next time he bothers you, come to me. That windbag doesn't have as much reach as he thinks he does. I'm only sorry your momma didn't call me first when you needed bail money. And for the record, I knew all along you were innocent. Everyone in this town did."

"Thank you, Mr. Elliott. You were a lifesaver, believe me."

"Nonsense. It would have been the least I could do for your father."

"Sir, could I possibly ask a small favor?"

"Anything, Rebecca."

"Joe Gallagher."

"What about him?"

"Judge Brown has managed to prevent him from hiring help with his hay crop, because I'm working with him. I'm his therapist."

"I just talked to Gallagher. He didn't say anything about that. We talked about his land. There's a parcel I've been trying to get him to sell. That's a standing joke between us. Has been for years. That boy will never sell. He likes to tease me every now and again. Someday he plans to build a house on that parcel and raise a big family."

Rebecca frowned, confused.

"When does Joe start cutting?" Hollis asked.

"Tuesday. Next week will be the first full week of sunshine we've had."

"You're right. Everyone is scrambling to get in the first cutting. I've got my balers tied up with my crop at the moment, but I'm not willing to let the judge get away with this. No, sir. It's not right. Let me see what I can figure out."

"I appreciate that, sir."

"Don't you worry." He grinned and patted her back. "I'll beat the judge at his own game. I'm good at that."

"Thank you."

"I don't suppose your mother is here?"

"She should be somewhere around here. I spoke to her before I left. She was bringing a few of the elderly ladies from the church."

"Your mother is a good woman. Heart of gold. A godly woman, as well."

"Yes, sir, she is."

"Do you mind if I ask you a personal question?"

Rebecca shook her head.

"Would it bother you if I…" He hesitated and cleared his throat as a red flush crept up his neck. "I'd like to ask your mother out to dinner."

She smiled. "That would be really nice."

"You're sure? I don't want to overstep my bounds. The way I figure it, your mother's been widowed fourteen years, and my dear wife has been gone twenty. I'd like nothing more than conversation and a meal now and again, with a lovely lady who understands ranching and cares about this valley as much as I do."

"You don't need my permission, Mr. Elliott. But if you feel you do, you have it."

"Thank you." He grinned. His dark eyes had a definite spark in them. "Now have a good time today. We won't do this again until next year."

Rebecca stood with a smile on her face as Hollis moved to greet his guests and check on the events. Her mother deserved a second chance at companionship, and maybe a little romance. Deserved it more than anyone she knew. Her heart swelled with joy at the possibilities that lay ahead for all of them here in Paradise.

Chapter Twelve

Rebecca curled her feet beneath her and relaxed against the leather sofa. "What did you think of our little church, Abi?"

"I have to admit that it was a pleasant surprise. Everything. The sermon, the people. It's been a long time since I've sat in a pew."

"Any particular reason?" Rebecca asked.

"Oh, lots of reasons. None of them of any merit." Abi paused and turned her head. "Before you start digging into my psyche, I should mention that I think that's your phone ringing."

Rebecca scrambled from the couch and raced to her room. Dumping the contents of her purse on the bed, she rifled through an assortment of papers along with souvenirs from Friday's barbecue. When had Casey have time to put all this stuff in her purse? Finally, at the bottom of everything, she located her cell.

Virginia Simpson. She tapped "accept" when she saw the familiar number.

"Virginia?"

"I know this is short notice, Rebecca—however, a

situation has arisen here. I'm leaving for Denver late tonight. Could you possibly come up to the house? I've wanted to talk to you for a long time. Now I find that I cannot put it off any longer."

Rebecca blinked, speechless for a moment at the unexpected request. "Um, yes. Sure. No problem. I'm happy to take a ride up there."

"When? Would now be too inconvenient?"

"Now?" Rebecca glanced at the clock at her bedside. "Okay. I'll make it work. Um, your father? Will he be there?"

"No. The judge isn't here." Virginia paused. "When shall I expect you?"

"I'll leave right away. Give me a few minutes to make arrangements for Casey. She's sleeping, and I don't want to wake her."

Rebecca ended the call and stared at her cell for a moment before dropping it, her wallet and car keys back into her purse. Something niggled at her. What was she forgetting?

The judge.

She tensed when she realized that she hadn't received any harassing calls from Judge Brown in several days. Did that, along with the fact that Virginia had summoned her out of the blue, mean something?

Admittedly, talking to Virginia was something she'd been meaning to do for a long time. Meaning to and avoiding. How was she going explain to her former mother-in-law that the woman's father was harassing her? Who would believe that an elderly respected community member spent his spare time prank dialing her? Were the calls even actionable?

It didn't matter. Virginia should know. It was time. Time to take back her life. Time to move forward.

Rebecca glanced down at her navy church dress. She pulled up the sleeve and took a long look at the disfiguring scar. Next to the healing sutures Sara had given her, the scar seemed especially ugly and mocking. Opening the closet, she yanked a short-sleeve blouse from a hanger, along with a pair of slacks.

She changed her clothes and stood looking at herself in the full-length mirror. No more hiding. The scar had been her secret for too long. Sara was right; the scar needed to be revised. A lot of things in her life were ready and waiting to be revised.

Sliding her feet into flats, she shoved everything back into her purse before closing her bedroom door.

"Abi, I hate to ask you a favor on your day off—"

"Please," Abi interrupted. "Ask away. I owe you plenty, and you made that wonderful lunch."

"Would you mind watching Casey for me for a few hours? That was her other grandmother on the phone. She asked me to stop by, and it's about a twenty-minute drive each way."

"Of course. That's a pretty easy favor. Take your time." Abi waved a hand and continued to type on her laptop. "I'm working on the piece about Joe. I want to have it ready for his approval tomorrow. This is good stuff, if I do say so myself. I think I might submit a feature article to the *Denver Post*, as well. With his permission, of course."

"I don't want to burst your bubble, but Joe splashed all over the Denver paper probably isn't going to excite him."

Abi sighed. "I suspected as much."

"You have my cell number, right?"

She nodded.

"Casey's still napping," Rebecca said.

"I meant what I said. Take your time. We'll play board games when she wakes up."

"Thanks, Abi."

Rebecca grabbed a bottle of water from the fridge and headed out the door.

"I was just looking for you."

Rebecca looked up, surprised to see Joe. He was smiling as he strode toward her. Smiling had to be a good sign. Right?

She offered a cautious smile in return, not sure what the protocol was after spending the day together yesterday. "You okay?" he asked.

"Yes."

"What do you think about you, me and Casey heading to Patti Jo's for a late lunch?"

"I wish I could. Virginia Simpson has summoned me to the castle. I'm leaving now."

"That explains why you look so tense." He paused. "I'm not doing anything else. I'll drive you."

"You don't have to do that." She unlocked the Honda.

He shot her a steely gaze. "I'll drive you."

"Why?"

"Sometimes we need backup."

"Oh?"

"Sure. The Lone Ranger and Tonto. Butch Cassidy and the Sundance Kid. Kirk and Spock. Han Solo and Chewbacca."

"Bert and Ernie?"

Joe laughed. "Exactly. I'm starting to realize how

much we're alike, Becca. Most of our problems in life stem from our inability to ask for help when we need it."

Her eyes rounded. "Excuse me?"

"You heard me. Speaking as one stubborn cowboy to another, you have to recognize when you need reinforcement. You can't be afraid to ask for help, and you can't be afraid to accept it."

She gingerly massaged the tender spot on her forehead. The only thing she recognized at the moment was that the idea of meeting with Virginia had already given her a headache. "Okay, I'm too stressed to argue, especially when there's a possibility you might be right."

"Of course I am." He nodded toward the barn. "Now wait right here, Ernie, and I'll get my truck."

"You sure have been quiet," Joe said once they arrived in Four Forks.

"Sorry. A lot on my mind," Rebecca returned.

"Do you know why she wants to see you?" Joe asked as he guided the truck up the mountain road to the Simpson home.

"No clue," she murmured. "And I don't mind telling you that alone makes me nervous."

"That's an understatement. You've been staring out the window and sighing for the last twenty minutes."

"Have I, really?"

He nodded. "Hey, look at that. Smiley is back on duty. The gate is even open. I guess he's expecting you." Joe gave the sour-faced guard a friendly wave as they passed by the security booth.

He drove the truck around the circle drive to the front door, where he unbuckled his seat belt.

"Joe, this time you have to wait in the truck."

"I can do that. I'll park over there, by the tennis courts."

"Okay." She glanced at the house and then away several times, attempting to bolster her courage.

She could do this. She could do this.

"Rebecca?"

"Hmm?"

"You know that promise you wanted me to keep?"

"Yes?" She said the word slowly.

"I know this won't be easy, but it's time for you to take care of what you wouldn't let me take care of."

She gave a quick nod "You're right. I know you're right. I'm going to tell her everything. I'm going to move forward."

"You can do this, Becca."

"Can I? If I wasn't such a coward, I would have taken care of this years ago."

"You're doing it now. That's what matters." Joe stared at her and frowned. "You look like you're going to pass out. I think we better say a quick prayer." He took her hand and held it against his heart. "Lord, give Becca the words to say today. Guide her and protect her. Amen."

Rebecca leaned forward and pressed a soft kiss to his cheek. "Thank you," she whispered.

"Ah, you're welcome."

He came around and opened the passenger door and helped her down. "Remember. I've got your back."

"You and God. Yes. You're right. She nodded and walked slowly past the high columns to the generously proportioned front door.

Virginia answered on the first knock. She was unsmiling, and she seemed even more solemn than usual.

There was something weighing heavily on her mind. She glanced from Rebecca to Joe's truck. "Thank you for coming."

Rebecca clutched her purse tightly as Virginia ushered her into the large entrance way. Her heels echoed on the marble floor.

"Did you fall?" Virginia looked from Rebecca's forehead to her arm. "Oh, my. Stitches, as well?"

"I was thrown from a horse."

"You're riding again?"

"I am. Not well, apparently."

Virginia frowned. "How unfortunate."

"Part and parcel," Rebecca murmured.

"Shall we sit in the living room?" Virginia asked.

"That's fine."

She looked quickly around as they passed from the entrance, through French doors and into the living room. Even after all these years, very little had changed in the room from the days when she and Nick would visit his family. He'd been an up-and-coming legal prodigy, mentored by his grandfather. But the pressure of meeting his grandfather's expectations seemed to be the catalyst that started spinning Nick's life out of control. They stopped visiting Four Forks. Nick rarely did anything, but work. He hardly noticed that he had a wife and a child.

Virginia smoothed her white linen slacks as she perched on the silk brocade couch. With a hand, she beckoned for Rebecca to sit next to her.

"I thought maybe it was time for us to discuss the future," Virginia said.

"The future? Whose future?"

"Casey's. Yours. Mine."

Rebecca nodded. She folded her hands in her lap and took a deep breath. "I hope you understand that before I can deal with the future, I need to deal with the past."

"I meant it when I said I knew you were innocent, Rebecca. I can't apologize enough for what my father put you through. What I allowed."

"That's not what I meant." She glanced around, praying she still had the courage to do what must finally be done. "Where did you say Judge Brown is?"

"He's in Denver. My father had a stroke yesterday morning. That's one of the reasons I wanted to talk to you."

"Oh." Rebecca froze. "How's he doing?"

"Please keep him in your prayers. I know it seems as though he doesn't deserve them, but he needs them. He's lost most of the use of his right side. His doctors have told me that full recovery is doubtful. With his other medical issues, we're hoping to keep him comfortable in a facility in Denver until his condition stabilizes and we can decide what's next."

"I see. What do you want me to tell Casey?"

"Nothing for now. I was in Denver all day yesterday. Jana is with him now. I'm closing out the house and will leave tonight."

"Maybe this isn't the time for us to talk. I don't want to add to your stress. You have a lot going on."

"I think we've put this off for far too long."

Rebecca nodded. "You're right."

"I now have power of attorney for my father's estate. I discovered he's been harassing you. His lawyer tells me he's been harassing Joseph Gallagher, as well." Virginia shook her head. "I wish you would have told me."

"I couldn't."

"Trust me, it will stop. Immediately."

"Thank you."

"Tell me about my son." Virginia took a deep breath and met Rebecca's gaze. "I haven't wanted to know. It's taken me two years, and I'm finally ready to face the truth. Nick had a drinking problem like his father. That much I am sure of."

Rebecca hesitated. Was Virginia really prepared for what she had to say?

"Nick… Nick was an alcoholic. When he drank, he became physically and verbally abusive. Never in front of his daughter." Rebecca held her hands tightly in her lap, her nails biting into her skin, as she admitted the truth aloud. A truth she had never revealed to anyone before.

"Oh, no, no." Virginia's words were a soft painful wail. She covered her mouth with her hands and closed her eyes. "You poor child."

"Nick often got a little carried away." She unfolded her hands and moved her fingers over the rough scar.

Virginia's gaze moved to Rebecca's arm and her face paled.

"That's what he would say. 'I got a little carried away. I didn't mean it.'" Rebecca swallowed. "This scar…it's from one of the times when he got a little carried away."

Silent tears ran down Virginia's cheeks. "I think I've suspected as much all along, which makes me as guilty as my son." She raised her face. "Nick made you lose control of the car, didn't he?"

Rebecca nodded. "Nick was furious because I took the car keys after he'd obviously had too much to drink. He took off his seat belt and grabbed the wheel." This time she closed her eyes, remembering that horrible night. It happened in an instant. The car had veered off the road, skidded as she fought for control of the wheel, and finally crashed. Then everything had been very silent, the only sound was the rain tapping on the windshield.

"I'm sorry," Rebecca whispered. The apology was for Virginia and maybe for Nick, as well.

She raised her head and met Virginia's gaze. "More sorry than you know. I should have demanded that he get help long ago."

"We can't fix people. You couldn't fix Nick. I couldn't fix his father." She wiped her tears and sniffed. "Yet you never told anyone."

"No. For years I believed it was my fault. My secret. My shame. It's taken a long time for me to understand that was wrong thinking."

"Why didn't your lawyer use this information in court?"

"I wouldn't let him. This was my daughter's father, and I honestly believed, deep down inside, that the guilt was mine. Those were the darkest days of my life, until I finally turned everything over to God."

"My father needs to know."

"You're the only one who can talk to your father. I can't do that to him. I doubt if he'd believe me anyhow."

"This just might destroy him. Nick was everything to the judge."

"There was a time when he was everything to me, too."

"Who's that man who drove you here?"

"That's Joe Gallagher."

"May I ask how he fits into your life? Into Casey's?"

"I don't know. I'm rebuilding my life one day at a

time. Joe's a good man, a good friend, but I don't know what the future holds."

"The Lord brought you back here for a reason, Rebecca. Stay close to Him. Don't throw away your second chance."

"I won't."

"Thank you for shielding Casey." She took Rebecca's hand in hers. "You sacrificed yourself for your daughter."

"I'd do it again in a heartbeat. Casey is the best of Nick and me. I see him in her all the time. She has his sense of humor, and she's smart. Smarter than both Nick and I. Maybe she'll grow up to be a lawyer."

"Or maybe she'll be a rancher. A horsewoman, like her mother," Virginia said.

"Whatever she wants to be. Casey has a full life ahead of her."

"Thank you. Thank you for telling me the truth. Despite everything, you've given us another chance. I'm grateful."

"I want to live in Paradise. I want Casey to grow up with a close relationship with her father's family. Do you think we can do that?"

"Yes. I want the same things."

Rebecca stood alone on the steps of the Simpson home and took a deep, cleansing breath as she looked around, almost expecting the world to have changed.

It had. Things were different, she realized. For the first time in a very long time she was free from the secrets of her past. The accident could no longer hold her hostage, nor could the awful memories.

Up ahead, Joe stood next to the truck, waiting for her. He was a good man and what Virginia said echoed in her head. The Lord had given her a second chance and she was going to do everything she could to hold onto it.

"How'd it go?" He moved to open her door. Taking her arm, he helped her step up into the cab of the truck and waited for her answer, concern on his face.

"That was probably the hardest thing I've ever done in my life. It was like burying Nick all over again. Yet it was also about forgiving him and saying goodbye to the past. I can finally close the door." She released a breath and leaned back against the seat. "I'm exhausted."

"What about the judge?"

"He won't bother either of us again."

"Becca, I'm so proud of you."

"You know what? I'm proud of me, too."

Rebecca nodded toward the packet on Joe's desk.

"This is it. We're finished, right?" Joe asked with a smile.

"We're finished as soon as you sign off on the photos and the video clips."

"I did."

"The write-up Abi did, too?"

"All signed and dated." He grinned and handed the stack to her.

"I'll take it back to Rod and Abi."

"No more 'turn slightly to the left, Mr. Gallagher.' 'Hold those reins with your right hand, Mr. Gallagher.' 'Give us a smile for the camera. Chin up. Hold that pose.'"

She raised a brow. "Now you're plain exaggerating. It wasn't that bad."

"Yeah, it was."

Rebecca cleared her throat. She frowned, trying to figure out the best way to broach the next subject.

"Okay, now what's wrong?" he asked.

"The team wants to talk to you."

"Say goodbye and all?"

"Um, not exactly."

"What exactly does 'not exactly' mean?"

"They're outside. Maybe I should let them explain."

"Oh, no." Joe shook his head and groaned. "I've got a real bad feeling about this, Becca. Can't you give me a heads-up?"

"It's not my place."

His shoulders sank. "Okay, Fine. Bring them in."

Joe offered a weak smile as the rest of the OrthoBorne team filed into his office.

Rod stepped forward. "Mr. Gallagher, we've been talking."

Joe's eyes rounded. He swallowed.

"We've decided to stay."

"Come again?" He blinked and shot a "help me" look at Rebecca.

"We're going to harvest the hay with you. It's the least we can do for all you've put up with."

Joe raised both hands. "That's not necessary."

"It is," Rod said. "Rebecca told us you're having a hard time getting help." He looked at Abi and Julian and smiled. "We're here and we're free. You can't hardly beat a deal like that, even in Paradise."

He turned to her again. "You told them?"

"It sort of came up in conversation," Rebecca said.

Joe opened his mouth and closed it. He scratched his head. Finally he looked up at Rod. "What do you know about cutting and baling hay?"

"I watched about a dozen videos on YouTube this morning. Today, I went out to the barn to inspect your equipment. I don't see any reason why I couldn't relieve you on the windrower. I used to work in the garden department of my local greenhouse. I've worked a forklift many times. Not much difference between that and your skid loader."

"Gotta love the internet." Joe chuckled.

"Especially WebMD," Rebecca muttered.

When Joe jerked his head around to look at her, she realized there was a good chance that pushing his buttons might not be the best approach.

"So how long after you cut are you going to bale?" Rod asked.

"We've had a run of good weather. Counting today, we've had four days of sunshine. The hay is prime for cutting. The forecast is in our favor. Humidity is back to normal, which is next to nothing in Colorado. You can't do better than cut one day, rake and bale the next. We're just going to give it our best shot."

"We?" Rod asked.

"I'm probably out of my mind." Joe scratched his head. "But I'm considering taking you up on your offer."

"That's great," Rod said. He offered a grin filled with enthusiasm.

"I'd like to help, as well. What can I do?" Abi asked with a smile.

"Well, um…" Joe swallowed.

"Never mind. I'll stand around and look good. That should be plenty."

Rebecca laughed. "Oh, I can think of a dozen chores you and I can do while Joe is cutting hay. No worries.

I'll make you a list, and then get you the keys to the truck."

"I can cook," Julian said quietly.

"What did you say?" Rebecca asked.

"I said, I can cook."

"Since when?" Abi asked, surprise lacing her voice.

"I attended Le Cordon Bleu College of Culinary Arts in Scottsdale on full scholarship."

"Wh-what?" Abi sputtered.

"Why are you working at OrthoBorne?" Rod asked.

"It pays better."

Joe's cell phone rang and he raised a palm to silence the room. "Yes, sir... Yes, sir... Looks like Wednesday, possibly Thursday, as well." He paused, blinked and then raised his brows in stunned surprise. "Yes, sir. Thank you."

He turned slowly to stare at Rebecca. "That was Hollis Elliott. When we're ready, he'll send over a team with equipment to rake and bale."

"A team?" she asked slowly.

"That's what the man said. Do you know anything about this?" he asked.

Rebecca shrugged and glanced away. "I might have mentioned that you were baling."

"That's all?"

"Hollis is a generous man."

"Yeah, right."

"Well, Joe," Rebecca said with a wink, "speaking as one stubborn cowboy to another, you have to recognize when you need backup. You can't be afraid to ask for help and you can't be afraid to accept it."

Joe gave a nod of approval, a slow smile appearing on his lips as if he recalled saying those same words to her, not so long ago. "Well done, Becca. Well, done."

Chapter Thirteen

"*Rebecca? Is that you?*"

Rebecca whirled on the heel of her boot, sending dirt and gravel flying. "Where are you, Abi?"

"In the horse barn."

She strode across the yard and stepped into the darkened building. A shaft of light from the window streamed inside, illuminating dust motes dancing wildly in the air along with tiny bits of straw. Evidence that someone had been cleaning stalls.

"Where?"

"Here." Abi popped her head up from a stall and leaned on the rail, pitchfork in hand.

"I've been looking all over for you."

"Sorry, I was bonding with Princess." Her eyes widened as she looked Rebecca up and down. "Aren't you a mess?"

"Me?" Rebecca glanced down at her clothing. "What about you? You've got more straw in your hair than on the ground. And you're covered with dirt."

"Apparently you haven't looked in a mirror lately. There's grease all over your face."

"Of course there is. The lawn mower broke down, and I've spent the last hour fixing it. I'm now convinced Joe keeps half the equipment around this place running with rubber bands and bubble gum." She looked at Abi. "What's your excuse?"

"Nothing so glamorous here," Abi said as she stepped out of the empty stall and carefully hung the pitchfork on the wall. "Although I can tell you that I've never had so much fun getting dirty."

Rebecca laughed.

"How's the barn look?" Abi waved a hand around her kingdom. "The horses and I are now on a first-name basis."

"You are now a professional mucker. The stalls are beautiful. Even Princess is impressed."

"What's next? Let's not waste time here chatting." Abi snapped her fingers. "There's work to be done."

"Julian says dinner is ready."

Abi pulled her phone out of her pocket and rubbed the screen on her sleeve. "Oh, my, it really is dinnertime. Why, it's been hours since lunch."

"Quite a lunch it was, too."

"Yes. You're right." Abi frowned. "Except that with all those extra hands from Elliott Ranch, you know there weren't any leftovers."

"Did you see their faces?" Rebecca asked. "I think they were stunned. Only Gallagher Ranch brings hot gourmet meals out to the ranch hands in the field."

"They'll be standing in line to work with Joe once the word gets out." Abi yanked off her gloves and tossed them on a stool.

Rebecca nodded. "Julian has totally redeemed himself, don't you think?"

"You've obviously forgotten about your stitches."

"I haven't. Then again, I know what it's like to be crucified for an accident."

"True," Abi said. "You know, I have to admit, this has been a very good couple of days. I am beginning to understand why you like ranch work so much."

"It is satisfying, isn't it? Sunrise to sunset. Nature all around. Man in his element."

"Yes, satisfying until I remember three a.m."

"What do you mean?" Rebecca grabbed two rags from Joe's stack of clean work rags and tossed one to Abi, who began to wipe her face.

"It's sort of like cowgirl Cinderella. Exactly as you said, toiling away, sunrise to sunset. Only she never gets to actually go to the ball. I mean, it really never stops here, does it? Three a.m. always arrives. You keep going and going and going, in perpetuity. At least with my job, I eventually get to type 'The End.'" She turned to Rebecca. "Am I right?"

"On a ranch you bring in the harvest and you take the cows to market."

"That's not exactly what I meant when I said going to the ball."

"I know, which is why ranch life is referred to as a calling. Because it keeps calling you back."

Abi offered a flat laugh. "You can say that again. In fact, you can say it a couple dozen times. I have new respect for Joe Gallagher. For you, too, for that matter. This home-on-the-range life is not for the fainthearted." She ran her hands through her hair, releasing a flurry of straw.

"Tell me about it. However, it does beat doing paperwork all day long," Rebecca said.

"Are you trying to talk yourself out of your upcoming bonus and promotion?"

"Shh." Once again Rebecca felt the need to glance around to be certain they weren't overheard. "That is definitely not a done deal."

"Once you deliver the Gallagher goods it is. And they are all but delivered. Do you want to be promoted and work from home, or not?" Abi asked.

"I do. I really do. It means more money and job security. I'm excited at the possibility of staying in Paradise with my family. The thing I hadn't considered is that as a senior case manager I'll have significantly less direct patient care and double the paperwork."

"Maybe you should rethink your career track. It's obvious that you were born to be a rancher. Anyone can see that. Why you're playing around doing anything else is a mystery to me, Rebecca. This is clearly what you're meant to be doing."

"I'd have to have a ranch for that to happen, Abi."

"Like that will be tough. Look around you. Have I mentioned I know a rancher?" Abi stomped her feet, knocking off as much debris as possible. "Come on. We can decide what we want to be when we grow up, later. I want food."

As they walked out, Joe and Rod met them in the yard. Joe stopped walking and his eyes rounded as he assessed first Abi and then Rebecca, his gaze taking in their disheveled and dirty clothes.

Rod sniffed the air. "Ewww. Which one of you two smells like eau de horse? No offense ladies, but you can't come to the table smelling like that."

"It's me, and I'm proud of it," Abi said. "You know, someone has to do the dirty work around here while you guys are out there with those other macho men, playing on those funny looking tractor thingies and that fancy Old MacDonald Bobcat."

"Hey, I resemble that remark," Rod said with a grin. "Did you see me on that baler? The good news is, we can consider the hay officially harvested."

"Really?" Rebecca looked to Joe for confirmation.

Joe took off his hat and wiped the sweat from his forehead with a cotton bandanna. "Yeah. Never could have done it this fast without Rod's help. Hollis Elliott's guys went to town, as well. I can finish pulling the bales off the field tomorrow. But you folks may consider yourself done."

Abi and Rod offered up a loud cheer and exchanged high fives.

"That's great, isn't it?" Rebecca asked Joe.

"Yeah. For sure." Joe twitched his nose and sneezed. "Abi, I'm going to need you to stand ten paces back."

"I get the hint," Abi said.

"That wasn't exactly a hint," Rod said. "Come on. There's a hose over there. I'll hose down your boots."

"Okay, but let's hurry. My stomach is rumbling," Abi said, racing ahead.

Rebecca smiled and fell into step beside Joe as they walked toward the cottage where Julian had dinner waiting.

"Things have worked out well, haven't they?" she asked him.

"They have, and you never even said 'I told you so.'"

"I'm not an 'I told you so' kind of gal," Rebecca replied.

They walked around Rod's rental SUV, her Honda and the farm truck to cross the gravel drive. As they approached the little house, Rebecca looked up and stopped in her tracks.

The large terra-cotta pots in front of the cottage over-flowed with tall crimson geraniums. The deep green foliage was ripe with buds.

"What's this? Who planted the pots?" she asked, turning to Joe.

"Technically, Julian did."

"Technically?"

"He needed something to do between meals, and I sure wasn't going to let him loose on the ranch. I sent him to town for flowers and potting soil. He planted some on the back porch, too." Joe nodded as he examined the pots. "Did a nice job, didn't he?"

"Why would you have him plant flowers?"

"Maybe I like flowers."

"Do you?"

"I'm not opposed to them. Truth is, they're for you. I know you've been too busy to plant and I…well, I wanted to say thank you."

"For what? My time here has been a comedy of errors."

"That's not true."

"Excuse me, but as I recall, it was so bad that you kicked us off the ranch last week." She chuckled.

"That may have been a knee-jerk reaction on my part."

Rebecca smiled. "That's one way to look at it."

He cleared his throat and glanced at her and then away. "Becca?"

"Yes?"

"I am indebted to you for talking to Mr. Elliott. You saved the day." He offered a sheepish smile. "I know

I talk a good game, but you recognized that I really needed assistance even though I didn't want to admit it. Thank you."

"You're very welcome. Glad I could help."

Rebecca knelt to examine the flowers. Stroking a velvet petal with a finger, she took a deep breath. "I'm not going to be here long enough to enjoy these blooms."

"Is there a rush? You said you have more certification stuff to check off."

"Just that paperwork you've avoided and the manufacturer DVD. We've covered everything else." She looked up at him. "Except for your grumbling, you've been an exemplary patient. A quick study, as well. Just as you promised you would be."

"Maybe we could talk about that."

"Talk about what? Your grumbling?"

"No. For that I can only apologize."

"Apology accepted."

Joe nodded. "Look Becca, we've come a long way, don't you think? I mean, well, it seems to me that things have changed lately. Gotten back to where we can trust each other again." He looked at the ground before slowly, hesitantly, meeting her gaze.

"I hope so, Joe." She rubbed her arm, a nervous gesture she still hadn't overcome.

"How's the incision?" he asked.

She pushed up her sleeve and let him see the clean line of stitches. "They're healing nicely. I've got an appointment to have the sutures removed tomorrow."

When Joe gently wrapped his fingers around her wrist to examine the wound, she stilled at his touch.

"It's healing." He met her gaze, his eyes tender with emotion. "Like you and me. We've reconciled the past.

Maybe it's time to talk about where we go from here."
His words were a soft murmur.

"Oh?" Rebecca swallowed.

The front door burst open and Julian stood on the
porch, hands on hips and a spatula in his hand. "The
boeuf bourguignon is getting cold, people."

"We'll talk later," he said, releasing her arm.

Rebecca nodded and followed him up the steps to
the cottage.

Something she hadn't felt in a long time began to
bubble up inside her. Hope. Had Joe truly forgiven her
for the past? *Did she dare to hope that he wanted to
consider the future?*

The sound of voices drifted to Joe as he passed by the
side of the cottage on his way home after evening chores
were completed. Though he knew he shouldn't, he
slowed his steps. Nothing good ever came from eaves-
dropping, yet he couldn't help himself. He grinned. He'd
blame his mother. It was no doubt genetic.

"So what do you think, Abi?" Julian's voice rang out.

"What are you babbling on about, Julian?"

"He's waxing philosophical now that he's headed
back to the big city," Rod said. "He's been doing it since
he served dessert tonight."

"What do you think about Paradise and this ranch
life?" Julian continued, ignoring Rod's jab.

"That's a no-brainer. Paradise is a wonderful town.
This ranch is terrific, and Rebecca is one blessed
woman."

"Awe, come on, Abi. That's a little over the top. Especially for you. I count on you to be a realist," Julian
returned.

"I am being a realist."

"Okay, then maybe you can shed some insight into what's going on with Rebecca and Joe."

"That's none of our business," she said.

"Oh, you're no fun. We're just talking."

"Gossiping is more like it."

"Whatever."

Joe could envision Julian shrugging his bony shoulders about now.

"I'm simply speculating. Do you think Rebecca's going to give up everything for a cowboy who runs a little ranch in the middle of Nowhereville?"

"That's none of our business, either," Abi retorted. "But for the record, Nowhereville is her hometown, and she and the cowboy have history. Personally, I'd take that package if it was offered to me."

"I was wondering about that myself, Abi," Rod chimed in. "She's got a chunk of change coming to her for this project. Do you think she's planning to stay in Paradise or go back to Denver?"

"You aren't supposed to know about the bonus," Abi snapped.

"It's common grapevine knowledge," Rod said. "If she brings the completed Joe Gallagher assignment to OrthoBorne on deadline, she's got a promotion and a mega-huge bonus in her pocket."

Joe swallowed, trying to digest what he was hearing.

Rod continued. "I can't believe Julian nearly blew it for her."

"What? You've never messed up before?" Julian asked, indignation in his voice.

"Plenty of times. But Rebecca has a twelve-inch souvenir down her arm thanks to you," Rod returned.

"It was an accident. What else can I do to make it up to her?"

"Stay out of trouble."

"Only twelve more hours, Julian," Abi warned. "And I agree, Rod. Rebecca deserves whatever she earned on this project."

"We haven't ever talked about it," Rod said. "But it's no secret that she's had a rough couple of years. She really deserves a chance to start over."

"Is that fresh off the grapevine, too?" Abi asked.

"*Denver Post*, Abi. I read the paper. Everyone in the office is aware. How could they not be?"

"Still, it's not right for us to talk about Rebecca when she's not here. Who has the keys? I suggest we head for town to pack up our stuff. We leave early tomorrow."

"Hey, I didn't mean anything by it. You know I care about Rebecca, the same as you," Rod said.

"I know." She sighed. "I just feel bad. She's a good person, and she deserves the best."

"Absolutely," Rod said.

"The best," Joe whispered as he shoved off the wall, his gut burning. Yeah, Becca deserved the best. He changed direction and walked behind the cottage and through the trees to the corral so as not to be seen.

The sound of a car starting indicated that the OrthoBorne group was indeed headed back to town.

Joe slammed the palm of his left hand against the top rail of the corral, causing the entire fence to vibrate. He'd nearly made a fool of himself. Again. Nearly put his heart on the line for the second time with this woman.

Hadn't he learned anything in twelve years? The first time he was a naive kid. At thirty-three, he should know better. He'd let down his defenses only to discover that Becca was stringing him along until she had a grasp on something better.

Joe Gallagher was an assignment. A means to an end. Nothing more.

He stared out at the slow-setting pink of sunset. Had she really been playing him all along?

"Joe?" Becca's cheerful voice called out.

He stiffened but didn't turn, willing himself to stay strong. One glance at her and his resolve would be shot to pieces.

"Did you want to talk?" She slid a booted foot on the bottom rail and relaxed her arms over the top one.

"No. I'm headed to the house. I've got to get up early and get those bales off the field in case it decides to rain."

"I'll help."

"That's not necessary. This is my job, and I can do it, thanks to you and OrthoBorne."

"Are you sure? I can ride the tractor while you—"

Joe held up a hand. "Becca, you're here to get me certified. It's never been part of your job description to be a ranch hand."

He refused to meet her gaze.

"I like working on the ranch," she said.

"Sure you do."

"What's that supposed to mean?" Annoyance now laced her voice.

He feigned interest in the sunset. Overhead the halogen lights, set on timers, sizzled to life.

"It means you've been very flexible. You've gone above and beyond to get this project completed. I'm very appreciative. Gallagher Ranch is appreciative. But your job is done."

"Terrific. Back to doing it all by yourself, I see. Good for you, Mr. Gallagher."

He clenched his jaw and struggled for control. "Look, I'm saying thank you. Everything has gone according to plan. The team has completed its assignment, the hay is harvested and you can tell OrthoBorne that you brought Joe Gallagher in on schedule."

He heard her soft gasp.

Silence stretched between them. In the barn a horse whinnied.

"Your certification?" she asked.

"I'll have that paperwork all filled out by morning. I can watch the DVD tonight."

"All right," she murmured.

He held up his myoelectric arm toward the sky and offered a bitter laugh. "I'm paid for. Doesn't get any better than that, does it?"

"No, I guess not."

He heard her footfalls on the dirt and gravel as she turned away. Then she stopped. "Have I done something wrong?" The softly spoken question drifted to him.

"Not a thing." Joe swallowed, determined to see this through. "You can hide the key under the mat when you leave. No rush. But I know you have things to do. Places to be."

Now Joe did turn from the fence. Becca's face was void of emotion. She stared through him for a moment, out into the deep darkness, before she turned and walked toward the house, her back ramrod straight.

Maybe if she stayed their paths would cross in town, then and again, but that was all. They'd go back to being strangers.

Julian was right. Becca deserved more than this little

ranch in Nowhereville, which was about all he could ever hope to offer her.

Funny thing was when he really thought about it, he didn't blame her. She had a child to consider this time around. It didn't seem necessary to do much praying on the matter. No, it was clear that once again this cowboy bit the dust.

He'd dismissed her.

Rebecca barely resisted slamming the door of the cottage. She paced the floor, grateful Casey was at her grandmother's. Mind made up, she headed to the laundry-room closet where cardboard boxes had been carefully broken down and stored. Yanking them out, Rebecca grabbed the packing tape from the shelf and savagely ripped strips of tape from the dispenser, slapping them on the boxes. When one was put together, she tossed it into the hall and started on another.

Energized by her anger, she began to shove laundry supplies into the same boxes, then sealed them with more tape.

Like an out of control tornado, releasing years of anger she moved to the kitchen. Slamming pots and pans, she tossed them into boxes, as well.

How dare he? How dare Joe Gallagher shut her out?

Opening another cupboard, her gaze landed on the refrigerator where a souvenir from the Fourth of July barbecue at Elliott Ranch was held in place by a flower magnet.

A photo of Casey and Joe. What would she tell her little girl? Casey had fallen in love with Joe, just like her momma.

Rebecca hitched a breath and a sob escaped.

Her knees buckled, and she slid against the cupboards down to the floor. Closing her eyes, she fought the tears that threatened.

"No. I am not going to cry." She swiped at her face with the back of her hand and then sat up straight, stirring up as much anger and indignation as she could muster. "No crying. I've come too far. I've endured much worse than this. I will not waste my tears on Joe Gallagher."

She licked away a drop of moisture from her lips.

How had this happened? This was a job. An assignment. A bunch of ordinary manila folders with patient-care plans. Assessment, intervention and goals. Period. It wasn't supposed to get personal.

Falling in love with Joe Gallagher hadn't been part of the plan.

Rebecca covered her face with her hands and allowed her shoulders to sag under the weight of her despair.

She hadn't imagined things, had she? They were growing closer and closer.

So what had changed? What did she do wrong? Whatever it was, the walls were up and Joe wasn't going to talk.

And figuring it out wasn't her priority. She had a daughter to think of. Casey was what really mattered.

Besides, if she'd learned one thing in the last few years, it was that Virginia was right. Fixing other people wasn't her responsibility. She wasn't to blame for someone else's issues.

She could train Joe in the use of his myoelectric arm, but she couldn't fix what was going on inside the cowboy.

Chapter Fourteen

Joe stood in the yard with the dogs at his heels. For the fifth or sixth time today, he'd forgotten what he was about to do next. His thinking had been muddled since the day began.

He blamed it on a sleepless night. Now he simply couldn't focus. Animals fed. Check. Hay bales in from the field. Check. Those chores had taken up the bulk of his morning. Maybe he'd just clean off the equipment and call it a day.

Overhead the clouds moved quickly and the sky had begun to darken ominously. Eighty percent chance of rain tonight. Like he trusted the weather guy anymore. Rain would be here long before tonight.

Across the yard he could see the cottage. The Honda was absent from its usual spot. Becca had probably gone into town. He'd promised to drop off the paperwork and DVD. May as well do that now before that slipped his mind, too. Joe strode into the barn, picked up the packet from the counter and headed across the yard.

With every plodding step toward the geranium-filled

pots, he once again began to second-guess the decision he'd made last night. Had he done the right thing?

Sure he had. It was time, once and for all, to bury the past. Joe dug in his pocket and pulled out the ring box he'd retrieved from his drawer this morning. Twelve years he'd been holding on to this dream.

Time to let it go. He'd bury this ring—literally—and finally lay his past to rest.

Alone on his land once more. Wasn't that what he wanted? A future he could control. Everything to return to normal?

He knocked several times first, then using his key to open the cottage door, he stepped inside and froze, stunned at the sight of neat stacks of sealed packing boxes in the entryway, all labeled with Becca's precise handwriting. Kitchen. Bath. Casey's room.

Becca hadn't wasted any time.

Joe walked slowly through the house, his boots echoing on the hardwood floors. The beds had been stripped. He paused in the doorway of Casey's pink bedroom. The room was empty, the blinds sadly drawn, blocking the view of the ranch.

Every single trace of Becca and Casey had been scrubbed and polished from the cottage. The place sparkled. Floors had been mopped, the windows cleaned.

It looked better than when she'd moved in.

He paused and ran a hand over his jaw. No. He apparently hadn't made the wrong decision. She knew it, too. Once again, Becca had wiped herself from his life, as though she'd never existed.

Yeah, it was time for him to do the same. Joe tossed the packet and DVD on the counter.

He closed the front door and stood on the porch.

Before he realized what he was doing, he kicked over a pot of geraniums with his boot, his frustration bubbling over.

Around him a cleansing rain began to fall. Tucking his myoelectric prosthesis safely beneath his coat to keep the expensive device safe from the moisture, he stepped off the porch and started walking.

And he kept on walking. Right out of Rebecca's life.

"I thought we were going to miss saying goodbye to you," Abi said as she hugged Rebecca.

"Sorry. The doctor's appointment took longer than expected."

"That's okay. We stocked up on Patti Jo's finest while we waited," Rod said with a laugh. "Though no doubt we're going to be going through Patti Jo withdrawal before the week is out."

The SUV had been conveniently parked outside the bakery, where Rebecca had pulled up only moments before in her Honda.

While Rod and Julian rearranged the equipment and luggage, Abi grabbed Rebecca's arm and pulled her to the curb.

"Are you all right?" she asked. "You look awful."

"I'm fine. Never better." Rebecca plastered on a jaunty smile. "A little insomnia."

"What's going on?" Abi demanded.

"Nothing."

"That might work with someone else, but not with me." Abi crossed her arms and stood waiting.

"Joe," Rebecca finally admitted on a hushed whisper. "Last night. He told me he was ready for me to leave Gallagher Ranch."

"Oh, Rebecca. And you believed him?"

"Of course I did. I was awake all night replaying his words over and over. He shut me out. I can't fight that. Besides, the way I see it, it's better to hurt now than to realize later that I'm making a terrible mistake. I've spent the last twelve years down that road."

Abi frowned and looked her up and down. "I never would have taken you for a quitter."

Rebecca jerked to attention at the words. "I'm not a quitter."

"Then get back to that ranch and fight for what you want. I mean it." Abi nodded. "And remember, you have my number. If you need someone to talk to, call me."

"I will. I will," Rebecca promised as she considered her friend's words. Overwhelmed, she reached out to embrace Abi in a bear hug.

"Excuse me," Julian interrupted, offering Rebecca an air kiss. "I need some love, too."

"Look at this, Julian," Rebecca said. She held out her arm, no longer ashamed of the other ugly scar. "The stitches were removed today."

"I'm so relieved," he said. "All is forgiven then?"

"Yes," Rebecca said.

"Okay," Rod said. "We've got to get going. We have things to do and it's starting to rain." Holding a hand in the air to catch the intermittent drops, he glanced up at the sky. "We'll be soaked if we stand here much longer." He looked to Rebecca. "We'll see you sometime soon at the home office, right?"

She nodded.

"Remember what I said," Abi called out from inside the vehicle.

Rebecca smiled and waved at the SUV as it pulled

away from the curb. She continued to stare until it disappeared down Main Street. Joe would be glad they were gone, but she would miss them. Especially Abi.

When all was said and done, the team had done a great job. She'd seen the prints, the video footage and read Abi's interview.

There was no doubt in her mind that she would get the promotion and the bonus.

Which was too bad.

Because she knew in her heart that she'd give it all up for a chance to stay on Gallagher Ranch. But that was silly. Her second chance was gone. No matter what Abi believed.

Joe Gallagher wanted things to go back to the way they were. Well, now he had his wish.

Rebecca got in the Honda and drove slowly back to the ranch, savoring her last drive. Drizzle tap-danced on her windshield, and the wipers sang a rhythmic song. She smiled at the riotous wildflowers in the fields along the route to the ranch as they swayed in the rainy breeze. The blooms stretched across the fields on either side of the road for miles until the tall conifers appeared. The stately pines led the rest of the way to Gallagher Ranch.

All she had to do was stick the boxes in the car and she was done. She'd stay at her mother's until she decided what was next.

By the time she parked outside the cottage the rain had stopped, leaving only muddy puddles in the yard outside the barn and the equipment garage.

In front of the cottage a pot had been overturned. She frowned, kneeling to carefully right the container, scoop the fallen soil back into the pot and pat it back into place around the flowers.

"You'll be just fine," she whispered to the plant.

Shaking the dirt from her hands, she picked up her keys from the ground and opened the front door.

The first thing she saw was the packet and the DVD. Joe had been here. Rebecca released a loud sigh of frustration.

She grabbed a box and headed to the car, popping open the trunk. Dumping it inside, she glanced around the ranch yard.

It was quiet. Almost too quiet. A shiver slid over her. Something wasn't right.

Rebecca walked to the horse barn. Blackie was in his stall, as was Princess. Gil and Wishbone were in the back of the barn snoozing on their backs.

She'd miss the ranch animals when she was gone. Miss the morning rides with them into the pasture. The smells of sunrise on Gallagher Ranch. Memories rushed in, overwhelming her. She swallowed hard and kept moving.

Pulling open the equipment garage only told her that the farm truck was gone. Joe was out there somewhere. Alone, per his request.

When the squawk of the CB radio rang out into the silence, echoing against the metal walls of the garage, Rebecca jumped.

"Joe Gallagher. Need help..."

The radio sizzled and crackled, cutting off his words. She waited for moments, hoping for more. Finally, she picked up the radio's receiver and depressed the button on the device as she spoke. "Joe. Message received. This is Rebecca. Come in, Joe."

She waited again, but there was no response.

"Where are you, Joe?"

Nothing. Was she the only one who'd heard him? Should she call Sam? She tamped down panic, instead formulating a plan.

It would be faster to check the ranch herself. In the last weeks, she'd memorized nearly every inch of the land.

Rebecca ran straight for the barn. She approached the chestnut mare's stall, and then hesitated. Yes, she'd been cleared to ride by the doctor, but was she ready, after the way Princess had tossed her?

Her stomach didn't think so. It didn't matter. She had no choice.

"Are we ready, Princess?" she whispered in soothing tones to the horse, as she stroked her mane. "We have to be. Joe needs us."

Rebecca put on a rain slicker and quickly tacked up the horse. She whistled for Gil and Wishbone. The dogs rallied to her, running in eager circles, ready for action. She mounted and rode out across the yard to the pasture.

Did they get any sorrier than him?

Joe sat on a boulder massaging his ankle. He'd driven out to the far corner of the ranch and broke an axle in a shallow water-filled creek, which he would have seen if he'd been paying attention and not thinking about Becca as he drove through the sudden downpour. Sure, he could blame it on the rain, but he and God both knew it was his own fault.

Overhead a hawk soared, making circles, as though the bird was examining Joe's predicament and no doubt laughing.

Yeah, he was alone on his ranch. Things were back to normal, exactly the way he'd claimed for weeks that he wanted them to be. Now he had all the time in the world to ponder his words which were coming back to haunt him.

Where was Becca now? Come evening, if not sooner, she would be long gone. She was never coming back.

He'd accused his brother of being foolish for not going after the love of his life, and lo and behold, the woman loved him so much she'd come back.

Happily-ever-after for Dan.

Not so much for him.

No. Joe Gallagher had to learn everything the hard way.

He'd lost the only woman he'd ever loved.

Twice.

Even he had to admit that was quite pathetic.

Yeah, he was in a fine fix all the way around. The truck was out of commission, and he'd twisted his ankle crawling out the passenger door after it'd ended up sideways in the creek bed. To make things even more fun, his phone was dead because he'd forgotten to charge it, and the CB had gotten wet, offering him little more than a snap, crackle and pop when he turned on the thing.

Joe was more than aggravated. He shoved his Stetson to the back of his head, grateful that while he'd lost his dignity, he still had his hat.

A glance at his watch reminded him that he'd been out here two hours now. He'd finished off the water and the granola bar in his jacket pocket an hour ago. He was damp and tired. His ankle hurt.

It was going to get cold real soon, too. There was only a few more hours of daylight. Yeah, he was turning into a pitiful excuse for a cowboy.

He rubbed his hands over his face and started to

pray. Hopefully the good Lord wasn't laughing so hard at how he'd messed up his life that He would miss the prayer that was just sent up. After all, He wasn't used to hearing from Joe so often. He might not even recognize his voice.

The pounding of hooves on the land filled the silence, becoming louder and louder. Joe's head snapped up at the sound. A horse and rider appeared in the distance. Silhouetted against the dark clouds on the horizon, a woman in a taupe Stetson approached at a rapid clip, with two dogs racing alongside.

Becca?

When she was inches from him, she stopped, reined in Princess and stared down at him, shaking her head but saying nothing.

"What are you doing out here?" he asked. "You aren't even supposed to be on a horse."

"I can go back if you want." She clucked her tongue and lifted the reins.

"No. No. Wait. I'm sorry."

"Finally we agree on something," she muttered.

He frowned.

"I've been cleared to ride. I went to the doctor this morning."

"Good. That's good." His heart began to beat funny in his chest as he stared up at her on Princess. She looked good. Real good. More important, she hadn't left the ranch.

Becca glanced around, her eyes rounding when she turned in the saddle and saw the truck. "What happened?"

"I had a little accident."

"Good thing you have backup, huh?"

He narrowed his eyes. That was as close as she'd probably ever come to an 'I told you so'—however, he was in no position to point out the obvious.

"How did you find me?"

"The CB radio. All I could get was that you needed help."

"Yeah, but how did you know where to find me?"

"I didn't. I prayed and rode the fence line. Gil and Wishbone told me you were here."

Hearing their names mentioned, the dogs began to bark and run in circles around Princess.

"Sit," Becca commanded. The dogs immediately obeyed. She looked back over at the creek. "What did you do to the truck?"

Joe glanced away. "That's a long story."

"No bars on your cell?"

"Forgot to plug it in last night." He stood and grimaced as he balanced on one boot.

"Are you okay?"

"Twisted my right ankle. It's not broken or anything. Just needs a little ice and I'll be fine."

"Sure you will. Maybe I should call an ambulance."

"Not funny."

She shrugged, unsmiling. "I thought it was really amusing."

"You mind if we ride double back to the ranch?"

Becca slid off Princess and led the horse close to him. "I mind and so does Princess. You ride and I'll walk."

"No way. I'm not doing that."

"Take it or leave it, Gallagher."

This time it was his eyes that rounded. "You drive a mighty hard bargain."

"Oh, you have no idea. Do you want help getting on the horse?"

"I can manage."

"Of course you can."

She held Princess steady as he hobbled over and ungracefully dumped himself into the saddle.

Becca was silent as they walked for the next thirty minutes. When they got close to the barn, she stopped.

"What do you want to do?" she asked.

"Let's get Princess taken care of first. Then if you could help me up to the house, I can handle things from there." He glanced over at the Honda. "You've already got it packed up."

"Only just started, but it turns out I don't have as much stuff as I thought. My baggage seems to thin down every day."

"What about Casey?" Joe asked.

Becca turned her face away, revealing nothing. "No big deal. She has a room at my mom's, too."

"But she likes this one. It's pink."

"Joe, I'm done here. Let's not get all morbid. You had your say yesterday. Besides, the truth is you really didn't need much help from me to start. A much-deserved kick in the pants, maybe, but that was about it."

"Hey, no need to be insulting," he said as he rode into the barn. He slid down from Princess, grimacing as he landed. Grabbing the top stall rail, he propped his boot on the rung. "So you got your bonus and the promotion. What's next?"

Becca stared at him. Her jaw sagged slightly, and she released a small gasp. "Is that what this is all about?" She didn't wait for an answer. "Who told you about the bonus and promotion?"

He shrugged.

Becca paced across the barn. "Seriously, you never even bothered to ask me?"

"What's to ask? You did a great job and now you're done."

"Yes. That's right. I got that bonus for doing my job. So what? It doesn't change anything. It wasn't even my idea. As for the promotion, it means I get to stay in Paradise, and that is everything to me."

She turned and met his gaze. "We had a second chance, Joe. Except you insist on living your so-called back-to-normal life here all by yourself."

Joe inhaled sharply at the words he himself had been thinking just a short while ago.

"I can't make you ask for help, Joe. I can't make you reach out to me. That's what cuts deep." Once again she paced back and forth. "I get that other-shoe-dropping mentality. I used to sing the exact same song when I arrived at the ranch. But haven't I proved you can trust me?"

"It wasn't about you."

"What does that even mean, Joe?"

"It means that I'm terrified you'll find out you don't really want to be here. On a ranch in the middle of nowhere with a handicapped man. I'm scared I'll let down my guard, and you'll decide you want to be with someone who can give you what you really deserve. It's been twelve years, Becca, and I still can't offer you anything but hay, cows and a house in the middle of nowhere."

"So basically you turned me away to save yourself?"

Joe sighed. "Yeah, when you put it that way, it does sound pretty sorry."

"If you hadn't dumped that truck, I would have been out

of here. Long gone. We're both so pigheaded and afraid, that we're missing out on what's right in front of us."

She walked up to him, getting smack-dab in the middle of his personal space.

"Do you love me, Joe Gallagher?"

He took a deep breath. "I keep telling myself that you don't fall in love with someone in three weeks. But my heart says that you do if you've been in love with her all your life."

Her eyes widened.

Joe neatly wrapped his arms around her. His left arm was gently around her waist, capturing her close, and his prosthesis rested on her hip, assuring her he would never let her fall.

Becca put her hand up to gently touch his cheek.

"I also need you to have faith in yourself, Joe. Otherwise you'll never have faith in us."

He closed his eyes and then opened them. She was still there, as beautiful as ever. She met his gaze, unwavering.

"I'm sorry, Becca. I'm sorry. I do believe in us. I was afraid."

She smiled, and her hand caressed his face.

Joe tipped his hat back with a finger, and the Stetson rolled off his head onto the floor. Didn't matter. Cowboys couldn't kiss properly with their hats on. Everyone knew that.

"Careful with your foot. Don't fall," she murmured.

"I got this covered."

His head lowered inch by inch until his lips rested on hers. Becca's hat fell to the ground as he closed his eyes and kissed the love of his life over and over again.

"Oh, Joe," she murmured. Looking slightly dazed, she held on to his biceps. "What are we going to do now?"

"Becca, do you love me?"

"I love you, Joe Gallagher."

"Seems pretty simple to me. Let me show you something." He pulled the ring box out of a pocket of his Levi's and handed it to her.

"What is this?"

"It's the ring I bought for you twelve years ago."

Her eyes welled with moisture, and she licked her lips. "I've wasted so much time. I've made so many wrong decisions."

"Stop that. This is all about us. We're right where we're supposed to be, right now."

Becca opened the box and stared at the marquis-cut diamond. She released a small gasp. "It's beautiful."

"Not real big."

"I said it's beautiful. The prettiest thing I've ever seen." She looked up at him. "What did you plan to do with this ring?"

He swallowed. "There is only one thing I ever wanted to do with this ring. Becca, will you marry me?"

"Yes," she breathed softly.

Joe's own breath caught, his chest swelling with happiness when he saw the love in her eyes.

Becca held out her hand and he slipped the diamond on her finger.

"What do you think? Should I exchange it?"

Becca splayed her fingers against his heart and examined the ring on her hand.

"Never." She smiled. "It's perfect."

Joe reached down and lifted her fingers using his prosthetic hand. He kissed each of them tenderly.

"I love you, Joe."

He sighed. "I love you, too, Becca. Forever."

Epilogue

Joe slid off Blackie and plucked a stalk of sweet grass from the ground and bit into it. First signs of spring. Clover and orchard grass were starting to come up in the pasture, as well. Raising his face to the sky, he inhaled.

Yes. Rain was on the way. That was okay. Better than snow. The long winter had finally passed. Now it was the time of renewal and rebirth for the land.

Behind him a horse whinnied. Gil and Wishbone barked a vigorous note of welcome, turning in eager circles. Joe turned, as well. Where was Mushy? He whistled, and the new pup came running from under a bush, with his black-and-white tail dancing as he ran.

Joe looked up in time to see a horse and rider approach.

Becca. His wife.

"How's the Gallagher Ranch foreman today?" Joe asked.

"Good." She glanced at the sky. "It's going to rain." Becca shuddered.

"What's the matter?" he asked?"

"I smell manure, and it's about to make me gag."

"I guess your smeller is working."

"In spades."

He gazed up at her, realizing once again what a blessed man he was. "I thought you were in town."

"I was. Oh, and that tractor part won't be in for another week. I stopped by to check for you."

"That's not good. How am I supposed to till your garden without the tractor?"

"It will wait another week. It's not like we don't have plenty to do around here."

"You're right," he agreed. "And we did promise the church they could have their Easter sunrise service out here on the ranch this year. Getting ready for that will keep us running."

Joe cocked his head. He was missing something here, and he wasn't sure what. Then it hit him. "Didn't you have a doctor's appointment?"

"I did."

"Everything okay?"

"More than okay." A smile lit up her face.

"What could be more than okay?"

"We're having a baby."

Joe nearly swallowed the blade of grass in his mouth. "A baby?" He almost choked.

"Well, if you want to get technical, we're having two babies."

This time he did choke.

Becca slid from her mare and came over to slap him on the back. "Are you okay?"

"When were you going to tell me about two babies?"

"I was thinking up all sorts of ways to surprise you. But then you asked." She shrugged. "I have a hard time keeping secrets."

"Twins?"

"You can blame your mother for that one. They run in your family, not mine."

"When?" he sputtered.

"You know these things take nine months. There's only ten or twenty days difference in the gestation period between my babies and your cows. Your cattle and I may be giving birth right around the same time."

"You don't say?" Joe stood there stunned for a moment, then he swiftly moved to cover her lips with his own.

"Mmm, that was nice," Becca murmured.

"I love you, Becca. Have I said that enough lately?"

"I love you, too, and you can never say it enough." She paused. "I'm thinking it's going to be boys."

"What? Did the doctor tell you that?"

"No. I've just got this gut feeling. The doctor said they can confirm in a few weeks." Becca punctuated the words with another quick kiss. "What do you think about Joseph and Jackson?"

Joe laughed. "What if it's girls? My sisters are twins."

"I'm telling you. It's boys."

"You're not even going to consider girls?"

"I like baby girls as much as the next momma, but my babies are little boys."

"I'm thinking it might be time to take that parcel of land that Hollis Elliott has been begging me for and finally build my big house."

"So he was right?"

"Who?"

"Hollis. He told me you'd never sell that land. You were bluffing me."

"Apparently so. I'd do anything to keep you here at Gallagher Ranch. You should know that by now."

She shook her head.

"I may need to hire a new foreman, as well. Too bad, I was nearly finished breaking in the new one. And I really like her."

"Not so fast. I'm not retiring for quite some time. Eight more months, to be exact."

"How long can you keep riding a horse?"

"The doctor said that as long as I feel safe, he'd approve walking my horse until my third month."

"Not really?"

"Yes. However, after some prayer, I've decided that I'm really making decisions for the three of us. Joseph Jr., Jackson and me. So today will be my last ride until after the babies are born. You can buy me a new all-terrain vehicle instead of a horse."

He rubbed a hand over his face and grabbed a water bottle from his saddlebag.

"Joe, are you all right?"

"Not really. I'm still pretty much flabbergasted. How'd I get so blessed?"

"By keeping your eyes on Him."

"Do you think Casey will be okay with this?"

"Are you kidding? More than okay. She's been green-eyed ever since Amy told her Dan and Beth are having a baby."

"Wow, our boys and Dan's son will grow up together."

"The Gallagher tradition marches on." Becca sighed. "Thank you, Joe."

"For what? Aside from the obvious, I think it's pretty clear I didn't do much, yet I've never been so happy.

Why, when I go to town I can hardly get anything accomplished for people asking me why I'm smiling."

Becca laughed. "You've done plenty. You gave me a second chance in Paradise." She reached up and put her arms around his neck and whispered against his mouth. "Thank you, cowboy."

* * * * *

Any day she could see Sammy was a good day. But she was pretty sure Jack was about to turn down her nanny offer. And then she'd have to tell Penny she couldn't take the apartment, and leave.

The thought of being away from her son after spending precious time with him made her chest ache, and she blinked away unexpected tears as she approached Jack and Sammy.

Sammy didn't look up at her. He was holding up one finger near his own face, moving it back and forth.

Jack caught his hand. "Say hi, Sammy! Here's Aunt Arianna."

Sammy tugged his hand away and continued to move his finger in front of his face.

"Sammy, come on."

Sammy turned slightly away from his father and refocused on his fingers.

"It's okay," Arianna said, because she could see the beginnings of a meltdown. "He doesn't need to greet me. What's up?"

"Look," he said, "I've been thinking about what you said." He rubbed a hand over the back of his neck, clearly uncomfortable.

Sammy's hand moved faster, and he started humming a wordless tune. It was almost as if he could sense the tension between Arianna and Jack.

"It's okay, Jack," she said. "I get it. My being your nanny was a foolish idea." Foolish, but oh so appealing. She ached to pick

Sammy up and hold him, to know that she could spend more time with him, help him learn, get him support for his special needs.

But it wasn't her right.

"Actually," he said, "that's what I wanted to talk about. It does seem sort of foolish, but...I think I'd like to offer you the job."

She stared at him, her eyes filling. "Oh, Jack," she said, her voice coming out in a whisper. Had he really just said she could have the job?

Behind her, the rumble and snap of tables being folded and chairs being stacked, the cheerful conversation of parishioners and community people, faded to an indistinguishable murmur.

She was going to be able to be with her son. Every day. She reached out and stroked Sammy's soft hair, and even though he ignored her touch, her heart nearly melted with the joy of being close to him.

Jack's brow wrinkled. "On a trial basis," he said. "Just for the rest of the summer, say."

Of course. She pulled her hand away from Sammy and drew in a deep breath. She needed to calm down and take things one step at a time. Yes, leaving him at the end of the summer would break her heart ten times more. But even a few weeks with her son was more time than she deserved.

With God all things are possible. The pastor had said it, and she'd just witnessed its truth. She was being given a job, the care of her son and a place to live.

It was a blessing, a huge one. But it came at a cost: she was going to need to conceal the truth from Jack on a daily basis. And given the way her heart was jumping around in her chest, she wondered if she was going to be able to survive this much of God's blessing.

Don't miss
The Nanny's Secret Baby *by Lee Tobin McClain,*
available August 2019 wherever
Love Inspired® books and ebooks are sold.

www.LoveInspired.com

LIEXP0719

Inspirational Romance to
Warm Your Heart and Soul

Join our social communities to connect
with other readers who share your love!

Sign up for the Love Inspired newsletter
at **www.LoveInspired.com** to be the
first to find out about upcoming titles,
special promotions and exclusive content.

CONNECT WITH US AT:

Facebook.com/groups/HarlequinConnection

 Facebook.com/LoveInspiredBooks

 Twitter.com/LoveInspiredBks

Earn points on your purchase of new Harlequin books from participating retailers.

Turn your points into **FREE BOOKS** of your choice!

Join for FREE today at
www.HarlequinMyRewards.com.

Harlequin My Rewards is a free program (no fees) without any commitments or obligations.